LEGACIES OF BETRAYAL

I FOLLOWED HIS recommendation: when I killed, I laughed. I let the ice-wind pull my hair free, and I felt hot blood against my skin. I ran far and strongly, daring my brothers to keep pace. I was like the berkut, the hunting eagle, free of the jesses, out on the rising air, high up on the horizon.

That was what we were back then; that was what we all were. Minghan *Kasurga* – the Brotherhood of the Storm.

That was our ranking name, the one we used to differentiate ourselves.

In private, we were the laughing killers.

To the rest of the galaxy, we were still unknown.

THE HORUS HERESY®

*Many of these titles are also available as abridged and unabridged audiobooks.
Order the full range of Horus Heresy novels and audiobooks from*
blacklibrary.com

LEGACIES OF BETRAYAL

Let the galaxy burn

BLACK LIBRARY

A BLACK LIBRARY PUBLICATION

Brotherhood of the Storm first published in hardback
© Games Workshop Ltd. 2012
Serpent first published in the Horus Heresy Weekender Programme
© Games Workshop Ltd. 2013
The Divine Word first published in the Black Library Weekender Anthology Vol. I
© Games Workshop Ltd. 2012
Heart of the Conqueror first published in the Horus Heresy Weekender II Programme
© Games Workshop Ltd. 2012
Veritas Ferrum, *Strike and Fade*, *Butcher's Nails* and *Warmaster* first published as audio dramas
© Games Workshop Ltd. 2012
Riven and *Kryptos* first published as eBooks
© Games Workshop Ltd. 2012
Honour to the Dead, *The Eightfold Path*, *Guardian of Order*, *Censure* and *Lucius, the Eternal Blade* first
published as audio dramas © Games Workshop Ltd. 2013
Lone Wolf first published as an eBook
© Games Workshop Ltd. 2013
Hunter's Moon, *Wolf's Claw* and *Thief of Revelations* first published as audio dramas
© Games Workshop Ltd. 2014

A BLACK LIBRARY PUBLICATION

Hardback edition first published in Great Britain in 2014.
This edition published in 2015.
Black Library,
Games Workshop Ltd.,
Willow Road,
Nottingham, NG7 2WS, UK.

10 9 8 7 6 5 4 3 2 1

Cover illustration by Neil Roberts.

A CIP record for this book is available from the British Library.

UK ISBN: 978 1 84970 836 4
US ISBN: 978 1 84970 837 1

See Black Library on the internet at
blacklibrary.com

Find out more about Games Workshop
and the world of Warhammer 40,000 at
games-workshop.com

Printed and bound by CPI Group (UK) Ltd, Croydon, CR0 4YY

THE HORUS HERESY®

It is a time of legend.

The galaxy is in flames. The Emperor's glorious vision for humanity is in ruins. His favoured son, Horus, has turned from his father's light and embraced Chaos.

His armies, the mighty and redoubtable Space Marines, are locked in a brutal civil war. Once, these ultimate warriors fought side by side as brothers, protecting the galaxy and bringing mankind back into the Emperor's light.
Now they are divided.

Some remain loyal to the Emperor, whilst others have sided with the Warmaster. Pre-eminent amongst them, the leaders of their thousands-strong Legions are the primarchs. Magnificent, superhuman beings, they are the crowning achievement of the Emperor's genetic science. Thrust into battle against one another, victory is uncertain for either side.

Worlds are burning. At Isstvan V, Horus dealt a vicious blow and three loyal Legions were all but destroyed. War was begun, a conflict that will engulf all mankind in fire. Treachery and betrayal have usurped honour and nobility. Assassins lurk in every shadow. Armies are gathering.
All must choose a side or die.

Horus musters his armada, Terra itself the object of his wrath. Seated upon the Golden Throne, the Emperor waits for his wayward son to return. But his true enemy is Chaos, a primordial force that seeks to enslave mankind to its capricious whims.

The screams of the innocent, the pleas of the righteous resound to the cruel laughter of Dark Gods. Suffering and damnation await all should the Emperor fail and the war be lost.

The age of knowledge and enlightenment has ended.
The Age of Darkness has begun.

CONTENTS

BROTHERHOOD OF THE STORM

Chris Wraight

~ DRAMATIS PERSONAE ~

The Primarchs

JAGHATAI KHAN	Primarch of the White Scars
HORUS LUPERCAL	Primarch of the Luna Wolves

The V Legion 'White Scars'

SHIBAN KHAN	Brotherhood of the Storm
TORGHUN KHAN	Brotherhood of the Moon
TARGUTAI YESUGEI	Stormseer

Imperial Personae

ILYA RAVALLION	Departmento Munitorum
HERIOL MIERT	Departmento Munitorum

I. SHIBAN

I REMEMBER MUCH of what he said even now, but we all learned quicker from example than words. That was the way we were made – we watched, and we acted.

We took delight in the speed we travelled. Perhaps we went too far, too fast, though I regret nothing. We were true to our nature, and in the final test that was what saved us.

I do remember much about him from that time, back when our instincts were simpler. Some examples, some choice lessons, stay with me even now, and I am better for it.

Of all the things he said, or was supposed to have said, only one truly struck at my heart. He said: 'Laugh when you are killing.'

If we had needed an epigram, if anyone had ever asked what made us what we were, then I would have told them that.

No one ever asked. By the time anyone cared enough about us to seek us out, everything had already changed. We were suddenly needed, but there was no time to think about why.

I followed his recommendation: when I killed, I laughed. I let the ice-wind pull my hair free, and I felt hot blood against my skin. I ran far and strongly, daring my brothers to keep pace. I was like the berkut, the hunting eagle, free of the jesses, out on the rising air, high up on the horizon.

That was what we were back then; that was what we all were. Minghan *Kasurga* – the Brotherhood of the Storm.

That was our ranking name, the one we used to differentiate ourselves.

In private, we were the laughing killers.

To the rest of the galaxy, we were still unknown.

I LIKED CHONDAX. The planet that had given its name to the whole stellar cluster suited our style of war, unlike magma-crusted Phemus or jungle-choked Epihelikon. It had big, high skies, unbroken by cloud and pale green like *rejke* grass. We burned across it in waves, up from the southern landing sites and out into the equatorial zone. Unlike any world I had known then or have known since, it never changed – just a wasteland of white earth in every direction, glistening under the soft light of three distant suns. You could push your hand into that earth and it would break open, crystalline like salt.

Nothing grew on Chondax. We lifted supplies down from orbit in bulk landers. When they were gone, when we were gone again, the earth closed over the scorch-marks, smoothing them white.

It healed itself. Our presence there was light – we hunted, we killed, and then nothing remained. Even the prey – the greenskins, which we call the hain, others the ork, or kine, or krork – failed to leave a mark. We had no idea how they supplied themselves. We had destroyed the last of their crude space-vessels months earlier, stranding them on the surface. Every time we cleared them out of their squalid nests, torching them and turning the earth to glass, the white dust came back.

I once led a squadron a long way south, covering three hundred kilometres before each major sunset, back to where we had fought them in a brutal melee that had lasted seven days and stained the ground black with blood and carbon.

Nothing remained as we passed over the site, nothing but white.

I checked my armour's locators. Jochi did not believe me; he said we had gone wrong. He was grinning, disappointed to find nothing, hoping some of them might have survived and holed up again, ready for another fight.

I knew we were in the right place. I saw then that we were on a world that could not be harmed, a world that shrugged off our bloodstains and our fury, and made itself whole when we passed on.

That observation was the root of my liking for Chondax. I explained it to my brothers later as we sat under the stars, warming our hands indulgently by firelight like our fathers had done on Chogoris. They agreed that Chondax was a good world, a world on which good warfare could be conducted.

Jochi smiled tolerantly as I spoke, and Batu shook his scarred head, but I did not mind that. My brothers knew they had a poetical character for a khan, but such things were not disdained by Chogorians as I had been told they were in other Legions.

Yesugei once told me that only poets could be true warriors. I did not know what he meant by that then. He might have been referring to me particularly or he might not; one does not ask a zadyin arga to explain himself.

But I knew that when we were gone, our souls made hot and pure by killing, Chondax would not remember us. The fire we warmed ourselves by, its fuel brought down by lifter like everything else, which in the old fashion we would not extinguish with water nor kick over when dawn came, would leave no stain.

I found that reassuring.

✠ ✠ ✠

WE WENT NORTH again. Always moving, always seeking. That was how we liked it; we would have quickly withered had we been forced to stay locked down in the same place for long.

I took my brotherhood over the plains; five hundred of us, pristine in our crimson-rimmed ivory armour. Our jetbikes cut swathes in the earth beneath us, churning it up and throwing out furrows behind. We rode them flamboyantly, knowing that none could master their thunderous power like we could. When the third sun rose, making the empty sky glow, our inscribed pennants flashed and our weapons glittered. We hurtled like earth-tied comets, strung out across the flat land in an arrowhead of silver, whooping our joy and our glory and our purpose.

When the third sun rose on Chondax, there were no shadows. Everything came to our eyes in razor-edged blocks of colour. We looked at one another and saw details we had never seen before. We saw the bloom in our leather-brown faces, and realised how old we were, and how long we had been on campaign, and marvelled that we felt more savage and vivacious than we had as children.

On the seventh day, when the suns were at their apex, we saw orks on the horizon. They were heading north too, driving in long columns of battered, clumsy armoured vehicles that sent gouts of soot into the air and gave away their position.

As soon as I saw them, my heart leapt. My muscles tensed, my eyes narrowed, my pulse quickened. I felt my fingers itch for the feel of my guan dao glaive. The blessed weapon – two-metre metal shaft, single curved blade, a work of close combat genius – had not drunk blood for many days; its spirit longed for the taste again, and I did not intend to disappoint it.

'Prey!' I roared, feeling the tight, cold air buffet my exposed face. I rose up in the saddle, letting my bike sway beneath me, peering into the sun-glare of the horizon.

The greenskins did not turn to fight. They kept going, ploughing on in their smoke-choked convoy as fast as they could.

When he had first led us to Chondax, they would have fought us. They would have rushed at us, mob-handed, bellowing and stampeding with spittle flying from their ragged mouths.

But no longer. We had broken their spirit. We had chased them across the face of the world, rooting them out, beating them back, cutting them down. We knew that they were mustering somewhere, trying to summon up some kind of defence in numbers, but even they must have sensed that the end was coming.

I did not hate them. In those days I did not know what it was to hate an enemy. I knew how strong, how clever, how resourceful they were, and I respected that. In the earliest days they had killed many of my brothers. We had learned together, the two of us, learning where our weaknesses lay, learning how to fight on a world that gave us nothing and was uncaring of our feuding presence. They could travel fast when they wished to. Not as fast as us – nothing in creation was as fast as us – but they were wily, creative, brave and fierce.

It may have been sentiment operating, but I do not believe they hated us either. They hated losing, and that gnawed at their spirit and took the bite out of their blades, but they did not hate *us*.

Years earlier, on Ullanor, it had been different. We had nearly been undone by them. They had come at us in an endless, formless green tide, overrunning everything, drunk on strength, unbounded in their magnificent, beautiful way of war.

In the end it was Horus who had turned them back. Horus and he had both fought there – I saw it myself, if only from a distance. That was where things had finally turned, where the back of the beast had been broken. All that remained on Chondax were the dregs; the last gritty remnants of an empire that had dared to challenge ours and had almost prevailed.

So I did not hate those that remained. I sometimes imagined how I would feel if we ever came up against a foe we could not defeat, where nothing remained but to fall back, again and again, weakening further with every encounter, watching the lifeblood slowly drain out of those around us as the noose tightened.

I hoped and believed that I would do as they did, and keep fighting.

I DID NOT need to give my brothers orders – we had done the same thing many times. We powered to full speed, sweeping up on either flank of the convoy in split formation.

It was a sight to make the blood race and the heart sing: five hundred gleaming jetbikes, thundering in arrowhead squadrons of twenty, their engines deafening, their riders whooping. We spread out across the dazzling sand, superb in our livery of white, gold and red, throwing up a storm of eddying dust in our wake.

Until then we had been cruising, letting our bikes sweep us into range. Now we were racing, our long hair snapping around our shoulder guards, our blades flashing in the light of the suns.

We homed in on the enemy vehicles – big, bulky carriers on half-tracks or mismatched wheels – swaying and rocking as the greenskins pushed the wheezing engines hard. Streams of smoke roiled out of gaps in the armour plating. I saw individual orks perched in gun-positions, swinging round to aim at us with patched-up rocket launchers and muzzle-blackened beam-weapons.

I saw their tusked mouths open – they were shouting something at us. All I heard was the rattling roar of the jetbikes, the blast of the wind, the throaty growl of the xenos engines.

Our jetbikes had spinal-mounted heavy bolters, but we kept them quiet. None of us fired – we swept in close, swerving away just before we came within range of the enemy guns, making our observations and plotting out our individual runs. We were searching for the weak links, the places we would start.

Erdeni got his angles wrong and shot in too close. I turned in the saddle to see him take a rocket right in the chest, burning out from a greenskin half-track and corkscrewing wildly before hitting him. He was hurled out of his saddle by the explosion. Before I surged out of range, I saw him crash into the ground, rebounding and rolling as his heavy armour dragged him along.

I made a note then that, if he lived, Erdeni would pay penance. Then we got to work.

Our bikes pounced, kicking in close, weaving and rolling through the hurricane of incoming fire. We opened up with our heavy bolters, a fractured, explosive roar that briefly drowned the thunder of the engines. We cut into the convoy, searing past tottering half-tracks, kindling devastation in our wake.

I was at the head of the arrow, gunning my mount hard, yelling out my savage battle-fury, diving clear of energy bolts and rockets, feeling the percussive judder of my bolter laying waste to all before me.

I was lost in the vitality of it. The suns were up, we were in close-packed, furious combat and the ice-clear air was racing over our armour plate. I have never wanted more than that.

The convoy broke. Slower vehicles had their armour penetrated first, and they rocked and bucked with explosions. Monstrous engines took shots to tractor units and crashed, nose-first, into the earth. Trailers swung upwards, tumbling and rolling. Scrap fragments spun high with the force of internal explosions. Jetbikes streaked past, scything like thrown spears through the carnage.

I closed on my chosen prey, standing in the saddle, guiding my speeding mount with my legs and pulling my glaive from its back strapping. My nineteen brothers of the minghan-keshig came in close alongside me, committed to the same trajectory. We spun and raced through the dense hail of bursting energy weapons and solid rounds. Jochi was there, as were Batu and Jamyang and the others, all crouched over the plunging chassis of their bikes with their blood up and rapture in their eyes.

My prey was at the centre of the convoy – a huge eight-wheeler, crowned with an unruly spine of guns and swivelling grenade launchers. A platform had been mounted high on a shaky looking suspension array, around which hung thick plates of looted armour painted in splashes of red and green. Many dozens of orks jostled for position up there: some armed, some operating the vehicle's mounted weapons. Two massive smokestacks vomited fumes at the rear as the whole structure bounced and tilted, crashing along with the rest of the collapsing convoy.

They were not stupid, nor were they slow. A storm of spitting beams streaked out at us, burning past our ears and ploughing up the earth beneath. I took a hit on my pauldron and slewed hard to my left; behind me another bike was downed in a careening, plummeting orgy of blurred flame and wreckage.

At the last moment I jumped, propelled high by my power armour and thrown clear onto the platform itself. I crashed through the barrier and onto the tilting surface, swinging my guan dao round in a bloody arc as I landed. The disruptor blazed, leaving streaks of shimmering silver in the air as the blade whipped across.

I gloried in the use of the glaive. It danced in my fists, spinning and punching, hurling ork bodies clear from the platform. I ploughed through them, breaking bone and shattering armour. Orks reeled away from me, staggering and yowling.

I *roared* with pleasure, my limbs burning, my shoulders wreathed in a fountain of sun-glittered blood. My hearts pumped, my fists flew, my spirit soared.

A big one got close, its left arm mangled by a bolt-detonation. It came right at me, head low, claws grasping. It carried a rusty cleaver; the blade swung round.

The guan dao lashed out, taking the monster's arm off at the wrist. Then it switched back, so fast the blade-edge seemed to cut the air itself in a smear of crackling energy, bursting its head open in a cloud of blood and bone.

Before the body had crashed to the deck I was moving again, cutting, whirling, leaping, swaying. My brothers joined me, throwing themselves from their bikes and onto the platform. There was barely room for us all; we had to kill quickly.

Jochi took out one of the gun operators, driving his blade into the creature's spine and ripping out the chain of bones with a flourish. Batu got into trouble taking on two at once, and was punched heavily in the face for his error. His bloodied chin snapped back, and he staggered to the edge of the platform. Projectiles hammered into his breastplate, but they failed to knock him off.

I didn't see how his fight ended – by then I was closing in on the warlord. It lumbered towards me, shoving its own kind out of the way in its eagerness to get into combat. I laughed to see that; not from mockery, but from approval and delight.

Its skin was dark and puckered with greying scars. It swung a huge, iron-headed hammer in two hands, and the weapon growled with moving blades.

I swerved away, missing the grinding teeth by a finger's width. Then I spun back in close, my guan dao shivering with angry energy as it worked. I hit it twice, taking chunks of its heavy plate armour, but it didn't fall.

It swung again, hurling the hammerhead in a bludgeoning arc. I ducked sharply, using the pitch of the platform, veering away and down, with the back-sweep of the glaive to balance me. We were like dancers at a death ceremony, weaving back and forth, our movements fast, close, heavy.

It lashed out again, its face contorted with frothy rage, piling its immense strength into a shuddering, whistling transverse sweep. If that strike had connected I would have died on Chondax, thrown from the moving platform and driven into the dust with my back snapped and my armour shattered.

But I had seen it coming. That was the way of war for us – to feint, to entice, to enrage, to provoke the slip that left the defence open. When the hammer moved, I knew where it was going and just how long I had to get around it.

I leapt. The glaive glittered as it cartwheeled, the blade turning in my hands and around my twisting body. I soared over the ork's clumsy lunge, up-ending the shaft of the guan dao and pointing it down, seizing it two-handed.

The beast looked up groggily, just in time to see my sun-flashed blade plunge through its skull. I felt the carve and slap of its flesh and skull giving way, gouged into a bloody foam by the plummeting energy field.

I clanged back to the deck, wrenching the glaive free and swinging it around me in a gore-flinging flourish. The ravaged remains of the warlord slumped before me. I stood over it for a single heart-beat, the guan dao humming in my hand. All around me I could hear the battle-cries of my brothers and the agony of our prey.

The air was filled with screams, with roaring, with the grind and crack of weapons, with the swelling clouds of ignited promethium, with the hard burn of jetbike thrusters.

I knew the end would come quickly. I didn't want it to end. I wanted to keep fighting, to feel the power of my primarch burn through my muscles.

'For the Great Khan!' I thundered, breaking back into movement, shaking the blood from my weapon and searching for more. 'For the Khagan!'

And all around me, my brothers, my beloved brothers of the min-ghan, echoed the call, lost in their pristinely savage world of rage and joy and speed.

✠ ✠ ✠

WE DID NOT move on until all of them were dead. When the last of the fighting was over, we stalked through the wreckage with short blades in our hands, finishing off any xenos who still breathed. When that was done, we doused the vehicles in their own fuel and set them alight. When that fire died down, we went back over the remnants with flamers of our own and plasma weapons, atomising anything bigger than a man's fist.

You could not be too careful. They were good at coming back, the greenskins, even after you thought you had killed them about as completely as you imagined possible.

Sometimes, in the past, we had not been careful. Being careful was not in our blood, and it had cost us. We had tried to learn, to better ourselves, to remember that warfare was not always a matter of glorious pursuits.

By the time we left, heading back north, the mounds of charred metal were already being eroded and smothered by wind-carried earth. Nothing remained, nothing endured. It was like a dream. Or perhaps we were the dreams, sliding across the blank surface of an indifferent world.

We left four brothers of the minghan behind us, including Erdeni, who had escaped penance by having his chest knocked inside out. We did not burn them. Sangjai, our *emchi*, extracted their seed and stripped the armour from their bodies. Then he laid them out, their bare skin open to the suns and the wind, and we took their bikes and equipment with us.

On Chogoris we had observed such customs so that the beasts of the Altak had something to feed on when the moons were up. We had never been a wasteful people. No beasts lived on Chondax save us and the hain, but the custom had followed us out into the stars and we had never changed it.

We had tried to learn, to better ourselves, but we did not change everything. The core of us, the things that set us apart and made us proud, those were the things we had carried from the home world and kept safe, guarded like a candle-flame cupped in a palm. I thought then that all of us in the Legion felt the same way about such things. Back then, though, I was blind to many truths.

A DAY LATER, and we reached our resupply coordinates.

Yes, we saw the bulk lifters from a long way out, descending and ascending in columns. They were huge: each one carried hundreds of tonnes of rations, ammunition, machine parts, medicae supplies; everything needed to sustain a mobile army on the hunt. In the years that the Chondax campaign had been fully underway they had been in ceaseless demand, plying their routes between the carriers hanging in orbit and the forward stations on the ground.

'We will have no use for them soon,' I observed to Jochi as we passed a lifter coming down – a bulbous leviathan buoyed by shimmering heat-wash from its landing thrusters.

'There will be other battlefields,' he said.

'Not forever,' I replied.

We swept past the landing sites. By the time we reached the main garrison complex only one sun still remained above the horizon, burning orange in a deep green sky. Shadows barred our path, warm against the pale earth.

The supply station had always been temporary, built from prefabricated components that would be lifted back up to the fleet when no longer needed on Chondax. Only its defence towers, looming up from the outer walls and bursting with weaponry, looked like they would take any time at all to dismantle when the time came. White dust ran up against the walls in smooth dunes, wearing at the rockcrete and the metal. The planet hated the things we had built upon it. It eroded them, gnawed at them, trying to shake off the specks of permanence we had hammered into its perpetually shifting hide.

Once the jetbikes were in the armoury hangars, I gave the order for my brothers to go to the garrison's hab units and make the most of their short rest period. They looked happy enough to do so; their endurance was immense but it was not infinite, and we had been on the hunt for a long time.

I headed off to find the garrison commander. Even as night fell, the dusty streets of the temporary settlement were thronged with activity – loaders moving between warehouses stacked with munitions and supply crates, servitors scuttling from workshops over to armoury bays, auxiliary troops in V Legion colours bowing respectfully as I passed them.

I found the commander in a rockcrete bunker at the heart of the garrison complex. Like all the other mortals he wore protective clothing and a rebreather – Chondax's atmosphere was too thin and too cold for ordinary humans; only we and the orks tolerated it unaided.

'Commander,' I said, ducking under the doorway as I entered his private chamber.

He rose from his desk, bowing clumsily, hampered by his environment suit.

'Khan,' he replied, speaking thickly through his helmet's mouthpiece.

'New orders?' I asked.

'Yes, lord,' he said, reaching for a data-slate and handing it to me. 'Assault plans have been accelerated.'

I glanced at the data-slate he gave me. Text glowed on the screen, laid over a map of the warzone. The symbols indicating enemy formations had shrunk together, falling back towards a single point to the north-east. Locator symbols of V Legion brotherhoods followed them, coming in from all directions. I was pleased to see that my minghan was at the forefront of the encirclement.

'Will he participate?' I asked.

'Lord?'

I gave the commander a hard look.

'Ah,' he said, realising to whom I was referring. 'I don't know. I have no data on his whereabouts. The keshig keep it to themselves.'

I nodded. That was to be expected. Only my burning desire to see him in battle again – this time at close quarters – had made me ask.

'We will leave as soon as we can,' I told him, affecting a smile in case my manner with him had been excessively brusque. 'Perhaps, if we make good progress, we will be the first at his side.'

'Perhaps you will,' he said. 'But not alone. You are to combine with another brotherhood.'

I raised an eyebrow. For the whole length of time we had been on Chondax, we had operated on our own. Sometimes we had gone without resupply or redirection for months at a time, out on the endless flats with nothing but our own resources to draw on. I had enjoyed that freedom; we all had.

'You have full orders waiting for you, security-sealed,' said the commander. 'Many brotherhoods are being combined for the final attack runs.'

'So who are we joining?' I asked.

'I do not have that information. I have location coordinates. Forgive me – we have much to process, and some data from fleet command has been… lacking in detail.'

I could believe that, and so did not blame the man before me. I must have let my smile broaden wryly, for he seemed to relax a little.

We were not a careful people. We were bad with the details.

'Then I hope their khan knows how to ride,' was all I said. 'He will have to, to keep up with us.'

IT WAS NOT long before we met.

My refitted brotherhood powered smoothly north-east. Many of our jetbikes had been replaced or repaired by the armoury servitors, and the sound of their engines was cleaner than it had been. We had always taken pride in our appearance, but the short break in operations had allowed some of the grime to be scrubbed from our armour plates, making them dazzle under the triple suns.

I knew my brothers were restless. As the long kilometres passed in a glare of white sand and pale emerald sky they became ever more impatient, ever more anxious to see signs of prey on the empty horizon.

'What will we do when we have killed them all?' asked Jochi as we sped along. He was powering his jetbike casually, letting it slew and buck in the headwind as if it were a living thing. 'What is next?'

I shrugged. For some reason, I was not much in the mood to talk about it.

'We will never kill them all,' said Batu, his face still purple with bruising from his fight on the platform. 'If they run out, I will breed more myself.'

Jochi laughed, but the sound had a faint edge to it, a faint note of trying too hard.

They were skirting around the issue, but we all knew it was there, sliding under the surface of our jokes and speculations. We did not know what lay ahead for us once the Crusade was over.

He had never told us what he had planned; perhaps, when alone with his own counsel, he shared the same quiet misgivings we did. I found it hard to imagine him having misgivings, though. I found it hard to imagine anything approaching uncertainty in his mind. Whatever the future held for us when the fighting was done, I knew that he would find a place for us within it, just as he had always done.

Perhaps Chondax had got under our skin. It made us feel ephemeral and fleeting sometimes. It made us feel as though we had no roots any more, and that the old certainties had become strangely unreliable.

'I see it!' shouted Hasi, riding out ahead. He stood up in the saddle, his long hair streaming out behind him. 'There!'

I saw it then myself – a puff of white against the sky, indicating vehicles travelling at speed. The trail was nothing like that produced by the greenskins – it was too clean, too clear, and moving too fast.

I felt a tremor of unease, and quickly quelled it. I knew what drove it – pride, an unwillingness to share command, resentment that I was being ordered to.

'Let us see who they are, then,' I said, adjusting course and making for the plume of dust ahead. I could see them slowing up, wheeling around to meet us. 'This brotherhood with no name.'

I DISMOUNTED TO greet my opposite number. He did the same. Our warriors waited some distance behind us, facing one another, still perched on their idling mounts. His force looked to be the same size; five hundred mounts, give or take.

He was taller than me by a hand's width. The skin of his bare head was pale, his chin angular and his neck thickly corded. He wore his hair short, cropped close to the scalp. The long ritual scar across his left cheek was raised and vivid, indicating that the incision had been made in early adulthood. His features were blunt, not the sharp, dark ones I was used to.

He was Terran, then. Most of us from Chogoris shared similar attributes: brown skin, oil-black hair worn long, wiry frames that bunched with muscle even before implantation boosted it further. That uniformity, so we had discovered, came from our lost origins as colonisers. The Terrans of the Legion, drawn from the cradle of our species long before the Crusade had come to us, were more diverse: some had flesh the colour of charred firewood, for others it was as pale as our armour.

'Khan,' he said, bowing.

'Khan,' I replied.

'I am Torghun,' he said, speaking in Khorchin. That did not surprise me; it had been the language of the Legion for the hundred and twenty years since the Master of Mankind had made himself known to us. The Terrans had always adopted it quickly, eager to take on the trappings of their newfound primarch. They found it easier to speak our language than we did theirs. I do not know why that was.

'I am Shiban,' I said, 'of the Brotherhood of the Storm. By what are you known?'

Torghun hesitated for a moment, as if I had asked him something impolite or strange.

'Of the Moon,' he said.

'Which moon?' I asked, since the Khorchin term he used did not specify.

'Terra only has one moon,' he said.

Of course, I thought, chiding myself. I bowed again, anxious to ensure that a state of courtesy existed between us, whatever else might differ.

'Then I am honoured to fight with you, Torghun Khan,' I said.

'The honour is mine, Shiban Khan,' he said.

IT WAS NOT long before we were moving again. Our brotherhoods travelled alongside one another, staying in the formations each of us had adopted prior to being brought together. My warriors adopted their arrowheads, his grouped into loose ranks. Other than that, there was not much to differentiate us.

I like to think that I noticed some minor disparities from the start – some subtle way in which they handled their bikes or carried themselves in the saddle – but in truth I am not sure I did. They were as competent as we were, and looked likely to be as deadly.

I and my minghan-keshig rode intermingled with Torghun and his, at my suggestion. I was determined that we should come to know a little of one another before we were thrown into action. We spoke to one another as we rode, shouting over the thudding of the jetbike engines, leaving the voxes off and enjoying the power of our natural voices. That came naturally to me, but Torghun initially seemed awkward with it.

As the plains roared away beneath us, blasted into clouds of white dust by the powerful backdraught of our machines, our conversation opened up a little.

'Were you on Ullanor?' I asked.

Torghun gave a dry smile, and shook his head. Ullanor had by then already become a badge of honour for the Legions involved; if you had not been a part of it, you needed a reason why.

'On Khella, bringing it to compliance,' he said. 'Before that, though, we'd been on secondment with the Luna Wolves, so I've seen them fight.'

'The Luna Wolves,' I said, nodding with appreciation. 'Fine warriors.'

'We learned a lot from them,' said Torghun. 'They have interesting ideas on warfare, things we'd do well to study. I've become a believer in the secondment system – the Legions have grown too far apart. Ours in particular.'

I was surprised to hear him talking like that, but tried not to show it. As I saw matters, he had it backwards – if there was fault on anyone's part for the V Legion's isolation then it lay with those who overlooked us and pushed us to the margins. Why else were we on Chondax, chasing down the remnants of an empire that had long since ceased to be a threat to the Crusade? Would the Luna Wolves have taken on that work, or the Ultramarines, or the Blood Angels?

But I did not say any of that.

'I am sure you are right,' I said.

Torghun drew close alongside me then, narrowing the gap between our moving bikes to less than a metre.

'Earlier, when you asked me what our designation was, I hesitated,' he said.

'I did not notice,' I said.

'I'm sorry for that. It was discourteous. It's just… it has been a long time since we used those names. You know how it's been – we've each of us been on our own for a long time.'

I held his gaze uneasily, not really understanding his intent.

'There was no discourtesy.'

'My men rarely call me khan. Most prefer "captain". We've got used to being the 64th Company, the White Scars. It helps, to use those terms – the other Legions, for the most part, use them too. For a moment, I forgot the old designation. That's all.'

I did not know whether I believed him.

'Why the 64th?' I asked.

'It's what we were given.'

I did not ask any more than that. I did not ask who had made that choice, or why. Perhaps I should have done then, but such things had never really interested me. The practicalities of war had always consumed me, the demands of the immediate, of the matter-at-hand.

'Call yourself what you want,' I said, smiling, 'as long as you kill hain. That is all he will care about.'

Torghun looked relieved when I said that, as if something he'd worried about divulging had turned out, in the end, to be a minor matter.

'So will he be there with us?' he asked. 'At the end?'

I looked away from Torghun and out to the horizon ahead. It was empty – an unbroken line of bright, cold nothingness. Somewhere, though, they were gathering to face us, to force the final battle for a world they had already lost.

'I hope so,' I said, earnestly. 'I hope he is there.'

Then I stole a quick glance at Torghun, suddenly concerned that he would look down on that sentiment, that he would see it as somehow laughable.

'But you can never tell,' I said, as lightly as I could. 'He is elusive. They all say that about him.'

I smiled again, to myself that time.

'Elusive. Like a berkut. That is what they all say.'

II. ILYA RAVALLION

I SAW ULLANOR for the first time from the crew deck of the fleet lander *Elective XII*. The fighting had only been over for three standard months by then and local space was still crawling with warships. We dropped rapidly through the midst of those huge, hanging giants, and the dark sweep of the planet's surface rose up to fill the realview portals.

It was odd, to see it with my own eyes at last. For so long, Ullanor had dominated my every waking thought. I could reel off statistics – how many billion men had been transported on how many million troop carriers, how many crates of raw supplies had been lifted down from how many cargo conveyers, how many casualties we'd taken (actual) and how many xenos we'd killed (estimate). I knew facts that almost no other person in the Army knew, perfectly useless ones, like the grade of plasteel used in standard ration boxes, and absolutely essential ones, like the time it took those boxes to move to the front line.

Some of those statistics would never leave me. Other people, I imagined, regretted not being able to retain information; I regretted never being able to lose it.

As a young woman I had thought of my eidetic habits as a curse. As it turned out, the Imperial Army valued my aptitudes. I'd made it all the way to general with them, and so had become one of those many greying, anonymous, unsung members of the war machine. We didn't get much praise once the fighting was over, and we got plenty of abuse from stressed field commanders while it was under way, but if we hadn't existed then there would have been no victories to celebrate. War didn't just happen on the whim of warriors – it was planned, orchestrated, fed by supplies and enabled by transportation.

We had been the Corps Logisticae for a while, then a division within the naval administration, then – briefly – overseen by Malcador's people. Only shortly prior to the Warmaster's appointment had we been hived off into a full Departmento, with all the bureaucratic advantages that brought us.

Departmento Munitorum. A dour name for a necessary job.

Mistakes had been made, certainly. Confusion over planetary coordinates, non-standard equipment reaching the Legions. For a while we even had two expeditionary fleets operating under the same numerical designation at opposite sides of the galaxy.

I tried to relax in my cramped seat, feeling the buffeting movement of atmospheric entry. I wasn't looking forward to what was to come once we made planetfall, so worked to take my mind off it by looking at the view.

The world's surface looked ravaged. Dark clouds raced across its surface, broken and straggling like snarls of wire wool. The land beneath was a puckered mass of ravines and defiles, worming through continents like masses of tiny cranial folds.

Only on one zone of Ullanor had that disorder been tamed. Before setting off I'd heard stories from Mechanicum contacts about what had been done to the remnants of Urrlak's fortress, and back then I hadn't quite believed them – they liked to boast about what they could do to worlds once they got their augmetic hands on them.

As I gazed out of the portal and down onto what they had done, I believed them. I saw the route of the victory procession, a scar of rockcrete hundreds of kilometres long. I tried to estimate how wide the ceremonial plaza I was looking at could have been – two hundred square kilometres? Twice that? It glistened under the broken cover of clouds like polished ebony, a colossal plain of stone smoothed out for the sole purpose of giving the Emperor a suitable site for his triumph.

What a piece of work is mankind, I thought then. What infinite faculties we have given ourselves.

The shuttle plunged down towards the cloud cover. I began to feel nauseous, and looked away.

I knew that the Emperor had long gone; returned, so they said, to Terra. I also knew that the Warmaster – as we then had to think of him – was still aboard his flagship, but I didn't know how long he planned to linger. It would have been helpful to know that so we could start to think about resupply for the 63rd Expedition, but there was no sense in trying to pin a primarch down to specifics, especially not *that* primarch.

In any case, my mission did not concern the Warmaster. It concerned one of his brothers, one about whom I knew very little, even from hearsay, and who had a reputation for being – among other things – hard to track down.

I didn't like the sound of that. I didn't like the thought of spending weeks waiting for an audience, and I liked the thought of being granted one even less.

I closed my eyes, feeling the structure of the lander begin to shake.

The things we do for the Emperor, I thought.

✠ ✠ ✠

HERIOL MIERT LOOKED tired, as if he hadn't slept for days. His dark green uniform was creased and the lines under his eyes were deep, as if they'd been etched in ink.

He welcomed me into his makeshift headquarters with the shuffling, slightly glassy look of a man who really needed to see a bed soon.

'First time on Ullanor, general?' he asked as we walked up the stairway to his private office.

'It is,' I said. 'And I missed all the action.'

Miert laughed – a weary chuckle.

'We all did,' he said. 'We're the ones still standing.'

We entered his room: a modest steel-frame box perched atop a column of prefabricated admin units (Terran origin, I guessed, from the frame press-marks). We were a long way from where the Warmaster's investiture ceremony had taken place, but through the windows I could just make out the grandiose towers on the horizon. A few lonely Titans still walked out across the huge expanse of stone, their immense outlines hazy in the drifting cloud.

I began mentally cataloguing their types – Warlord, Reaver, Nemesis – and had to stop myself.

'So how are you, colonel?' I asked, sitting down on a metal chair and crossing my legs.

Miert sat opposite me, and shrugged.

'Things are easing off now,' he said. 'I think we can be proud, all things considered.'

'I agree,' I told him. 'What's your next assignment?'

Miert smiled.

'Retirement,' he said. 'Honourable discharge, then home to Targea.'

'Congratulations. You've earned it.'

'Thank you, general.'

I envied Miert a little. He'd done his duty and had got out while the going was good. At that stage, still several years away from my own retirement, I had very little idea what role lay ahead for me. The gossip running through the Army hierarchy was about large-scale demobilisation. We were running out of planets to conquer, after all.

Not that retirement didn't appeal. Others had done it, and I'd seen what kind of life could be lived after the fighting was over. I didn't want to slog over the figures forever; the idea of going on indefinitely, of one's service ending only in death, that struck me as almost uniquely depressing.

'So you wish to know about the White Scars,' Miert said, sitting back in his chair.

'I was told you know as much as anyone here.'

Miert laughed again, cynically.

'Possibly so. Don't assume that amounts to much.'

'Tell me what you know,' I said. 'It'll all be helpful.'

Miert crossed his arms.

'Liaising with them has been a nightmare,' he said. 'A nightmare. It's mostly been Luna Wolves here, and they're a dream: they do what they say they're going to do. They keep us informed, they make sensible requisitions. The Scars – well, I never know where they are or what they want. When they finally turn up they're very, very good – but what use is that to me? By then I have reserve battalions running out of food and unused kit sitting in warehouses halfway across the sector.'

He shook his head.

'They're frustrating. They don't listen, they don't consult. We've lost men over it, I'm sure.'

Miert gave me a sidelong look then.

'Is that what you're here for?' he asked. 'Is that why you want to see him?'

I smiled tolerantly.

'Just the facts, please,' I said.

'Sorry. From what I hear, they have no close links with the other Legions. They're not hostile exactly, just... not close. They've retained too many habits from Mundus Planus.'

'Chogoris.'

'Whatever. In any case, it's a strange place. They don't use standard rank designations. They don't even use ordered companies – it's all "of the hawk" this and "of the spear" that. You can imagine how hard that makes it to coordinate with anyone else.'

'What of the primarch?' I asked.

'I know nothing. As in, literally, I know nothing. The other ones call him the Khan, but all White Scar captains are called khan, so that doesn't help. I don't even know where he was fighting at the end. He was seen, so I'm told, on the primarchs' balcony when the Emperor was here, but it's hard to get any reliable accounts of what happened before that.'

Miert smiled to himself – the look a man gives when he's spent too long grappling with impossible tasks but will soon be free of them.

'And they're obsessed with courtesy,' he said. 'Courtesy! When you meet them, be sure to learn their titles and use them correctly. They will know all of yours. If you carry ceremonial weaponry, anything of value, they'll want to know about that too.'

I didn't carry anything of value. My life was too organised, too exact, to bother with antique swords. I wondered if I should try to source something.

'What of the Stormseers?' I asked.

'They have a role,' said Miert. 'We just don't know what it is. There are different theories: that they're just like Librarians; that they're entirely different. There's a rumour Magnus the Red thinks highly of them. Or maybe not.'

He spread his hands, admitting defeat.

'You see?' he said. 'It's hopeless.'

'This Stormseer, the one you've arranged for me to meet,' I said. 'Is he senior? Does he have the ear of the Khan?'

'I hope so,' said Miert. 'He was hard enough to find, and I had to call in a few favours. Don't blame me if he's not, though – we honestly did what we could.'

I didn't feel like I was learning very much.

'I'm sure you did, colonel,' I said. 'We will have to make do and hope for the best. Unless there was anything else?'

Miert gave me a slightly impish look.

'You may have noticed a superficial likeness to the Sixth Legion, the Wolves of Fenris,' Miert said. 'You know, the whole barbarian thing.'

He rolled his eyes.

'Don't bring it up,' he warned. 'We've been burned by that before. It makes them very annoyed.'

'Why?'

'I don't know. Envy? But, seriously, leave it alone.'

'Then I will, colonel,' I said, feeling more pessimistic about the upcoming meeting with every equivocal morsel of information that emerged. I needed more. I needed details. Those were the things that made me function. 'Thank you. You've been helpful.'

I TOOK A crawler – an Augean RT-56, Enyiad variant by its track-pattern – out from the triumph plain and into the badlands beyond. It was uncomfortable and hot. The air tasted of grit, and it was impossible not to imagine the stench of ork spoor lurking under it all.

He didn't make himself easy to find, just as Miert had warned. I never got the impression that he was deliberately being difficult, just that he had absolutely no concern whether I stumbled across him or not. His locator beacon flickered in and out of existence as we travelled, blocked by the dense ranks of undulating rock around us. When I finally homed in on it, we had been travelling for over four and three-quarter hours.

I did what I could to make myself look presentable before disembarking – smoothing down my greying hair and adjusting the creases of my dress uniform. Perhaps I should have made more effort. Physical appearance had always been the least of my concerns, a trait that age had only accelerated.

Too late now. I took a swig of warm water from my canteen and dabbed some on my sweating forehead.

He must have seen us coming. Even then he made no effort to come to us, remaining high up on a long ridge that was too steep for the crawler to negotiate. I left it at the base, stepping out on the dusty surface – the true surface – of Ullanor for the first time since making planetfall.

'Stay here,' I told the crawler's crew, including the security detail Miert had sent out with me. I had little concern for my own safety, but I did worry about somehow offending him by going up mob-handed.

Then I started to climb. I was not in the greatest shape – years of filing reports in Administratum vaults had not given me a battle-hardened body and I'd never bothered much with juvenat treatments.

I wondered what he would make of me when he saw me – a slight, hard-faced woman in a general's uniform. I felt my skin grow sweaty again as I laboured, and the creases I'd smoothed in my uniform crumpled. I would look frail to him, possibly ludicrous.

I stumbled as I reached the top. My foot slipped on loose scree, and I staggered against the rock. I reached out with my right hand, hoping to catch hold of the lip of the ridge. Instead of stone, my fingers clamped onto an armoured hand. It held me firmly.

I looked up, startled, to find myself staring into two golden eyes set in a leather-brown face.

'General Ilya Ravallion, Departmento Munitorum,' said the owner of the face, inclining his head politely. 'Be careful.'

I swallowed, holding onto his gauntlet tightly.

'Thank you,' I said. 'I will.'

HIS NAME WAS Targutai Yesugei. He told me that as soon as I'd dusted myself down and recovered my breath. We stood, the two of us, on the ridge. The dry gullies and defiles of Ullanor ran away from us in every direction, a maze of charred debris and gravel. Above us, dark clouds drifted.

'Not much of a world,' he said.

'Not any more,' I agreed.

His voice was like the voice of every Space Marine I had ever encountered – low, resonant, held quiet, echoing up from his barrel chest like crude oil slapping at the sides of a deep well. If he ever chose to raise it, I knew it could be terrifyingly loud. Back then, though, it was a curiously calming sound to hear, out there in the aftermath of devastation.

He wasn't as tall as some I'd met. Even clad in his armour plate, I had the impression of a certain wiriness; a compact, lean frame under sun-hardened flesh. His bald head was crowned with a long scalp-lock that snaked down around his neck. Tattoos had been inked into the skin on his temples. I couldn't make out what they signified – they looked like the letters of a language I didn't understand. He carried a skull-topped staff, and wore a glistening crystalline hood over the shoulders of his armour.

Amid a lattice of other ritual scarring, he had a broad, jagged mark running down his left cheek, from just under the eye socket almost to the chin. I knew what that was. For a long time that custom had been the only thing I'd known about them. They did it themselves once they'd been inducted – they made the scars that gave the Legion its name.

His eyes seemed golden. His irises were almost bronze, and the whites were a pale yellow. I hadn't expected that. I didn't know then whether all of them were like that, or whether it was just him.

'You fight on this world, Ilya Ravallion?' he asked.

He spoke Gothic awkwardly, with a thick, guttural accent. I hadn't expected that either.

'I did not,' I said.

'What are you doing here?'

'I was sent to seek an audience with the Khan.'

'Know how many he grants?'

'I do not.'

'Not many,' he said.

A half-smile played over his brown lips as he spoke. His skin creased with every smile, wrinkling at the eyes. He looked like he smiled often and easily.

In those early exchanges, I could not decide whether he was toying with me or whether he was serious. His clipped delivery made it hard to divine his meaning.

'I was hoping, lord,' I said, 'that you might assist me.'

'So you do not wish to speak to me,' he said. 'You use me to get to him.'

I decided to stick to the truth.

'That is correct,' I said.

Yesugei chuckled. It was a tight, hard, wind-dried sound, though not without humour.

'Good,' he said. 'I am… intermediary. That is what we do, the zadyin arga – we speak from one, to the other. Worlds, universes, souls – is much the same.'

I was still tense. I couldn't tell whether things were going well. A great deal rested on the meeting I had been sent to arrange, and it would be hard to go back having achieved nothing. At the very least, though, Yesugei was still talking, which I took as a good sign.

All the while I took in details, storing them away, my mind working automatically. I couldn't help myself.

His armour is Mark II. Indicates conservatism? The skull on his staff is unidentifiable; Chogorian fauna, no doubt. Equine? Check with Miert later.

'If you had your audience,' he asked, 'what would you say?'

I had dreaded that particular question, though it had been bound to come up.

'Forgive me, lord, it is for his ears only. It concerns business between the Fifth Legion and the Administratum.'

Yesugei gave me a shrewd look.

'And what would you say if I reached into your mind, right now, and took the answer? Do not think you are shielded from me.'

I stiffened. As soon as he made the suggestion, I knew he could do it.

'I would prevent you, if I could,' I said.

He nodded again.

'Good,' he said. 'Though, in case you are worried, I would not do it.'

He smiled at me again. Against all expectation, I found myself beginning to relax. That was strange, standing as I was next to a towering, armoured, genhanced, psychically-charged killing machine.

Spoken Gothic surprisingly poor. A reason for unsatisfactory communication with centre? Had assumed linguistic aptitude; may have to revise.

'I admire perseverance, General Ravallion,' Yesugei said. 'You work hard to find me here. You always work hard, ever since you start.'

What did that mean? I hadn't expected him to have researched me. As soon as I thought that, though, I admonished myself – what did I think, that they were *really* savages?

'We know you,' he went on. 'We like what we see. I wonder, though, how much you know us? You know what you let yourself in for, dealing with White Scars?'

For the first time, his smile ghosted with something like menace.

'I don't,' I said. 'But I can learn.'

'Maybe,' he said.

He turned away from me, looking back out over the smoulder-dark landscape. He didn't say anything. I hardly dared to breathe. We stood next to one another as the clouds scudded overhead, both of us locked in silence.

After a long time like that, Yesugei spoke again.

'Some problems are complex – most are not,' he said. 'The Khan does not grant many audiences. Why? Not many people ask.'

He turned back to me.

'I see what I can do,' he said. 'Do not leave Ullanor. If news is good, I will find way to contact you.'

I struggled to hide my relief.

'Thank you,' I said.

He gave me an almost indulgent look.

'Do not thank me yet,' he said. 'I only say I will try.'

A deep, raw humour danced in those golden eyes as he looked at me.

'They say he is elusive,' he said. 'You will hear that a lot. But listen: he is not elusive, he is at the centre. Wherever he is, that is the centre. He will seem to have broken the circle, drifted to the edge, right until the end, and then you will see that the world has come to him, and he has been waiting for it all along. Do you understand?'

I looked him in the eye.

'I don't, Khan Targutai Yesugei of the zadyin arga,' I said, sticking to my policy of honesty and hoping I'd got the titles right. 'But I can learn.'

III. TARGUTAI YESUGEI

I WAS SIXTEEN years old. Those were the years of Chogoris, though, which are short. If I had been born on Terra, I would have been twelve.

I sometimes think our world forced us to grow up quickly – the seasons pass in rapid succession, and we learn the skills of survival very soon. Out on the high Altak, the weather can change so suddenly, from frost to baking sun, that you need to be nimble on your feet. You have to learn how to hunt, to feed yourself, to make or find shelter, to understand the tortuous, swaying politics of our many clans and peoples.

But perhaps we did not grow up quickly enough. In the days after the Master of Mankind came to us, we found that our warrior ways – our speed, our prowess – made us strong. We did not pause to reflect on what our weaknesses were. It was left to others to show us those, by which time it was too late to change them.

Before He came I did not know that there were other worlds, populated by other men with other ways of being. I only knew of one sky and one earth, and they seemed both infinite and eternal. Now that I have seen other earths and marched to war under their strange skies, I find my mind returning to Chogoris often. It is diminished in my imagination, but also more precious. I would go back if I could. I do not know if that will ever be possible.

More than a century has passed since I was a child. I ought to be wiser, and I ought to have left my memories behind me, but we never leave our childhood behind us: we carry it with us, and it whispers to us, reminding us of the paths we could have taken.

I ought to be wiser, and not listen, but I do. Who does not listen to the voice of their memories?

I WAS ALONE then. I had gone into the mountains of the Ulaav, walking the high ways. Those mountains are not tall, not like those of Fenris or Qavalon. They are not as majestic as the mighty Khum Karta, where our fortress-monastery was raised, many years later. The Ulaav are ancient mountains, worn down by millennia of winds from across the Altak. In summer a rider can crest the summits and never leave the saddle; in winter only berkut and ghosts can endure the cold.

I had been sent there by the khan. Those were the days when we were always at war, whether it was with one another or against the forces of the Khitan, and a boy with golden eyes was a prize worth much to all sides.

Later, I read accounts of those wars written by Imperial remembrancers. I struggled to do this as, to my shame, I never learned their language as well as I should have. Many of us in the Legion had such struggles. Perhaps Khorchin and Gothic were too far removed from one another for easy comprehension. Perhaps that was why we and the Imperium were always at cross purposes, even in the beginning.

In any case, those remembrancers referred to places I have never heard of and men who never lived, like the Palatine of Mundus Planus. I do not know where they got those names from. When we were fighting the Khitan we called their emperor by his title – Khagan, a khan of khans. We had no idea what his family name was, though I found it out later. He was called Ketugu Suogo. Since we keep so few records of our own, this knowledge is scarce. I am possibly one of the few left who knows it, and when I am gone, his name will be gone too.

Does that matter? Does it matter that we were fighting a man who never lived on a world that I have never heard of?

I think it does. Names are important; history is important.

Symbols are important.

I WAS ALONE because I had to be. The khan would not have sent such a precious commodity into the mountains if he could have helped it; by choice, he would have surrounded me with men of his keshig, sworn to protect me should the enemy get wind of my vulnerability and seek to snatch me away.

Unfortunately for him, the test of heaven only worked on a single mind. We had strange and bashful gods on Chogoris; they only showed themselves to lone souls, and only where the land rose to meet the infinite sky and the veil between realms was thin and perilous.

So, even knowing what danger waited for me, the khan's warriors left me at the foot of the mountains, and I made my way up into the heights alone. Once I started walking I did not look back. The air was already biting, whistling under my rough kaftan and chafing against my flesh. I shivered, huddling my arms to my chest and keeping my head down.

The valleys of the Ulaav mountains were famously beautiful. Melt-water created lakes of cobalt in the shadowed laps of the peaks. Pine forests ran down sheer rock-shoulders in cloaks of dark green, dense and glossy like lacquered armour. The sky above the summits was glass-clear, so intensely blue it hurt the eyes to look at. Every-thing there was hard, stern, clean. Even in my half-chilled state, I was moved by it. I understood, as I neared the high places, why the gods lingered there.

Aside from that, I felt nothing – no visions, no magical powers, no bursts of supernatural strength. The only mark of my unique-ness was my eyes, and they had done nothing thus far but bring me trouble. If it had not been for the khan I would likely long since have been killed, but he recognised my potential before I did. He was a far-sighted man, with a vision for Chogoris that I was too young to understand. He also knew how useful I could be to him if he was right.

I climbed higher, following tracks that were seldom trodden and which were little more than pale impressions on loose stone. By the time I stopped, my head light from the thin air, I was high up on the eastern scarps and could see how far I had come.

Both of Chogoris's moons were up, even though the sun had not yet set in the north. I was looking out across the vast expanse of the eastern Altak – the endless plain of scrub-grass that ran away further than anyone had ever travelled. From my vantage, I could see tiny sparks of camp fires out in the wilds, separated by huge, empty distances and overlooked by the lowering sky.

Those lands were the khan's, though in those days they were still contested by other tribes and clans. Beyond them, over the eastern horizon, lay the realms of the Khitan.

I had never seen so far. I sat down, leaning against a shelf of bare rock, gazing out across the vista before me. Night-birds wheeled high above, and I saw the first stars come out in the frost-blue sky.

I do not know how long I sat there, a single soul exposed on the flanks of the Ulaav, shivering as night fell across the world.

I should have made a fire. I should have begun the work of

making a shelter. For some reason, I did nothing. Maybe I was fatigued from the climb, or dizzy from the sparse air, but I stayed where I was, cross-legged, gazing out across the darkening Altak, mesmerised by the tiny golden lights glowing out on the plain, held in thrall by their silver counterparts in the arch of heaven above.

I felt that I was in the right place then. I did not need to do anything, or change anything, or move anything.

If something was going to happen, it would happen to me there. I would wait for it, as patient as an aduu under halter.

It could find me. I had done enough travelling.

I WOKE SUDDENLY.

It must have been much later – the sky was velvet dark, pocked with a glittering cloak of stars. Distant campfires still twinkled out on the plain, now sunk into deep, deep blue. It was bitterly cold, and the wind rustled the dry branches around me.

One by one, I saw the fires across the Altak die. They winked out of existence, leaving the plain even emptier – just a void, broken by nothing.

I tried to move. I found that I could glide upwards, swimming through the air as if it were water. I looked down at myself and saw a sleek, feather-lined body. I rose quickly, circling higher, feeling the breeze lift my trembling wings.

The mountains fell away below me. The curve of the world's horizon dropped. In the east, over where the lands of the Khitan lay, I saw more lights going out. The whole world, all of it, was sliding into darkness.

I hovered, tilting a little in the high winds. I called out, and heard the *crii* of a night-bird. It felt like I was the only living thing in creation.

Soon I was alone with the stars. They continued to burn silver in the space above me. I flew ever higher, beating my wings against thinning air.

I came amongst them. I saw lights burning in the vaults of heaven. I saw fires raging and curls of flame flickering in the darkness. I saw things I did not recognise, mighty iron-clad things with prows like ploughshares, torn apart and reduced to drifting pieces. Forces too immense for me to comprehend were fighting across the trackless void.

So these are the gods, I thought.

I passed among the wreckage of those things, marvelling at the shapes and symbols carved on shards of spinning metal. I saw a many-headed snake-creature embossed upon one fragment; the head of a wolf on another. Then I saw a sign I recognised – a lightning strike in gold and red, the eternal mark of the khans.

Part of me knew those things were visions, and that my body remained where I had left it on the slopes of the Ulaav. Another part of me, perhaps the wiser, recognised that I was seeing something real, something more than real, something that underpinned reality like the poles of a *ger* underpin the fabric.

Then, like the fires on the Altak, the fires in the stars faded away. Everything went dark. I knew, though, that I was not falling asleep again. I knew that something else was coming for me.

I WAS OUT on the plain. It was noon, and the sun burned white in the empty sky. The wind came down from the mountains, rustling the scrub-grass and tugging at my kaftan.

I looked down and saw a cup in my left hand. It was earthenware, like all the cups of the *ordu*. Blood-red liquid filled it nearly to the brim.

I looked up again, shading my eyes against the piercing sun, and saw four figures standing before me. Their outlines were shaky, as if broken by heat-haze, except that it wasn't hot.

All of them had the bodies of men and the heads of animals. One had the head of a blue-feathered bird with amber eyes; one had the head of a serpent; one had the head of a red-eyed bull; one had the decaying head of a fish, already yellowed with putrescence.

All of them looked at me, shimmering in the direct light. They lifted their arms and pointed.

None of them spoke. They did not have human lips to speak with. For all that, I knew what they wanted me to do. Somehow their thoughts took shape in my own mind, as clear and distinct as if I had summoned them up myself.

Drink they told me.

I looked down at the cup in my left hand. The liquid within was hot. Froth had collected around the rim. I felt a sudden thirst break out. I lifted the cup halfway to my mouth, and my hand trembled as I did so.

I knew something important was in there, but I held back. My instincts warred within me.

Drink they told me.

The tone of their command gave me pause. I did not know why they wanted me to do it.

It was then that I saw Him. He came from the opposite direction. He had the shape of a man too, but the halo of light around Him made it hard to make much more out than that. I could not see His face. He was coming towards me, and I knew, without knowing how, that He had travelled from a long, long way away.

He gave me no command. Other than that, He was like the four beast-figures. There was some relationship between them, something I could sense but did not understand. The Four were scared of Him. I knew then that if I drank from the cup, then I would be defying Him – if I did not drink, I would be defying them.

We all remained like that for the space of many thoughts. The Four pointed at me. The man wreathed in light walked towards me, never seeming to come any closer.

Drink they told me.

I lifted the cup to my lips. I took a sip. The liquid had a complex taste: sweet to begin with, then bitter. I felt it flow down my throat, hot and vital. As soon as I had started, I felt an urge to keep drinking. I wanted nothing more than to swallow it all down, to drain it to the dregs.

Drink they told me.

After that one sip, I put the cup down, crouching carefully and resting it on the earth before me. For all my care, it spilled a little, staining my fingers. Then I took a step away from it.

I bowed to the Four, not wishing to give offence. I spoke, not really knowing where my words came from.

'It is courteous to take a small amount,' I said. 'That is enough for us.'

The Four lowered their arms. They did not command me again. The man stopped walking, still just where He had been when I had first seen Him.

I felt that I had disappointed all of them. Perhaps, though, I had disappointed Him less than I had them.

The vision began to fade. I could feel the hardness of the real world reasserting itself. The sunlit plain before me rippled like water, and I saw gaps of darkness under it.

I wanted to stay. I knew that my return to the world of the senses would be painful.

I looked again at the man, hoping to make out something of His face before the dreaming ended.

I saw nothing but light, flickering and wheeling around a core of brightness. There was no warmth in that light; just brilliance. He was like a cold sun.

When His light was taken away, though, I felt the loss of it.

I WOKE, FOR real that time, shuddering from the chill. My limbs ached, and were as red as raw meat. I tried to move and felt spikes of agony in my joints. Everything hurt – I felt flayed.

It was dawn. Below me the plains were milky with mist. I saw an arrowhead of birds scud across them, moving just like our formations of mounted warriors did. Pale lines of smoke rose up through the mist, the last remnants of the fires that had burned through the night.

I forced myself to move. After a while, the worst of the pain began to ebb. I jogged and waved my arms, unstiffening my knees and my elbows. Blood started to flow around my body again. I was still very cold, but movement helped.

I could still remember my visions. I knew what they were. Uig, the khan's old zadyin arga had told me to expect them. That was the test of heaven – once the visions came, they would never leave.

I didn't know how to feel about that. On the one hand, it was confirmation of what I had always believed about myself. On the other, it presaged a life of loneliness.

A zadyin arga was not a warrior. He did not travel the plains in lacquer armour fighting for his khan: his life was a solitary one, shackled to the gers, protected at all times and forced to root through entrails and scry the stars. The position was one of honour, but not of the highest honour. Like all the boys of the tribe, I had dreamed of riding the steppes, taking war to the enemies of my brothers and of my khan.

As I stood, shivering upon the slopes of the Ulaav, watching the mist boil away from the plains, I contemplated telling them that the test had failed; that my golden eyes were nothing more than a strange, harmless affliction.

I even began to wonder whether the things I had seen had been nothing more than dreams, the kind that everybody has. I tried to make myself believe that.

Then I looked down at my hands. The ends of my fingers were still stained red.

I stuffed those hands into the sleeves of my clothes, unwilling to look at them. Slowly, I started to walk back the way I had come.

I had passed from one way of being into another during that night. The change was profound, and over the wearing years I would gradually learn just *how* profound – back then, though, it felt like almost nothing had changed. I was still a child, and I knew nothing of what powers had been stirred into life within me.

Even now, more than a century later, I am still a child in that respect. We all are, those of us with power: we know so little, we see so imperfectly.

And that is both a great curse and a great blessing, for if we knew more and saw more perfectly then we would surely go mad.

IT TOOK ME longer to travel down from the heights than it had taken me to climb them. I stumbled often, slipping down loose banks of scree with my numb limbs. When the sun came up fully, my pace improved. I stopped only as I neared the level of the plains, back at the head of the valley I had walked up the previous day.

I saw what remained of my escort's camp from a distance, and immediately knew that something was wrong. I crouched down beside the trunk of a tree and screwed my eyes up, peering down a long, meandering river-course to where the khan's warriors had left me.

The aduun were gone. I saw bodies on the ground in awkward poses. I felt my heartbeat quicken. Twelve warriors had come with me into the mountains; twelve bodies lay on the ground around the remains of the fire.

I moved closer to the trunk. I had no idea what to do. I knew that I needed to get back to the khan's side, but also that I was now dangerously exposed. The plains were no place to travel alone – there were no hiding places out on the Altak.

I would have waited there longer had I not heard them coming for me. From somewhere higher up, I heard the snap of branches

and the loud, careless voices of soldiers singing in a language I
didn't know.

A single word flashed through my mind, chilling my blood.

Khitan.

Somehow I had passed them on the way down – they must have
been hunting for me up in the highlands, and only dumb luck had
carried me past them undetected.

They were close, rooting through the undergrowth. For all I knew
there were more of them, crawling across the Ulaav like ants out
of a kicked nest.

I didn't stop to think. I ran, darting out of the cover of the trees
and tearing down to where the khan's men had been killed. Even
as I skidded and slipped down the steep path I could hear the cries
of the Khitan as they caught sight of me and lumbered into pursuit.

I ran as hard as I could, feeling my lungs burn as my breathing
became heavy. I ran like an animal runs, fuelled by fear. I didn't
look back.

My only thought was to get clear of the hunters, to get out into
open ground, to find the khan. He led the mightiest warband on
the Altak, one that grew every day. He would be able to protect me
even if the Khitan who chased me numbered in hundreds.

But I had to find him. Somehow, I had to stay alive long enough
to find him.

I knew his reputation. I knew that he moved around without
warning, shifting from place to place to keep his enemies guessing.
Even Uig, who could see all paths, had called him the berkut – the
hunting eagle, the far-ranger, the elusive.

Such thoughts did not help. I forced my mind to remain fixed on
the task. I kept running, leaping over briars and swerving around
boulders. The voices of my hunters followed me, and I heard their
boots thud against the earth.

I had no more choices to make. All the ways of the future had narrowed down to a single course, and I could do nothing but follow it.

I ran down from the mountains and out into the plains-grass beyond. I had no plan, no allies, and little hope. All I had was my life, newly enriched with visions of another world. I intended to fight for it, but did not yet know how.

IV. SHIBAN

WE KNEW THEY would make a fight of it in the end. Once there was nowhere left for them to run, they turned and faced us.

They had chosen a good place to make their stand. High in Chondax's northern hemisphere, the endless white plains eventually crumpled into a maze of ravines and jagged peaks, a scar on the open face of the world that was visible from space. We had never penetrated far into that region, opting to clear the orks from the plains first. It was natural defensive terrain – hard to enter, easy to hide in.

When our auspex operators had seen it from orbit, they had called it *teghazi*: the Grinder. I think that was their idea of a joke.

I stood in the saddle, looking out at the first of the many cliffs rising up against the northern horizon. I could see long trails of smoke rising from the heart of the rock cluster.

I raised magnoculars to my eyes and zoomed in. Metal artefacts had been placed amid the stone, glinting in the bright sunlight. The orks had built walls across narrow ravine entrances, using material stripped from their own vehicles. Knowing that they would not need them again, they had turned their only means of movement into their only means of defence.

I approved of that.

'They are well positioned,' I said, scanning across the fortifications.

'They are,' said Torghun, standing beside me and also using magnoculars. Our two brotherhoods spread out behind us in their assault formations, waiting for the order to advance. 'I see fixed weapons. They've got numbers.'

I swept my view across to the nearest of the ravine mouths facing us. Walls were clearly visible, placed further back between the jaws of the ravine and strung across the gulley floor in a line of metal panels and bolted struts. I could see orks patrolling along the top of them. As Torghun had noted, there were weapon towers lodged higher up the ravine slopes.

'This will be difficult,' I said.

Torghun laughed.

'It will, Shiban.'

In the days since we had joined forces, I had not found it easy to understand Torghun. Sometimes he would laugh and I would not know why. Sometimes I would laugh and he would look at me strangely.

He was a good warrior, and I think we both respected one another when it came to blades. We had destroyed two more convoys before we had arrived at the Grinder, and I had seen at first-hand how his brotherhood fought.

They were more structured than we were. I rarely gave my brothers orders once an engagement started: I trusted them to look after themselves. Torghun gave his warriors orders all the time, and they followed them instantly. They used speed, just as we did, but were quicker to adopt fire positions when the combat became more static.

Some tactics I never saw them adopt. They never pulled back, feigning retreat in order to draw out the enemy.

'We don't retreat,' he had said.

'It is effective,' I had replied.

'More effective to let them know you'll never do it,' he had said, smiling. 'When the Luna Wolves go to war, the enemy knows they'll never stop coming forwards, all the time, wave after wave, until it's over. It's a powerful reputation to have.'

I could hardly argue against the record of the Warmaster's Legion. I had seen them fight. They were impressive.

So, as I scanned the greenskins' defences, I had little idea what Torghun would propose. I feared that he would advocate waiting until other minghan reached our position, and I did not relish disputing with him. I wished to maintain our momentum, since I knew that other brotherhoods would already be entering combat on the far sides of the huge ravine complex. If we were to gain the honour of fighting alongside the Khagan – who would surely be at the heart of the action – then we would have to remain at the forefront of the closing circle.

'I do not wish to wait,' I said firmly, putting my magnoculars down and looking at Torghun. 'We can break them.'

Torghun did not reply immediately. He continued looking out at the distant cliff-faces, scanning for weaknesses. Eventually he stopped and looked at me.

He grinned. I had seen that grin before; it was one of the few gestures we shared. He grinned before he entered battle, just as I did.

'I think you're right, brother,' he said.

WE CAME IN hard over on the left flank of our target, building quickly to attack speed, burning across the plains in close-packed squadrons. I crouched low in the saddle, gripping the controls of my mount, feeling the animal grind of the engines, the hard vibrations of the blazing thrusters, the violent urgings of the caged machine-spirit. My brothers spread out on either side of me, speeding across the white earth in perfect formation.

The ravine entrance we had chosen was narrow – two hundred metres across, as the auspex read it – and clogged with defenders. We skirted wide, using the cliffs jutting out on either side of its jaws to mask our approach. I felt my braided hair whip against my shoulder guards. We ate up the ground, devouring it, tearing it up in a blaze of furious motion.

We had timed our run to coincide with the rising of the third sun. As it emerged behind us, flaring silver, blinding the defenders to our advance, I cried out to greet it.

'For the Khagan!' I roared.

'For the Khagan!' came the thunderous, rapturous response.

I relished that: five hundred of us on the charge, thundering into range at searing velocity, wreathed in a dazzling corona of silver and gold, our jetbikes bucking and swerving. I saw Jochi alongside me, hurling out battle-cries in Khorchin, his eyes alive with blood-lust. Batu, Hasi, the rest of my minghan-keshig, they all hunkered forwards, all straining at the leash.

The first volleys of defensive fire snapped and bounced around us, a motley rain of solid rounds and crude energy bolts. We weaved amongst them, goading our jetbikes ever faster, glorying in their superb poise, rush and tilt.

The jutting cliffs zoomed up to meet us. We came around, leaning heavily, scraping the ground before racing into the mouth of the valley beyond.

We cleared the cover of the cliffs, and our senses were overrun by a crashing, coruscating storm of incoming fire. A hurricane of projectiles spiralled out of the walls ahead of us, blowing up in our faces and hurling bikes end-over-end.

A rider close to me took a direct hit. His mount disintegrated, ripped apart in a shower of metal and promethium, flying crazily across the ravine and slamming into the ground in a smear of flame and debris. Warriors were hurled from their saddles, had holes punched through their armour, were sent careering into the rock walls where they exploded in massive, blooming fireballs.

None of us slowed. We hurtled down the ravine, maintaining attack speed, ducking and swaying around the lines of fire, rising above it to widen the field before plunging back down to ground level and letting it streak over our heads.

I poured on more power, feeling my bike shudder with the strain. The land around was a mess of streaked, blurred white – only the metal walls ahead remained in focus. I felt shots graze against my bike's forward armour, nearly throwing me out of line. More of my brothers went down as the torrent of flak and shrapnel took them.

The walls screamed closer. I saw orks leaping about on top of them, waving their weapons and roaring challenges. Gun towers zeroed in on us, swivelling to let loose before we hit them.

We opened up. A pounding cacophony of heavy bolter fire snarled out, filling the ravine with a ragged hail of ruinous, withering destruction. The walls disappeared behind bursting clouds of explosive devastation. Metal plates snapped and dented, blowing apart in a hail of splinters. I saw greenskins thrown high into the air, their bodies shredded open by the flood of shells.

Just then, as he had promised they would, Torghun's heavy support opened fire. His auxiliary squads had broken off, making the most of the screen of our frontal assault and securing high ground on either side of the ravine. They possessed tools of devastation that we didn't carry: lascannons, missile launchers, barrel-cycling autocannons, even an esoteric beam-weapon they called a 'volkite culverin', something I had never seen before.

Their barrage was devastating, igniting the air around it, cracking into the barrier ahead of us and dousing it in a cataract of raging, swimming energy. Huge rents were blown open. Panels, struts and spars went spinning, tearing through the curtains of flame. Missiles streaked in, angling through the storm of destruction, whistling past us and crashing into the burning ork lines beyond. Neon-bright spears of energy snapped and fizzed, sending lurid glows racing along the rock walls.

I picked my target, aiming for a fire-rimmed breach in the walls. I hurtled through the inferno towards it, feeling sheets of flame sweep and shimmer across me. I swung over almost to the horizontal, letting an ork missile whine past. Then I rocked back upright, kicked in a final boost and shot clean through the ragged gap in the walls.

Something must have hit me as I burst through the defences. I felt a thud somewhere under the bike's undercarriage, and it spun away hard right. I grappled with the controls, barely arresting a fatal spin.

The world slurred around me, rocking and spiralling. I could hear other jetbikes streak through the gouges in the walls and turn their heavy bolters upon the defenders. I had a brief glimpse of the ravine on the far side – studded with ramshackle barricades and choke-points, crawling with whole gangs of orks, all of them teeming with brutish fury. Gunfire, thick and incessant, criss-crossed the narrow defile, broken by airborne bursts and flak clouds.

I swung around, diving under a flurry of incoming rounds before gunning my faltering drive unit again. Trailing smoke, my bike lurched and bucked before it gave out completely, throwing me into a sharp dive.

The rocky ground rushed towards me in a sickening plummet. I leapt, hurling myself from the saddle. I hit the ground hard and rolled away, hearing the sharp crack of my bike impacting on the ravine floor, followed by the whoosh and bang of its fuel tanks going up.

I jumped to my feet as wreckage rained down around me, my glaive already poised. I'd come about two hundred metres beyond the walls. I could see the barrier from the other side – the scaffolding collapsing, the ammo-lifters going up like torches, the shuddering impacts from Torghun's punishing long-range fire. Bodies were everywhere, falling from the tottering parapets, swarming over the rock. The air was dense with an incredible fog of noise – screams, bellows, jetbike engines throttling up, cannons discharging.

Greenskins were already homing in, knots of them, firing at me from makeshift carbines and pistols and lumbering to the charge. I felt the ping and crack of the solid rounds as they ricocheted from my armour. I heard their bestial, throaty war-challenges. I smelt the stench of their anger.

I flicked the guan dao's energy field on, feeling the shaft tremble as it powered up.

By the time they closed on me, I was more than ready.

I whipped my upper body around, punching out with the guan dao. The crackling edge dug deep into the leading ork's face, slicing open its flesh and sending the creature staggering backwards in a bloody, flailing froth.

Another threw a wild hack with a cleaver, biting into my pauldron but failing to penetrate the ceramite. I plunged my glaive into its stomach, twisting it round, liquefying the hard flesh. More piled in, and I tore through them, spinning and stabbing. The guan dao sang in my hands, spiralling around me in a glistening net of sparkling power. Greenskins were thrown clear, their armour cracked, their bodies broken.

I barely heard the thunder and rush of the battle around me. My mind drilled down to the core of combat, and I lost myself in it, unaware of the flaming sky above me, unaware of the scores of jetbikes tearing past with their weapons blazing.

I rotated, swiping a greenskin's head clean off, then darted back, cracking the heel of the guan dao into the skull of another. I eviscerated, gouged, ripped, snapped and blinded, boosted by my armour, my strength, my vicious artistry.

One of them, a huge tusked monster with rusty iron pauldrons, threw itself bodily at me, somehow evading my blade and getting under my guard. We collided with a jarring thud and both sprawled to the ground. The creature landed on top of me, and the stink of it clogged in my nostrils. It butted my face, and the force of the blow cracked my head back. My vision swam, and I saw blood wash across my eyes.

I was pinned. I tried to bring the glaive, still clutched in my left hand, around to dig into the monster's back. It saw the movement and twisted to block it with its own weapon – a spiked maul already covered in a slick of blood. The guan dao's energy field detonated on contact, shattering the maul-head in a shower of metal fragments, lacerating both of us.

The greenskin jerked back up, loosening its grip, clawing at its eyes and bellowing with pain. With a huge heave, I pushed it clear and swung the glaive round in a whip-lash figure, aiming for the stomach. The blade cut deep, driving between armour plates and severing the ork down to the spine. I wrenched the shaft back out, hauling hard with both hands. The monster bisected, its torso disintegrating in a sucking swamp of ripped muscle, blood and bone.

I heard another movement from behind me and whirled around, primed to swing again.

Jochi stood there, his armour streaked with red, his bolter in hand, surrounded by heaps of ork corpses. Behind him I could see the ramshackle barrier coming down, slowly toppling as the fires ripped through it. My brothers were everywhere, harrying, pursuing, slaying, tearing like vengeful ghosts through the teeming hordes.

'This is good hunting, my khan!' Jochi observed, laughing heartily.

I joined him in his mirth, feeling the cuts across my face open up.

'And not done yet!' I shouted, shaking the blood from my blade, turning to find more prey. Jetbikes shot overhead, powered onwards by whooping, shrieking riders.

Under their wheeling shadows, we launched back into the fight.

THE BATTLE IN the ravine did not let up once the walls had been broken. More barriers had been strung across the winding gorges ahead, clogging the routes leading deeper into the interior of the Grinder. Greenskins had dug themselves in wherever they could. They poured out of their refuges, lurching at us in waves, scrambling over the rocky ravine floor in their haste to blood us. We were dragged deep into melee combat, assailed from all sides as we cut our way down the long defiles and gulches.

Many of my brothers remained mounted, sweeping up and down the long valley and taking out enemy fire positions with a speed the defenders could not match. Others advanced on foot, as I did, racing to bring combat to the greenskins.

When we got in close, we smelt the blood and sweat on our prey. We heard their broken roars and felt the tremors of their massed tread. Even as we cut them down we relished their skill and their savage bravery, appreciating what superlative creatures we were purging from existence.

Jochi had been right. When the last greenskin was gone, it would be a sad day.

My only concern was Torghun's slow advance. We surged onwards, punching our way far up the gorge, torching every barricade we came across and slaying freely. I had expected Torghun's brotherhood to be close behind us. We would have welcomed the cover of their heavy weapons squads.

We began to lose them. They needed to be quicker.

After fighting our way to the first intersection in the twisting ravine system, I withdrew from the combat, letting my warriors take the fight to the enemy.

'My brother!' I shouted into the vox, using the channel that Torghun and I had designated for private messages between us. 'What keeps you? Are you sleeping? We have them on the run!'

I had intended my speech to be light, just as I always spoke when in the midst of battle. Perhaps I might even have laughed a little.

Torghun's reply startled me.

'*What are you doing?*' he responded. Even over the comm-link, I could hear the anger in his voice. '*Consolidate your position, captain. You are getting strung out. I will not match this pace. We have not secured our entry points.*'

I looked around me. The battle was chaotic and free-flowing, as battles always were. The horde of orks swelled down the ravine floor, huge and sprawling, met by a thin line of White Scars warriors, tearing at them with furious energy. We had already been slowed. We had to break them quickly, to rush at them before they could gain momentum, to hurl them back, again and again.

The task was urgent, and could not wait. The Khagan would be advancing quickly towards the heart of the Grinder. Other brotherhoods would be racing to meet up with him. I dreaded being left behind.

'We are advancing,' I said. I reported this as a matter of fact, and no longer smiled as I spoke. 'We must advance. We are breaking them.'

'*You cannot. Hold your position. Do you hear me? Hold your position.*'

The tone of command astonished me. For a moment, I struggled to find the words to respond.

'We are advancing,' I repeated.

There was no alternative. He had to understand that.

Torghun didn't reply. I heard him curse at the other end of the link, and just made out the muffled crack of munitions going off in the background.

Then he terminated the connection.

Jochi, who had been fighting close by, came up to me, looking quizzical.

'A problem, my khan?' he asked.

I did not reply immediately. I was troubled. I considered ordering my warriors to pull back, to consolidate our position and wait for the Terrans to reach us. That would have maintained the harmony between us, which I was loath to break.

We were brothers, he and I. The thought of strife between brothers was repellent.

Then I looked out across the ravine, and saw the carnage we were creating. I saw my minghan in the full splendour of their unrivalled ferocity. I saw my warriors fighting as they had been created to fight – with passion, with freedom.

'There is no problem,' I said, marching past Jochi and back towards combat. 'We break them.'

WE FOUGHT ON. As the suns began to sink, we fought. Once the light failed, turning the ravines into pools of oily darkness, we fought. We donned our helms and used our night-vision preysight to hunt them down, always advancing, always rushing them.

They resisted ferociously. Not since Ullanor had I seen them fight a battle like it. They staged rallies, orchestrated ambushes, hurled suicide fighters right into our midst. Every barricade cost us, every gun-pit took lives before we could clear it out. We maintained the punishing pace, never letting them regroup, never letting ourselves slow. Our blood mingled with theirs. The ravines slopped with it, turning the pale dust a deep red.

In the cold hour before dawn when all three suns were still below the horizon, I ordered my brothers to halt at last. We were deep into the Grinder by then, surrounded by jumbled, overhanging terrain of ever deeper gorges and rising shelves of white rock. Curtains of fire streamed at us from all directions. Groups of greenskins had looped round, stealing back through the treacherous country and spilling into territory we had already won. They bellowed at us from the shadows. Cries echoed from the surrounding cliffs, amplifying and distorting. It sounded like the land itself was goading us.

I remembered Torghun's admonishment. I considered the possibility that he had been right, and that my eagerness to advance had compromised us. His brotherhood was still a long way from our position, making steady but measured progress towards us. I could not shake the suspicion that he was moving deliberately slowly.

'We will hold here,' I ordered, conveying the command to Jochi and Batu to relay to the others. 'At first light, we renew the attack.'

THE SITE I chose was the closest thing in the vicinity to a defensive bastion. A wide plateau of rock rose up from the tumbled, broken landscape, offering a commanding position over the terrain around it. Its sides were sheer on three sides, while the fourth dissolved into a shattered slope of cracked rock and scree. It was not perfect – we were still overlooked by peaks on the far side of the ravine, and there was precious little cover on the plateau itself.

Still, it gave us the chance to stem our growing losses, to bring some shape back into the battle. We fought our way to the plateau, scrambling up plunging rents in the rock, slipping and sliding on the loose stone. Once we had seized it we dug ourselves in along the edges, giving us firing angles into the gorges below. I sent our surviving squadrons of jetbikes after the main static firebases, but did not permit them to go further once they had destroyed their targets.

As I had known they would, the greenskins saw our halt as weakness. They poured towards us, bursting out from hidden caches and up from tunnels we had not properly destroyed. They surged up the steep sides of the plateau, clambering over one another in their eagerness to get at us. They were like an army of ghouls, their skin almost black in the gloom, their eyes burning red.

From then on, we were hard-pressed. Hemmed in, we fought like they did – ferociously, artlessly, brutally. They clambered up, we hewed them down. They clawed at us, dragging any warriors who broke formation into their pits of roaring horror. We shot and stabbed at them, sending their flailing bodies cartwheeling away into the darkness. We hurled grenades into their splayed maws, recoiling as their torsos blew open in shreds of flying sinew. They surrounded us, turning the plateau into a lone island of sanity amidst a heaving storm-swell of xenos blood-mania.

I remained at the forefront, where the combat was heaviest, wielding my guan dao two-handed, carving through greenskin flesh as if it were a single, vast, amorphous organism. I felt my hearts pumping hard, my arm muscles searing with pain. Sweat slicked my face under my helm, trickling down the underside of my gorget. They ran at our blades, using their bodies to wear us out, to slow us down, to punch gaps for others to crash through. Their bravery was phenomenal. Their strength was immense. Their commitment was total.

We were surrounded, we were outnumbered. Such a thing was rare for us – we did not let ourselves get pinned down often. Our Legion had never been chosen for missions where objectives had to be held for extended periods, not like the dour Iron Warriors or the pious, golden Imperial Fists. We had always looked down on such garrison work and pitied those who were condemned to it. I could not imagine us ever distinguishing ourselves in warfare of that sort – under siege, fighting with our backs to the wall as the skies burned above us.

For all that, we were Legiones Astartes. We fought with the precision and resolve of our long conditioning. We never yielded. We paid for that bastion on Chondax with our blood, gripping on tight to the handhold, gritting our teeth and digging in deep. When one of us fell, we exacted a toll of vengeance, closing ranks and ratcheting the already staggering violence up a further notch.

I believe we could have held out there indefinitely, letting the greenskin waves crash against us until they were exhausted and we could move on again. As it was, that supposition was not tested. I saw the streaks of missiles spin out of the night, slamming into the rear flanks of the enemy and breaking the momentum of their advance. I saw the bloated beams of lascannons snap out in massed volleys, silently reaping their dreadful toll. I heard the low growl of heavy bolters and autocannons, loosed in rolling, dense barrages.

I looked up, out across the seething mass of alien bodies, and saw glints of white and gold moving up the ravine from the south. Gunfire flashed, jetbike thrusters roared into life.

I regarded the development with mixed emotions: relief, certainly, but also annoyance.

Torghun had reached our position at last.

BY THE TIME the first shafts of dawn-light filtered down the ravines, the greenskins were dead or fleeing. For the first time, we let the survivors go. We had enough on our hands – equipment to salvage, armour to repair, the wounded to get back into fighting shape. The plateau looked desolate in the growing sun's light; a hazy land-scape of corpses and smouldering jetbike carcasses.

I did not see Torghun for a while, even after his brotherhood had joined us there. I had much to detain me, and I was not eager to speak to him. I busied myself with my own warriors, working hard to get them ready for war again. Despite everything, I was keen to keep advancing. I could see grey columns of smoke rising up ahead of us, and knew that the circle around the orks was closing fast.

I was still looking north, trying to gauge the best route for the advance, when Torghun finally came to me. I turned, sensing his presence before I saw him.

He was wearing his helm, so I could not read his expression. I assumed he was angry – when he spoke, his voice was tight, but resigned.

'I don't want to fight with you, Shiban,' he said, wearily.

'Nor I with you,' I said.

'You should have listened.'

I found the questioning of my tactics a novel experience. Torghun was within his rights to do so, of course, but it wore at my pride as khan, and I could not think of an adequate response.

'Just tell me this,' he said. 'Why does it matter to you so much?'

'Why does what matter?' I asked.

'To reach the Khagan. Why are you determined to do this, putting our formations, our warriors, in jeopardy? We don't even know he's on the planet. Tell me. Help me understand.'

His words surprised me. I knew that Torghun was more cautious than I was; that his way of war was different. It had not occurred to me that he did not place importance on fighting alongside the greatest of us.

'How can you not wish for it?' I asked.

I actually felt sorry for Torghun then. I assumed that he must have missed something in his ascension, or perhaps forgotten it. He called himself a White Scar; I wondered if the name meant any more to him than his Legion designation. For me, for my brotherhood, it was everything.

I felt I had to try to explain, even if my hopes of making myself clear were not high.

'War is not a tool, my brother,' I said. 'War is life. We have been elevated into it, we have become it. When the galaxy is finally cleansed of danger, our time will have ended. A brief time, a speck of gold on the face of the universe. We must cherish what we have. We must fight in the way we were born to fight, to make art of it, to celebrate the nature given to us.'

I spoke fervently. I believed those things. I still do.

'I saw him fight, once, from a distance,' I said. 'I have never forgotten it. Even from that one glimpse, I saw a possibility of perfection. Each of us has a part of that perfection within us. I long to witness it again, to see it close at hand, to learn from it, to become it.'

Torghun's blood-stained helm gazed back at me blankly.

'What else is there for us, brother?' I asked. 'We are not building a future for ourselves – we are creating an empire for others. These warlike things, these grand, terrible inspirations, they are all that we have.'

Still, Torghun said nothing.

'The future will be otherwise,' I said. 'For now, though, for us, there is only war. We must live it.'

Torghun shook his head in disbelief. 'I see they breed poets on Chogoris as well as warriors,' he said.

I could not tell whether he was mocking me.

'We do not distinguish between them,' I said.

'Another strange habit,' he said.

Then he reached up and unfastened the seals on his helm. I heard the locks hiss as they were undone. He twisted the helm off and mag-locked it to his armour.

Once we were looking with our own eyes it was easier to understand one another. I do not think my words had done much to convince him.

'I do not fight in the way you do, Shiban,' he said. 'Perhaps I do not even fight for the same things that you do. But we are both of the Fifth Legion. We must look for common ground.'

Torghun looked up, past me and into the north.

That was where *he* was. That was where he was fighting.

'We must be at the forefront of the assault, even now,' Torghun said. 'How soon can your brothers be made ready?'

'They already are,' I said.

'Then we travel together,' said Torghun, his expression sombre. 'In unison, but I will not slow you.'

In the morning light, lit only by one sun, his skin looked darker than before, almost like one of us. He had conceded a lot already. I could appreciate that.

'We will find him, brother,' he said. 'If he is there to be found, then we will find him.'

V. TARGUTAI YESUGEI

TO FLEE ONTO the Altak, that had been a bad decision. Had I stayed in the mountains, I might have had some chance of evading my pursuers. Out on the plains, it was impossible.

I sometimes reflect on why I made the choice that I did. I was a child, of course, but I was not a stupid one – I would have known that the wooded valleys gave me a better chance to escape from the Khitan, even if the prospect still remained slim.

Perhaps I was fated to make the choice I did. I dislike the idea of *fate*, though. I dislike the idea that the things we do are ordained for us by higher powers; that our actions are like shadow-plays performed for their amusement. Most of all, I dislike the idea that the future is set, running away from us in clear lines that we are compelled to follow, with only the illusion of a sovereign will to comfort us on the journey.

Nothing I have learned since my ascension has convinced me that I am wrong to think those things. I have learned of the deep metaphysics of the universe, and the long, tired games of the immortals, but I retain faith in our ability to choose.

We are the authors of our actions. When the test comes, we can go in either direction: we can triumph, or we can fail, and the universe cares not which.

I do not think it was fate that carried me out of the Ulaav and into the empty spaces of the Altak. I think I made a poor decision, born from fear.

I do not blame myself for that. All of us, even the mightiest, even the most exalted, may make such mistakes.

FOR A WHILE, I was faster. The Khitan in the mountains were armoured and wore curved steel plates over leather jerkins. I could hear the clatter of their jointed arm-guards even as I sprinted, and knew that they would tire quicker than I would.

I headed south, running hard out of the shadow of the highlands and down across the open plains. The earth was firm and dry beneath my feet. The wind was dawn-fresh, cold and spare.

Ahead of me was nothing. The Altak undulated gently, like an ocean of green, but there were no deep valleys for me to hide away in. A man or beast could be spied for kilometres on the plains. That was my hope – that I would see the Great Khan's entourage from a distance and be able to get to it in time.

I felt my breathing grow ragged and my feet, bound in soft leather, ache. I had not eaten since the day before, though for some reason that didn't affect my stamina. I remembered my vision of the four figures and the drink they had given me, and wondered how close to reality that vision had been. I could still taste something at the back of my throat – a bitterness, like spoiled milk.

For all their armour-encumbered clumsiness, I worried that I could not pull away from the pursuing Khitan. The noises of their footfalls, their heavy breathing, their clinking weapons, all of it followed me out across the plains. I turned my head as I ran, expecting to see them close behind me.

They were not. I had far outpaced them, and they laboured in my wake, running on foot like I did. My hearing seemed to be sharper, as did my eyesight. As I watched twelve of them come after me, puffing and swearing, I felt that I could see right into them. I saw the flame of their souls burning within their chests.

That startled me. My perception had been changed. Everything – the world around me, my pursuers – was more vivid than it had been.

I found that terrifying, even more so than the prospect of being killed. New sensations boiled within me, bubbling up under my skin and making my cheeks flush and my palms hot.

I felt powerful, but also powerless. I knew enough of the ways of the seers to know that whatever had been birthed in me on the mountain needed tutoring.

I turned away from the Khitan, and ran harder. The physical exertion helped a little. I felt the grass flatten under my feet, and the curses of the soldiers recede as they lost ground.

I scoured the horizon ahead, desperate for some sign of the Khan. I cursed his evasiveness then.

I saw nothing – just sky and earth and haze between them.

I KNEW THAT the foot soldiers would not be the only ones. No one travelled far on the Altak without steeds, and the lands of the Khitan were far away.

Once the soldiers realised that I would outpace them, they began to blow split-bone horns. The sound of their warnings rang out across the open spaces, travelling far on the gusting wind. Then they fell back, panting, content to let me race away from them and knowing I would not get far.

I kept going. I felt as if I could run forever. My light kaftan, which had failed to keep me warm in the high places, let my legs stride out. As the sun rose higher into the sky, my muscles warmed up properly. I could feel the heat on my clean, brown limbs, and it spurred me on further.

Then I heard the noise of the aduun. I heard their hooves drum on the packed earth, and without looking back I knew there were many of them. I kept my head down, and scoured the way ahead, fruitlessly, for any kind of break in the featureless landscape.

They caught up with me quickly. An aduu can outpace a man many times over and gallop tirelessly. Those of the Altak are fine beasts, with dark hides and powerful limbs. I heard their throaty breathing and the slap of their long tails.

I cast a despairing glance at the horizon a final time. The Khan was nowhere to be seen. I had placed all my hopes in finding him, and I had failed.

As the hoof-beats rang in my ears, I stopped running and turned to face my killers. Of all the crimes of our people, none was worse than showing fear to an enemy, and I resolved to make my death a good one.

I saw a line of mounted troops come at me, racing across the plain with poise and skill. They wore plate armour, overlapping and glinting in the sunlight. One of the riders carried a long spear with a tail of thick hair pinned just below the blade. Pennants streamed out behind them, brightly coloured and cracking in the wind.

One of them rode out ahead of the others, bearing down on me quickly. I saw a steel helm crowned with a spike, bronze-lined armour pieces, churning hooves, a loop of rope whirling out at me.

The lasso slipped over my shoulders and pulled tight around my waist. The rider hurtled past, yanking me after him. As the lasso closed, I was jerked off my feet and hurled to the ground. I hit the earth face-down.

For a moment I thought he intended to drag me along, but the pressure slackened immediately. I pushed myself back up to my knees, the rope knotted around my midriff and blood running down my chin.

The rider brought his steed around and dismounted, clasping the other end of the rope all the while. He walked up to me and grinned, tugging at the rope like I was a beast on a leash.

'You run fast, little one,' he said. 'But not fast enough.'

His tone made me angry. My arms were still free, and though I didn't have a weapon, I could still fight.

I launched myself at him, pushing up from the ground. I had no plan of attack, no thought about how I would grapple with a man nearly twice my weight and wearing full armour.

And it happened then.

The path of my life turned, slipping from one course to another. It was so sudden, when it finally came. Perhaps my visions on the Ulaav had been nothing more than delirium, or perhaps they had given me a true glimpse of some deeper, darker reality. It matters not. Something had awakened within me, and it chose that instant to make itself manifest.

When I look back, thinking of Chogoris, the lost world I loved, that is the moment I see, etched forever in my mind like acid-washed steel. That was the moment that sundered us, turning my destiny away from the plains and into the stars, out into the void where both horror and wonder waited for me in the immortal darkness.

I did not know it then. I did not know it for many years afterwards. None of that alters the truth.

It happened then.

I lunged out, stretching both fists in front of me like a wrestler going for a hold. Piercing, blinding light burst from my hands, crackling and spitting like splinters of lightning.

It was painful. I cried out in agony. Coruscation swarmed all over me, swimming across my flesh in a haze of heat and scouring energy. The world exploded in a hail of silver and gold, spiralling and thrashing, blazing madly, roaring in my ears and burning in my nostrils. It suffocated me – I could feel my lungs blistering. I lost my feet. I lost everything.

I saw the broken outline of the soldier reel away from me. I heard his cries of shock and pain. I saw him scratch at his eyes. The rope that had bound me exploded in a cloud of sparks. I staggered backwards, my fists clenched, still surging with gouts of hard, clear incandescence. Raw elemental power, the stuff of the other universe, thundered out of me, bleeding me, hollowing me.

I have no idea how long I was lost in that state, blazing like a pearlescent firebrand, reeling across the plains and vomiting destruction. It might have been seconds, it might have been far longer. I remember the vague impression of riders circling me, their outlines broken amid the torrent of white fire, unwilling to come close in case they were burned. I remember the faces of the four man-beasts swaying before my mind's eye, pointing at me with their hooked, cruel fingers.

Drink they told me.

I fell to my knees. The inferno raged, burning my flesh but not consuming it. My whole body locked rigid, clenched in spasms, convulsing.

The first I saw of him was a dark shape against the fire. He walked through it, pushing the curtains of energy back as if they were sheets of rain. It didn't hurt him.

He knelt over me. He seemed gigantic – far taller and broader than any living man should be. I looked into his eyes, blinking away tears as fire spilled from my own, and saw something familiar in them.

I remembered the light-wreathed figure of my vision. For a moment, I thought the man before me was the same person. Soon I realised that he wasn't, but felt sure that there was some link between them.

Then I felt the crushing weight of his authority sink down upon me. The flames around me guttered out, flickering into nothing and rippling into the wind. Like a man casually snuffing a candle, he staunched the torrent of bleeding madness. Even then, locked in bewilderment and pain, my mind numbed, part of me knew how astonishing that was.

He remained stooped over me. His helm was spiked, like those of his men. His armour was elaborate and finely made, with gold and red beading arranged around a breastplate of white bone panels. I saw a long scar running down his left cheek, as I had been told the Talskar people wore. His eyes were deep-set and intense. I had never seen such eyes.

Perhaps I had been wrong about my hunters. Perhaps they were not Khitan.

Panting, shivering, I still clung on to the hope of a noble death. I tried to hold his gaze, sure that he had come to kill me.

I could not do it. Something about that giant overwhelmed me. I saw his face swim before my eyes, breaking up like a reflection in water. He seemed to be peering into my soul, shriving it, flaying it. I felt myself losing consciousness.

'Be careful,' he said.

Then I passed out, and the rising darkness was as welcome to me as sleep.

SIX DAYS LATER, I awoke.

I learned, long afterwards, how dangerous that time had been for me. My inner eyes had been opened in the Ulaav, but I had not been shown how to use them. I could have died. I could have suffered worse than death, as could all those around me.

He had prevented that. Even then, long before the Master of Mankind had shown us the path to the stars, he had known how to control the fires that raged within the minds of the gifted.

He did not have the gift himself, as far as I know. I never saw him summon fire, nor bring the storm to bear on his enemies. He used his warrior's body – that magnificent, enhanced body – in the cause of war and nothing else. I cannot believe, however, that he did not have some innate knowledge of the paths of heaven. He was made to be a player in the other universe, to contest those who remained on the far side of the veil, and so he must, like his brothers, have had some understanding of the hidden deepness of things.

Back then, though, all I knew was that he had captured me, and that, under the laws of the Altak, I was his slave. Having been denied an honourable death, I resigned myself to a life of drudgery. The khan – *my* khan, the one I had served until then – would not be able to rescue me. I had seen the nature of my new gaoler, and knew that he far surpassed any other warrior of the plains, including my kin-lord.

He was at my side when I awoke. I lay on a bed of furs within a large *ger*. A fire burned in the central pit, and the air was red and smoke-filled. I could hear voices murmuring in the shadows. I heard the sound of sword-edges being filed, arrows being fletched.

He looked at me, and I looked at him.

He was massive. I had never seen a man so domineering, so nakedly potent, so replete with coiled power. His big, lean face flickered in the shadow and flame.

'What is your name?' he asked.

His voice was low. It thrummed deeply in the murmuring space.

'Shinaz,' I said. My mouth was dry.

'No longer,' he said. 'You shall be Targutai Yesugei, the child who ran and the man who fought. You shall be a zadyin arga of my household.'

His words were not presumptive. By the custom of the Altak he owned my life, at least until such time as another warlord could take me from him by force or I could somehow escape. I doubted that either thing were possible.

'You come to me at the beginning, Yesugei,' he said. 'I am the Khan of many khans. You are joining the ordu of Jaghatai, the tide that shall sweep across the world and make it anew. Be thankful that I took you before you returned to your old khan. If I had faced you in battle, you would have died.'

I said nothing. I was still groggy from sleep and sickness. I could not see his face clearly, and his voice had a strange, unsettling quality. I lay back on the furs, feeling my breast rise and fall gingerly.

'You shall be trained, like the others,' he said. 'You shall learn to use what you have been given. You shall learn when to use it, and when not to use it. In all these things, you will follow my word of command. No other man shall ever tell you how to use your gifts.'

I watched his lips move in the lambent darkness. As he spoke, I saw fleeting remnants of the visions I had seen from the mountain. I saw those broken vessels, burning amid the stars. As he talked of conquest, I remembered the insignia on those pieces of charred metal.

A wolf. A many-headed snake. A lightning strike.

'I have brought a new way of war to the world,' he said. 'To move fast, to remain strong, never to rest. When the Altak is ours, we shall take this war to the Khitan. After that, we shall take it to every empire between earth and sky. They shall all fall, for they are sick, and we are healthy.'

My heart beat shallowly in my breast. I could feel the heat of fever in my cheeks. His words were like the words of a dream.

'All empires fall,' he said. 'All empires sicken. This is the lesson we have learned. This is the lesson that you shall learn.'

I saw the scar move on his face as he spoke. In the blood-red light, it looked alive, like a pale snake clamped to his skin.

'We will not serve empires,' he said. 'We will remain in motion. We will not have a centre. Wherever we are, that is the centre.'

I knew he was telling me something important, but I was too

young and too sick to understand it. Only later, much later, was I able to look back on those words and recognise the truth of what I was being told.

'Will you serve me, Targutai Yesugei?' he asked.

Back then, I assumed the question was rhetorical. I was a child. I had no idea how long it was possible for a human to live, what it was possible for a human to become. I thought that only trivial things were at stake: my life, the feuds between clans, the old cycle of war on the Altak.

Now, knowing what I know, I am not so sure. Perhaps, even then, I had a choice to make.

'Yes, my khan,' I said.

He looked at me for a long time, his eyes shining in the blood-light.

'Then you are Talskar now,' he said. 'You will be marked, like we are. You will bear the white scar on your face, and all will learn to fear you.'

Firelight rippled across his bone armour plates.

'For now, we are unknown,' he said. 'It will not always be so. A day will come when we will be revealed, fighting in the way that I will teach you.'

His eyes were like jewels in the night, burning with hungry, boundless ambition.

'And when that day comes,' he said, 'when we are revealed at last, I tell you truly, zadyin arga – the gods themselves will cower before us.'

VI. ILYA RAVALLION

HE CAME FOR me five days later, just as he'd said he would. I'd been kicking my heels in the wastes of Ullanor all that time, trying to find something useful to do. I hadn't been very successful – the fleets in orbit were beginning to break up. The war was over, and already new battles had been identified.

I catalogued things. I submitted reports to my superiors. I read the notes I'd made after meeting the Stormseer.

The summons came with no warning. I was in Miert's complex looking over some of his shoddily done datawork when my secure comm-bead pulsed.

'You have your audience, General Ravallion,' came the message. *'Be ready in an hour. I send a lander to your location.'*

I had no idea how Yesugei had obtained access to the Departmento's grid. My immediate reaction was to feel a swell of nerves bloom in the pit of my stomach. I had served in many warzones and argued my corner with many powerful military commanders, so did not consider myself easily overawed, but this…

This was a *primarch*, one of the Emperor's own sons.

I tried to imagine what he would be like. I had heard different things about them: that they were constantly engulfed in light, that their armour shone like the sun, that they could kill with a word or a gesture and their gaze alone could flay skin and crack bone.

I had plenty of time to speculate. Typically for the White Scars, the lander arrived late. It eventually came down in a flurry of dust just north of the complex's perimeter. From my window I saw its white flanks and its gold-and-red lightning-strike sigil, and felt a fresh twinge of nervousness.

'Control yourself,' I said out loud, adjusting my newly acquired weapon belt a final time before leaving for the lander. 'He is just a man. No, more than a man. What, then? Flesh and blood. Human. One of us.'

But I didn't know if even that were true. I was faced with a problem of categorisation, something that I'd always found difficult.

'On our side,' I settled on, feeling sick with anticipation.

THE LIFTER WAS a Legiones Astartes variant Horta RV local-space shuttle – a late issue pattern. I knew everything about it. Fixing on the details helped my mood.

Yesugei was waiting for me in the crew-bay. He was wearing his ivory armour, and looked enormous in the confined space. He bowed to me as I climbed up the ramp to join him.

'Are you well, General Ravallion?' he asked.

I bowed in turn, trying to hide my anxiety with, I suspect, little success.

'Very well, Yesugei,' I said. I had learned by then, after much research, that Stormseers did not take the title 'khan'. They didn't take any kind of title at all; their name, and their calling, seemed to be enough. 'My thanks again, for arranging this.'

The boarding ramp to the lander closed behind me with a whine of servos. I heard airlocks clunk closed, and the craft's engines begin to power up.

'Pleasure,' he said, sitting back against the metal walls.

The dimensions of the lander fitted Space Marine physiology; everything, even the benches and the restraint harnesses, was far too big for me. I sat opposite Yesugei and fiddled with the straps, my feet barely touching the floor. He didn't bother using a harness, and sat serenely, his gauntlets resting on his knees.

'May I ask, general,' he said, 'you have met primarch before?'

The engines continued to power up, and I saw dust billowing up on the far side of the tiny viewports.

'No,' I said.

'Ah,' said Yesugei.

With a muffled roar, the lander took off, hovering over the apron for a few moments before generating lift. Out of the corner of my eye, I saw the dry valleys of Ullanor begin to fall away.

'In that case, may I offer advice?' he asked.

I smiled grimly. I could already feel uncomfortable waves of vibrations running through my body, and the walls of the crew-bay shook like a drum skin. We were climbing very fast. I wondered if the pilots made any allowances for the nature of their passengers.

'Please do,' I said. 'No one else has been able to.'

'Address him as Khan,' said Yesugei. 'That is not what we call him, but it is proper address for you. Look him in the eye when speaking, even if you find difficult. The shock of first meeting can be... bad. It will pass. He will not try to intimidate. Remember what he was created for.'

I nodded. The lander's violent ascent made me feel nauseous. I pressed my hands firmly against the rim of my seat and felt moisture on the inside of my gloves.

'I am told, by those who know, he is not like his brothers,' said Yesugei. 'He can be hard to read, even for us. On Chogoris we use hunting raptors. We call them berkut. His soul is one of theirs: far-ranging, restless. He may say things that seem strange. You may think he mocks you.'

I saw the sky in the viewports fade into black, and the tiny points of stars emerge. We had broken into the upper atmosphere incredibly quickly. I tried to concentrate on what Yesugei was telling me.

'Remember only this,' he said. 'A berkut never forget the shape of the hunt. In the end it always comes back to the hand that loosed it.'

I nodded, feeling light-headed.

'I will remember,' I said.

I caught my first glimpse of our destination in the far distance: a warship, vast and battle-scarred, its curved prow painted white and its marker lights blinking in the void.

I knew its name from the records: the *Swordstorm*.

Capital-class. Huge. Retro-fitted for speed – those engines are enormous. Was that sanctioned by Mars?

I knew he was in there. That was where he was waiting.

'Try to understand him,' said Yesugei calmly. 'He may even like you. I have seen stranger things.'

WE TOUCHED DOWN in one of the *Swordstorm*'s hangars, and then things moved quickly. Yesugei escorted me down long corridors, up elevator-shafts, across huge halls thronged with menials and servitors. I heard singing in a language I didn't understand, and laughter echoing along service corridors. The entire ship had an air of furious, good-natured, slightly chaotic energy. It smelt cleaner than the Army cruisers I was used to, with an underlying aroma of something like incense rising from the polished floors. Everything was brightly lit and copiously decorated with the colours of the Legion – white, gold and red.

By the time we reached the Khan's chambers I had no idea how far we'd come – such enormous battleships were more like cities than vessels of war. We eventually stopped before a pair of ivory-inlaid doors flanked by two enormous guards in ceremonial armour. I recognised the cumbersome outline of antique Thunder Armour, heavily altered and edged with gold. Unlike Yesugei, the guards wore their helms, which were slit-visored and gilded, and topped with horsehair plumes.

As the Stormseer approached them, they bowed, then grasped two heavy bronze handles set into the doors.

'Prepared?' asked Yesugei.

I could feel my heart hammering. Light was bleeding out of the cracks under the doors.

'No,' I said.

The doors opened.

FOR A SPLIT second, I saw absolutely nothing. I had the blurred impression of a corona of light, dancing in front of me as if reflected from water. I could sense enormous energy, enormous power burning away, thundering within its bonds like the caged heart of a reactor.

At the time I was unsure if I was sensing him as he truly was, my unpractised gaze piercing some carefully constructed veil of artifice and into his true nature beneath, or whether the sickness of the ascent from Ullanor had simply addled my senses.

I only knew one thing: that I had to keep my feet, to keep my eyes open. Yesugei had said it would pass.

'General Ilya Ravallion of the Departmento Munitorum.'

As soon as he spoke, the details of the room sank into focus, like an old physical pictograph being developed in a bath of chemicals. The chamber was large, with grand, high windows that flooded it with filtered light from Ullanor's sun.

I bowed my head clumsily.

'Khan,' I replied, disliking the thin sound of my voice in contrast to the richness of his.

'Sit, general,' he said. 'There is a chair here for you.'

I walked towards it. As I did so, I began to take in my surroundings. The walls were panelled with dark, sleek wood, like Terran mahogany. A thick rug lay under my feet, woven coarsely with images of arid plains and spear-carrying riders leaning in the saddle. I saw an antique bookcase lined with old leather-bound books. There were weapons hung against the walls – swords, bows, flintlocks, armour from other ages and other worlds. Smells of earth and metal rose up to meet me, acrid with the tang of buckskin, burned charcoal and burnishing oils.

I sat in the seat that had been prepared for me. I heard the gentle ticking of an old clock on a stone mantelpiece and the very faint, very distant hum of starship engines.

Only then did I have the courage to look at him.

His face was the same leather-brown as Yesugei's. It was a lean face, noble and fiercely intelligent, and proud. His scalp was bald save for a long top-knot of ink-black hair bound with rings of gold. An aquiline nose ran down a wind-toughened, moustached face. His eyes were sunk deep under bony brows, and they glittered like pearls set in bronze.

He sat at ease, his immense body stretched back in his own chair, which was twice the size of mine. One gloved hand rested on an ivory arm, the other hung casually over the edge. I had the image of an apex-feline lounging in the dappled shade, resting its tremendous strength for a moment between hunts.

I could barely move. My heart was thudding.

'So,' said the Khan. He spoke in a cultured, patrician drawl. 'What did you wish to speak to me about?'

I looked into his glittering eyes to reply. It was then that I realised, with a lurch of horror, that I couldn't remember.

YESUGEI JOINED US then, standing at his primarch's shoulder and calmly explaining the circumstances of our meeting on Ullanor.

I learned later that he'd been at my side the whole time, staying close in case I'd been overwhelmed. That was a kindness I have never forgotten.

As he spoke, and as the Khan responded, I recovered myself. I sat up straight in my chair, recalling my mission in all its detail. Even then I was struck by the irony of the situation – the one thing I had always been able to rely on, my memory, undone in an instant by the figure before me.

'So what more do they want of us?' asked the Khan drily, still speaking to Yesugei. 'More conquests? Faster?'

His tone was that of a weary patriarch, indulging the paltry concerns of subjects far below him in stature and nobility. Unlike Yesugei, his spoken Gothic was perfect, albeit with the same dense accent as his Stormseer.

'Lord,' I said, hoping my voice didn't shake as I spoke, 'the Departmento has no complaint about the speed of the Fifth Legion's progress.'

Both the Khan and Yesugei turned to look at me.

I swallowed, and felt the dryness at the back of my throat.

'The matter is rather different,' I went on, holding the primarch's gaze with difficulty. 'Senior strategeos have found it challenging to retain an adequate picture of your movements. This has consequences. We cannot keep you resupplied as we would like. We cannot arrange coordination with your accompanying Army regiments. You are due to rendezvous with the 915th Expeditionary Fleet, but we still do not have confirmation of your onward destination.'

The Khan's face was like a mask. His expression didn't alter, although I could sense his disappointment.

I felt ludicrous. He was a total warrior, a machine bred by the Emperor to destroy worlds. He didn't want to discuss supply chains.

'Do you think, general,' he asked, 'that you are the first to complain of this to me?'

His tone – casual, courteous, disinterested – was crushing. I doubt he meant it to be, but it was all the same.

They can kill with a word.

'No, lord,' I said, trying to hold my nerve, determined to keep to my mission. 'I am aware that seventeen Legion-level communications have been made from Terra to your command staff.'

'Seventeen, is it?' he said, his lids heavy. 'I lose count. And what do you hope to add to them?'

'Those delegations did not have the honour of speaking to you in person, lord,' I said. 'I had hoped that, if I could explain the situation clearly, then we might be able to determine a revised framework for logistics liaison. It is something the Departmento would dearly like to negotiate.'

As soon as I used the words 'revised framework for logistics liaison', I knew I'd lost him. He looked at me directly, half-bemused, half-irritated. He shifted in his chair, and even in that miniscule movement I sensed something of the futility of what I was trying to do.

He hated being seated. He hated talking. He hated being cooped up inside the walls of his battleship. He wanted to be on campaign, lost in the pursuit, deploying his phenomenal strength in the eternal chase.

He never forgets the shape of the hunt.

'Are you Terran?' he asked.

The question came from nowhere, but I remembered Yesugei's words and didn't blink.

'I am, lord.'

'I thought so,' said the Khan. 'You think like a Terran. I have warriors in my Legion who are Terrans, and they think like you too.'

He sat forwards a little in his chair, clasping his gloved hands together in front of him.

'This is what you want,' he said. 'You want to see the Legions march out from Terra in ordered lines, plodding like aduun, each one leaving a trail behind it leading back to the home world along which you can plot your convoys of arms and rations. You think like this because your world is one of complexity – of cities, of settled nations – and such a world needs tethering.'

He was right. That was what I wanted.

'That is not what we want,' said the Khan. 'On Chogoris we learned to fight without a centre. We took our arms and our mounts with us. We moved as the pattern of war dictated. We did not tie ourselves down. We have never done that.'

His deep-set eyes held me as he spoke. His voice was never raised. He was not angry with me; he spoke calmly, like an austere parent patiently explaining a simple matter to a child.

'The armies we fought were bigger than ours,' he said. 'Our movement was our advantage. They could not strike at our centre, because we had no centre. We have never forgotten that lesson.'

I understood then why all our delegations had failed to make an impression on him. The White Scars were not hard to organise because of carelessness – it was a point of principle for them, a doctrine of war.

Perhaps I should have said nothing then and accepted the failure of my mission, but I was unwilling to let the matter lie. Fighting on Chogoris on horseback was one thing; a Crusade of trillions across the galaxy was another.

'But lord,' I said, 'after Ullanor, there *are* no bigger armies. We are advancing, not defending, and such work requires coordination. And, forgive me, but surely you agree that there are no threats to Terra. Nothing remains that could harm us.'

The Khan looked at me in his frosty, jaded way. My words had not impressed him. I felt the full weight of his disappointment, and that alone was hard to bear.

'*Nothing remains that could harm us*,' he repeated softly. 'I wonder,

Yesugei, how many times, and in how many forgotten empires, those words have been spoken.'

He was no longer addressing me. He had moved on, discussing the paths of history with his own kind. I had been cast aside, just like all the others who had attempted to drag him back into the rigid structures of the Imperium. I was nothing to him; the work of the Departmento was nothing. The months of travel, of research, of preparation, they had all been for nothing.

I was furious with myself, and burned with frustration. At that point I assumed that I sat face-to-face with the greatest and most powerful warrior I would ever meet, and that I had squandered the opportunity to influence him.

I was wrong about that, as it turned out, on both counts.

HE BURST IN with no warning, no prior announcement. The doors thudded back on their hinges, startling me.

He swept into the room, clad in a thick wolf-pelt mantle that swayed with his resounding strides. His armour was white gold, swirled and rich like mother-of-pearl, rimmed with hammered bronze and with a lustrous, garnet-red eye emblazoned across the breastplate. He radiated enormity – of body, of mind, of spirit. He moved with a generous vigour, with confidence, with a soldier's swagger.

I had seen picts of him, of course. We all had. I had never expected to witness him up close, to be in the presence of such a figure of legend and whispered rumour.

I shrank back in my chair, clutching the arms of it tight, fearful that I would pass out or do something stupid.

The Khan leapt to his feet, hurrying to greet him with a smile breaking out across his face. I was instantly forgotten; a mundane smudge against the splendour of reunited gods.

'My brother,' said the Khan, embracing him.

'Jaghatai,' said Horus Lupercal.

My heart was thudding in my chest. I became terrified that one of them would turn on me and ask me what I was still doing there. I wanted to leave, but I wouldn't have dared to move, not without being given permission, so I stayed where I was, wishing the chair would fold up over me.

I should have been filled with awe and joy at the sight of the Warmaster. I should have felt my heart bloom with pride and gratitude that I, one mortal among trillions, had been placed in the presence of the Emperor's chosen. For whatever reason, the only thing I felt was fear. I saw my knuckles turn white. I said nothing. It felt as if a cold wind had raced through the chamber, chilling it and making my soul shiver.

Yesugei was introduced to him, and the Stormseer took it in his stride, as calm and phlegmatic as ever. Then Horus's gaze – his terrible, searching gaze – moved beyond his brother and settled on me.

My heart seemed to stop. I was powerless to react, or even to look away. It was a pure, primal terror; that of prey that knows it cannot escape.

'And who is she?' Horus asked.

The Khan placed his hand on his brother's arm.

'One of the Sigillite's bureaucrats.' He glanced briefly in my direction. 'She has my countenance.'

When they turned away, falling into conversation with one another once more, I felt as if an iron vice had been loosed from around my heart.

Where the Khan had been hard to deal with, Horus was overwhelming. The two primarchs were of similar build – the Khan might even have been slightly taller – but it was obvious to me why Horus had been chosen to be the Emperor's instrument; the dynamism of his gestures, the openness in his face, the sense of effortless power that cascaded from his ornate armour and spilled out across the room. Even amidst the inexplicable dread that reached up to choke me, I understood why men worshipped him.

I struggled to reconcile what I saw with what I felt. The Khan and Horus were obviously brothers. They talked and goaded one another like brothers, speaking of galaxy-spanning matters that I could not understand as if they were pieces of trivia to toy with and argue over. For all that, they were not equals. The Khan was dominating, brooding, austere, magnificent.

Horus was… *something else.*

The encounter between them was a brief one. By the time I dared to listen, it was almost over.

'For all that, believe me, I am shamed by this, brother,' said Horus, looking apologetic.

'You should not be,' said the Khan.

'If there had been any other choice…'

'You do not have to explain. In any case, I have already given you my word.'

Horus looked at the Khan gratefully.

'I know,' said the Warmaster. 'Your word means a great deal. To our Father, too, I am sure.'

The Khan raised an eyebrow, and Horus laughed. Laughing freed up his features. The Warmaster's habitual demeanour was one of raw, passionate exuberance, as if some reflected glory or perfection of the Emperor's will lingered in the cut of his martial features.

'It isn't all bad,' Horus said. 'Chondax is barren, suited to your Legion's strengths. You'll enjoy the hunting.'

The Khan nodded readily enough, though, to me, it looked like the gesture of one who knows that the best is being made of a poor situation. 'We are not hungry for glory,' he said. 'Running down Urrlak's dregs needs to be done, and we are equipped to do it. But what then? That is what concerns me.'

Horus clapped his gauntlet onto the Khan's shoulder. Even that simple movement – the faint shift of posture, the upward sweep of his arm – gave away the primarch's warrior-balance. Every gesture was so painfully elegant, so beautifully efficient, so tightly packed with self-assured, superabundant power. They were both creatures of a more exalted plane, shackled only loosely to the stuff of mortal existence.

'Then we should fight together again, you and I,' Horus said. 'It has been too long, and I miss your presence. Things are uncomplicated with you. I wish you would not hide yourself away.'

'I can usually be found, in the end.'

Horus shot him a wry look.

'In the end,' he said. Then his expression became serious. 'The galaxy is changing. There is much I do not understand about it, and much I do not like. Warriors should remain close. I hope that I can call upon you, if the time comes.'

The two primarchs looked one another in the eye. I could imagine them fighting together, and I shuddered a little at the prospect. Such an alliance would make the foundations of the galaxy tremble.

'You know you can, brother,' said the Khan. 'That is always how it has been between us. You call, I answer.'

I could hear the sincerity in his voice; he meant it. I could hear the admiration, too, and the warmth. They were hewn from the same stone.

I held my breath. For whatever reason, I felt that something significant, something irrevocable, had taken place.

You call, I answer.

After that they left the room together, marching in step, locked in conversation. Yesugei went with them.

The chamber fell still. I could hear the ticks of the clock, as loud in my ears as my own heartbeat. For a long time, I couldn't move. My cloying sense of dread faded slowly. When I finally unclenched my fingers from the arm of the chair, I was still trembling. Thoughts and images raced through my mind, jostling in a mad rush of dazzling impressions.

Only slowly did it dawn on me that I had been abandoned in the heart of a Legion battleship with no obvious means of finding my way out. I guessed that my rank would count for little in such a place.

That wasn't the worst of it. I had seen – just briefly – the way in which the Great Crusade was really ordered, and it made my tiny role seem even more insignificant than I had thought. We were nothing to them, those armour-bound gods.

As I reflected on that, the idea of trying to debate war policy with a primarch felt less like vainglory and more like insanity.

Still, I had seen them. I had witnessed what countless career soldiers would have happily died to witness. Despite my failure, that was worth something.

I got up from the chair shakily, steeling myself to go back into the corridor outside. I didn't relish the prospect of meeting those guards again.

As it turned out, I didn't have to. Yesugei returned, slipping silently back through the doors and giving me a conspiratorial smile.

'Well,' he said. 'That was unexpected.'

'It was,' I replied. My voice was still weak.

'Primarch and Warmaster,' said Yesugei. 'You did well.'

I laughed, more for the release of tension than anything else.

'I did?' I said. 'I almost lost consciousness.'

'It happens,' he said. 'How you feel?'

I rolled my eyes.

'I made a fool of myself,' I said. 'This was a waste of time – of your time. I'm sorry.'

Yesugei shrugged. 'Do not apologise,' he said. 'The Khan does nothing wastefully.'

He looked at me carefully.

'We leave for Chondax soon,' he said. 'We have orks to hunt. The Khan knows the task ahead. He listened to you. He asked me to tell you, if you wish, you may join us. Our *kurultai* needs counsellor, one with experience, one not afraid to speak truths we do not wish to hear.'

Yesugei smiled again.

'We know our weakness,' he said. 'All things change. We must change. What do you think?'

For a moment, I could hardly believe it. I thought he might be joking, but I guessed that he didn't joke much.

'Are *you* going to Chondax?' I asked.

'I do not know,' he said. 'Maybe not yet. Joining us – it will not be easy. We have ways strange to outsiders. Perhaps you would be happier in your Departmento. If so, we understand.'

As Yesugei spoke, I made up my mind.

It was a thrilling feeling, a leap into the unknown, something that was as out of character as my temporary forgetfulness had been earlier. Given the events of the past few hours, it was not hard for me to believe that fate had offered me a chance to make something of myself, to become more than an unnamed cog in an infinite machine. I was near the end of my active service; such a chance would never come again.

'You are right that I do not understand you,' I said. 'I barely know anything about you.'

I tried to keep my voice steady, to sound more certain than I really was. I felt like laughing, half from excitement, half from fear.

'But I can learn,' I added.

VII. SHIBAN

IT TOOK TWO more days before we reached the centre. Torghun and I fought together in that time, blending our different skills. We made an effort not to countermand one another. On occasion, I would be hungry to push on, and he would not protest; on others, I would accede to his desire to secure an area before we left it.

It was not always easy. My warriors did not operate readily with his. We did not mingle much; I met only one of his lieutenants, a dour warrior named Hakeem, and even then barely exchanged two words. For all that, we learned from one another. I came to see that Torghun's way of war had things to recommend it. I hoped that he felt the same way about ours.

By the time we broke into the core of the Grinder, we had taken more casualties than we had during years of prior campaigning. My own brotherhood was ravaged, down to barely two-thirds of its original strength. I did not regret that. None of us did. We had always known that the greenskins would fight hard for their final foothold, and those who had died had died like warriors.

If there had been more time, though, I would have mourned Batu, who had always been close to me. I would also have mourned Hasi, who had been a cheerful soul and who would have achieved great things had he survived.

Sangjai retrieved their immortal elements, and so a portion of them was destined to live on in the actions of others. As ever, we preserved their armour and their weapons, and left their mortal bodies to return to the earth and sky of Chondax. Even in the ravines, sheltered from the worst of the wind, we could see them begin to wear away to nothing. I knew that the plateau, the place we had fought so hard for and with so much bloodshed, would now be blasted clean again – bone-white, empty, echoing.

I had seen the monuments raised to the Imperium on Ullanor, and had marvelled at them. They would last for millennia. Nothing like that would remain to mark our presence on Chondax. We were like ghosts there, flitting across the wastes, killing briefly before our presence was scrubbed from existence.

But the combat was real enough. The ruthless, ceaseless, brutal combat – that was real. By the time we reached the core we were weary, driven into fatigue by the unflagging resistance of the orks. My armour was dirty-brown from bloodstains. My breastplate was chipped and dented, my helm scored by blade marks. My muscles, hardened to a life of constant warfare by habit and genetic proving, never lost their dull ache. I had not slept for days.

But when we crested the last rise, coming to a halt along the lip of a long cliff-edge and gazing out into the object of our exertions, our spirits lifted.

We saw the final mountain, the rusting fortress of the enemy, and we smiled.

IT WAS A broad, circular bowl, carved out of the broken landscape like the gigantic scoop of a spoon. We stood on the southern edge of it, looking north into its centre. We could just make out cliffs on the far side, half-lost in dust and distance. The floor of the depression was smooth and empty, a barren expanse of naked rock that gleamed in the light of the suns. The land ran away from us in a shallow curve, sweeping down nearly two hundred metres before levelling out.

In the centre of the bowl stood the citadel – a spike of rock, jagged and cracked by time, hurled upward from the bare stone like a hunting lance piercing a carcass. It rose up over two hundred metres, breaking into a series of slender pinnacles that glistened like splintered bone in the sunlight.

The orks had had a long time to work on it. They had looped walls around it, and towers across it, and twisting stairways slung between the slender rock turrets. The flanks of the citadel bristled with guns, and columns of soot-black smoke belched from its base. Enormous machines growled away within – engines, generators, forges. I guessed that those things had been taken from one of their cavernous space-going hulks, perhaps one that had crashed into the world a long time ago and had been slowly turned into the heart of their last redoubt.

The citadel had many gates, each with heavy lintels of rust-crusted iron. Thousands of greenskins milled about on the ramparts above, bellowing their challenges into the clear air. Many thousands more, I guessed, sheltered further within, waiting for the attack they knew was coming.

Near the top of the haphazard pile of interlocking structures, lodged among a cluster of lopsided walls and precarious weapons platforms, was a mass of bolted metal sheets in the rough image of a giant greenskin head. I saw ten-metre long tusks and flaming eye sockets, each the size of a man. Slaps of red and yellow paint had been thrown across its angular skull. Slivers of lime-green light danced across the surface, indicating the presence of rudimentary shielding.

The structure might have been some quasi-religious artefact, or perhaps a den for the shaman-caste, or an elaborate garrison for their elite warriors. Perhaps their leader resided in there, squatting like a bloated insect in the dark while its minions died around it.

That level of artifice surprised me. We had never seen orks build such structures, even during the slaughter of Ullanor.

As I gazed at it, I guessed the truth. The greenskins learned fast. We had always known that about them. If they were not utterly exterminated by the forces ranged against them, they would eventually turn any weapon back against its bearer. Even here, hammered into submission and bereft of hope, they were still working on new tools of destruction.

They had seen what weapons we had used to lay them low, and the inspiration had lodged deep in their brutish minds. Somehow, driven by some astonishing capacity for replication, they were still labouring.

They were building a Titan.

I noted the routes up to that grotesque head – the tottering gantries, the rough-cut stairs, the clattering elevator-shafts. I memorised them quickly, knowing that once we were inside the citadel I would have no time to orientate myself.

By then I could hear distance-echoed reports of gunfire from the far side of the wide depression. My helm-display showed the signals of other brotherhoods closing from the north, east and west. Already some squads had broken out of cover and were streaking down the long slopes of the bowl towards the citadel. The guns on the walls opened up, hurling their shells in long arcs at the incoming jetbike squadrons.

I turned to Torghun, who, as ever, stood at my side.

'Ready, brother?' I asked.

'Ready, brother,' he said.

I held my gauntlet up, open-handed, in the Chogorian way. He clasped it. If we had been warriors of the Altak, we would have cut our palms, allowing the blood to mingle.

'The Emperor be with you, Shiban Khan,' he said.

'And with you, Torghun Khan,' I replied.

Then we activated our blades, gunned our engines, and broke into the charge.

As khan, I could have taken one of my brotherhood's remaining bikes from its owner, but chose not to. I saw no reason to deprive any of my warriors of their mount just because I had lost mine.

So I ran, just like the others around me whose jetbikes had been downed. We surged down the slope, crying out and letting our blade-edges hiss with energy. Over a hundred of us sprinted alongside one another, whooping and roaring, swinging our glaives and tulwars around our heads. The remaining jetbikes thundered overhead, laying down a crashing layer of heavy bolter fire and screaming ahead to the walls.

I watched them soar with envy and with joy. I saw the superb control of their riders, the way they banked and thrust in the sparkling sunlight. They were so natural, so effortlessly deadly. I wished to be among them.

Deprived of that raw power, I ran hard, using my own native speed and my armour's peerless machine-boost. I felt my muscles work, shot-through with hyper-adrenaline and combat-stimms. My brothers charged with me, kicking up dust from their pumping limbs.

At the edge of vision I could see other warriors spill into the depression. Dozens crested the rise, then hundreds. Entire brotherhoods broke from cover, streaking into the open. I did not wait to count, but before I reached the walls there must have been thousands of us in the attack. I had not seen such White Scars numbers since making planetfall. We were together again, reunited in the splendour of our full, dreadful potential. The noise of it – the voxed battle-cries, the massed drum of boot-falls, the percussive clamour of the jetbikes – it thrilled me to my core.

The entire bowl filled with the whoosh and crack of incoming fire. Primitive flak-bursts studded the air, downing several bikes even before they had come within bolter-range of the walls. Artillery crashed out at us, ploughing up the wind-worn rock and scattering whole squads of charging warriors. Massive, snub-barrelled guns opened up, lobbing shells into our path and ripping up the terrain.

I felt my secondary heart kick in, and relished the blood pumping through my veins. My long hair whipped in the racing wind. My guan dao trembled from its death-hungry disruptor field, eager to bite into flesh again.

I leapt over smoking craters and swerved round heaps of blazing wreckage, building up speed with every stride. We were like a bursting tide of ivory, spilling into the depression from all directions and racing towards the flaming pinnacle at its centre. Everything moved, everything hurtled, everything streaked and blazed in a smear of white, gold and blood-red. Shadows of jetbikes raced across us as they wheeled into their searing attack runs. The walls ahead were already burning, cracked open and leaking acrid columns of smoke.

We gained one of the many gates, freshly devastated by volleys of heavy bolter strikes and missile-fire. Orks rushed out to meet us, slavering with rage. They were bigger than any I had seen on Chondax, almost as big as some of the monsters we'd seen on Ullanor. They lumbered right at us, stumbling over their own clawed feet just to get into blade-range. We crunched back into them, bursting through what remained of the gates, spinning, hacking, blasting, punching, gouging. Two hordes – one blinding white, one sickly green – crashed together in a morass of blades, bullets and flailing limbs.

I surged up a tangled slope of rubble, my glaive flying around me. Orks lurched down, shoving aside debris and kicking up dust.

I thundered into them, dragging my guan dao in whirling arcs. Its edge sliced clean through iron plate, skin and bone, flinging scraps around it as it flickered back and forth. I cut them down before they knew I was even within range. Every stroke whistled cleanly, delivering crushing levels of force before springing away again and moving on to the next target. Throughout it all, my brothers' gunfire roared away, blasting exposed armour pieces into shrapnel and shredding flesh into chunks of bloody meat.

In those moments, tearing into battle under the incandescent light of three suns, we had become the storm. We were irresistible: too savage, too skilled, too swift.

I tore on upward, fighting past the ruined gates and into the tottering maze of the ramshackle citadel beyond, flanked by Jochi and others of my minghan-keshig. More orks threw themselves at us, swinging down from corrugated roofs and burning webs of scaffolding. I punched one full in the face with my ceramite gauntlet, splintering its skull into bloody shards, before spinning away to crunch my boot into the stomach of another. My glaive threw gore around in swathes, streaking my armour and spraying my helm lenses.

'Onward!' I roared, pumped with aggression and energy. '*Onward!*'

My brothers swept along with me, racing up ladders to reach greenskins on platforms and charging up stairwells to purge them from the ramparts. When one of us was thrown down, another took his place. We gave them no room to breathe, to think, to react. We used our speed and our power in turn, swivelling away from danger only to surge back in with our power weapons spitting. The citadel became clogged with bodies – thousands of them – all locked in close combat amidst the burning towers, slaying and being slain in great, bloody droves. The deafening noise of it, amplified and distorted in the claustrophobic narrows, made the towers tremble and shake down sheets of dust.

As I fought my way up, I lost sight of Torghun. Only my own brothers, those whom I had led across the Crusade for a hundred years of warfare, kept up with me. We raced together, blasting aside all who came before us, shouting and laughing for the sheer exuberance of it. My armour clanged from repeated solid-round impacts, but I never slowed. The blades of the enemy came at me in clumsy swipes, but I thrust them aside and slew their owners. I heard the screams and bellows of greenskins ringing in my ears, and it only fuelled my drive to kill. I inhaled the stench of ork bodies and ork filth and ork blood, a hot musk of alien excreta. Everywhere, every stinking corner of that shoddy place, rang with the clash of weaponry; every rusty facet flashed with the reflected burn of gunfire.

That made me feel alive. I felt unstoppable. I felt *immortal*.

'For the Khagan!' I cried, my chest burning and my eyes blazing as I powered upward, ever upward.

I knew he would be there, somewhere. I would kill and kill, slaying with abandon, purging every last one of them, driving my body beyond all limits of endurance, just for the chance to see it.

Whatever Torghun thought, I had faith. I would see him fight again.

And after that, everything that had happened on Chondax, all the long, long years of hunting, it would all be vindicated.

I knew he would be there.

As we sprinted, I caught glimpses of the combat down in the lower flanks of the citadel. Pitched battles raged across every surface. Gun platforms and defence towers were snarled up with overflowing scrums of close combat, pitting whole gangs of greenskins against tight knots of embattled White Scars. Fires broke out everywhere, fed by burst fuel-dumps in the bowels of the structure. Thousands of warriors were still streaming across the depression to join the fight, tearing across the plains and into combat. Thousands of defenders rose to meet them, staggering out of their smouldering dens and bunkers with fierce, violent desperation lit up in their twisted faces.

As for us, we'd burned faster and higher than any others. We broke out of a shattered and burning elevator shaft, clinging to the yawing metal struts before flinging ourselves clear. We burst out onto a wide, flat metal platform strung up amid the finger-like pinnacles of stone. Jochi was with me, as were dozens of my brothers, their armour charred, cracked and glistening with gore.

At the far end of the platform hung the lower jaws of the huge ork head I had seen from the cliffs. It was even bigger than I had guessed – twenty metres tall and wide, a bulbous mass of riveted scrap and rust-crusted wreckage, suspended amid a sclerotic tangle of walkways and buttresses like some giant iron dirigible.

I started to give the assault order, but the words died on my lips. The structure issued a low, grinding bellow that made the rickety gantries around us shake and tremble. I struggled to keep my feet as the flimsy platform beneath me swayed wildly.

A heavy metal panel detached from the base of the grotesque artificial head, peeling away and clanging against the far end of the platform. Then another fell, revealing a glowing, smoke-filled void on the inside. I heard the sound of pistons withdrawing, and the hiss of heavy lifting gear wheezing into action. Earth-brown smoke belched out of the gap and rolled across the platform towards us.

'Kill it,' I ordered, bracing myself against the juddering metal, taking my guan dao one-handed and drawing my bolt pistol.

I fired, joining the torrent of bolter-rounds thundering out from my brothers. The barrage lanced into the ragged opening at the base of the head structure. I heard echoing explosions from within as the rounds went off, and muffled wails of rage. Something had been hit. Something was in pain.

Only then, roaring and slurring, did it emerge.

It burst out of the base of the head, crashing through the remaining walls with a drunken, lurching gait and throwing the remnants aside in a shower of smoking metal. A huge, muscle-bunched arm shot out, then another, hauling a vast and swollen body after it. A grossly distended head emerged, hung with low-slung jaws and drooling lips, clustered with weeping sores and marked with festering scarification.

I saw two yellow, watery eyes sunk deep below a low, knobbly brow. I saw tusks grind against one another as the creature roared again, and gobbets of thick spittle flying from its gaping maw. When it moved, its obese frame shuddered, shaking the bones and armour-fragments that clung to it like barnacles around the yawing hull of a ship.

I had never seen one so big. When it moved onto the platform, the bracings below it twisted under the weight. Its arms were encased in cages of metal, from which tubes ran directly into its flesh and sinew. Iron gauntlets encased its fists, each one of them bigger than my torso. Ripples of green energy sluiced across it, spitting and fizzing where they met the creature's skin.

It *stank* – a pungent mixture of bestial musk, engine oil and the sulphurous discharge of shield generators.

I had seen chieftains of their kind before of course; giant bulls that had roared their defiance to the heavens and charged into battle with reckless abandon. Those monsters were driven by savage lusts of battle, the burning desire to crush, to slay, to destroy and to feed.

This one was different. It was fused with clanking technology, bolted into its armour like one of our lobotomised weapon servitors. Had they learned that from us too?

And its anger was different. The noises it made, the way it moved, the swimming lack of focus in its animal eyes; all of that was different. I knew then that I was seeing what happened to the greenskin when nothing remained but defeat. They did not keep blindly raging, nor did they plead for mercy, nor did they learn at last how to fear their enemy.

They went mad.

'Bring it down!' I roared, aiming for its head.

We opened up with everything we had left. We fired rounds directly at it and watched them explode across its shielding. I saw Jochi launch himself into a charge, ducking and wheeling under the fire-lines to bring his blade in close. He was swatted clear with a vicious backhand and sent cartwheeling over the edge of the platform, his breastplate crushed. I saw others try the same, all of them moving with their habitual speed and prowess. None of them even got close – they were crunched aside by those iron gaunt-lets, knocked to the ground as if they were children. The monster waded forwards, flailing with cybernetic arms, vast and monstrous and slobbering with febrile madness.

I holstered my pistol and grasped my guan dao two-handed, already breaking into the charge that would carry me into range. It saw me coming and lurched to meet me, swinging its huge arms in clumsy, devastating sweeps. I dived under one of the gauntlets and twisted around, aiming my glaive into the creature's wrist.

The biting edges ground up against the shield in a shower of sparks. A sharp bang was followed by a stink of cordite, and the shimmering barrier over the creature's forearms flickered out.

Before I could take advantage, the beast swung back at me, keeping its other fist low. I tried to scrabble away, but its gauntlet slammed heavily into my side.

I was hurled clear, clattering across the platform, my blade still clutched in my hand. The world spun around me, and I had a brief glimpse of the fortress's topmost pinnacle above me swing-ing across the sky.

I skidded to a halt, knowing that the monster would be right behind me. I leapt to my feet and angled my blade back. I connected again, severing one of the cables that looped from its shoulders. Fluid cascaded over me, hot and stinking. As my blade's disruptor slashed through, it ignited, dousing us both in flaring green flames.

I pressed the attack, zigzagging the guan dao in a blur of speed, going for the active shielding.

I had no chance. For all its huge bulk, it was fast. An iron-clad fist shot out, catching me below the throat and crashing into me with the force of a skidding Rhino. I was sent sprawling for the second time, nearly blacked-out from the impact and hurled hard over to the far side of the platform. I saw the fire-tattered edge coming and blurrily tried to grab on to something. My gauntlet almost closed on a splintered stump of wreckage, but the corroded metal collapsed under my grasp.

I clattered over the edge, my armour gouging sparking trails in the steel. I looked down and saw the sheer sides of the citadel drop away below me, two hundred metres of empty air before the mass of burning structures near ground level.

In that split second, suspended over collapsing shards of rust and about to plummet, I saw death coming for me.

Then a hand grasped my wrist. I was hauled back, away from the crumbling edge, my armour-clad bulk heaved back onto the platform as if I weighed nothing.

As I was dragged back up, I stared – disorientated and fog-visioned – into a pair of glittering eyes set deep in a scarred, brown face. For a split second I gazed into those eyes, rigid with shock.

Then a huge body swept up and over me, followed by the rush of a fur-lined cloak and the sound of boots striding purposefully into combat.

Even then, my mind did not process what had happened. For a moment I did not know what I was seeing.

Then the fog cleared. My senses returned. I looked up, daring to believe, and saw at last who had saved me.

I do not know how he had made it up to the platform undetected. I do not know how long he had been fighting to get there. Perhaps his approach had been masked by the noise and violence of the melee, or perhaps he had been able to conceal his presence somehow.

Nobody was ever able to tell me where he had been while the assault was underway, nor how he had managed to enter combat at just that moment, without warning, without announcement.

I do not know whether he did such things deliberately, to add uncertainty to the shape of the battle, or whether it was just how matters were fated.

None of that mattered. The Khagan, the Great Khan, the complete warrior, the primarch of the V Legion, had unveiled himself at last.

He was there, right before my eyes, on Chondax.

He was there.

MY FIRST INSTINCT was to rush into battle at his side, to pick myself up and add my blade to his.

I immediately saw how pointless that would be. He had come with his keshig, a whole phalanx of giants in bone-white Terminator plate, and even they did not come between the Khan and his prey. They hung back around the platform edges, silent and massive, ensuring that nothing – greenskin or White Scar – intervened. Below us, the battle continued unabated, but up on the platform, under the shadow of that massive, ruined alien head, only two warriors fought.

He was tall, lean even in his ivory armour. A heavy crimson cloak hung from his shoulders, lined with mottled *irmyet* fur and covering the fine gilt curves of the ceramite plates beneath. He carried a *dao* sabre with a glass-polished blade that flashed in the sun. His shoulder guards were gold, engraved with flowing Khorchin characters and the lightning-strike sigil. Two Chogorian flintlocks nestled at his belt, ancient and opulent, studded with pearls and bearing the guild marks of their long-dead makers.

On Ullanor I had seen him fight from a distance, marvelling at the tremendous destruction he wrought amidst the congested fields of total war. On Chondax I saw him fight at close quarters, and it took my breath away.

I have never, before or since, seen swordsmanship like it. I have never seen such balance, such contained savagery, such unrelenting, remorseless artistry. As he whirled the blade around, sunlight shone from his gilded armour like a halo. There was a cruelty to it, a razor-edged note of aristocratic disdain, but there was also splendour. He handled his blade as though it were a living thing, a spirit he had tamed and now forced to dance.

Yesugei had said that only poets could be true warriors. I understood then what he meant: the Great Khan distilled the sprawling language of combat to its core of dreadful, merciless purity. Nothing was extravagant, nothing was wasteful – every stroke carried the full measure of murder within it, just enough and nothing more.

He hammered the maddened beast back, step by step, forcing it towards the far end of the platform. It raged at him, bellowing in a burbling frenzy of fury and misery. It swung its gauntlets wildly in massive, bone-breaking arcs, hoping to swipe him from the platform as it had done with us.

The Khan stayed close to it, his cloak swirling as he worked back and forth, sending his blade darting out and cutting back, using the long curved edge to carve through the creature's shambolic armour and bite deep into the addled flesh beneath. Whole sections of shielding were shattered, overloading the generators on the creature's back and making the tangled wiring burst and pop.

It tried to smash him to the floor with a wild haymaker, and he spun out of the challenge, plunging the edge of the sabre down hard as he moved. The ork's severed gauntlet-clad fist clanged to the metal, taken cleanly at the wrist and doused in a spray of steaming blood.

The monster raged on, its eyes wild and froth bubbling from its open maw. Its other fist swung round, as fast as the blow that had felled me. By then the Khan had already moved, pivoting on one foot and angling his blade back to meet the incoming sweep.

The gauntlet crashed against the dao, and I felt the platform shudder from the impact. The Khan held his ground, bracing his sabre two-handed, and the creature's iron fist cracked open, exposing a bloody, pulpy claw within, striated with cabling and corroded piston-sleeves.

The greenskin was weaponless then. It reeled away from the onslaught, and its roars became weaker and more desperate.

The Khan went after it, maintaining the icy, austere ferocity of his attack. His blade flashed out, slicing a weeping chunk of blubber from the creature's torso; then it switched back, cutting a long gash across its chest. Armour pieces shattered and fell like rain from its heaving shoulders, mingling with the slurry of blood that pooled and bubbled at its feet.

When the end came, it was quick. The beast rocked back onto its haunches, its stomach streaming blood and its jaws hanging limp. It stared up at its killer, its tiny eyes swimming with fluid and its chest trembling.

The Khan raised the dao high, holding it in both hands, his feet planted firmly.

The greenskin made no move to protect itself. Its damaged face was a piteous, weeping mess, marked by abject wretchedness and bewilderment. It knew what was being destroyed. It knew what had been lost.

I did not like to see that face. It was an ignoble end for something that had fought so hard and for so long.

Then the sword whistled down, trailing lines of gore as it plunged. The beast's head fell to the platform with a dull, booming thud.

The Khan withdrew his blade with a cold flourish. For a moment he stood over the vanquished warlord, gazing imperiously down at it, his long cloak lifting in the smoke-drifted air.

Then he stooped to retrieve the beast's head. He swivelled smoothly, holding the agonised skull high above him in one hand. Blood streamed from the beast's fleshy neck cavity, slapping against the metal floor in thick slops.

'For the Emperor!' roared the Khan, and his voice rang out across the bowl and high into the sky.

From below us, from the levels where the fighting still burned, a massed shout of acclimation rose up, overmastering the animal howls of the surviving orks and the crackle and rush of the flames.

I heard them answer him, hurling the same word up into the air, over and over.

Khagan! Khagan! Khagan!

That was the moment when I knew we had won at last. Years of ceaseless campaigning had finally come to an end.

The war on Chondax had ended in the only way it could have ended: with our primarch holding the head of the defeated enemy in his fist, and with the voices of his Legion, the ordu of Chogoris, rising in savage joy towards the vaults of heaven.

I joined them. I cried out his name, my fists clenched with euphoria.

I was glad we had won. I was glad that the white world was cleansed at last, and that the Crusade would grind onward, taking another step on the road towards galactic hegemony.

But that was not the main source of my fervour. I had seen the terrible power of the Great Khan unleashed – the spectacle I had coveted for so long.

It was not a disappointment.

I had seen perfection. I had seen the poetry of destruction. I had seen the paragon of our warrior breed in the full flood of his matchless glory.

My joy was complete.

✠ ✠ ✠

I MET TORGHUN one more time on Chondax.

It took many hours to subdue the citadel entirely. The greenskins, true to their nature, never stopped fighting. By the time the last of them was hunted down and killed, the fortress had begun to disintegrate around us, consumed by explosions from below and raging fires from above, and we had to withdraw.

I led what remained of my brotherhood out onto the plain at the base of the depression. Many tasks remained for us: we needed to make a tally of the slain, to direct Sangjai to those wounded who might live, to recover what we could of our fleet of damaged mounts for onward transport.

I remember only fleeting impressions from that time. My head was filled with visions of the Khan, and it made me distracted. Even as I worked, I could not shake the images of him in action. I rehearsed the blade-manoeuvres he had made, over and again, running through them in my mind and resolving to adopt those that I could once back in the practice cages.

Amidst all the devastation, with the fortress before us blazing and smoking in its ruin, all I saw was his curved dao flashing in the sunlight, his gilded armour moving smoothly under the cloak, his jewel-like eyes that had looked, briefly, into mine.

I would never forget it. One does not forget the fury of living gods.

Other brotherhoods, nearly a dozen of them, had done the same thing as we had and were reordering themselves in the aftermath of the battle. Once the bulk of my brotherhood had been extracted and had regrouped, I went to find Torghun. I guessed that the minghan would disperse quickly, and I did not wish to leave without making the appropriate courtesies.

When I found him, I saw that his brotherhood had fared better than mine. I learned later that they had fought with honour, seizing many of the gun mounts on the walls and destroying them. Their actions had allowed many other squads to break through the perimeter without enduring the losses that we had taken.

He had done well, and had enhanced his reputation for solid, competent command. For all that, though, I could not help but pity him a little. He had not seen the things that I had seen. He would leave Chondax with only a glimpse of glory from afar.

'Did he speak to you?' Torghun asked me, showing more interest than I had expected.

He had taken his helm off – the lenses were cracked and useless – but otherwise he looked almost unscathed.

'He did,' I said.

I was in much worse shape. My battleplate was riddled with dents, breaks and gouges. My gorget was shattered from where the beast's gauntlet had hit me and much of my suit's sensory array was inoperative. The fleet's armoury would be busy with us for months before we would be ready to deploy again.

'What did he say?' Torghun asked, pressing me for answers.

I remembered every word.

'He commended us on our speed,' I said. 'He said that he had not expected to be beaten to the summit. He said that we were a credit to the Legion.'

I remembered the way he had walked up to me after the beast was dead, watching tolerantly as I had struggled to bow before him. His armour had been pristine – the creature had not so much as scratched it.

'He told me that speed was not the only thing, though,' I said. 'He said that we were not berserkers like the Wolves of Fenris, that we could not forget that we had responsibilities other than breaking things.'

Torghun laughed. The sound was infectious, and I chuckled at the memory.

'So his advice was similar to yours, in the end,' I said.

'I'm glad to hear it,' Torghun said.

I looked out across the wide depression, over to where orbital landers had already come down from the fleet, ready to begin the long process of resupply and refit. Mortal auxiliaries were beginning to make planetfall, shuffling out in their awkward environment suits to liaise with the warriors of the Legion.

I saw a woman walking among them, a grey-haired official wearing a transparent dome-helmet over her suit. It seemed to me that she was in charge of the others, though she didn't look Chogorian – she looked Terran. I wondered what she was doing there.

'So what now for you?' asked Torghun.

I shrugged, turning back to him.

'I do not know,' I said. 'We await orders. And you?'

Torghun looked at me strangely then, as if trying to decide whether to tell me something important. I remembered how he had looked during our first conversation, when he had struggled to explain his brotherhood's name and customs. It was much the same then.

'I can't say,' was all he told me.

It was an unusual reply, but I did not press him. I thought little of it, for mission orders were often restricted and he was entitled to keep his brotherhood's business to himself.

In any case, I had secrets of my own. I did not tell Torghun what else I had seen the Khan do. I did not tell him that he had turned away from me quickly after our brief meeting, distracted by an approach from one of his keshig.

I could recall every word of that exchange too, every gesture.

'A message, Khagan,' his Terminator-armoured bodyguard had said.

'From the Warmaster?'

The keshig had shaken his head.

'Not from him. About him.'

'What does it say?'

There had been an awkward pause.

'I think, my lord, that you might wish to take this on the flagship.'

After that, I had seen an expression on the Khan's face that I had never expected to see there. Amidst all the pride, all the assurance, all the martial majesty, I had seen a terrible shadow of doubt ripple across those haughty features. For a moment, only a moment, I had seen uncertainty, as if some long-buried nightmare had rushed back, inconceivably, into waking thought.

I will never forget that look, imprinted for the briefest of seconds on his warrior's face. One does not forget the doubts of gods.

Then he had gone, striding away to whatever tidings they were that demanded his attention. I had been left on the platform, surrounded by those of my brotherhood who had survived the final assault, wondering what news could have prompted such a rapid departure.

At the time, the episode had troubled me. Facing Torghun, however, with the fortress of our enemies in ruins and the strength of the Legion gathering around me again, I found it hard to reconstruct that emotion.

We had triumphed, just as we had always triumphed. I had no reason to suppose that it would not always be so.

'You were right,' I said. 'Earlier, you were right.'

Torghun looked amused.

'What do you mean?'

'We should learn from the others,' I said. 'I could learn from you. This war is changing, and we need to respond. I did not defend well, back in the gorges. A day will come when we will need to master these things, not just the hunt.'

I am not sure why I said all that. Perhaps the lingering memory of the Khan's unexpected anxiety had dented my confidence.

Torghun laughed. He was not laughing at me that time; I think we had both come to understand one another too well for that.

'No, I don't think you should change, Shiban Khan,' he said. 'I think you should remain as you are. I think you should stay reckless and disorganised.'

He smiled.

'I think that you should laugh when you are killing.'

I FOLLOWED HIS recommendation: when I killed, I laughed. I let the ice-wind pull my hair free, and I felt hot blood against my skin. I ran far and strongly, daring my brothers to keep pace. I was like the berkut, the hunting eagle, free of the jesses, out on the rising air, high up on the horizon.

That was what we were back then; that was what we all were. Minghan Kasurga – the Brotherhood of the Storm.

That was our ranking name, the one we used to differentiate ourselves.

In private, we were the laughing killers.

To the rest of the galaxy, we were still unknown.

THAT WOULD CHANGE. Soon after Chondax we would be dragged headlong into the affairs of the Imperium, hauled into a war whose origins we had missed and of whose causes we knew nothing. Powers that had barely registered our existence would suddenly remember us, and our allegiance would become a matter of import for both gods and mortals.

The story of that war has yet to be written. As I stand now, gazing at the stars and preparing for the fires we shall unleash upon them, I do not know where the fates will lead us. Perhaps this will be the mightiest of our many endeavours, the final examination of our species before its ascendance into mastery.

If I am truthful to myself, I find it hard to believe that. I find it more tempting to think that something terrible has gone awry, that the policies and stratagems of ancient minds have faltered, and that our dreams hang over the abyss by a thread of silk.

If that is so, then we will fight to the last, putting our mettle to the test, doing what we were bred to do. I take no joy in that. I will not laugh as I kill those whom I have always loved as brothers. This war will be different. It will change us, perhaps in ways we do not even begin to guess.

In the face of that, I take some comfort in the past. I remember the way we used to fight: without care, with vigour, with abandon. Of all the worlds where we laboured, I will remember Chondax with the most fondness. I could never hate that world, no matter the cost in blood to us of its taking. It was the last time that I hunted in the way I was born to – untrammelled, as free as a falcon on the steep dive.

Above all, nothing will rival the memory of that final duel. If I live to see the ruin of everything, if I live to see the walls of the Imperial Palace broken and the plains of Chogoris consumed by flame, I will still remember the way he fought then. That perfection is fixed in time, and no force of malignity can ever extinguish what was done, there, before my eyes, atop the last spire of the white world.

If Yesugei were here with me, he would find the right words. I am no longer confident that I have the gift for it. But were I forced, I would say this.

There was a time, a brief time, when men dared to challenge the heavens and take on the mantle of gods. Perhaps we went too far, too fast, and our hubris may yet doom us all. But we dared it. We saw the prize, and we reached out to grasp it. In fleeting moments, just fractures of time amidst the vastness of eternity, we caught glimpses of what we could become. I saw one such moment.

So we were right to try. We were right to attempt it. He showed us that, less by what he said than by what he did, what he *was*.

It is for that reason that I will never regret our choices. When the time comes, I will stand against the darkening heavens, keeping his example fixed before my eyes, drawing strength from it, using it to make me as lethal and imperious as he. And when death finally comes for me, as it will, I will meet it in the proper way: with my blade held loose, my eyes narrow, and warriors' words on my lips.

For the Emperor, I shall say, beckoning fate. *For the Khan.*

SERPENT

John French

'And a serpent came even to that paradise.'

– from *The Fall of Heaven*, compiled from various ancient sources
Work proscribed 413.M30

THE MAGUS STARED at Thoros. Her arms were red to the elbows, and the white silk of her robe hung heavy with dried blood and fresh sweat. The man at her feet was still alive, twitching in the remains of his skin. Blood ran down the edge of the silver dagger in the magus's hand – a thick drop formed at its tip, glittering red-black in the burning coal light. Around them the magus's throng of followers waited, wide eyed and unsure of what exactly they were seeing or how exactly they should react.

They had done this many times and thought themselves hidden, but Thoros and his priests had simply walked into the centre of the ritual as though they were expected.

Looking into the magus's eyes, Thoros wondered what she saw when she looked back at him. A messenger of the gods? A monster? A revelation? He had shed the dark cloaks that had hidden his form during his journey here, and he stood now as he had upon Davin: a spindle-limbed figure in rough-spun robes. Gold torques circled his neck and wrists, each worked in the image of a snake with red jewelled eyes. Five of his priests stood behind him, swathed in pale robes, staffs clutched in scaled fingers. Their red, slitted eyes looked out on the world, unblinking.

The cavern around them was iron, a hollow space beneath the great furnaces above. Heat shimmered from the glowing mouths of kiln vents in the high roof. The cultists had been using it for years, and the spilt blood and muttered prayers itched at the edge of Thoros's senses.

He did not like this place. He did not like its iron smell, or the dull stink of the minds that infested its forges. He had come here only because it was the will of the gods that this world become theirs, and that it should fall before the war came. It was to be reborn – a high blessing for an unworthy planet. The throng of the magus's followers that filled the cavern were the beginning. But they had yet to see the true face of those they served.

Thoros tilted his head, letting the magus tremble under his gaze. She was afraid; he could taste it, an edge of fear spicing the human stink in the cavern's air. And why should she not be? She was used to power, to having others obey her commands. Now an emissary of her gods had come to her, and she no longer liked the face of the powers she had knelt to. He knew this was true; he could see it in the mirror of her eyes.

+It is coming, exalted one.+

The ghost voice of his priests whispered in Thoros's mind. He smiled.

+Yes, my kin,+ he responded. +The moment is close. The gods will show us the way.+

On the floor, the skinned man shuddered, vomited blood and then went still. The magus did not look at him, his sacrifice already forgotten. The rest of the kneeling cultists still did not move. The fear coming from them was a raw perfume to Thoros's senses.

Cattle. Cattle led by their spite and jealousy. Cattle that nursed their small hatreds, and dreamed of taking power from those that ruled them. It was to be expected; such desires bound mortals to the gods, but they were still little more than beasts waiting for the herdsman's lash. They called themselves the Eightfold Door. They were weak, and they were desperate – in their hearts they had never truly believed that their prayers would be answered.

'By the blood,' the magus intoned, her voice shaking as she raised the dagger to point at Thoros. 'By the seven silver ways and five chalices of night, I bind and command you...'

Thoros shook his head slowly, never taking his eyes from hers.

'Small things,' he hissed, taking a step forwards. 'Petty things.'

Around him whispers and shadows gathered, brushing his skin, filling the cavern. The gods had blessed him – nay, *made* him for this. From the moment his mother had brought him to the Serpent Lodge, a twisted child with the red eyes of the chosen, to the time he had seen beyond the doors of sleep and glimpsed the gods beyond – all of it had been preparation. Out beyond the walls of this cavern was a world, and in the sky of that world hung stars, around which other worlds circled in an eternal dance. All sleeping, all waiting for a new age that they could not know was coming. That was why the gods had seen him safely across the sea of souls to stand here at this moment: to ready the sleeping Imperium to awaken.

The magus was truly shaking now. Thoros heard the seed of speech in her mind and spoke before she could, his voice a rattling whisper.

'*Quietnessss.*'

The magus did not move or reply, though at his back Thoros sensed his attendant priests shifting. Slowly he reached across his waist and pulled a blade from the fold of his robes. The handle settled into his fingers.

'You are called by the high servants of the gods.' He took another step forwards. The gazes of a thousand eyes brushed his skin. 'This world will belong to them.' He paused, lips cracking over pointed teeth. 'But you – you are mine, now.'

The stillness snapped. The magus leapt at Thoros, a dagger in her hand.

The gathered cultists rose to their feet in a roar. Thoros felt their cries echo through his soul in that endless instant, their rage as hot as a furnace. Across the cavern other knives were slipping free of sheaths. He could feel it all: each ritually sharpened edge, each uncoiling muscle, each heart surging with fear and hatred. The murder lust bathed him, filled him and remade him.

He slid past the magus's thrust, and his knife came up and opened her stomach. She fell, blood sheeting down the white silk, mouth gasping for air, mind pleading for mercy as her soul rushed to meet her gods. He felt the shadows whisper in glee as she screamed.

Thoros's ghost voice rose into the gathering darkness. +The gods speak!+

+They speak,+ his priests echoed as one.

A pillar of jagged light stabbed up from amongst them, splitting the gloom with green fire. The five priests rose into the air, lightning winding around them in endless coils. Frost spread across the cavern ceiling, strangling the heat from the kiln vents. Where the fire touched the circle of cultists, it burned them to ash.

Thoros turned from the collapsing magus, his hand rising to become a black serpent of smoke. The serpent uncoiled down his arm, winding around his body, his skin burning and freezing at the nether-creature's touch. The remaining cultists surged at him, knives raised, eyes wide with fear. He felt the serpent encircle his throat; he opened his mouth to swallow it.

A cultist broke from the throng. He was huge, bare chested and slicked with sweat. Silver rings clattered from folds of skin as he charged. Thoros felt the man's dagger punch between his ribs, felt its point burst his heart, blood pouring into the cavity of his chest.

Fire and ice pulsed through him. He looked down at the fat cultist; the man pulled back to stab at him again, black droplets scattering from the knife as it ripped free.

Thoros opened his mouth, feeling his jaws dislocate wider and wider. Shadows spilled from his throat, boiling through the air, coiling around the cultist before his second blow could fall. The black cloud flowed on, twisting through the charging throng. They fell, their eyes blinded by nightmares, sweat turning to frost across their bare skin.

Every mind within the cavern screamed.

They see it now, thought Thoros as shrieks ripped from a thousand mouths. They see the primordial truth.

HUNTER'S MOON

Guy Haley

ARE THE NETS done? Boy! Are the floats stowed, no more are broken? That glass costs more than you're worth... Yes? Good, good. Sit down then, we have some time before the tide is right.

Oh, don't look so fearful boy, you'll survive. Off Old Ven I learned the sea, as you're going to learn it from me. Be thankful. Ven was the best, and his knowledge I give to you.

Still frightened? You shouldn't be. I'll tell you a thing, of Old Ven and how he died. There are worse things in this life than felphins or nautilons – much, much worse. Let me tell of them. I know, because I was there the day the hydra came to Pelago.

I was on my seventeenth voyage, a boy not much older than you. So long ago now, but I remember it right enough. If only I could forget...

WIND TEASED CURLS of white from black water. Our boat rocked, gentle as your mother's arms. It was a peaceful night, a night for calm after a hard day.

The ocean is a bitter foe, but we had triumphed, we three – me, Old Ven and Sareo. Our baskets were full. Not like the poor catches you see now, no! Our limbs ached with work well done, our hearts satisfied. All lived. A good day, boy. A good day.

Ven sat cross-legged in the cup of the hull, Sareo by him – not far from where you're sat now, if you can imagine it. Their faces were craggy in the orange light of the boat's firebowl. They enjoyed the warmth, enjoyed the motion of the steelcord bundles as they rolled with the water.

I was like you. I did not enjoy the night or the sea then. I gazed into the deep, terrified yet entranced. It has that effect. You'll know soon enough. You'll see.

Old Ven watched me. 'Your cousin still fears the water, Sareo?' he said, as though I wasn't there. 'Even now?'

'There is much to fear,' Sareo replied. 'The ocean is not safe. If you taught me nothing else, you taught me that.'

'Still, if he feels that way, why become a fisher?'

Sareo laughed. 'What else is there to do, Ven? He must fish, or he will starve.'

Ven called out to me, then. 'Hey! Hey, young one! Come away from the side. We sail home tomorrow. Come and sit with us. Keep an old man company. I have heard all Sareo's stories before.'

Sareo tutted and came to fetch me.

'Do you not hear our captain, Tidon? Come away now.'

But I was distracted. Such wonders had I seen that night! 'Down there, in the water... So much light. Are they spirits?'

'They are only sea-lights,' he replied. 'The actions of small creatures. That is all. They are harmless.'

I pouted. 'Something else you have learned in the collegium?'

'Aye, something else I have learned. Now come. You dwell too much on fear. Let us rest, and pass the time in pleasant company, for tomorrow we work hard. This catch won't salt itself.'

I came reluctantly to the fire. Ven frightened me, if truth be told. So old and stern, never a smile, but I was young and foolish and did not see his wisdom until it had left this world.

'You need not fear so much, young one,' he said. 'I have sailed these seas for fifty years, and no harm has come to me.'

'You are luckier than many,' I murmured.

Sareo looked up sharply. 'Show some respect, cousin!'

'Hush now,' said Ven. 'It is fine, Sareo. I was terrified for many voyages. But I trust to my vessel. Nothing can hurt a man through steelcord.' He patted the woven hull of the boat. 'Not if he sails well, and pays attention to what the ocean tells him. Look up. Go on! Look into the sky. You watch the lights in the water with fear. Consider the men who sail the night in their ships of steel and fire – do they fear the starlight, up there? Theirs is the deadlier sea. And yet they come, they go. They ply their ocean as we ply ours.'

I frowned. 'They are safe in their vessels. But they are just men. They would be as afraid as I on this sea.'

'Are you sure?' the old captain said, his eyes almost sparkling. 'The star giants are their allies. I saw them once, clad all in metal and taller than the tallest man. They came to Pelago when I was a boy. I have never seen the like before or since, but although I am old now, it is not a memory easily forgotten. How can you say that the off-worlders are just men, when such giants serve them?'

'This is true?' I asked, filled with excitement. 'You saw the giants?'

Sareo smiled. 'He saw them all right. In the collegium, there is a *pict* – a… a true picture – of the giants. In this pict there is a boy, he comes no higher than the knees of the visitors. It is our own Ven. Ven, standing with giants!'

I could scarcely imagine it. 'I have not been told this!'

'You do not ask, and so remain in ignorance,' Ven chuckled. 'When you attend the collegium, you will learn much – why the lights shine in the sea, why the sun rises, why the giants came to us.' He looked to Sareo, who nodded.

'It is so. Cousin, the engine of our boat, the clothes that you wear, that flashlight you so love. All things of wonder from the stars, they work not for magic but for clever artifice. You will learn all this, and more.'

Ven sighed. 'Aye, the old ways are dead. No gods in the sky or the sea now. Only giants.'

I looked past the rising sparks of the fire, into the night where the stars blazed thickly, and thought of the giants in their sky-ships.

I saw something there, a fast moving light upon the horizon.

'Cousin, captain – look!'

Sareo followed my gaze. 'What?'

'A star. A falling star!'

'Steady, boy,' said Ven, squinting into the darkness. 'My eyes are old, I cannot see.'

I scrambled to the side, rocking the boat with my movements. 'There! Upon the morningward horizon.'

'I see it. It is growing closer,' Sareo gasped, placing a hand upon my shoulder. 'Do not leap about so, Tidon!'

I paid no attention. I hurried back to the gunwale, my fear forgotten, and hung off the rigging.

Ven muttered grimly to himself. 'I see it now.'

We watched as the light grew to a ball of fire, big as a torch flame. The air itself trembled. Nightgulls took from their watery roosts, and felphins fled the growing glare.

The light roared overhead, smaller fires chasing it. Night turned to day. The ocean went from black to a sheet of rippled bronze.

Then it was gone. A sheet of lightning lit up the sky. A single peal of thunder rolled.

All returned to dark. Ven stood, hands on his stiff knees. The boat rocked as waves washed out from the distant impact.

'That was no star,' he said. 'It was a sky-ship. Come, we must go to them, and lend what aid we can.'

DAWN CAME, STRIPING the sky with lashes of light. The ocean glowed orange, and amidst the patches of burning fuel was a blocky shape, hard lines all at odds with the curve of the waves. It filled me with great fear, but Ven sailed on, his hand steady on the tiller.

Let me tell you boy, myths and legends are one thing when in their proper place... but in front of you, like that... Ach, you'll never understand.

We drew close. The sky-ship was dull blue, all streaked and scored. It lay canted at an angle, a skerry made all of metal. The prow of the ship was out of the water, a wheelhouse with many brilliant windows at the top. They glinted in the sun, scorched though they were.

It dwarfed our fishing smack, ten times its length, maybe twenty. Its true size was hidden by the waves. Not even the biggest house in the village would have come close to it.

Sareo pointed. 'To the front, captain. The wheelhouse. Let us look for a way in.'

'You're no expert in star vessels, cousin,' I snorted.

'No, but Ven is.'

The old captain kept his gaze level. 'I am not. I have seen them but twice. I will bring us a little closer.'

As we came in, Sareo rose from his perch. 'I see something!' he said, leaning out. 'What is that, Ven, that sigil?'

Again, Ven's eyes failed him. 'Describe it to me, all I see is a smear of blue.'

'Blue it is – a field of blue with a many-headed serpent set upon it.'

The captain was silent for a moment. 'Are you sure?'

'It is blackened... but aye, I am sure.'

'Then it may be a badge of the Legions.'

The word was unfamiliar to me. 'Legions?' I asked.

'The giants, Tidon,' Ven snapped. 'Young fool, do you know nothing?'

'But why is it here?'

'I do not know. For that we must venture inside.'

'There, then. There is a door.' I pointed out a square hatchway aft of the wheelhouse, made of the same metal as the hull, a perfect seal around it made to keep out the cold night in the sky.

Ven deftly brought us below the hatchway. The bulk of the ship glimmered in the dark water beneath our keel. 'Sareo, Tidon, go in.'

Sareo turned. 'You will not come with us, captain?' He looked doubtfully at me. He thought me too young, and I was.

'If only I could…' Ven muttered. 'I am old. I will wait here. But I am still the best sailor! Each member of a crew must play to his own strength.'

There was a roiling in the surface of the sea. Air bubbled from beneath the star vessel, carrying with it strange, chemical smells.

The Legion ship lurched, casting up a wave that sent our little boat bobbing away.

'Go quickly,' the captain urged us. 'We have little time.'

Ven brought our boat in to the sky-ship again. It gently kissed the hull of its distant cousin. I leapt first, for all my fear, and then came Sareo.

The hull was sloped enough that we could clamber easily to the door. It was surrounded by thick, black and yellow striping and strange symbols. Some were pictographs clear in purpose, others stencilled boldly in the script of the giants. I could not understand it.

'What says this, cousin?'

Sareo stared, puzzling out the unfamiliar sounds. 'Access… Access Hatch Four. And these, they are instructions to work the door machinery.'

'A machine? Like our engine?'

'No, not alike. Different. Dangerous.'

'Can you open it?' I asked.

He grabbed a handle sunk into a circular recess in the skin of the ship, and tried to twist it round. It would not move.

'The mechanism is not functioning. There are instructions.' He paused, mouthing silently to himself. 'Stand back, the words say to stand back. No. Go further, behind that faring. Careful you do not slip into the sea! There. Duck down. Cover your face. Do not be afraid of the noise. Now, I must turn this… and depress this.'

A shrill noise came from the downed ship's door. Sareo ran to take refuge beside me. A smooth, metallic voice spoke.

'Warning. Warning. Warning.'

There were four flashes of fire. Smoke drifted on the breeze.

I unwrapped my arms from my head. 'Is it… Is it done?'

'Aye,' Sareo replied.

We went back to the door. The paint was marred by starburst patterns of black. Sareo bent down and twisted the handle again. This time it turned.

'Now help me.'

We heaved open the door, and gazed down into the sky-ship's interior. A sense of dread welled up within me. 'It is dark in there, Sareo. How do we know it will not sink and drown us both? No! Don't go in!'

Sareo lowered himself into the opening. 'Stop being so foolish. I will not let you drown. It's perfectly safe. Follow me cousin, follow me.'

I FOLLOWED SAREO into a short corridor, half-lit by the wondrous lamps of the Imperium, some of which now burned erratically. The vessel sloped sternwards, and water lapped not far from the hatch. Lost lamps shone greenly in the depths.

Sareo moved quickly and surely. 'Do not be afraid. The giants will thank us. We are their rescuers. Think of that!'

'But, the lights...' I whispered. 'The water...'

'Stay calm. The vessel is surely holed, and will take on water as readily as any craft of Pelago. We must hurry. There is no profit to be had going aft. Let us head upwards, to the wheelhouse. It is still above the water. The pilots might live.'

We made for another doorway up the corridor. It was difficult going. The ship was wallowing, rolling onto its side, and we were forced to brace our feet against the wall and the deck, proceeding like glimmer crabs picking over a reef.

Sareo banged on the sealed hatch.

'Can you open it?' I asked.

'No, we must force it open. See, there are tools in that alcove there.'

I scrabbled at a panel in the wall, painted over with strange words. 'Here?'

'Aye.'

Sareo pushed me out of the way and pressed the panel's edge. It opened and I looked inside, unsure what I was searching for.

'Is there a pry bar, Tidon?'

'Yes, cousin.'

The work was hard, and the ship's interior close and hot. We sweated to pull the door open, fingerwidth by fingerwidth. Fearsome noises haunted the ship, but with Sareo with me, I did not take fright.

We squeezed through the gap we made. On the other side, the way was wider, set with rows of large seats facing each other. Between, two corpses lay on the deck – one in blue, one in grey.

I could not believe my eyes. 'They are... so huge...'

'They are dead,' Sareo replied flatly.

'What happened?'

'They killed each other.'

They were locked together even in death. A knife jutted from a

join in the blue giant's armour. What had killed the one in grey,
I could not tell.

'Why do they fight? I thought them all brothers.'

'I do not know, but it augurs ill. There is another door. Perhaps
in there, in the wheelhouse, we will find answers.'

We clambered over the corpses. The second door yielded as
unwillingly as the first. The ship rolled further to starboard as we
worked, spurring us to greater action.

We forced it wide to reveal a broad cabin full of dead devices.
Two massive forms were strapped into a pair of seats, back to back,
by the fire-blacked windows. A pair of half-men – creatures of flesh
joined with their machines – were also within. None showed any
sign of life.

I looked around in confusion. 'Is this the wheelhouse? I see no
wheel. How does so large a ship sail with no wheel?'

'It is not a ship as you would understand it, cousin. It is science.
The wisdom of the stars.'

Sareo made forwards, pulling himself up the sloping deck. Both
the seated giants were in grey armour, hung all about with pelts
and charms.

'Such savages!' I choked, covering my mouth. 'They stink!'

'Their customs are different to ours, that is all. Look not to their
trinkets – look instead at the craft of their machines, and then
tell me if it is they or *us* who are the savages.' Sareo leaned down.
'Help me here.'

Sitting, their lifeless eyes were level with ours. I stood back as
Sareo fiddled around the base of the first giant's helm. He hit upon
a catch, and it came free.

He passed it to me; it filled my arms and was almost too heavy
for me to carry. Beneath the helmet the giant had a thick red beard
and braided hair, and tattoos writhed over his face. The tips of long
teeth protruded between his lips.

Sareo pressed fingers to the warrior's thick neck.

'This one lives…'

He went to the second and removed his helmet too, more quickly this time. It was only then that I saw the giants' blood staining the deck beneath our feet.

'This one does not.'

Sareo was distracted, looking for some other sign of injury, and did not see the first giant move.

I cried out to warn him. 'Sareo!'

The giant grabbed Sareo's shoulder in one armoured gauntlet, forcing him to his knees.

'What… What are you doing?' he slurred.

'We are here to help!' I pleaded. 'Please, you are hurting him!'

The giant looked down at Sareo with puzzlement. He let go. Sareo tumbled forwards with a gasp.

The savage warrior slammed at the belts that crossed his body. He fell from his seat, stood unsteadily and looked at us with pale yellow eyes.

'Atmospheric re-entry. Too violent.' He shook his head. His long braids swung.

'We have to get off the ship,' Sareo insisted, his voice pained. 'We are sinking.'

'Sinking?'

'You are in the water, the oceans of Pelago. Follow us. Quickly now!'

The grey warrior moved falteringly. I cowered.

'Come on, Tidon!' Sareo called back.

We pushed out of the wheelhouse. The gap we had made was not wide enough for the warrior, but he grasped the edge of the door and forced it back.

We stumbled down the gangway and over the corpses. The giant wrenched at the second door, and then his strength was spent.

The slope was steepening, threatening to tumble us into the water below. The warrior stumbled. Sareo steadied him on one side, I on the other. I dropped his helm, and it splashed into the water.

'Tidon!' Sareo cried.

'I'm sorry!'

The giant was so weak, but we pushed and pushed until he hauled himself up through the hatch and out into the sunlight. He staggered down the unsteady hull towards the fishing smack. Ven steered as close as he could.

'Quickly, quickly!' he called.

Sareo gestured urgently. 'Onto the boat, sir giant.'

The warrior fell onto it, his weight lifting the stern out of the water, and lay still. Ven tried to rouse him, but he was unconscious. Instead Ven wrestled feebly to pull the giant further on.

The sky-ship was slipping lower into the ocean. 'Get aboard!' the captain shouted to us. 'To the prow, both of you! Your weight might counterbalance his!'

Sareo looked back. 'There may be more surviv–'

'You have no time! We must be away, or the wreck will drag us all down with it!'

The lip of the open hatch reached the water. A foamy rush spilled over, and the ship began to sink faster. Sareo shoved at me urgently, and I leapt the gap.

Ven beckoned wildly. 'Now, Sareo, now!'

He jumped, but landed awkwardly with a cry of pain.

'Sareo!'

'It is his shoulder,' I explained. 'He... the giant... He hurt him.'

Sareo grunted. 'In error. It is only bruised. Come now, Tidon, to the prow!'

Our weight stabilised the boat enough so that Ven could work the engine. He swung us out and around, away from the sky-ship. 'Tidon, raise the sail. We must be quicker!'

I set the canvas swiftly, catching the wind. We drew away as the wheelhouse vanished under the water. The ocean boiled. Wave slapped into wave, foam swirled, and then there was nothing, as if the ship had never been.

'The ocean takes everything,' Ven murmured. 'Even a sky-ship is no proof against it.'

WE SET SAIL for home. Sareo and I managed to get the giant further into the boat, and our ride became smoother. Daygulls wheeled, their cries like the cries of the dead upon the waves.

I was seated by the giant when he awoke. He groaned, sat and stared about him. He was fierce, his gaze uncompromising. None of us could hold it.

'Where am I?' he demanded.

'Pelago,' said Ven. 'Fifth world of the sun of Gollim.'

The giant stood. Steelcord is a tough fibre, but the boat was flimsy beneath his great weight, and it rippled under his movement. He examined it, then the sea, then each of us, with a look of distaste.

'A backwater world. Have you even acceded to compliance?'

Ven nodded. 'We have. We welcome you, our saviour.'

'Welcome me not, for you do not know what follows me. You, old one – you are the captain of this vessel?'

'I am Ven. This is my sister's son, and his cousin.'

Sareo and I bobbed in turn. The grey warrior ignored our awkward bows.

'Then I direct you to take me to the nearest point of Imperial authority. I have grave news that must be delivered.'

'We saw violence on your ship,' I said. 'The giant in blue–'

The grey warrior whirled around. In one stride, he crossed the deck to where I stood, causing the boat to rock alarmingly. He towered over me. His lips drew back, showing the full, inhuman length of his teeth. Sareo and I shrank back.

'You will not speak to me of this again,' he growled before turning away, leaving us gasping and afraid. 'Make haste, little captain. Set your sail, or all is lost.'

FOR THE FIRST day after his rescue, the grey warrior would not talk with us. He took little food, and drank sparingly of our water. He evidently had some sea-craft himself, for he remained out of the way as we went about our business. We were wary of this lord of the stars, who sat brooding over some unfathomable woe.

Near noon on the second day, he suddenly broke from his silence as we worked on the remainder of our catch.

'You do not trust the water.'

Ven looked at him strangely. 'To swim in these waters is to die, sir giant. Pelago is mostly ocean, and it is an ocean deadly to man.'

The giant stirred himself and stood tall.

'Are you unharmed, sir?' asked Sareo.

'I am, thanks to you. You have saved my life. Normally, that would suffice to put me in debt of honour to you. But I have seen things of late that have robbed me of my trust. I misjudged you, I misspoke and I have abused your hospitality.'

He locked eyes with Sareo, and this time my cousin did not look away.

'I am mighty Torbjorn, company champion of *For*, renowned for my skill at arms the breadth of the galaxy. My honour is my life, and I have sullied it. Let me make amends and labour beside you.'

With that, he began to work. The giant was as good a sailor as any I have known since, and he told us that in his youth he had plied the seas of his far-off home world – seas even more deadly than our own. With his aid we made good progress, and soon our catch was all salted in its barrels and the ship was clean.

When our course was set, he told us his story, a manner of story few are privileged to hear.

'War rages in the heavens, little sailors. Brother pitted against brother. Foul treachery is at hand. The Imperium is ripped asunder.'

'We know nothing of it,' said Ven. 'We only knew of hope and of unity.'

'Hope is embattled. Unity is no more. But there is perhaps a little comfort – my brothers have died, but not in vain. We were sent by our father, Leman of the Russ, the Wolf King. In the wake of Magnus's perfidy, we went quietly, in fives and tens, to watch over the primarchs of the Legions – the lords of those you call giants, and brothers to my Lord Russ. A guard of body in name, a guard of loyalty in fact. My pack was to go to Alpharius of the Alpha Legion, those of blue you saw. We set out into the warp as doubt engulfed the stars.

'We could not know that Alpharius had already turned against our beloved Emperor. We were received as brothers by the remnants of the 88th Expedition, feasted and honoured. Into the primarch's presence we came, three days after our arrival. He was a lesser being than our own lord, not much bigger than his sons, with a troubled face under a drawn brow. Would I have marked his perturbation well then my brothers would not have died.

'"I am Alpharius," he said. "To what do I owe the honour of a guard of the sons of the Russ?" His words were hard, and only then did I know he saw through our purpose. Our ruse was distasteful to us, but not dishonourable – we were there to guard him if he proved true and, if not, to act in guard of the Imperium. There is no higher calling than that. He bade us kneel, but we did not, for the *Vlka Fenryka* are proud, and our lord is more than the equal of Alpharius. This angered him. He was ignoble and rash. He railed against us, shouting imprecations for our rightful scouring of Prospero. And then, his sons attacked.

'Brother Egil died first, his armour split by bolts. Then Grivnir, although he accounted for two of theirs before he fell. Six of us remained, hemmed in by the Alpha Legion high in the galleries about us. They underestimated us. Theirs is the way of stealth and manipulation. Ours is that of open battle, and of fury. We fell hard among them, blades swinging, howling out our wrath and sorrow.

'Helgist died, then Skalagrim, but the traitors paid the blood-price for their deaths. I fought, my brothers Engal, Gunnir and Holdar at my side. We closed so they could not bring their bolters to bear, for we are their betters when it comes to blade's sating. Holdar and Engal gained the stairs to the gallery, staying the storm of fire with their corpse-makers.

'I and Gunnir faced their lord. We are the Legiones Astartes, Space Marines of the Emperor, Wolf Guard, and the favoured sons of Russ. But he was mightier still, a primarch. Gunnir rushed in first, axe descending. With one sweep of his arm, Alpharius knocked him down. I pressed my own attack, sword in hand. Together we duelled.

'Long did our fight proceed, a blur of weapon and might's art that I will never again experience. If that is to be my last battle, so be it, for it was a contest worthy of the sagas. I have been unmatched in war, but I could not prevail there alone. Gunnir saw his chance. He re-entered the fray, curving his axe down at the traitor's leg. He lost his life for it, but distracted our foe long enough.

'I ended Alpharius with my pistol. Primarch or not, he died by my hand with a bolt to his head.'

I spoke up. 'What happened then?'

'We fought free, the three of us, to their embarkation decks where we seized a Stormbird drop-ship. It was a miraculous escape, but we skulked through an asteroid field like chastened dogs until we arrived here, and their final surprise was sprung – for a pair of them had stolen on board with us. As Holdar battled one within the ship, the other sabotaged the engines, and we were clawed down into the well of your planet's gravity.'

Ven seemed concerned. 'I know a little of star vessels. Did you sail upon the tides of the warp?'

'No, we did not venture into the empyrean,' said Torbjorn, gently. 'A Stormbird has no such capability, little captain.'

Sareo's expression grew haunted. 'But that means…'

'Yes. I am sorry. The traitors are coming here. Nevertheless, hope remains. I sent a message to my kin. They come also.'

WE SPOKE LITTLE as we sailed the final day. A storm beset us, and our attentions were focused on our craft. Torbjorn stood at the prow, weathering all that the sea could throw at us.

Our fears did not subside with the tempest. With clear night skies, we glanced often to the stars, seeking movement.

The sky-ship came as we approached land the next morning. A small cove, not far from this village – you know it, don't you boy? You have seen the stone cairn there. I know you have broken the ban and gone to see. What young man would not? The craft flew in from the sun, roaring round the headland as it slowed its approach.

I laughed in relief. 'The wolf's head, sir giant – they carry the emblem of a wolf's head!'

Torbjorn laughed as well. 'It is one of our craft, the *Hunter's Moon*! My brothers are here!'

Surf carried the boat in to shore and we jumped down, pulling it out of the waves. Torbjorn did not lend his strength to ours. He stared at the sky-ship at the edge of the dunes, apprehensive.

'Something is not right,' he murmured.

The ramp opened.

Out strode six giants clad in rich, indigo blue. Their leader was ornately attired – bareheaded, his scalp gleamed coppery in the sun.

Torbjorn's face twisted in an enraged snarl. 'No! It cannot be! I slew you!'

He reached for a pistol that was no longer there. The other giant raised his gun.

Pray you never hear that sound, boy – the terrible, terrible sound of Legion weaponry.

Ven was right beside me one moment, and the next he was gone. Scraps of his flesh spattered over me as he collapsed into the surf. Sareo turned to flee, but his arm was blasted from him, his body shredded, and he fell.

Torbjorn roared in defiance. 'Die, traitors!' He ran at the giants in blue, as they all opened fire upon him.

He made it less than ten paces before he was cut down. Torbjorn had fought his last.

No more guns spoke. I opened my eyes. The remains of my cousin and my captain rolled in the rush of the tide at my feet.

'No, no…'

The leader levelled his gun at me, its muzzle a black eye staring the promise of death. I shook with terror. For an age, I waited to die.

wThe others followed. Sparkling in the sunlight, the jewelled eyes of the many-headed serpent emblazoned upon their armour plates transfixed me as they left.

I did not dare move as the sky-ship lifted from the ground and flew from my sight.

MUCH TO MY shame, I survived, boy. The giants never returned, but I will never forget that day. That golden afternoon of bloody surf haunts my nights still.

I tell you, whatever fear you may have for the ocean, there are far worse monsters swimming in the sky's night. I know, because I have seen them.

I was there the day the hydra came to Pelago.

VERITAS FERRUM

David Annandale

THE EXPLOSIONS RIPPLED along both flanks of the *Veritas Ferrum*. The blasts were twin broadsides, as the Iron Hands strike cruiser drove between its enemies. With Night Lords to port and the Alpha Legion to starboard, there was no question of evasion. There was only, for now, a choice of foe.

As the *Veritas* was bracketed by the fire of the two smaller cruisers, her void shields flared with the brilliance of a new sun. The glare was so intense that, for an instant, the oculus showed nothing but white blindness.

Standing at his command lectern, Captain Durun Atticus raised his bionic rasp of a voice over the din of alarms and the rumble of secondary blasts. 'Damage report, Sergeant Galba!'

'Void shield collapse over port-side stern, captain. Fire in that landing bay, and in the serf barracks.'

'Seal the sector. Divert its power to the shields.'

Galba looked up from his post just beneath the lectern. 'Captain, the survivors–'

Atticus silenced the sergeant with a sharp gesture. 'They're dead either way. Anyone in that sector is a casualty. Let's not add to their numbers. Do it, damn you!'

Damn the arithmetic of war. Damn Horus. Damn the turncoat cowards who were filling the near orbit of Isstvan V with the wreckage of ships, the flames of treachery, and the ruin of the Emperor's dream.

'*And damn me too,*' Atticus muttered.

Galba paused over his controls. 'Captain?'

'Nothing.'

But it wasn't nothing, was it? What was it he had said to his men, laughing with that bionic larynx of his – *laughing* – as the *Veritas* had begun its journey through the warp to the Isstvan System? He had said that it was not true that the Legions knew no fear, because he had a great one, and his fear was that they would arrive to find that their primarch, Ferrus Manus, had already crushed the War-master's rebellion without them.

After Callinedes – after Fulgrim's craven ambush – and after the warp storms had calmed, Lord Manus had raced hard for Isstvan, taking the fastest, least-damaged ships, and filling them with his most experienced Avernii veterans. Atticus had given over half his complement of warriors to the primarch's folly. But now the *Veritas Ferrum* had finally dropped out of the warp at the system's Mandeville point, and into a vision of hell.

Atticus descended from the lectern and strode to the oculus. Littering the far orbit of the Isstvan star was a graveyard of loyalist ships. Some had been caught as they attempted to escape, but many more were simply torn apart by enemy fire as soon as they emerged from the immaterium.

The Iron Hands second wave had been virtually obliterated.

'Hard to starboard!' he ordered, sweeping his eyes over his crew. 'Will none of you ask if I am relieved that my fear has not come to pass?'

The battle was not over, but the terrible truth was that it seemed as though it soon would be.

He jabbed a finger at the nearest enemy ship that hove into view as the *Veritas* began its turn. 'I want everything hitting that Alpha Legion bastard.' If he still had lips, they would have parted in a murderous smile. 'So the individual is unimportant, is it, Alpharius?' he spat. 'Then what we're about to do won't hurt you at all.'

With the slow majesty of a glacier, the *Veritas* rounded on its prey. The Alpha Legion ship, the *Theta*, tried to evade by rising above the ecliptic, but it was too slow, and too late. Concentrated lance and torpedo fire from the *Veritas* overwhelmed its void shields. They went down in a flickering cascade, and the *Theta*'s running lights died just before the Iron Hands main barrage struck it amidships.

The blow was devastating. The *Theta* broke in half.

Galba called out from his station, 'The Night Lords vessel is firing again.'

'Noted, sergeant. Countermeasures.' Atticus looked at the bisected cruiser before them. 'Helmsman,' he ordered, 'take us *through*.'

The prow of the *Veritas Ferrum* drove into the dissipating fireball where the core hull of the *Theta* had been. The two sections of the Alpha Legion vessel seemed to fold in upon the *Veritas* in an embrace of the void. There was a glancing impact that brought down the starboard prow shields, but then the *Veritas* was clear. Behind them, the Night Lords vessel's flank was exposed to the wreckage – the ship was manoeuvring into an evasive turn, but there was no time. The shattered rearward bulk of the *Theta* slammed into it, lighting up the void as her reactor went critical.

The sound that came from Atticus's voice box was a growl of satisfaction. 'Sergeant Galba?'

'Shields holding. Just.'

Ahead, there was a clear path. Atticus turned to the vox-operator. 'Any word from the dropsite?'

'Nothing I can confirm, captain.'

They had received only fragmentary vox chatter since their arrival. Broken distress calls from voices that claimed to be Iron Hands, lamenting the death of their primarch, but never any direct responses to hails from the *Veritas*. Atticus returned to the command lectern. 'More lies, then,' he said. He would not believe that Ferrus Manus had been killed. Not unless he saw the primarch's body before him. Perhaps not even then.

He would not believe it. Yet deep down he knew there was nothing left to salvage from the dropsite, and he felt his soul filling with a hatred that he would carry to his grave.

Galba's auspex blared a proximity alarm. 'Capital ships, dead ahead!'

Atticus could not sigh any more. So much of the weak flesh was gone, the many basic human mannerisms given up and replaced by the strength of metal. So he did not sigh – he tightened his fists instead, bending the rails around the lectern. 'We must retreat. If we do not, if nothing of the loyalist forces survived the slaughter on the surface, what then? What then for our Legion?'

The vox-operator whirled to face the lectern. 'Signal! Thunderhawks. Two, outbound from the debris field, requesting aid.'

The war-arithmetic loomed before Atticus once more. 'Put it on main speaker.'

Static crackled through the open channel. Then came a voice.

'This is Sergeant Khi'dem, Salamanders 139th Company. Our carrier vessel was destroyed. We need recovery.'

Atticus looked at the tactical hololiths before him. So few allied ships left. The *Veritas* was the only one close enough, and with even the illusion of freedom to act. But the arithmetic was unforgiving.

'I'm sorry, sergeant. We cannot help you. This is the Tenth Legion strike cruiser *Veritas Fe*–'

'We have a number of your brothers and those of the Raven Guard aboard. We lost many to save them. Is that worth nothing?'

'Do you have our primarch?'

There was a long moment of silence. *'No.'*

'Then, I regret–'

'Three Legions have fought for the Emperor, and now face annihilation. Are they to be abandoned, their sacrifice forgotten? Will you grant the traitors an absolute victory? Will there be no witnesses to what was done this day on Isstvan Five?'

Atticus cursed. He cursed Khi'dem. He cursed the entire galaxy.

'Helmsman, set course to intercept. Recover those ships.'

He hated the piece of his soul that rejoiced at the decision. He wished he had replaced it with bionics, too.

THE VERITAS FERRUM closed with the Thunderhawks. On both its flanks, the great warships of the Sons of Horus and the Emperor's Children were approaching. A noose was closing around the Iron Hands.

The *Veritas* slowed to take on the two gunships, even as the traitors opened fire. The starboard landing bays were closing when the torpedoes struck the port side. Then the already terrible damage became catastrophic.

The explosions were thunder that built upon thunder. Atticus felt his ship's wound through the command interface like a blade scraping the length of his ribs. The bridge klaxons were the *Veritas* screaming in pain.

But the Iron Hands still had the vector of escape. Atticus pounded the railing of the command lectern. 'Go!' he roared.

The *Veritas* ran. The tear in its flank was huge. It bled air and flame and tiny, armoured figures into the void. The ship was rocked by yet another torpedo hit.

Galba was hunched over his post as though the screens themselves were his enemies. 'Fire spreading, captain. Over a hundred legionaries lost to the void.'

'Many times more than the Thunderhawks were transporting,' Atticus raged. 'I'm *sure* our guests are worth it.'

He felt it then, the final excision of mercy from his being. The last weakness, killed one battle too late. And now, with only one desperate path remaining, a calmness as cold as the grave descended upon him.

'Make the jump.'

Galba was staring at him. 'Captain, the hull is compromised–'

'Make the jump. *Now.*'

The *Veritas Ferrum*'s warp engines flared. The bleeding ship plunged into reality's scream, and Atticus gazed into the maw of a future as pitiless and uncertain as he.

RIVEN

John French

'It is not the dead I pity but the living. Those left at the threshold of ending are the ones who bear the burden of death. They are the ones who have to learn to live, knowing that nothing can be as it was.'

– from *Lament for the Phoenix*,
penned by the Primarch Fulgrim in 831.M30

'*When do we free him?*'

The voice was the first that Crius had heard since he had woken in the prison of his armour. It was low and deep, like the sea surging against a cliff. Static cracked and popped as the vox-system came to life in his helmet. The darkness remained, pressing against his eyes.

'*When we reach the edge of the sun's light, Boreas,*' said a second voice, further away but still close.

'*Is he awake in there?*' asked the first voice, the one called Boreas. '*Perhaps.*'

Small jolts of electricity ran up Crius's spine. Power was slowly seeping into his armour systems – enough for him to feel, but not enough for him to move. That was the point, of course. In this state his armour was as complete a prison as any cell, its fibre bundles paralysed, its servos locked.

This is not Khangba Marwu, he thought, and the months of silence in Terra's great gaol rose and drained away as the realisation hardened. *I am no longer chained beneath the mountain.* His armour was vibrating against his skin, steady and slow, like an electric pulse.

I am on a ship, he realised.

He had spent most of his life on ships, journeying between wars across the scattered stars, and the sensations of a vessel under power were as familiar to him as the beat of his own hearts. At least they had been, before he was returned to Terra, before Crius, Lord of the Kadoran and veteran of nearly two centuries of war, had become an Iron Hands legionary of the Crusader Host.

Before he had been forgotten.

Light touched his eyes. Ice-blue numerals ran across his sight. He tried to focus on the scrolling data but found that he could not. The connections between his flesh and augmetics itched; the scrambler that the Custodians had used to subdue him had shorted out half of the connections.

He began to inventory the details of his situation. He had no weaponry beyond his own body. Not normally the greatest of problems, but he had no control of his armour, and it was likely to be power starved. His augmetics were functioning far below optimal parameters. Even if he could get control of his armour, his combat effectiveness was fifty-nine per cent of optimal. That, of course, was based on the presumption that there were no other bindings holding him in place.

Not forgetting that you were too old for the warfront before you were sent to Terra, said a voice at the back of his thoughts. *Not forgetting that factor.*

Then there was the question of what enemy he would face. He recalled the voices he had heard, rolling their pitch and tones through a mental analysis. No auditory markers of the Custodians, but the vocal range was outside a human norm – deeper, textured by muscles and structures that mortals lacked. The conclusion formed in his mind with the smallest possibility of error: Space Marines.

He had new gaolers then, but why?

Irrelevant. That they were Space Marines was enough to skew the combat outcome. *Even if I could move I would likely still lose,* he thought.

Hatred rose through him then – hatred for those who had betrayed the Emperor, hatred for those who had imprisoned him, but most of all hatred for his own weakness. He should not have become weak enough that his only use was as a figurehead; he should not have allowed himself to be imprisoned; he should have been with the rest of his clan and Legion as they struck down the traitor Horus. He should...

He shut down the chain of thoughts, containing them and allowing their heat to flood him but not dull his logic.

'The truth of iron,' he muttered to himself, 'guide me.'

Something scratched on the outside of his helm. He froze, muscles tensed and poised. Gas hissed around his neck. Seals clunked open and his helmet lifted away. His eyes dimmed as light poured into them, and his sight fizzed briefly before resolving to clarity.

A broad face looked back at him. Tanned and scar-knotted skin covered flat and muscle-thickened features; it was the face of one of the Emperor's finest, the face of a Space Marine. A close-cropped strip of hair ran down the centre of the warrior's skull, and a pair of dark eyes watched Crius without blinking. Crius stared back, his indigo lenses set into a face divided between scarred flesh and chromed ceramite.

He sat in a throne at the centre of a chamber of tiered stone. Chains wound across his body, linking to manacles at his wrists and fixed to cleats in the floor. The walls of the chamber were black, smooth and flecked with crystal that sparkled in the light of dimmed glow-globes. Banners hung from the walls, their gold, black and crimson thread tattered by bullet holes and charred by fire. The domed ceiling above was a mosaic of white and black tiles forming the emblem of a clenched fist.

The Space Marine who had removed Crius's helm wore yellow armour with a black-on-white cruciform device on his shoulder. There was a stillness about him that reminded Crius of the memorial statues that guarded the graves of the honoured dead.

Imperial Fists, he thought. *The praetorians of Terra. Of course.*

The Imperial Fists legionary stepped back, and Crius saw a second figure standing further back, watching in silence, his armour swathed in a white tabard crossed with black, his hand resting upon the pommel of a sheathed sword. He looked into the figure's hard, cold sapphire eyes. Crius's gaze did not waver.

'His armour, my lord?' said the Imperial Fists legionary standing over him. 'Should I activate it?'

Boreas, Crius thought. That was what the other voice had called him.

'I would not do that,' he said and looked up. Boreas met his gaze, the hint of a frown forming on his brow. 'And if I were you, I would also not release these chains.'

'What?'

'Because if you do,' Crius continued, calmly, 'I will kill you both.'

Boreas glanced at his silent comrade, then back to Crius. 'Do you–'

'Yes, I know who he is,' growled Crius.

'I would not wish to believe you a traitor, Iron Hand,' said the second Imperial Fists legionary.

'Treachery…' Crius said the word slowly. 'Tell me, if you had been buried beneath a mountain, chained beside those with the blood of true traitors, then what thoughts would you have nursed in the dark? What would you wish on those who bound you there?' The focusing rings of his eyes twitched. 'If Sigismund, First Captain of the Imperial Fists, were sitting here in my place, what would *he* be thinking?'

Sigismund narrowed his eyes. 'I would be considering how I might best serve the Imperium.'

'Truly?' sneered Crius.

Sigismund carried on as if he had not heard. 'Now that we have passed beyond the bounds of the Solar System, I am charged by Lord Dorn to give you his orders.'

Crius shook his head slowly, not breaking Sigismund's gaze. 'My sword is *my* primarch's to order, and the Emperor's to command. You are neither, and nor is Rogal Dorn.'

Boreas surged forwards, anger cracking his stony features. His hand was already bunched into a fist. 'You dare–'

Fast, registered Crius. *Very fast.*

But Sigismund moved faster and put a hand on Boreas's shoulder.

'Peace, Boreas,' said the Lord of Templars. Boreas glanced at his commander, and something passed between them in that glance.

Crius opened his mouth to speak. Sigismund spoke first.

'Ferrus Manus is dead.'

Crius heard the words. He felt his brain process them. He felt their meaning spread through him. He felt… nothing.

The instant stretched out, and still there was nothing. Not the feeling of his armour against his skin, not the ache of his shorted augmetics, not the pulse of blood in his limbs. There was just the rush of silence and a sense of falling, as though a hole had opened up in the universe and swallowed him. He was falling, and there was just emptiness above and below.

Ferrus Manus is dead. The words rang in his mind.

Somewhere in his memory, a grim face turned to look at him, unsmiling.

'And who are you?'

'I am Crius. First Vexilla of the Tenth Legion,' he had swallowed in a dry throat. *'I am your son.'*

'So you are,' Ferrus Manus had said.

'How?' he heard himself say.

Sigismund was watching him as he had before, with not a flicker of emotion in his eyes. 'He fell in the counter-strike on Isstvan.'

'When?'

'It's unclear,' said Boreas.

'*When?*' asked Crius, feeling his lips pull back from his teeth.

'It has been two hundred and fourteen days since we heard the news,' said Sigismund.

Crius processed the number. Half of his mind dealt with it as cold data, while the other half howled. Muscles tensed across his body. His armour creaked and the chains rattled.

All this time, they knew. They knew, and yet they said nothing until now.

He breathed out, fighting down the fire that crawled through him, feeling a measure of control returning. The Imperial Fists just watched him.

Ferrus Manus is dead. No. No, it was impossible.

They knew, and yet they said nothing.

Crius's thoughts tumbled through the widening void of his mind even as his mouth formed words. 'What of the rest of the counter-strike?'

'We do not know, not for certain.' Sigismund blinked and for the first time broke Crius's gaze. 'The Alpha Legion, Night Lords, Iron Warriors and Word Bearers went to Horus. Vulkan is missing. Corax has made himself known to us, and he reports that the Raven Guard are gone, save for the few thousand he brought with him.'

Crius gave a small nod. A few moments before, this new information would have shocked him. Now his numb mind simply absorbed it and processed it. A high-pitched buzz rang in his ears. He swallowed but found that his mouth was paper dry.

Ferrus Manus is dead…

There will be a way for him to return. He is the Gorgon, he is iron, he cannot die.

'My Legion?'

'We do not know. Some may have survived the massacre. Some may not have reached the Isstvan System. There may be many of them still out there.' Sigismund paused and moved a step closer. 'That is what Lord Dorn wishes of you – that you find any of your brothers that you can.'

Ferrus Manus is dead...

He failed us. He broke the bond of iron. He fell and left us to live on without him.

'And then?'

'Bring them back to Terra.'

'For a last stand.' Crius heard the hollowness in his own laughter. 'The few against the coming storm?'

'Yes,' said Sigismund, and Crius saw something in the Imperial Fists legionary's blue eyes – a flash of something dark and empty, like a shadow in a hole. 'Do you consent to this endeavour?'

Crius looked away. His eyes clicked as they studied the chains that held him, taking in every mark left by their forging. The air tasted of cold stone, weapon oil and armour plate.

Ferrus Manus is dead...

Crius looked back to Sigismund and nodded.

Sigismund drew his sword. Crius noticed then the chains that circled the templar's wrist, linking arm and weapon. Lightning crackled up the blade, and for a second he watched it dance in Sigismund's eyes. Then the sword cut down, and the chains holding Crius sheared with a ringing sigh.

Boreas keyed a control on his wrist, and Crius felt full connection to his armour tingle up his spine. He stood slowly, the movements of armour and body stiff. He looked down at the manacles on his wrist. Boreas came closer, a brass key in his hand, but Crius considered what he had glimpsed in Sigismund's eyes. He waved Boreas away, the severed links of chain clinking against his armour.

'No,' he said, and turned to Sigismund again. 'Leave them.'

'As you wish,' said Sigismund with a small nod. 'This ship is the *Oathbound* – she will carry you on your search. Boreas here will go with you.' He clenched his fist and brought it up to his chest. 'I hope we meet again, Crius of the Kadoran.'

Crius returned the salute and watched as Sigismund turned and walked from the chamber.

DATA SCROLLED ACROSS Crius's eyes as he watched the stars, the binaric runes blending with their pale light. Around him, the bridge crew moved and whispered, passing spools of parchment and data-slates, mind-interface cables trailing behind them. He did not sit upon the command throne – this was not his ship after all, nor was it truly his command. Instead, he stood before the bridge's main viewports, listening, watching, waiting, just as he had a dozen times before.

Here I stand, he thought, *waiting for the dead to speak from the night.*

His eyes clicked without him willing it, as though blinking.

Ferrus Manus is dead.

It had been months since he had heard those words, yet still they spun through his waking thoughts and dreams. Crius had remained awake since they had left the Solar System, standing here on the bridge of the *Oathbound* when she emerged from the warp, listening to the song of the ship when they passed through the realm beyond. He had tried to find calm in the Cant of Iron and the Calculations of Purpose, but every time he had reached out for peace it had slipped away from him. He had waited for the storm within him to end, for the cold process of logic to assert itself and leave him as he was before, with fury in his hand but iron in his heart. Instead, with every passing day, and then every passing month, he had felt the hollowness growing in his hearts.

We were not made for this, he thought. *What we needed to survive this sorrow was cut away in our forging.*

'The machine is strong, and logic can lay open any realm of understanding.'

The words of Ferrus Manus spoke to him from the shadows of a distant memory. *'But without the hands and minds of the living they are nothing. We live and bend iron to our will, but iron can break, machines fail and logic can become corrupted. Life is the only true machine. Cut too much away, and we lose ourselves. Remember that, Crius.'*

Crius's eyes clicked as they refocused, and the memory faded. At his back he heard the click and hum of Boreas's approach.

'Twelve jumps,' said Crius, without turning. 'Twelve times we have sat dead in the void while the astropaths sift the aether for any trace of my kin. Twelve cycles of silence.'

'We must succeed, no matter how long it takes. That is our oath.'

Crius nodded but did not reply. Boreas stepped closer. Crius could feel the warrior's eyes upon him, but did not turn away from his view of the stars.

'Terra must have every blade to defend it when Horus comes,' said Boreas.

'You are certain that he will?'

'Lord Dorn believes so.'

'Why?'

'How else could Horus hope to win this war?'

Crius shrugged and turned to look at Boreas. Dark eyes looked back: sharp, unyielding and utterly without emotion.

'You are so certain this is about winning?' asked Crius.

'What else could it be about?'

Crius looked back at the stars.

'Oblivion,' he said. The moment stretched in silence.

Another amplified voice rang across the bridge. 'Lord Crius.'

Crius turned to see the shipmaster of the *Oathbound*. Casterra was an old man, his eyes bright green in a face scarred by time and the ice-winds of Inwit. Though human, Casterra had served the Imperial Fists in war for nearly seventeen decades, and the Empire of the Inwit Cluster for a decade before that. Strong and steady, the old captain was like a pillar shaped to support great weight.

'Lord,' said Casterra with the slightest pause, 'the astropaths have something.'

'What was the essence of the sending?' asked Boreas. Casterra looked from Crius to Boreas and back.

'The image of a mountain,' said Casterra. 'A great crater descends from its pinnacle into its heart. The mountain's heart is dark, its fire long cold. The astropaths say that the dream of the mountain's heart presses on them still. They say it tastes of flint and lead.' The man paused. 'Secondary imagery is standard code metaphor for a system in the Arinath Cluster.'

Crius nodded his thanks and turned away. Boreas waited, watching.

'Ignarak,' said Crius at last. 'That is what the Medusan-born call it – the silence of mountains that once burned, and will burn again.'

'What does it mean?' said Boreas.

'It is a summons,' said Crius. 'A summons to a gathering of war.'

FOLDED IN THE light of a dying sun, the *Thetis* lay in the silence of the void. The *Oathbound* hung at a distance, the power of her reactor held in check for fight or flight. Crius watched the vast, black bulk of the other vessel as the Storm Eagle crossed the distance between the two ships.

The *Thetis* had been born in the skies of Mars. Black stone and unpolished iron skinned her bulk from engines to hammerhead prow. She was like a forge-city set to float among the stars, her bloated body filled with workshops, furnaces and storage facilities. The last time Crius had seen her, she had been the queen at the centre of a fleet of lesser craft, the lights of lifters and bulk transports darting around her docking bays like fireflies. Now great wounds marked her iron skin, and scorches darkened her hull. Her docking bays were lightless caves. The fortress of her spine was a tangled ruin of broken architecture. Blank holes of gun barrels, sensor arrays and viewports looked out upon the stars from beside ragged craters. Projected across the inside of Crius's machine eyes, she looked like a corpse floating in black water.

She is alone, thought Crius, the couplings of data and probability in his mind reaching uncertain conclusions. He cancelled the image but kept his eyes dark to the inside of the Storm Eagle. Petals of polished metal had closed over the lenses of his eyes, and only the glowing cascade of constant data broke the blackness of his world. Somewhere to his left, he heard the scrape of Boreas's armour as he shifted in his mag-harness. The growling purr of the engines ached through Crius's limbs and armour.

He preferred it this way, preferred the inside of his own thoughts. It reminded him of a time before he knew of his father's death, when the world was made of straight lines of logic and strength.

What happens to a Legion when its primarch dies? His thoughts spiralled on as the Storm Eagle slid through emptiness towards the *Thetis*. *What happens to his sons without his hand to guide them? What will become of us?*

'Crius.'

Boreas's voice broke the spiral of his thoughts, and he shook himself and opened his eyes. They had reached the *Thetis*, he realised.

The Storm Eagle's hull creaked as she settled, the engines and systems sighing as they cycled to sleep. Boreas was standing, looking down at Crius with that carved-stone expression that only ever broke to show anger. The light gleamed from the templar's armour, catching the eagle wings etched into the golden yellow plate. A cloak of black and red hung down Boreas's back, and the skull upon the pommel of his sheathed sword winked at Crius with eyes of jet.

'Are you ready for this, Crius?' he asked, and for a second Crius thought he saw a flicker of emotion in the warrior's dark eyes.

Pity? he wondered. *Is that all that remains for us?*

He nodded to Boreas, unclamped the mag-harness, and rose. The servos in his leg stuttered. Error-data and pain stabbed through his body. He cursed silently but did not let it show upon his face. The malfunctions in his augmetics had become worse since they had left the Solar System, as though the metal added to his flesh echoed the fractures in his soul.

Or rejects the weakness growing in me, he thought, as he checked the thunder hammer at his back and the bolt pistol locked to his thigh.

'I am ready,' said Crius at last, and they turned to face the ramp of the Storm Eagle as it lowered. For a second his eyes dimmed at the brightness of the light, then rebalanced. Their gunship sat at the centre of a floodlit circle in an otherwise gloomy cavern. He turned his head, taking in the echoing space that extended to darkness on either side. Assault craft covered the deck, silent and cold, their hulls marked by damage. Stormbirds, Thunderhawks and assault rams crowded together with craft of a dozen other configurations. He recognised the colours of Salamanders, Night Lords, Raven Guard, Imperial Army regiments and the Adeptus Mechanicum, all jumbled together like the store of a scavenger. The air was like the breath from an open furnace door.

Twelve figures waited for them. Crius's eyes flicked over them, noting the scratched and dented black battleplate and the markings of five different clans of the Iron Hands. Each of them wore armour that looked as though it had been repaired many times over, growing in bulk each time. Crius recognised none of these legionaries, but it had been almost a decade since he had been sent to Terra, and the hundred thousand faces of a Legion could change much in that time.

'I am Crius,' he said, and heard his voice echo. 'One-time chief of the Kadoran, and Solar Emissary of Ferrus Manus.' He paused, turning to indicate Boreas. 'Beside me stands Boreas, Templar of the Seventh Legion. I come with tidings and orders from Rogal Dorn, Praetorian of Terra.'

The Iron Hands did not move or respond. Crius frowned.

'To whom do I speak, brothers?'

'I am Athanatos,' said a static-laden voice. The speaker's face was a black iron skull, with a pierced grill for a mouth. Blue light burned cold in the skull's eye sockets. Cables punctured Athanatos's scalp, trailing back into the gorget of his armour. The plate itself was a mixture of patterns and designs fused together around its wearer. Crius registered the details of the hunched shoulders, weapon-tipped arms and secondary pistons visible through gaps in the arm and leg plating. Droplets of moisture clung to the dented plates, as though they had been scattered with rain. 'I know your name, Crius of the Kadoran,' added Athanatos. 'I stood under your command on Yerronex. Few still thought you among the living.'

Crius sorted through legionary records and images in his memory, until he found the face of a line sergeant with grey-steel eyes. If it had not been for the name, he might never have thought it to be the same warrior.

'Of what clan-companies are you?' asked Crius.

'Of what we were, nothing remains.' Athanatos paused, static scratching at the edge of the words. 'Brother.'

Crius swept his gaze over the circle of Iron Hands. 'These who stand beside you?' He noticed their stillness again. Like Athanatos, their armour was sheened with moisture. *Why is the air so hot?* he wondered.

'The few that came from the fields of slaughter,' said Athanatos. 'We are of the *Thetis* now.'

'You were on Isstvan Five?'

The pause lasted for several long heartbeats.

'Yes, Crius of the Kadoran. We were there,' said Athanatos, his speaker grill popping and crackling. 'And on Gagia, and Sacrissan, and Agromis.'

'These places are not known to me,' said Crius.

'They are places of battle, places of vengeance and death to the betrayers,' said another of the Iron Hands, standing near Athanatos.

Crius looked at him. His face was bare, without the mark of augmetics, but the iron was in his eyes. Interface sockets dotted his layered armour, and cables hung from the base of his skull like a cloak of snakes. His lips pursed and a frown etched its lines between the service studs on his skull.

'I am Phidias,' he said, as if in answer to the question Crius was about to ask. 'I am commander and keeper of the *Thetis*.' Crius thought he caught a flicker within Phidias's stare, perhaps a brief flare of emotion. 'It is good to see another of our kind amongst the living.'

'How many of your Legion are with you?' demanded Boreas. Athanatos turned his head slowly to look at the Imperial Fists legionary.

'Our strength stands before you, son of Dorn.'

So few... Crius felt the leaden weight in his stomach swell. When he had last seen the *Thetis*, she had carried three thousand warriors under arms. An image of corpses scattered under fire-soaked skies filled his mind before he could control it. *How many are lost and dead at our father's side?*

'Rogal Dorn asks that you return to Terra,' said Crius. 'To stand there with our brother Legions.'

'Asks?' said Athanatos.

'Or demands?' added Phidias.

'The strength of all Legions must be gathered to defend Terra,' said Boreas, taking a step forwards. Crius could see the lines of the templar's face harden. 'You must return with us, as Lord Crius says.'

'Lord Crius...' Athanatos purred the words, as he nodded to the severed chains still hanging from Crius's wrists. 'What is he lord of?'

Boreas was moving to reply, but Athanatos spoke again.

'Your strength failed long ago, Crius of the Kadoran. We will not return with you. We will not turn away from what lies before us.'

'What of the signal you sent into the void?' demanded Boreas. 'The gathering of war?'

'We are here,' said Phidias.

'And the other survivors, the rest of the Legion?'

'We have not seen any others of the Legion since the massacre,' said Athanatos.

'Not until now,' Phidias muttered.

Details clicked into place in Crius's mind, completing patterns and closing off possibilities. He let out a long breath as the realisation formed. He felt a sudden need to shiver despite the heat crawling in the air.

'The signal is not a summons,' he said. Boreas turned to look at him. 'It is bait.'

'We draw our enemies to us,' nodded Phidias.

'There are hunters amongst the stars,' said Athanatos. 'They seek us now as they have ever since we escaped Isstvan. They will have heard our summons. They know enough of us to understand its meaning. They will come, and we will face them.'

'With a handful?' asked Boreas.

'With every weapon we have,' replied Athanatos.

'If you had a hundred times the numbers...' said Crius, then shook his head. 'You will perish here, brothers.'

'Perish...' Athanatos echoed, rolling the word through the hot air.

'How can you hope to do anything other than die here?'

Athanatos laughed then, a crackling growl of noise that clattered in the silence like grinding gears.

'This is no longer a war of hope, brother – this is a war of vengeance and extermination.' He shook his head. 'The primarch is gone, the Great Crusade is done and soon the Imperium will follow. All that matters is that those who brought us to this end will share our graves.'

Boreas snarled. Crius heard the blade begin to scrape from the templar's scabbard. He turned and fastened his hand on the grip of the half-drawn sword and met the Imperial Fists legionary's burning eyes. Around them, he could hear the high-pitched whine of charged focusing rings and the clunk of firing catches as volkite and bolt weapons armed.

'No,' said Crius. 'Your death or theirs will serve no purpose here.'

Boreas stared back, his face a blank setting for the rage in his eyes. Crius felt the servos in his hands whine as they strained to hold the sword still. Slowly, Crius released his grip and turned back to Athanatos.

'Forgive our kinsman of the Seventh. Your words...' Crius paused, his tongue still behind his open teeth. His eyes clicked and refocused. 'Your words surprised him.'

'You are wrong when you say that death serves no purpose,' said Athanatos. 'Death is all there is now.'

What has become of these brothers? wondered Crius as Athanatos turned away, armour creaking and hissing. Phidias and the rest of the Iron Hands turned to follow.

'We will remain with you,' Crius called out. Boreas caught his eye but said nothing. 'For now.'

'You speak as though there were any other choice,' said Athanatos as he walked away.

'Madness,' breathed Boreas.

Crius did not reply. He and Boreas stood on the bridge of the *Thetis*, on the peninsular of shaped granite that lay beneath her command throne and above the servitor-filled canyons of the control systems. The whole chamber was five hundred metres long and half as wide. Pillars reached up to a vaulted ceiling a hundred metres above the deck. Black iron braziers hung from chains, adding their coal-glow to the cold green and blue of hololith-screens.

Silent crew sat at their consoles, heads bowed, cables snaking from the folds in their charcoal robes to link to the banks of machinery. Tech-priests in white and red robes moved between the machines like ghosts.

Raw heat filled the air even here, which smelt of worn metal and electrical charge. To Crius, it felt both familiar and unsettling, like a friend's face subtly scarred.

Phidias sat in the command throne above and behind them. A host of cables swarmed over him, linking him to the ship's systems. Athanatos and the other Iron Hands had vanished after they had left the hangar deck – they had not appeared again.

Crius turned his eyes back to the display showing the empty void around the *Thetis*. The display was a polyhedron of blue light revolving above a dais of black crystal. Data runes swam through the holo-projection, tracking the position of void debris with the *Thetis* at its centre. The *Oathbound* was out of sight in the shadow of a planetoid which rolled slowly through the near reaches of space. Phidias had told Boreas to order his ship away, and that she was to remain silent, no matter what occurred. No threat had needed to be spoken for all to understand that if the *Oathbound* did not obey then she would be destroyed. Boreas had given the order.

Crius turned slowly to look at the templar. A charge of restrained control and focused rage surrounded Boreas, like hard and soft steel forged together to make a blade.

'What strength they have will end here, wasted for spite,' said Boreas.

'They do not intend to die here,' Crius said after a long moment of silence. 'That is not our way.'

'They are not like you. They are like no Iron Hands I have ever met.'

Yes, thought Crius. *They are like another Legion, or a shadow cast by the past...*

They had not been allowed to leave the bridge, and on their journey from the hangar decks he had seen no sign of any other Iron Hands – just servitors, and serfs hooded in tattered grey. He took a deep breath, and wondered again why it was so hot.

'A ship with a carcass-house of assault craft, but only a "handful" of warriors...' said Boreas, letting the words hang. 'And now Athanatos is nowhere to be seen.' He looked at Crius, his face grim. 'Secrets,' he muttered softly, as though following the thread of his suspicion.

'No, *reasons,*' said Crius. Boreas held his gaze. 'They are still my brothers. Even if they have changed. We are still kin. We are still...'

...the sons of a dead father. The thought caught in his mind and he felt the tide of emptiness rise inside him again.

'*Look.*' The word echoed from vox speakers across the bridge. Crius's mind snapped clear as he looked up at the command throne. Phidias's voice rumbled through the air again. '*They come.*'

Crius turned his eyes back to the hololith display. At the edge of the projection, red marker runes of enemy ships blinked into existence. Names began to form beside the spreading clutch of ships.

'Sons of Horus,' Boreas breathed. 'They do not even hide their allegiance.'

'They want us to know who they are,' said Phidias. 'They want us to know it is them when they destroy us. In *that,* they have not changed.'

Crius read the data spilling from the enemy vessels. He recognised them all. Three of the ships were spear-hulled, skinned in sea-green adamantium and bronze. They had been born in the forges of Armatura and gifted to Horus by Guilliman – the Lord of the Ultramarines had named his gifts, *Spear Strike, Wolf of Cthonia* and *Dawnstar,* and there were few to match them for speed and ferocity.

The fourth ship, larger and blunter than the rest, had a history that stretched back to the first wars beyond the light of Terra's sun.

The Emperor had christened her the *Death's Child*, and she still bore that name in treachery.

'Two thousand legionaries,' muttered Crius, calculating the likely numbers. 'If we are fortunate then they will be under strength.'

'They are firing!' shouted Boreas.

Crius saw a spread of markers break away from the four ships. The torpedo clusters sped towards them.

'Twelve seconds to impact,' called a grey-robed crewman.

'Why do you not return fire?' called Crius. Phidias said nothing. The clatter of machines swelled through the bridge, the crew bent over a thousand tasks, but the *Thetis*'s guns remained silent. 'You must–'

The bridge pitched with the first detonations. Crius staggered and caught his balance. Alarm after alarm began to sound. Red fire leapt up. The reek of charring meat filled the air; crewmen were burning at their stations, their screams lost in the din. White gas vented into the bridge space.

Phidias did not move in his throne. Crius wondered if he was even aware of what was happening in front of him, or if his interfaced mind now saw only the darkness beyond the hull.

Another blow ran through the ship. The deck pitched and for a second the gravity failed. Mortal bodies flew into the air. Cables ripped free of flesh. Blood sprayed out, the droplets breaking into hanging globules.

Crius rose from the deck with the rest of them, tumbling end over end. Then the gravity cut back in and he crashed back down, rolling and coming up in a crouch. Boreas was next to him, already on his feet.

Around them, mayhem reigned in the smoke and flame.

'We have to find Athanatos,' shouted Crius. 'If Phidias will not listen, he must. They have to run, before they are overwhelmed.'

Boreas glanced at the chaos around them and nodded. As one they pulled themselves from the deck and made for the door. Behind them, the alarms screamed on.

✠ ✠ ✠

IN THE THETIS'S command throne, Phidias felt his ship shudder with anger. The *Thetis* was bleeding across her hull. Gas, plasma and machine fluid sprayed from fresh holes in her scarred skin. He felt each wave of damage as a stab of pain through what remained of his flesh. It was a small price to pay. An irrelevance.

The hololithic projection hanging in front of him swam with the red markers of enemy craft, closing fast.

'Turn to face them,' he said. 'Power to the engines.' A second later he felt the ship begin to obey. The crew and adepts on the bridge cancelled new warning alarms as they triggered. They knew better than to question the order.

This will be a great father of firestorms, he thought. *Perhaps this will be our last.* He shivered in his armour. *No, we are not done with this war yet. While we still have strength, we will never be done.*

'Enemy targets, thirty seconds from battery weapons range,' called out a battered signal officer. Phidias did not even nod; he knew already and could see the range to the three Sons of Horus ships draining down to nothing.

'Begin the rites,' said Phidias, over the noise of the bridge. 'Waken them.'

CRIUS HAD STOPPED at the sight of the doors, his flesh prickling, his breath stopped in his throat. Behind him Boreas halted, his eyes going up to trace the doors' height into the darkness above. Condensation covered the pitted adamantium. The air was very hot, as though they stood beside a fire. A steaming pool had gathered upon the threshold, its surface a black mirror disturbed only by the tremors of the void battle that wracked the ship. Crius had the overwhelming feeling that this place had been *waiting* for him to find it.

They had found it by accident. Running through the empty corridors of the *Thetis*, they had felt the tremors of battle, and seen the lighting dim and flicker, but found no sign of Athanatos. Then the doors had just been there, looming above them.

'A weapons cache,' said Boreas.

Crius shook his head but said nothing as he moved forwards. The pool on the threshold rippled around his boots. The chamber beyond *had* been a weapons cache once, he remembered. 'But a weapons cache does not sweat condensation,' he said. 'Nor does it flood an entire ship with heat.' Slowly he raised his metal hand, reached out, then paused just before he touched the door's surface.

'We should keep searching,' said Boreas.

Crius shook his head. Logic whirred in his mind, faster and more clearly than at any time since he had left Terra. Conclusions danced just beyond his reach, waiting for data to close off possibilities.

And at the core of all his thoughts was the certainty that all the answers lay on the other side of the doors before him...

He edged forwards. Boreas reached to pull him back.

Crius pressed his hand to the moisture-beaded metal. He felt the connection as a hot tingle that spread through his nerves. Traces of circuitry spread across the doors in luminous lines. Something out of sight released with a clang.

Crius pulled back.

A crack appeared in the surface of the doors and slowly widened. Beyond, the darkness peered back at them.

'ENEMY ARE FIRING,' called the signal officer. Warning sirens blared. Phidias waited, counting slices of time, watching the enemy ships in the projection. They were not coming straight at the *Thetis*, of course; the Sons of Horus knew the business of war too well for that. Two of the four ships – the *Spear Strike* and *Wolf of Cthonia* – were accelerating head on, while the *Dawnstar* and *Death's Child* had looped wide to close the *Thetis* in a pincer of firepower.

They meant to lace the *Thetis* with torpedoes and then close to take the ship in a boarding action. Phidias was sure of it. The Sons of Horus were still wolves at heart, for all that time and treachery had changed them. They would behave as wolves now, crippling and pinning their prey as a pack before delivering the killing stroke.

Macro-shells hit the *Thetis*'s void shields – first one, then another, then a deluge. Phidias watched the shields peel back; vast rainbow smears of energy glittering at the edge of his awareness. A hundred metre-wide globe of plasma struck the *Thetis*'s prow, and the ship trembled as a glowing scab of armour tumbled away. Phidias kept his gaze fixed upon the heart of the holo-projection, on the markers of the enemy ships. The whole ship shook as she plunged on into the wall of enemy fire.

He felt the wakening protocols begin to leech power from the auxiliary systems. The reactors howled feed-shortage warnings. Even if there had still been enough crew to man the guns, there would not have been enough power to light them.

'Prepare for launch,' said Phidias.

THE DOORS HISSED shut behind them. Crius stood in the dark, his eyes clicking and whirring as they searched for any scraps of light. Cold began to bite into the exposed skin of his face.

Temperature below life support threshold, clicked into his mind. *No immediate threat.*

A scrape of steel cut the silence as Boreas drew his sword.

Crius's eyes cycled to thermal vision. Cold – blue and black. Completely and utterly *cold.*

Data scrolled across his lenses. He ignored it, trying to make out any recognisable shapes in the smudges of blue in the black.

'Light projection,' he whispered, and his eyes lit up like stark lamps. Machines filled the space before him, marching away into the darkness, filling the space that had once swallowed Storm-birds and tank battalions. Stacks of cylinders and slab-like boxes lay amongst a tangle of pipework, and a low dais of polished iron stood in the clear space before the doors.

A sceptre of milled and polished metal floated a finger width above the dais's surface. The dais and sceptre device were the only things that seemed free of the frost that rimed the rest of the chamber.

'Artificial temperature control,' he muttered, panning the beams of his eyes though the dark. 'This chamber has been adapted, this machinery installed. This is the cause of the high temperatures within the vessel – the heat taken from here has to go somewhere.'

'Secrets,' growled Boreas, white mist hissing between clenched teeth.

Crius breathed in, paying attention for the first time to the taste of the still air: traces of machine oil and counter-septic filled his olfactory sensors. The focusing rings of his eyes clicked involuntarily as his logic processes ran to uncertain ends. He stepped forwards, his machine joints and armour creaking in the cold. Carefully, he moved past the dais.

The closest machinery loomed above him, glittering in a skin of ice. It stood slightly apart from the others, like a general at the head of an army. Thick clots of frozen fluids covered the points where tubes and pipes linked to the machine's top and sides. Crius raised his hand in front of him, splayed his metal fingers and touched the surface. Metal clinked on metal. Tactile sensors itched as they spoke to his cold mind: adamantium structure, with traces of silver and other unknown elements. A low pulse ached through his fingers. He moved his hand, tracing his fingers across the metal surface, until they met frost-covered crystal.

He halted, then flinched back.

He could see something through the tiny window his fingers had cleared in the ice.

'What is this?' Boreas's voice seemed to rise and vanish into the dark.

Computations clicked through Crius's mind, following paths of inference and possibility, forming conclusions.

'This is a tomb,' said Crius, his voice a dry whisper. Slowly he raised his hand again and scraped the frost from the glass. His eyes poured light into the space beyond.

An iron skull looked back at him.

Crius's mind stopped dead. The data was still scrolling across his eyes but he was no longer paying even the slightest attention to it. A ringing filled his ears.

The frozen form of Athanatos looked back at him from its cocoon of ice.

'How can you hope to do anything other than die here?' He heard his own question resonate in his mind, and Athanatos's reply from the pit of his memory.

'This is no longer a war of hope brother – this is a war of vengeance and obliteration.'

And with the memory came the inescapable inference of the accumulated data.

Cybernetic resurrection, breathed the logic in his mind. Athanatos is dead. They are all dead. They came from this sleep to greet us when we arrived and then returned to its embrace. They have turned the Keys of Hel.

'No.' He heard the word come weakly from his own lips. 'No, it is forbidden. Our father forbade us to open those gates.'

Ferrus Manus is dead.

Crius could not move. His thoughts were a spinning ruin, his eyes locked upon the caskets marching into the distance under their shrouds of frost. There were hundreds of them.

The deck shook beneath his feet. A spill of cracked ice fell from the ceiling, far above. The Thetis was within the battle sphere.

Death is all there is now, Crius.

The deck shook again. Blue lights were lit along the length of the chamber, and a dull crack echoed as the front of the casket split open. Gas vented from grilles and pipework. Crius stared, his eyes still blazing. Boreas's sword ignited.

Another crack rang out, and Athanatos stepped free. The deck rang under his tread, pistons surging in place of muscle. His weapons shed their casings of ice as they armed. He stood for a second, his joints breathing steam, his servos clicking.

Then he looked at Crius. His eyepieces glowed blue.

'You see now, Crius,' rasped Athanatos in a voice like the shattering of frozen iron. His deactivated power fist reached out and plucked the sceptre from the dais. Crius could see Medusan runes running around it in rings, each one now glowing with faint light. He could almost taste the exotic energies bound within its core. 'Now, you understand.'

PHIDIAS COULD FEEL his flesh quivering in sympathy with the ship as his interface links fed him the *Thetis*'s pain. There was blood in his mouth and more blood clotting on the inside of his armour.

'Weakness,' he growled to himself and forced his mind to focus.

The *Spear Strike* and *Wolf of Cthonia* had shot past the *Thetis* and were turning hard, firing as they came around. Turbo-lasers began to score her back, cutting deep and burning into her guts. The *Dawn-star* and *Death's Child* were closing, their prow and dorsal weaponry hammering the *Thetis*'s flanks. Phidias thought he could feel his own flesh cooking around his implant sockets.

Everything was as it should be, but everything was also terribly wrong.

The assault craft were ready, the boarding torpedoes poised to enter their launch tubes, but the wakened dead had yet to fill them. They should already be swarming into the lower decks of the XVI Legion ships. But they had delayed too long, or the wakening processes had failed. Athanatos should have called the rest from their sleep by now.

Phidias tried to signal him, but the only answer was the crackle of static. They needed to launch; they needed to strike at the ships attacking them *now*. They had no guns – all the power had been drained from them to keep the dead asleep and to push the *Thetis* into the battle.

Distortion washed across his vision. He fought down a sticky wave of mental fog. They needed time. If they could just survive a little longer…

'Bring us above them,' he ordered.

Reports began to cluster into Phidias's awareness as the engines strained. If they could loop above the enemy's plane of attack, then they could plunge back into the storm of fire when the wakening had completed. They could still have this moment of vengeance. His mind ran with recalculations. They could still do it. They could–

A synchronised spread of fire from the *Dawnstar* and *Death's Child* hit the *Thetis* in her spine. The shock wave rippled through the superstructure. Domes across the outer hull shattered. Hundred metre-tall spires tumbled away into the vacuum like splinters from a shattered spear.

Phidias dug his fingers into the arms of the throne, refusing to fall. He could taste burning. Something deep within his body had burst and was cooking in the heat of his machine links. His eyes focused on the holo-projection of the battle sphere, on the pulsing green marker of the *Oathbound* hiding in the shadow of the planetoid, seemingly forgotten by all.

They needed time, no matter what the cost, or their deaths would serve nothing.

With a grunt of effort, he opened a long range vox-link.

'Help us,' he croaked through bloody lips.

For a second nothing changed. Then the *Oathbound* began to move. Reactor readings flared to full life, pushing it out into the edge of the battle sphere. It accelerated, engines burning like captured suns.

Phidias saw all of this, and yet he knew that it would not be enough. The *Oathbound*'s guns were still out of range. Even as he thought it, the *Spear Strike* came around, momentum making her skid across the void as her guns fixed upon the *Thetis*.

Lances burned into the rear hull. Molten metal wept from the wounds, and the armour plating began to glow as the fire ate deeper and deeper.

'WHAT HAVE YOU done?' Crius's voice rang clear in the icy air, even over the thunder of the battle beyond.

Athanatos did not answer but turned to look at the rows of ice-covered caskets. Then Crius felt it – a shiver in the air, like a breath edged with static.

He opened his mouth to speak again, but Athanatos spoke first, the bulk of his body clattering with pistons and gears.

'The logic fails after a while. Have you noticed that? The pure flow of data and reason – after a while it just runs out. You keep trying to understand, to bargain with the reality of what has happened, but there is no understanding to be had, no bargain to be made.'

'You have–'

'The way of iron, the logic of the machine – it was meant to make us strong, to raise us above flesh.' Athanatos paused, and when his voice came again there was rage in the dead, electric drone. 'But it was a lie. Iron can shatter, logic can be flawed and ideals can fail.'

'What are you?' Boreas demanded, and Crius glanced at the templar. He had not moved, but there was a bound fury in his stillness. Slowly, Athanatos looked at him.

'I am the dead of Isstvan. A Word Bearers legionary took half my skull with a claw. I fell, like so many of us. Phidias took me from the battlefield – me and as many more as he could manage. Our flesh had failed, and our gene-seed rotted in our corpses, but enough of me remained.' Athanatos raised the sceptre and watched the data runes run across its surface. 'He knew the secrets of the Aegisine Protocols and the Scarcosan Formulae, the devices and processes from Old Night that our father placed out of our reach. Phidias remade me and gave me a second life, a life of ice and iron. For a long while I could not remember who I had been, but eventually some of the past returned. That is rare. Most of those wakened remember little.' Athanatos looked towards the caskets lining the chamber. 'But all remember what it is to hate.'

'The primarch forbade what you are,' growled Crius. 'Ferrus Manus–'

'Fell,' said Athanatos softly. 'I saw it, brother. I watched our father die.'

Crius felt cold spill through him. His mind was no longer functioning properly. He could not reason – he could only feel the ice forming splinters in his flesh and augmetics.

Ferrus Manus fell.

He failed.

Blackness rolled through his thoughts, spreading like a thunderhead, boiling with anger.

He left us. What remains of his authority, now?

Athanatos was looking at him, nodding. His eyes were blue suns in his iron skull.

'Yes,' Athanatos said. 'You see it now. That is what our father left to us, then. Not logic, not reason, but hatred. That is the lesson of his death. This will be the last war, fought for vengeance rather than reason. There is nothing else. No orders or oaths mean anything any more. You know this is true, Crius. You cannot deny it.'

'*I call it betrayal!*' roared Boreas. Crius saw a blur of lightning and polished metal as the templar's sword whirled. The blade struck Athanatos's hand, bit deep, and scattered blood and oil. The sceptre fell to the deck. Boreas cut again, his blade spinning low to slice into the Iron Hands legionary's leg.

Athanatos fell, and Boreas raised the blade above his head for a killing blow. Crius moved before he could think, his hands locking around Boreas's forearms. The Imperial Fists templar did not even pause but turned, whip-fast. The twist of force lifted Crius from his feet, and he was spinning through the air, crashing to the ground, rolling, coming up to meet an armoured boot descending towards his chest.

'Heretic,' spat Boreas. Crius heard the word, felt it cut even as Boreas's boot crashed into his breastplate. The shock rippled through him, but out of the corner of his eye he saw Athanatos rise to his feet, reaching for the sceptre.

Boreas was turning, his sword dragging lightning in his wake.

'No!' screamed Crius, and launched himself up. His shoulder stuck Boreas, and they fell together. Crius felt the field of Boreas's blade char the lacquer from his armour. They hit the deck with a dull crack. Boreas was already twisting beneath him, still holding on to his sword.

The deck was shaking. The whole room was shaking.

Boreas hammered his free hand up into Crius's face, and the metal socket around his left eye crumpled. Crius's sight crazed. Boreas struggled free, then rolled and rose up, the edge of his sword alight.

I fall here, thought Crius. *Like our father, I fall under the blade of a lost friend.* He looked into Boreas's cold, merciless eyes and felt relief flood his flesh. In his mind, the broken cogs of logic were still.

Boreas's sword crackled with an executioner's hunger. It rose high above Crius, shining like a sliver of a storm, and stabbed down.

Athanatos came out of the fog with a scream of pistons, striking Boreas across the left shoulder. The templar spun with the impact.

Crius felt cold spread through him, as though the chamber's melting ice was reaching into his body. Time seemed to slow to a trickle, to a fading pulse. Crius watched as Athanatos stepped in for a second blow, and realised that – dead or not – his Legion-brother would not survive this.

Athanatos was fast as only a Space Marine could be, but Boreas was faster.

The Imperial Fists legionary turned his stagger into a cut, and the edge of his blade sawed through the cables and pistons under his opponent's arm. Crius saw liquid glitter black in the blue light. Athanatos began to turn, but Boreas was already pulling his sword back for a kill stroke.

Crius rose to his feet. Pain dragged at his limbs. Blood cascaded from him. Cold was spreading through his chest. He advanced one step, his hand pulling the hammer from his back.

Boreas lunged. The tip of the sword met the already weakened armour under Athanatos's arm.

Crius felt his hammer activate in his hand. Darkness clouded his vision.

Boreas pulled his blade out through the front of Athanatos's chest. Crius roared.

Boreas turned, and their eyes met.

Crius's hammer blow shattered Boreas's plastron and lifted him from his feet. The templar hit the deck and did not rise.

Swaying with a hiss of complaining servos, Crius looked at Athanatos. The other Iron Hands legionary lay on the deck, his torso split open to show the metal components clicking amidst the ice-burned meat of his chest. Blood and oil formed a dark mirror sheet around him. Crius heard his own eyes whirring as they tried to focus. The deck trembled, and suddenly the numbing cold in his chest was all around him. He looked down at the dark fluid covering his torso and legs, pulsing from a wide wound in his ribs.

The deck came up to meet him as he fell to his knees. He met Athanatos's dying gaze. There was no sorrow or pity in those eyes.

'The dead must walk,' croaked Athanatos. 'For vengeance. We remember. The dead remember...'

His voice trailed off, static bubbling in his breath. His eyes dimmed, a final flicker of defiance in their depths, and then they were empty.

Crius turned his head slowly. His vision blurred into pixelated blocks. He could feel the void within him, the void that had been there since he had heard that his father was dead. It opened wide to greet him.

Pain and numbness ground together with each slow movement. The sceptre lay on the deck where it had fallen from Athanatos's hand, blood smearing the glowing runes. Crius reached for the device, grasped it and lifted it from the floor. It felt like clutching a lightning bolt.

Ferrus Manus is dead.

His eyes would not focus any more, but his fingers found the runes cut into the sceptre's length.

And so are we all.

He twisted each ring.

We are wraiths that remain in a dying land.

His fingers found the trigger stud.

And all that is left to us is vengeance.

Behind him, another casket opened with a crack of shattered ice; then another, and another. Figure after shambling figure stepped onto the deck. Crius felt the sceptre pulse, before it slipped from his fingers. The darkness reached up to meet him.

It felt warm and tasted of iron, like metal taken from a fire, like flesh and blood.

The last thing he saw, before night closed over him, were his dead kin marching to war, ice falling from their tread.

The Thetis rolled, her engines clawing the void for control. Close behind her, the enemy vessels closed in upon their prey. The dark mouths of launch bays opened across their hulls, but while their sisters closed into boarding range, the *Dawnstar* and *Death's Child* kept firing. Macro-shells cracked the *Thetis*'s outer hull, and plasma widened the wounds, preparing the way for the warriors waiting in the Dreadclaw pods and assault craft. They were close now, the whole engagement crammed into a battle sphere no more than a thousand kilometres in diameter. To the Sons of Horus, the *Thetis*'s death seemed inevitable, but even as they gave the order to board the wounded ship, the situation changed.

The *Oathbound* plunged in like a thrown dagger. A sheet of light reached from the Imperial Fists ship and struck the *Dawnstar*. Void shields collapsed, popping like oily water bubbles. The *Oathbound* fired again, accelerating hard. Plasma relays within the enemy vessel's hull burst, flooding compartments with sun-hot energy. In her engine spaces, thousands screamed as their skin burned in the heat.

The *Dawnstar* shook. Smearing fire across the dark, she turned to bring her guns to bear. Half drained of power, the *Oathbound* had one weapon still to fire.

High in the tower of her bridge, Shipmaster Casterra nodded to a servitor cradled in a knot of cables.

'Launch torpedoes.'

The missiles slid into the void, their internal thrusters igniting as they met the vacuum, powering them ahead of the *Oathbound*. Each was the size of a hab-spire, its warhead an artefact gifted to Rogal Dorn by the Adeptus Mechanicum priesthood of Mars.

A wall of interceptor rounds rose from the stricken *Dawnstar*. Torpedo after torpedo exploded before they could find their target.

Then one slipped through and struck the *Dawnstar* high on her flank, driving deep into the warship's guts.

The ship continued to turn, surrounded by a haze of debris and the flicker of failing void shields. Then the torpedo's vortex warhead detonated in a spiral of neon light and roaring darkness. The *Dawnstar* practically vanished, her hull fragmenting as unnatural forces pulled her apart from within. In the space where she had been, a glowing wound remained, howling with impossible sound before collapsing to emptiness.

The remaining XVI Legion ships faltered. The *Spear Strike* broke from her interception course with the *Thetis* and turned towards the *Oathbound*. The others cut their speed as they diverted power to shields and weapons.

The respite was enough. The *Thetis* pushed beyond her attackers, curving above them in a burning loop, and plunged back into the inferno-stained void between her enemies.

FROM HIS THRONE, Phidias watched the enemy ships rise to meet them. The *Wolf of Cthonia* and the *Death's Child* spun as they tried to bring their weapons to bear. The *Thetis* plunged on. Shards of armour the size of Battle Titans ripped from her flanks, liquid fire and burning gas billowing in her wake. The enemy spun and fired as they came about, peppering the *Thetis* with explosions.

On the edge of the engagement, the *Oathbound* turned as the *Spear Strike* closed. The Imperial Fists ship came around, lining up with her enemy. Both ships fired, their prows blistering with fire as their shields burst. Then they hurtled past each other, raking with rolling volleys. The *Spear Strike*'s belly was torn open by macro-cannon shells, ripping away gantries and sensor dishes in a ripple of detonations. The *Oathbound* took the return fire across her unshielded hull – a blaze of plasma found the yawning barrel of a battery cannon, detonating a shell in the breech, and suddenly explosions were ripping down the ship's entire flank.

She began to spiral, her engines pushing her on even as deck fires ate her from within.

On the *Thetis*'s bridge, Phidias listened to the *Oathbound*'s last signals in silence. Around him the servitors and crew bent to their tasks, murmuring in impassive binary and Medusan cant. Deep within the folds of his thoughts, he watched the data from his ship shining clear and bright. Damage indicators were a squall of deep red. Engine output markers flashed insistently.

He knew what it all meant. He could almost feel it in his body. They were on the verge of death, inside and out. It did not matter now.

At the edge of his awareness, the voices of the dead rose – some in monotonous flesh-voices, some in mumbled machine code. The dead marched to war, and that was all that now mattered. Hundreds of them poured from the icy heart of the *Thetis* to fill the ramshackle assault craft and boarding torpedoes.

Phidias waited, the screams of his ship and the whispers of his brothers washing over him.

The *Thetis* cut between the *Wolf of Cthonia* and the *Death's Child*. Fresh volleys of energy sliced out from both ships. The *Thetis* shook, and binaric screams filled the air, thick with the reek of burning metal.

In the cable-tangle of his throne, Phidias felt the ship's systems pulse with rage. He let the feeling rise in him, shutting out all his other sensations. The enemy vessels were so close that if they fired now they would hit each other.

'Launch,' he said, and his ship answered.

The *Thetis*'s engines cut out. Retro thrusters fired, fighting against the ship's momentum. Void locks opened along her flanks and gut, scattering craft into space on breaths of launch flame. They swarmed across the gap and found the hulls of their foes. Magma blasts boiled through bulkheads, graviton charges cracked armour, and the assault craft clustered around the breaches like flies on a bloody wound.

The first of the dead Iron Hands met the Sons of Horus on the gun decks of the *Wolf of Cthonia*. The corpses of gun crew littered the decks beneath the magazines, choked and crushed by explosive decompression. Oily flame-light shivered in the remaining pockets of atmosphere. The Iron Hands advanced, their weapons spitting death. The deck quivered beneath their slow tread.

Blast-doors down the deck opened with a rush of smoke-filled air. The Sons of Horus came through in tight wedges, heavy infantry shields held in a solid wall. They fired as they charged – bolt-rounds cut the air, slammed into armour and detonated. The first Iron Hands legionary fell, his re-forged body torn apart by multiple explosions. Then his brothers answered in kind. Volkite and plasma beams lit the darkness with neon light. Armoured figures vanished in washes of fire and false sunlight. Shields slammed into armour, sparks flew as chain-teeth scraped across ceramite. Iron Hands fell to blades, to hammers, to point blank blasts of energy and explosives. The dead died again in silence, the sounds of their ending stolen by the airless void.

And still the dead poured from the *Thetis*.

By the time the Iron Hands had taken the gunnery decks, a dozen other beachheads had formed across the *Wolf of Cthonia*. The Sons of Horus began to dwindle, falling back into close-pressed circles of defiance.

In the void, both the *Death's Child* and the *Wolf of Cthonia* continued to slide through the vacuum on their original trajectories. Within the *Death's Child*, the Iron Hands struck the ship's command citadel, dozens of them breaking into the towers and bastions surrounding the domed bridge. The Sons of Horus met the Iron Hands advance with walls of suppressing fire and ground it to a halt before signalling their counter-attack. Terminators waded through spent shell casings and heaped bodies, muzzle flare and the light of power fields reflected from their sea-green armour. For a while it seemed certain that the *Death's Child* would throw the dead back into the void.

Chance ended that hope.

Crawling with Iron Hands boarders and slewing in the void as she turned back towards the *Thetis*, the *Wolf of Cthonia* fired her torpedoes. Perhaps it was a mistake – perhaps panic, or a malfunction in a system on a ship that was being ripped apart from within. Launched blindly, the torpedoes streaked between the spinning vessels. One clipped the upper hull of the *Thetis* and spilled flame across her ruined towers. The rest hit the *Death's Child* just fore of her engines and detonated next to a primary plasma trunking.

The explosion almost ripped her in two. She began to spiral, her engines pushing her on even as propagating explosions ate her insides. The Iron Hands pressed on as the ship they had conquered broke apart.

On the *Wolf of Cthonia*, the Iron Hands finally reached the reactor decks and quenched the warship's burning heart. The *Wolf of Cthonia* became dark and silent. Faced with the death of her sisters, the *Spear Strike* ran for the system's edge and dived into the warp. Deprived of the total annihilation of her enemies, the *Thetis* settled to stillness beside the dying vessels like a predator settling to feed upon its kills.

When their task was done, the dead that still walked withdrew to the *Thetis* and the waiting embrace of cold oblivion.

THE VOICE REACHED Crius through dreams of ice. '*Waken!*'

The pain came first, as it always did. It began in his chest and spread through his remaining flesh, burning with an acid touch. Then the iron awoke.

More pain came, stabbing through him, shrill and needle-sharp. For a long moment he could feel each piston, servo and fibre of his body but could not move them. He was trapped once more, held by the dead weight of the metal he was bound to. Blood pulsed through his flesh and power through his limbs, beating like a distant drum. Sounds swelled in his ears: the clatter of machines, the scrape of tools, the burbling of servitors as they went about their tasks.

More pain came, and it did not fade. The instinct to thrash, to shout, to break free of the iron rose in him until it took all of his will to remain still. Then the moment passed.

His body became his own again. Sight returned. First came a cloud of static falling from the blackness like snow. Then shapes, then colours, then a face that he recognised.

'It is time,' said Phidias.

Crius nodded. A stutter of pain ran up his spine.

Ferrus Manus is dead.

As always the truth rose in his mind as fresh and raw as the moment he had first heard it. First emptiness, then the sucking blackness of sorrow, then anger redder than blood, then at last the hatred came. Cold, limitless and as dark as quenched iron, the hate took shape and became a need, a drive. He cut away all other emotions and thoughts, disconnecting them from his mind like redundant systems. Only the hatred remained, bathing in the light of his pain.

He turned from Phidias to look at the ring of Iron Hands that stood before him, their weapons in their hands, their eyes cold when they met his gaze. He looked back to Phidias.

'We are close enough to the Solar System,' said Phidias.

Crius said nothing but began to walk, and in his wake the Iron Hands followed in silence.

BOREAS LOOKED UP at Crius – the skin over the hard bones of the face was paler and the flesh thinner than when they had left Terra. The templar wore a black robe rather than his ruined armour, and chains linked thick manacles around his wrists and ankles to an adamantium collar which circled his neck. The links of the chains clinked together as he straightened. His wounds clearly pained him, but he would heal and live. Boreas's face showed no emotion, but Crius caught a flicker in the depths of the eyes. His mind processed possibilities as to what that could signify: anger, pity, resolve, recognition? He dismissed them all as irrelevant.

The hangar was as silent as when they had arrived all those months ago. The looted carcasses of landing craft and gunships still filled the dark cavern, and the hot air still pressed close. The golden and black hull of Boreas's Storm Eagle sat ready to launch, her lights creating a pool of light before the open embarkation ramp.

'We are at the edge of the light,' said Crius. 'We will send a signal once we have left. Your brothers will find you here.'

'You are… like them,' said Boreas, his eyes moving from Crius to the rest of the Iron Hands.

'They are my brothers,' replied Crius.

'There will be no end to this,' said Boreas quietly. 'All hope ends down the path you now walk.'

'Hope was lost long ago, Boreas.' Crius's voice was a low rasp. In his chest he felt the beating of the machines that had replaced his hearts. 'It was lost the moment our primarch fell, when our fathers became mortal in our eyes. This war will not end as you think, Boreas, nor as your lord wishes.' He paused and lifted his hands. The broken chains clinked where they still hung from his wrists. 'But I will fulfil my promise even though I do not return with you. If you wish this bond, it is yours. When the time comes, then you may summon us.'

Boreas held Crius's gaze for a long moment.

'How?'

'Ignarak. The silence of mountains that once burned, and will burn again. Send that message with one word bound to it. If we still endure then we will hear you, and we will answer.'

Boreas said nothing. His features had closed and hardened again, his expression unreadable. Crius took a step back, and made to leave the chamber. The two Iron Hands bracketing Boreas led him

up the ramp of the Storm Eagle, and Crius heard the pilot servitors burble to their craft in the language of machines.

At the top of the ramp, Boreas twisted to face Crius again.

'What word?' he called back. Crius looked up at the templar. 'In
the summons, what word will bring you?'

The hot air of the hangar billowed as the Storm Eagle's engines
began to keen with power.

'Waken,' said Crius.

On the ramp, Boreas stood for a moment in the rising wind and
then turned away.

STRIKE AND FADE

Guy Haley

WHERE THERE HAD once been many sons of Nocturne, now there were only four – Brother Jo'phor, grim Hae'Phast, the young neophyte Go'sol and the ever-silent Donak. They crouched among the rocks above the trail. None knew the others well, and that they had come together at all amidst the turmoil of the massacre was as great a miracle as any.

They spoke in whispers. They had not dared use the wider vox-net for days. Their voices barely carried above the wind and Donak's repetitive sharpening of his combat blade. Go'sol flexed his shoulders, stretching his numbed limbs.

'When will they come?'

Jo'phor quietened him with a raised hand. 'Patience, neophyte.'

'And stay still,' Hae'Phast added. 'Your motion will betray us to the enemy.'

Go'sol's face reddened at Hae'Phast's words.

'I am sorry, masters.'

'Do not be sorry,' said Jo'phor. 'This is not how your training should be, but you will be stronger for it.'

The Scout nodded. Hae'Phast grunted bitterly. 'If we live...'

The old warrior had no patience with the youth – whether that was his nature or merely anger at the recent atrocities they had witnessed, Jo'phor could not yet tell.

'Brother, mind the spirit of the neophyte,' he urged him.

'And what of *our* spirits? My dreams are tapestries of gross betrayal, our brothers slaughtered by those they once called friend.'

'Just have a care for the lad.' Jo'phor sighted down his weapon to where their improvised explosives had been planted. 'I worry more for Donak. He has not spoken at all since we found him. The flames of his eyes are low. The forges of his hearts have been quenched.'

Hae'Phast looked at him. 'You see? There are things too great for even a Space Marine to bear. Tell me you are untouched by it.'

Jo'phor spoke so quietly, his voice was barely audible.

'I am not untouched, brother. My hearts ache. My mind cannot contain the enormity of the slaughter. My eyes are sore with sorrow.' He turned to Hae'Phast. 'But my rage outmatches it all. We four are of different companies within the Legion, granted, but all of us were born of the fire and fury. Our brotherhood is unshakeable. There is succour for me in that, and power. Let *all* the other Legions turn upon the sons of Nocturne, for nothing can break the bonds between us. There *will* come a reckoning. That is what I say to any who doubt us.'

Hae'Phast nodded solemnly. When he spoke, he was calmer.

'And that is why we follow you, brother.'

'All is not lost,' said Jo'phor. 'That the traitors spend so much time scouring this particular area gives me hope. I do not believe that we are the last servants of the Emperor on Isstvan Five.'

Behind his visor, Hae'Phast chuckled. 'And if we are?'

Jo'phor shifted.

'Then we will fight to the very end. Silence now. The Night Lords are coming.'

They all held themselves as still as the rocks around them. They waited until the faint sound of engines reached their enhanced ears. Go'sol looked up.

'Do you hear that?'

'Bikers,' said Hae'Phast. 'Do we withdraw?'

Jo'phor shook his head.

'Too late. Look!'

A figure came around the curve in the track. He was clearly a legionary, but unarmoured and with welts criss-crossing his pale flesh. He staggered towards the defile where the Salamanders booby traps waited.

'Now?' Go'sol produced the detonator switch, but Jo'phor held up his hand urgently.

'Wait. That is no traitor who runs before them...'

The sound of bikes built to a roar as a figure in night-blue armour veered around the mountainside. He rode the narrow, uneven path with breathtaking skill.

He chased the stumbling figure, lashing him with a cruel whip, harsh laughter grating from his stylised helmet augmitters. Four other bikers followed, the lightning marks on their battleplate sullied with dry blood.

Hatred boiled up in Jo'phor's hearts. He looked at Go'sol – the Scout's face was flush with excitement.

'Wait for their captive to get clear.'

The lone legionary was still within the blast zone, but the bikers were gaining on him. Any longer and they too might escape the worst of it.

Jo'phor felt his guts twist. 'Now! Go'sol, *now!*'

There was a terrific explosion, the blast of multiple charges erupting out of the lengthening shadows. The leading Night Lord was hurled from the track like a rag doll, his bike plunging end over end down the steep mountainside.

His followers skidded to a halt, frantically scanning through the clouds of obscuring dust to see who had attacked them. Jo'phor surged forwards, aiming for one traitor who had removed his helmet. He would pay dearly.

A boiling jet of promethium from Jo'phor's flamer engulfed the warrior. He fell screaming from his mount, his burning flesh sloughing from his bones.

The others spun their bikes and opened fire. Treachery had left their skills undimmed, and bolter shells tore up the rocky terrain, but Hae'Phast and Donak fired with impunity from cover. One Night Lord raised a plasma pistol, before a bolter shot took him in the chest and he slumped over the handlebars.

There were two of the traitors left. One gunned his engine as his comrade intensified his fire, rearing up onto the hillside. Fishtailing madly, he rode his bike up the incline towards Jo'phor. He brought a chainsword down at the Salamander's head, but his bike slipped sideways on the scree-covered slope and he reached out to stay his fall.

His hand never touched the ground. A bolt exploded within the traitor's gauntlet, spraying ruined flesh and metal.

As the warrior fell, Jo'phor looked to his left; Brother Donak strode forwards, his weapon held level in both hands. He advanced calmly on the fallen Night Lord, putting a single shot through his eye lens.

The last traitor swung his bike around again to bring its twin bolters to bear, but Hae'Phast brought him down, blowing out his chest plate along with the ribcage it shielded.

The silence was sudden and horrifying. The air stank of propellant and murder. Jo'phor wrinkled his nose.

'Well fought, brothers. By a thousand pinpricks must we bleed them.'

'They died more easily than they deserved,' Hae'Phast muttered, advancing warily between the bodies. Then he turned to Go'sol. 'Quickly now, young Scout – "strike and fade". Let's strip the bodies.'

He went down to the dead, and Donak and Go'sol followed him, rifling through the saddlebags of the nearest bike.

Hae'Phast halted suddenly, doubling back towards them. 'What have we told you, lad? Leave the gun! Take nutrient packs, ammunition...' He stopped to put a bolt in the head of a traitor who stirred. 'Night Lords bolts fit a Salamander's gun. A Night Lords water bottle will quench a Salamander's thirst.'

Go'sol seemed unsure. 'It feels wrong.'

'These warriors were our cousins. They were raised up by the Emperor alongside us – their cause has been our cause, their lord brother to our lord. But now we are opposed. They are the enemy, and *we* are the righteous.'

Jo'phor did not hear his brother's words. He knelt beside the Night Lords' fallen captive and his hearts sank when he saw a fist-sized hole in the legionary's back. He rolled him over, seeing the emblem of the Raven Guard tattooed on his shoulder.

The legionary's eyes fluttered. Jo'phor took him in his arms.

'I have killed you, kinsman,' he murmured.

The Raven Guard's eyes focused. 'No, brother. You have saved me. Do not weep.'

'I would weep for us all, my friend – loyalist and traitor alike. To slay our own kind is no small thing, no matter the enormity of their crimes.'

'They are our own no longer. Darkness has overtaken them.' The legionary was wracked by a bloody cough. 'Listen to me. You must fight on. Fight and *survive...*'

'And you, survive with us!' Jo'phor urged.

The Raven Guard smiled and weakly shook his head. His eyes

closed. Jo'phor stayed with him, until the weak beating of his hearts had ceased.

When his brothers approached, Jo'phor pointed to the mountain peaks high above the trail. He did not speak, for in that moment he did not trust the authority of his voice.

As they made their way from the ambush, he went to one of the Night Lords corpses. With his knife, he scratched the mark of his Legion into the warrior's greave. The work was rapid, but fine – a dragon's head of pure, silver scores roaring outrage against betrayal.

'Let them see,' Jo'phor muttered. 'Let them see that the shadows of Isstvan harbour the flames of vengeance, and that those flames will burn them all.'

Then he departed, following his brothers away from the traitors' inevitable pursuit.

HONOUR TO
THE DEAD

Gav Thorpe

ACROSS THE PLAIN they march, the Titans of the Legio Praesagius, the mechanical giants of the True Messengers. The shadows of the behemoths pass over low buildings, eclipsing the marshalling yards on the outskirts of Ithraca as Titan after Titan follows in single file. The ground shakes to the thud of their ponderous steps.

Battle Group Argentus brings up the rear of the long line, the third such formation in the column. At the fore strides *Evocatus*, great Warlord, largest of the machines, whose adamantium skeleton was first raised a thousand years earlier.

After the Warlord come *Victorix*, *Deathrunner* and *Firewolf*. Classed as Scout Titans, the Warhounds are still many metres tall, capable of obliterating entire battle companies, pack-hunters that are a match for even the largest war engines.

Next is *Inculcator*, a Reaver-class engine, stalwart of the line, whose weapon systems can level city blocks and lay waste to lesser foes in a heartbeat.

Ancient war engines, old even when the Great Crusade began,

striding purposefully towards the mustering field. Old save for one machine – *Invigilator* brings up the rear of the battle group. Newly commissioned, the Reaver Titan's blue and gold livery is freshly painted, the threads of the banners hanging from weapon mounts coloured bright, metal gleaming with recently applied unguents and blessed oils.

Invigilator's commander leads the battle group. Princeps Senioris Mikal, veteran of many battles, hears the general order to halt. He eases his consciousness deeper into the mind impulse unit of his war engine to survey the scene, his senses moving from sight and sound and touch to thermal optics, frequency audit and tactile resonance.

For a moment he feels weak, a man of flesh and bone with a slowly beating heart trying to tame a colossus of metal driven on by the unimaginable energies of a plasma reactor. *Invigilator*'s crude awareness defies him briefly, almost petulant as Mikal imposes his will upon the machine-spirit.

Several kilometres ahead, the ships of the Mechanicum wait for the Titans to board. With magnified vision, Mikal sees the war engines of the Legio Infernus – the Fire Masters. Through the haze he sees dozens of Titans, black enamelled hulls decorated with yellow flames. Their column is breaking, spreading out between the super-lifters that will transport the Titans to orbit.

'Order to Argentus,' Mikal transmits. 'General halt. There seems to be some delay ahead. Our friends in the Fire Masters are being laggards. Princeps Maximus, what are our comrades doing? They are blocking our path into the mustering zone.'

There is no response, only static and a few seconds of garbled voices.

'Calth command, this is Princeps Mikal of the Legio Praesagius. Reporting communications fluctuation. What is the status of Ithraca embarkation?'

Still there is no reply. Only the hiss of a dead channel.

'Moderati Lockhandt, run full track diagnos–' The order becomes a gasp of shock. 'By the Omnissiah!'

The cloudy sky reddens with a false sun. Scarlet shadows dapple the landing field as miniature stars seem almost to descend from the heavens, their ruddy light glinting from the transports waiting for the Titans.

There is a moment of perfect silence.

Then the stars strike the landing field, smashing into armoured hulls, searing through drop craft in blossoms of devastating fire. The thunder of detonations is picked up by *Invigilator's* audio relays. Aghast, Mikal is speechless as great beams of energy lance down from orbit, obliterating temporary worker blocks and overseers' villas as they rip across Ithraca. In moments the city is aflame, bright and harsh in Mikal's artificial sight.

Half a kilometre above the landing field a lance beam slices through an ascending transport, carving its engines in a plume of escaping plasma. The ship's climb stalls, its momentum carrying it over the city in a declining arc.

A rough voice breaks through the crackle of transmission static.

'*...no control at all. Coming down in Ithraca, close to the admin... Repeat, this is Eighty-Three-TA*-Aratan. *We have been struck by orbital fire. No contr...*'

Mikal would look away but every sensor of the *Invigilator* is fixated upon the crashing ship, making him a reluctant witness as it ploughs through towering hab-blocks, trailing debris and wreckage.

As he tries to process this flurry of information, new sensor readings crowd Mikal's thoughts from the systems of *Invigilator*. Energy spikes erupt into life amidst the ruin of the landing site. The Fire Masters are powering their void shields. Miraculously, it appears that their Titans were unharmed by the extraordinary bombardment.

Yet the miracle is soon proven to be complicity.

War horns blare. Plasma destructors, volcano guns and gatling blasters unleash their fury against the Praesagius Titans at the head of the column. The distant sound of cannon fire and the snap of lasweapons seems muted and unreal. With their own void shields inactive, the True Messengers are easy targets, and dozens are executed in the space of a few heartbeats.

Invigilator responds more swiftly than its crew as alarm chimes and threat warnings ring across the bridge of the Titan.

'Raise shields!' Mikal snaps the order without thought, sending the command through the systems of his machine. 'All power to shields and locomotion.'

He feels the strength of *Invigilator* surge through him, the energy of the plasma reactor like fire in his blood as it crackles through void shield generators and flows into the Titan's legs.

The impetuous young machine, stirred from near-dormancy, wants to fight. The instinct to return fire is almost overwhelming, but Mikal cuts through the urge with cold reason. The True Messengers are outnumbered. Badly outnumbered. The *Aratan* was carrying much of their strength and the Fire Masters have a superior position.

'Battle Group Argentus, fall back to the city. All engines that can heed my command, fall back and regroup!'

Even as he says the words, *Invigilator* responds, swinging ponderously away from the devastation unleashed at the Titan fields, heading for the sanctuary of Ithraca.

UNABLE TO BELIEVE their eyes, the people packing the third floor balcony stare in amazement and horror at the destruction being set free across their city. The wrath of giants is being unleashed in a blinding display of fire and shell, laying ruin to great swathes of Ithraca's skyline. Most of the observers are wives and children of the Imperial Army regiments called to the Calth muster, their gasps and cries of fright lost in the tumult.

There is one whose eyes are not directed at the Titan battle, but instead her gaze is in the opposite direction, towards the centre of the city where the transport ship fell. Varinia's thoughts are of her husband, Quintus, stationed with his regiment. They said their goodbyes only hours before, and she knows he was at the government plaza to receive his company's muster order. She cannot see the buildings but the tower of fire and smoke rising from the crash site fills her heart with anguish.

A detonation close by, less than a kilometre away, rips her attention from thoughts of her husband. A Titan, a Reaver in black and red, stumbles at the far end of the avenue, its void shields flaring as it tramples across groundcars and topples into a five storey housing block.

The battle is getting closer.

'Pexilius,' she whispers. She dashes back into the stairwell landing from the balcony, thoughts turned to her infant child in the nursery two floors up.

She reaches the first landing at a full run, almost slipping in her haste as she turns at the next flight of steps.

Then the front of the hab-block explodes, showering glass and chunks of plascrete down the stairwell, the fire of the detonation billowing over Varinia as she dives into a corner. Roof beams and ceiling panels fall.

Dust clogs her mouth and nose, coating her pale skin and clinging to blond curls of hair. Her clothing is tattered in places, her face and arms scratched. There is a pain in her side and warm blood soaks her dress.

'Pexilius!' Her voice a scream, ignoring the agony of her wound, she clambers over a fallen beam and scrambles up the rubble-choked stairway. 'Pexilius!'

There are bodies, and parts of bodies, crushed in the tangle of fallen masonry. Someone croaks a cry for help, a broken-fingered hand reaching from the depths of the debris. She pushes past, heaving aside a fallen beam to get through. Varinia cannot stop to help. She has but one thought in her mind.

Three whole floors have been smashed by the stray missile. Reaching the floor of the nursery, Varinia sees the flimsy door hanging by one hinge. She pushes through.

'Pexilius!' She stops, coughing hard in the dusty haze, the pause giving sense a chance to return. Her son cannot reply; he is only a few weeks old. Instead she calls for the nurse. 'Lucretia? Lucretia? Anybody?'

The nursery is in ruins, the brightly painted walls covered with black blast marks. Half the ceiling has fallen in, completely burying the area where the cots had been lined.

Varinia screams again at the sight, every worst fear brought to stark life by the grim scene. She throws herself at the fallen tiles and plaster, cutting her hands and breaking her fingernails as she tears away lumps of masonry.

'Lucretia! Is anybody alive? Is there anyone here? Make a noise. Oh, please, someone be alive. Please let my little Pexilius be alive.'

Her tears wash into the caked dust on her face as she continues to dig.

A cough attracts Varinia's attention and she redoubles her efforts, aching limbs finding new strength. She hears rasping breath and pulls away a cracked ceiling tile to reveal the blood-covered face of old Lucretia. The nurse is twisted unnaturally, hunched over something.

There is a wide gash down the side of her head, her face slick with blood.

'Pexilius?' Varinia whispers the word, in dread more than hope.

'…just got him up… to feed…'

Varinia does not know whether this is good or bad, but then poor Lucretia shifts her weight, pain contorting her face, to reveal a blue-swathed bundle underneath her.

'My son! Lucretia, you saved him.'

Varinia nearly snatches the dazed child from Lucretia's weak grip, lifting his cheek to hers, holding him tight.

Another explosion mere blocks away reminds her that they are not safe. Cradling tiny Pexilius in one arm, she tries to move the pillar pinning down the nurse but it will not move. The old woman's eyelids flutter and she slumps, her chest unmoving.

'Thank you, Lucretia. Thank you, thank you, thank you…'

Varinia's tears of gratitude spill onto the dead woman as she leans forwards to kiss her wrinkled brow. Then she composes herself, for the sake of her son.

'Right, Pexilius, let's get you out of here.'

Her forced jollity cannot hold back the dismay she feels. Varinia heads back to the stairwell, picking through the rubble with her child clasped to her chest. She reaches the floor below and stops, suddenly wary.

The building shudders, more debris clattering from the ruined floors above. Again and again, something pounds the earth close by, slow and methodical. Varinia screams as an immense shadow looms beyond the broken windows and stops. With a rising whine, massive multi-barrelled cannons spin into motion, directed at some distant target. Knowing what is to come, Varinia dashes into one of the rooms adjoining the landing, shielding her son with her body.

The Titan opens fire.

The noise is deafening – the rapid boom of ignited shells, the shockwaves shattering what glass is left in the windows, causing a fresh storm of shards to hurtle around Varinia as she hugs Pexilius tight and throws herself against a wall.

She cries wordlessly, trying to cover her son's ears as best she can, her own eardrums throbbing with pain, the primal scream drowned out by the Titan's cannonade.

And then, numb silence.

Its mighty footsteps shaking the building, the Titan sets off once more, pitching the interior of the hab-block into darkness for a moment. Varinia sees a table, upended but intact. She seeks shelter behind this flimsy barricade.

'We'll stay here, little one, my precious son. We'll stay here and they'll come for us. Father is fighting now. But he'll be thinking of us. Yes he will. He'll be coming. He knows where we are and he'll come for us.'

As the din of the Titan's passing fades, Varinia curls into a protective ball around her child.

'We'll be safe here until father comes home.'

THE SCREAMS OF the fleeing crowds can barely be heard over the incessant blare of the Fire Masters' war horns. Their Scout Titans lead the attack, fast and mobile, driving the populace of Ithraca before them like cattle.

There is a harsh logic to their clamour: targets on the street are easier to destroy. The purpose of this cacophony is to rout the people of Ithraca from their homes and workshops, sparing the renegade regiments following in the Titans' wake the miserable task of clearing the buildings. There are tens of thousands of soldiers flooding into Ithraca now, on foot and in transports, the way paved by the terror unleashed by the Fire Masters.

Speed is essential. With surprise, the Word Bearers and their allies have gained the upper hand. With speed, they will seize victory.

At the head of the chase is Princeps Tyhe in his Warhound, *Denola*. Thousands pour through the streets in front of him, surging like waves down boulevards and alleys. He is one with his Titan, weapons spewing explosive rounds into the midst of the panicked crowds, gouging the ferrocrete roadway and shredding grounded civilian skimmers trapped by the press of the throng.

'Is it not beautiful, my sweet?' He caresses the interface of the mind impulse unit. 'See the ants spilling from their nests to be crushed. So weak and pathetic. But kill them we must! Our comrades in the Word Bearers require deaths, and deaths we shall give them. Deaths by the dozen! Deaths by the hundred, by the thousand!'

With *Denola* are two more Warhounds, splitting through the streets to herd the civilians of Ithraca to their doom, but Tyhe pays them no heed. He will not share the glory of battle. His is a world that consists only of hydraulically powered limbs and heavy servos, plasma cores and weapon systems, targeting arrays and autoloaders.

'Yes, yes! The death of this rabble will make us stronger. The Princeps Maximus swore to that. Fortunate was the day he heeded the call of Kor Phaeron and swore us to this cause. Have you ever known such freedom, such power? We have become one with the Machine-God through destruction! Gone are the shackles of the Emperor! The Machine-God is set free from the bonds of servitude to Terra. Horus has shown us the way and we follow gladly!

'They thought to make us a slave, glorious *Denola*. They muzzled us and told us when we could hunt. Yes, I feel the same savage glee that roars in your plasma heart. It beats as my own. When we are done clearing out the vermin, the true hunt will begin.

'Remember how the True Messengers fled from our guns? That will not save them. They will be shown the lie of their name, for there is no message more true than the one we bring. We are the harbingers of a new dawn, the heralds of death! We are the Fire Masters, the bringers of woe! And as we set the sorrow of our foe upon the fires of battle, it will raise us up beyond all–'

'Tyhe, you are moving out of formation.'

The warning from his fellow princeps is meaningless, just syllables barely understood through the pounding of blood and the thump of pneumatics. Tyhe laughs. He can feel piles of corpses underfoot as *Denola* strides along the street, the bodies pulped beneath the weight of its tread.

'The enemy are massing around the crash site of the Aratan. *Legion command is issuing orders to regroup. We cannot attack piecemeal.*'

The words irritate Tyhe, like the buzzing of a gnat. He simply ignores them, stalking further into the city, guns blazing.

THE UNDERSIDES OF the smoke clouds shrouding Ithraca are lit by the flare and flash of explosions and searing las-blasts. Two battles rage, both desperate in their own way. In the buildings and streets the traitor regiments of the Imperial Army sweep through Ithraca in long columns of tanks and transports. Artillery and self-propelled guns pound the city blocks from the outskirts, paving the way for the infantry with a creeping barrage. Street-to-street, the scattered forces still loyal to the defence of Calth sell their lives for every metre the enemy advance; each life expended to buy time for the shock of treachery to pass and the defenders to organise.

Aboard *Invigilator*, the ground battle pales into insignificance compared to the mighty rage of the Titans. The men and women hurling themselves at the traitor advance with desperate abandon, the horde of rebels pushing into the Ithraca – they are as nothing compared to the war engines that stride through the city. They crash through buildings and stomp across plazas, cracking ferrocrete underfoot as they manoeuvre to catch one another in deadly cross-fires. Flights of rockets and hails of shells rip through the choked air. The crackle of overloading void shields shatters windows and sets fire to tree-lined avenues.

The battle group have extricated themselves from the immediate threat of the Infernus assault, but several mighty Warlords of the Legio Praesagius have been brought down in the withdrawal. Their sacrifice has allowed Mikal and others time to get their war engines to full battle readiness.

Though outnumbered, the True Messengers will not surrender Ithraca meekly.

Away from the landing fields communications are better, though patchy, and Mikal can speak with the rest of Argentus. The traitors must have employed some kind of damping screen, and there is still no contact from Legion command or the other battle groups. For the moment Mikal must lead Argentus without any grander strategy to follow.

The *Aratan* becomes the focus of his efforts. Trapped on board are the principal engines of the Titan Legion, and if they can be salvaged then they could well turn the tide. The Fire Masters have apparently come to the same conclusion, and enemy Titans are also moving through the city towards the crash site. Battle Group Argentus were the least mauled by the traitor ambush, and lead the way for the six surviving Warlords of the True Messengers. If the Battle Titans can secure the *Aratan* and guard the area from infantry assault, there may still be a chance of blunting the enemy attack.

'*Evocatus*, take the lead and push on to the crash site,' commands Mikal. 'Pull down that broadcast station and the clear line of fire. Enemy Warlord, four kilometres to north-east. Warhounds, flank westward. *Inculcator*, support position theta.'

Affirmatives buzz back across the battle group vox-net, and the Titans break their close formation to disperse through the streets of Ithraca. With *Inculcator* moving along a parallel route, *Invigilator* advances. Loyal Imperial Army troops part ahead of the Reaver, the infantry cheering and raising their fists to the defiant war engines as they pass.

There has been no word from Calth command or the Ultramarines Legion. The Imperial forces are still reeling from the surprise attacks and the defence of the city rests upon the shields and weapons of a score of Titans, against three times that number. Mikal barely registers the shouts of encouragement from the infantry swarming around his machine, his mind enmeshed in the sensor net of his Reaver as he monitors the enemy's movements.

'*Victorix*, we need eyes ahead of advance. Five hundred metres. There was a Warhound hunting group to the west but they have disappeared from the auspex. Keep watch for them.'

'*Aye, Princeps Senioris*,' comes the terse reply.

'Keep communications to minimum, total encryption. If the enemy were able to scramble transmission, they may have possession of our cipher keys and protocols.'

The battle group advances swiftly, leaving behind the rag-tag formations of Imperial Army preparing to repel those who had but hours before been their allies. With the Warhounds scouting ahead, the larger Titans remain within a few hundred metres of one another in close support. An enemy engine, a heavily gunned Nemesis-class, has taken up a position directly ahead of their advance. Scanner returns suggest that the Nemesis is not alone, but all energy signatures are blurred by the background noise of the turbine mills and manufactories.

A kilometre further on, they come within range of unseen enemy artillery. *Evocatus* takes the brunt of the first salvo, the Warlord's void shields crackling and blazing as they absorb the shells. A building to the right and a few dozen metres ahead of *Invigilator* collapses in moments, spilling debris into the street. Through the smoke and dust, the Reaver's sensors pick up massed infantry and vehicles heading directly for the battle group.

'Enemy troops, half a kilometre. Several hundred infantry. Battle tanks, number unknown. *Inculcator*, *Deathrunner*, engage and suppress. *Evocatus*, we will continue to advance. Enemy artillery located on the outskirts of Demesnus parklands. *Victorix*, *Firewolf*, deal with the guns.'

Whether from bravado, madness or fear of failure, the enemy regiment attacks the Titans directly, pouring into the buildings across their line of advance. More shells and rockets fall, laying waste to city blocks around the war engines.

A lucky salvo engulfs *Invigilator*, and Mikal feels the pulse of the Titan's void shields straining to hold back the explosions. A generator fails, the mind impulse feedback feeling like a muscle spasm in Mikal's gut. In the heart of the Titan, enginseers and servitors race into action to repair the overloaded shield.

The enemy infantry are within range. *Evocatus* opens fire with its twin carapace-mounted gatling blasters, sending a torrent of shells into an occupied building in reply to the sporadic heavy weapons shots spitting from the windows and balconies. The front of the stuccoed building sags and implodes under the weight of fire, opening up its shattered interior like a gaping wound.

The Warhound *Deathrunner* breaks into a run, paired megabolters shredding squads of infantry as they try to move in the open. *Inculcator*'s lasweapons chew through a column of battle tanks rounding the junction ahead, turning three into blazing wrecks and blocking the advance of the others.

Mikal highlights the formation in his tactical display. 'Skallan, target that choke point. Full salvo.'

The apocalypse missile launcher atop the Reaver's carapace adjusts its trajectory under the coaxing of the moderati and then opens fire, sending a flurry of ten missiles screaming down the boulevard into the heart of the tank formation. Machines and men are ripped apart by the thunderous detonation, spraying the lower floors of the surrounding buildings with shrapnel and wreckage.

Assessing the damage inflicted by the battle group, Mikal reaches a conclusion. The tanks and infantry are nothing more than a distraction, intended to prevent the Titans from reaching the *Aratan* before the enemy.

'Threat minimal, this is a delaying action. Continue the advance, we cannot afford to waste time mopping up dregs. Nemesis is two kilometres, holding position.'

Mikal considers his options, absently strafing the shattered traitor company as they pass. The opposing Nemesis is only a single Titan, but its weapons are capable of ripping through void shields and slicing through armour. It is the perfect Titan killer. Its position gives it wide arcs of fire and would require a lengthy detour to outflank – a detour the battle group cannot afford to make. Sporadic sensor returns also indicate the presence of supporting troops, probably traitor Skitarii from the Fire Masters Legion.

Weighing up the possible courses of action, Mikal must decide if the risk of losing one or more of the battle group outweighs the time lost by an encircling manoeuvre. It is not an easy choice, but as Princeps Senioris he knows what must be done.

'Full attack on the Nemesis. If we can break through to the parklands then we have an open route to the *Aratan*. *Evocatus*, you must draw its fire from the west. *Deathrunner*, dare the gauntlet and deal with ground support. *Inculcator*, you and I will make the main attack.'

To the credit of his fellow princeps, there is no hesitation in their affirmative replies. Leaving the dead in their wake, the battle group presses on through Ithraca.

AMIDST THE CREAK of settling debris, Varinia hears voices. She cannot make out the words, but they are coming from down the stairwell. For a moment she wonders if they are other survivors, but their harsh, cruel laughter suggests otherwise.

Pexilius stirs in her arms as she stands up to survey the remains of the apartment. Broken furniture litters the dust-covered floor and the collapsed ceiling blocks off the only other exit. She spies a crawlspace, just large enough for her, where an inner wall has toppled. Pexilius murmurs and opens his eyes as she places him inside the dark space.

'Hush now, mother will be right back.'

Pushing him a little further into the gap, Varinia returns to the upturned table and tries to lift it. She hears the crunch of boots on the stairs through the broken doorway. The table is too heavy for her to lift completely but she needs something to cover the opening. If not, she might as well stand in the middle of the room. Gritting her teeth, she pulls up the edge of the table and takes a few steps, wincing at the noise as the corner drags through broken tiles. Arms already trembling from the effort, she lowers it gently and takes in a deep breath.

The voices are coming closer, echoing up the shattered stairway. Glass breaks under their approaching tread.

'Move, damn you,' she whispers.

There is the sound of rubble thudding down the stairs and a curse as one of the men stumbles. There are words she does not understand, but the tone of them needs no translation. Varinia seizes her chance, hauling the table up onto its side across the entrance to her hiding place. Ducking behind, she pulls a few stray ceiling tiles across the gap, leaving only a sliver of light.

Pexilius is fully awake now. He wriggles in his swaddling, yawning and blinking. Taking him up in her arms, Varinia backs as far into the hole as possible, shaking with fear. Her son seems to sense her fright, brow creasing. She strokes her fingers across his head to comfort him.

'Not now, little one, not now. Stay quiet for mother.'

Her agitation unsettles the infant and she recognises all too well an imminent cry.

'Please, Pexilius...'

Through the crack she has left, Varinia sees dark shapes at the doorway. Three men appear. They are dressed in drab Imperial Army fatigues. She does not recognise the regiment; there have been so many in Ithraca for the mustering that she always lost track during the conversations with her husband.

She wishes he were here now. She wishes her brave lieutenant would kill these damnable looters and take her and Pexilius to safety. Her tears start again, salty on her lips.

There is a sigh from Pexilius and he opens his mouth, eyes screwing shut. Hating herself, Varinia puts her hand over his face, terrified for the both of them. His distress is muffled, unheard amongst the sound of settling wreckage and the thud of the looters' boots. Holding her breath, sure that the pounding of her heart itself can be heard, Varinia is immobile, not daring to move a muscle lest she disturb the pile of debris above her.

Someone steps next to the upturned table, blocking out the light. Varinia stifles a gasp of fright, clenching her jaw tight. Pexilius struggles beneath her hand.

The men sound disappointed, snapping at each other. She sees fingers grabbing hold of the table. She shrinks back, trying to make herself as small as possible.

Five staccato bangs echo deafeningly in the room, cutting short a cry of pain. Something crashes against the table, dislodging the tiles.

A heavier tread thuds across the apartment. She realises she still has her hand clamped across Pexilius's mouth. For a moment she is filled with the terror that she has suffocated her child. She pulls her hand away, the lesser of the two evils, and Pexilius takes a gasping breath. She waits for his cries to start and cannot stop herself, her words little more than a breath.

'Hush, my beautiful boy. Hush. Mother is here. It won't hurt for long.'

She shrieks as light floods the hiding place, the loose debris above her wrenched away. Varinia finds herself staring into the wide barrel of a gun, pointed directly at her. She screams again before taking in everything else.

Behind the gun is an armoured figure, dwarfing any man Varinia has ever seen. She lets out a choked cry of relief, recognising the livery of the Ultramarines. The legionary has lost his helm and stares at her with cold blue eyes, his broad jaw set. His hair is dark, cropped short, and there is a golden stud in his brow above his right eye.

'Survivor. Nothing more. Move out.' The words are uttered without emotion.

As the warrior turns away, Varinia surges out of her hiding place, holding little Pexilius tightly. The sound of more gunfire drifts down the stairwell, startling her momentarily. She steps in a spreading pool of blood and almost slips, putting out one hand upon the overturned table to steady herself. The three looters lie scattered in the broken tiles and dust, lifeless eyes staring at the ceiling. Shuddering, Varinia covers her child's eyes and steps after the Space Marine.

Past him, on the landing, another Ultramarine stands at the window. In his hands he has a large, multi-barrelled cannon, carrying it as easily as a normal man hefts a lasgun. He fires at something in the street, and a torrent of shell casings spill to the floor. Varinia winces at the sudden noise, trying to shelter Pexilius from the din.

'Take your child to safety, woman.' The helmetless Space Marine gestures at Varinia as she attempts to protect her son. 'The Word Bearers and their treacherous allies have brought war to us all.'

Then he strides away, with Varinia at his heels.

'Wait! Please wait!'

He stops, seeming to stiffen, and turns his head. His gaze is harsh. 'We are heading for further battle. It will not be safe.'

'Safer than here,' replies Varinia. 'Please, take us with you.'

The Space Marine at the window speaks without turning. 'There is an evacuation point being set up in the Demesnus park. Go there.'

'On my own?' Varinia's limbs feel even weaker at the thought. 'That's nearly *five kilometres* away.'

Another Ultramarine descends from the floors above, fallen masonry shifting under his tread. He stops when he sees Varinia.

The three warriors seem to pause, exchanging words via their communicators.

'We won't be any trouble, I promise. I'll stay out of your way. *Please.* Please don't leave us here. There could be more… of them.'

There is another exchange between the Ultramarines, the one without his helmet remaining silent and grim-faced. He turns to look at Varinia and nods once.

'No guarantees,' he says. 'We are heading to the muster point. We will take you that far.'

The other two warriors head down the stairs, leaving him to wave Varinia onwards.

'Thank you, thank you so much. What are your names, so that I might praise them to my husband when we find him? Have you any news from the administration centre? He was there to receive orders.'

'A ship came down in the area of which you speak. Communications are fractured. Enemy forces converge on that position, but there are survivors still fighting…'

The words bring renewed hope to Varinia. As they reach the last flight of steps, she realises the Space Marine did not answer her question.

'Your names, please. I am Varinia, and this little one is Pexilius.'

The lead Ultramarine laughs, the sound strange through his armour's external speakers. He stops by the shattered remnants of the double doors leading onto the street.

'Our captain was called Pexilius. He would have been proud.'

'That is Gaius,' says the warrior behind her. 'My companion with the rotor cannon is Septival. I am Sergeant Aquila. Tullian Aquila.'

'Thank you, Tullian Aquila.'

'Do not thank me yet. Five kilometres through Ithraca is no easy journey today.'

✠ ✠ ✠

THE FLICKER OF firelight in the windows of the villa makes it look like the building is laughing at the destruction, eyes glinting with glee. Tyhe laughs with it, delighting in the death and misery that stalks Ithraca alongside him. His weapons are like fists of fire, obliterating everything he comes across. In his wake the streets are littered with corpses and wrecks.

The villa holds a few dozen desperate men. They think they have found safety but all they have located is their tomb. Tyhe has chased them for an hour, goading them with his war horns, forcing them back with his mega-bolter when they think to turn and fight.

Some tried to make a stand, turning their autocannons and plasma guns against his armoured form. They did not even over-load his void shields. In repayment, he wiped them from the mortal world, turning flesh to bloody ruin and vehicles to tattered metal. He has forced the survivors up the hill to a patrician's home overlooking the parklands. It gives him reason to destroy this place, sating a desire that has filled him since he first spied the column-fronted compound, lording it up over the common city below.

'An eyrie for the arrogant eagle, now to fall to ruin!' he cries, pleased by his own poetic tone. He throws out a full spectrum scan of the villa and the men hiding within. 'Fifty, no more. A fit-ting sepulchre we shall make of this fine palace, my sweet *Denola*. I wonder where the master of this house is now. Perhaps he still cowers within? Or maybe he flees the city, abandoning even his own slaves to save himself.

'Such shall be the fate of all tyrants. The liberation begins here and will end upon shackled Mars! The gears of war will grind the eagle to a bloody smear, and then we shall reclaim the galaxy! Horus shows us the way, and by the word of Lorgar has it been promised!'

He fires the turbo-laser, smashing through one wing of the villa, blowing out the power generators within. A gasline explodes and sheets of flame erupt from the windows, setting fire to the lawns and trees of the trampled gardens.

Tyhe steps easily over the wall of the compound as futile lasgun fire sparks from *Denola's* void shields. It feels like rain on his skin; persistent but not unpleasant.

'Cease your pointless resistance!'

His bellow roars from the Titan's external speakers. There are defiant shouts, small and weak, from the men trapped inside the building. Tyhe spots a handful trying to escape – he steers his engine through the gardens, trampling an orchard to block the rear roadway. He guns down the men emerging from the building and tears through the parade of windows into a ballroom beyond. Drapes are shredded and the lacquered wooden walls shattered into splinters.

'Let me lavish upon you the feast you deserve, my friends! You no longer feed from plates borne upon the backs of the conquered, but must now taste the ashes of defeat and humiliation. I shall heap upon you the just rewards for the lies you have spread, the misdeeds you have performed in the name of "compliance". It is *you* that shall comply, for you are mere men and we are *Denola*, immortal agent of the Machine-God!'

The sport provided by the ragged band of men does not last long, and they retreat into a basement, not daring to fight. Tyhe considers kicking his way in through the walls, but is not so desperate for their blood that he will risk becoming snared in the ruin.

He breaks away from the compound, descending the hill into the greenery of the park in search of a fresh challenge. Not far away, no more than ten kilometres, the Nemesis-class *Revoka* is carefully striding backwards along a tree-lined road, gatling blasters and volcano cannons blazing at an enemy Warlord. The other Titan's void shields are a riot of colours under the constant hail of fire, writhing and spitting with every shell impact.

The Praesagius engine cannot take any more punishment. With a flash that momentarily whites out all of *Denola*'s scanning systems, the Warlord's reactor detonates. Almost twelve city blocks become a glassy crater in that instant, mottled with grey as droplets of molten slag fall to the ground. It is all that remains of the war engine.

Tyhe can see that the enemy's sacrifice is for a purpose – *Revoka* is being outflanked. Two Reaver Titans are approaching from the south. He is too far away to intervene and watches as *Revoka* is caught in a withering crossfire. The Nemesis's shields try to hold back the fusillade but fail in spectacular fashion, flattening trees and ripping up the turf all around.

Exposed, *Revoka* turns its guns upon the approaching Reavers, but too late. The next volley dents armoured plates and slices through the Titan's carapace. A knee joint suddenly gives way, and *Revoka* collapses sideways. Surrounded by dust and flames, the great war machine crumples, armour buckling and tearing as it crashes to the ground.

Contemptuous of the great warrior they have felled, the enemy battle group marches on. Tyhe growls, the noise echoed and amplified by his Warhound as he cuts across the park. One of the Reavers stands as rearguard, protecting the others as they head towards the crash site.

The Reaver is bigger than *Denola*, with more firepower and better shielding, but Tyhe does not care. He is a wily hunter. Sooner or later, the Reaver will make a mistake and that is when he will pounce. He will avenge *Revoka*, but more than that Tyhe will savour the execution as its own reward. A Reaver would be a fine kill indeed, far better than the tanks and infantry he has encountered so far.

Powering down shields and weapons, *Denola* sprints into the cover of the hab-blocks surrounding the parkland, the Warhound's falling energy signature masked almost completely by the burning buildings.

'Repeat, Thunderhawk extraction in progress. Enemy Titans are closing on our position. General order to all companies – withdraw from Ithraca or fall back to rally point at sector sigma-secundus-delta.'

Aquila lifts his hand to the vox-bead in his ear and then lets it fall back, knowing from recent experience that although he can hear the words of his superiors, they cannot hear him.

There is an ornamental gate in the high wall of the park at the end of the street. The buildings to either side of the road are burning shells, but the battle has passed from this sector, the Titans moving on to continue their deadly conflict in the parkland.

Aquila can hear the constant rumble of distant thunder, knowing that it is no tempest but the barrage of heavy guns deciding the fate of the city. It is not lightning that brightens the sky but the flash of super-weapons fire and the flare of void shields.

'Fifteen hundred metres, straight across the park.'

'Open ground, no cover,' replies Gaius. 'It will be a deathzone.'

'All right, *seventeen* hundred metres, following the treeline,' counters Aquila. 'Slower going. We need to keep watch for traitor patrols.'

He turns his attention to the woman, Varinia. She leans against the gate, face bright red. Her child is slung across her chest in a papoose made from a torn curtain. True to her word, she has not slowed them down, but only because they are not moving at full speed, the terrain requiring that they advance more cautiously in case they should encounter a well-armed foe.

'No time to rest,' he tells her.

'Just... a moment... please...'

Her ragged breathing causes Aquila some concern, as does the blood that smears her leg.

'You cannot continue.' He looks around. The streets in this part of the city are deserted. 'Rest here and when you have recovered, make your way to the rendezvous point.'

She looks at him, confused.

'In the park.' He points north-west. The wreck of the crashed ship is plain to see, rising above the low buildings that are scattered across the grassy hills. 'Head towards the crash. You cannot go astray.'

'Sergeant, is that wise?' Septival's protest is restricted to the comm-link. 'The order is for general withdrawal. Ithraca is lost, my friend. It is just a matter of how soon and how many survivors we can extract.'

'Sep has a point,' adds Gaius. 'Ithraca is not an isolated event. All of Calth is under attack. The city will be abandoned in favour of higher value objectives. This will become hostile territory. If she stays here, she will die or be taken by the enemy.'

Conscious that the woman is close at hand and his words can be overheard, Aquila points across the parkland. The ground is pocked with fuming craters, the hillsides gouged and torn by the tread of Titans. Explosions have ripped up trees and the air is thick with ash from the burning meadows.

'She will not make it across that,' Aquila whispers. He raises his boltgun a little. 'She is dying of blood loss. Perhaps we should spare her the torment.'

'Sergeant!' protests Gaius.

'Be honest, we are most likely already dead as well. It would be a mercy.'

'Have you given up hope, sergeant?' Septival's disapproval is also clear.

'Any optimism I harboured was destroyed by the traitors' first salvo. The Word Bearers have caught us at our most vulnerable. It is likely that the Ultramarines Legion will perish on Calth.'

'We can't just give up.'

The woman's words take Aquila by surprise; he realises he has spoken louder than he intended. He looks at her and sees defiance rather than dejection. He cannot share her blind hope, but he does not want to delay the advance any longer.

'Gaius, carry her if you wish. The traitors will be upon the muster point before long. The Infernus Titans are entering the fray. We cannot be tardy if we wish to fight again.'

'As you say, sergeant.' Gaius stows his boltgun and scoops up Varinia, cradling her as easily as she holds her child. The legionary's head tilts to one side as he looks down at the baby. 'You are... *very small.* To think that once even our noble Sergeant Aquila was as tiny as you.'

'Enough,' says the sergeant. 'We head to the trees, and then north. Be vigilant.'

The three Space Marines break into a loping run, plunging into the smoke and fire.

A COLUMN OF Ultramarines vehicles powers along the road beneath *Invigilator* – three Rhinos, and the same number of battle tanks. There are others, scattered formations of blue-armoured figures making their way through the blasted woodlands not far from the Titan's position. The Reaver stands vigilant amongst the pavilions and villas bordering the park, a kilometre from the crash site of the *Aratan*. Princeps Mikal can see the bulk of the vessel, its ravaged hull steaming, on the northern edge of the parklands. The immense ship towers over burning trees and the ruins of buildings, nearly two kilometres long and three hundred metres high. On the broad-spectrum scanners, the wreck is a blazing mass of heat and radiation, blotting out every sensor signature within hundreds of metres.

'So few Ultramarines,' Mikal mutters. 'Not even a company. It is not only the Legio Praesagius that has been caught unawares by this treachery. They may help against these traitor Army scum, but bolters and volkites are no match for a Battle Titan.'

The rest of Battle Group Argentus is further to the east, providing a cordon against the traitors so that the Legion's Warlords can create a perimeter to protect the downed transport ship. The Battle Titans of Infernus are massing, four kilometres away, readying their strength for an all-out assault on the downed ship. Intense fire from the True Messengers lights up the skyline, holding back the traitor tanks and infantry trying to occupy the buildings overlooking the eastern stretches of the park.

Mikal performs a last sensor sweep but against the background flare of the *Aratan* there is nothing significant, only a scattering of signatures that could be loyal forces, trapped civilians or inconsequential enemy ground troops.

'Negative threat. This area is secure. Routing power from sensor screen to locomotion. We will conduct a patrol to the west and north before heading east to join the line.'

Invigilator turns from the park and steps over the tumbled ruin of the wall, into the gardens of a low manse. Leaving deep footprints in the lawns and crushing hedges, the Titan crosses to the north, a shortcut to the main highway leading around the park from the outskirts to the administration quarter. The power of *Invigilator's* plasma reactor drives the Titan on, every stride felt by Mikal as if he were a giant.

THE TRAITOR SHELLING has intensified. Most of it is directed at the hulk of the downed ship but errant rocket salvos and shell-fire scatters onto the park like explosive rain. Moving through the woods in the western border of the parklands, Aquila is not confident of the route ahead.

Not much can be seen through the trees, but the bellowing of war horns echoes all around, growing louder as the enemy Titans converge on the wrecked transport ship.

'If we press on directly, it is only a matter of time before we get caught in the bombardment.'

'We have more immediate concerns, sergeant,' says Septival.

He points to the east where a bridge crosses the narrow river, the road curving northwards along their line of advance. Hundreds of men in the colours of the traitor regiments are crossing, their column supported by super-heavy Fellblade tanks and armoured cars ploughing through the water.

'Not much a rotor cannon can do against them,' says Septival, 'and no way to avoid them if they spread into the trees.'

Aquila glances at Gaius. The woman cradled in his arms appears to be asleep, but that is not a good sign. She hangs limply in his grasp, but stirs for a moment, eyes vacant. The child is clutched to her chest, his little face stained from the smoke, but does not make a sound.

'That Reaver we saw would make a fine escort,' said Gaius.

'I concur,' replies Aquila. 'It will take a little longer but we have to move back into the city. If we make haste we should reach the muster before the Titan cordon is breached.'

There are nods of agreement from the other two and they turn west towards the park's edge, heading for the burning buildings beyond.

'FOOL,' TYHE DECLARES with triumph. 'Blinded by false devotion, as much as the flames obscure his scanners!'

At the princeps' urging, *Denola* steps through the fires raging within a destroyed power coupling station, the heat posing little threat to his beloved war engine. Masked by the thermal backwash, the Warhound stalks after the enemy Reaver. Moving swiftly, Tyhe closes the range to three hundred metres, using burning ruins to cover his approach.

His sensors detect people in the buildings close by, on the edge of the park, but he pays them no heed. He is entirely focused on the kill.

The Reaver presents an easy target, moving away with its back to him. Tyhe waits for a moment longer, analysing the street layout ahead. There is a smaller road running parallel to the highway, separated by tenements even taller than the Warhound. A perfect flanking route.

At two hundred and fifty metres, the Reaver stops. Tyhe feels active sensors wash over him.

'Too late,' Tyhe whispers. 'Far too late.'

Denola opens fire with its mega-bolter. Hundreds of high-calibre rounds stream up the wide road, ripping into the Reaver's void shields with an actinic flare of energy. Auditory sensors detect the failure of the void shields, their generators overloading with a crack of sonic pressure.

'Come on, you clumsy oaf! Fight us! Bring your weapons to bear!'

The Reaver staggers as the last shots slam into its carapace, causing only superficial damage. Tyhe powers up the turbo-laser and fires, the beams of energy slicing into the hip joint of the Battle Titan.

'Turn, you bastard! Retaliate!'

Tyhe is already moving towards the parallel road, increasing power to *Denola*'s legs. Once the Reaver brings its weapons to bear, he will already be at full speed, heading past the Battle Titan to come at it from the rear again.

The enemy princeps does not comply. Instead of turning to fight, he drives the Reaver forwards, crashing through the corner of a tenement in a shower of rockcrete fragments.

'No! No matter, you cannot run from us.'

Adjusting stride, *Denola* sprints along the second road, weapons recharging and reloading. They will be ready to fire into the retreating Titan's back as soon as they round the next corner. The enemy princeps is clever, but his machine is simply too slow to respond to the ambush.

✠ ✠ ✠

THE BLARE OF warning sirens seems muted. Mikal's body is awash
with manifold feedback, his shoulders and flanks feeling bruised
and sore. Emergency systems are like a soothing balm to his flesh
as the repair crew initiate damage control procedures.

'Shield status?'

There is a pause before his prime moderati, Lockhandt, replies.

'Not responding, princeps. All generators overloaded. That sneak
attack caught us good and proper.'

Mikal can sense the Warhound dashing after him. It will be less
than a minute until its weapons are brought to bear.

'Cease damage control. All power to locomotion and weapons.'

'Princeps? We have no shields.'

'No time. We need to kill this engine first.'

Under Mikal's urging, *Invigilator* slams into another tower block
as the Warhound reaches the junction behind him. The armour
holds out better than the struts and ferrocrete of the hab-tower. A
cascade of debris tumbles behind the Titan, filling the road.

'That will slow him down a little. Forget the launcher, overload
power to arm weapons. We are not finished yet.'

THE OUTER WALL of the building disintegrates as the traitor Warhound blasts through with its turbo-lasers, shattering masonry and
support beams to target the loyal Reaver beyond. Lumps of debris
tumble onto Aquila as he retreats from the window.

'Our sanctuary is short-lived,' he says. 'Septival, try to get an angle
on that Warhound. It is little enough, but the rotor cannon may
strip off a void shield. Gaius?'

He turns to see Gaius lowering the woman to the carpeted floor
by the doorway. The Space Marine looks up, and shakes his head.
Aquila can see that Varinia is still alive but her movements are
weak – she has lost too much blood. She strokes the head of her
son with a trembling hand, her eyelids fluttering.

'Gaius, get a visual on target. Guide Septival to the prime firing point.'

The building shakes again. The Warhound passes by the gaping windows, its mega-bolter churning out dozens of rounds a second.

Through the ruin of the far wall, Aquila sees the Reaver turning. Its weapon arms are raised, a short melta cannon and a multi-barrelled las-blaster. The Ultramarine glimpses a crackle of energy from exposed power cables and knows what is about to happen.

Septival knows it too. 'Does he not see that we–'

The Reaver opens fire, targeting the Warhound through the building. Pulses of laser energy obliterate the walls. The Warhound's void shields explode, the blast wave smashing into the already weakened structure.

There is a rumble from above as the ceiling gives way.

Gaius moves like lightning, hurling himself at Varinia. He crashes over her and the child as great chunks of masonry rain down. Armour splits with a loud crack. Aquila knows instantly that his companion has not survived.

Septival is also caught by the falling ceiling, the rotor cannon knocked from his grasp as a twisted support beam glances from his shoulder. The floor buckles under Aquila and pitches him through the widening gap into the storey below.

He tumbles down, fragments of rockcrete raining around him in the suddenly dazzling light as the roof is opened to the sky. He crashes into the rubble-filled basement level, stunned. The debris settles, clouds of dust billowing up from the ruin.

The whine of immense motors steals Aquila's attention. Looking up, he sees the traitor Warhound looming over the breach.

Somewhere above him, Varinia screams.

THE REAVER IS directly ahead of *Denola*, revealed by the partial collapse of the corner block. Its aim was off, smashing the hab-complex but missing the Warhound. Tyhe roars with laughter. One blast to the Reaver's unprotected bridge will end the duel.

A noise filters through the audio pick-ups. A scream of utter terror. The sound is pleasing to Tyhe and he glances down into the ruin of the building. He feels *Denola* responding too, elated by what it detects.

A young woman kneels in the rubble, bloodied and covered in dust. Her fear and anguish is palpable.

Something stirs in her arms. A child.

Two bright blue eyes look up at Tyhe, as startling as las-beams.

Slay.

The impulse surges through *Denola* but Tyhe hesitates. The infant shows no fear, blissfully ignorant of what it is looking at. Pure innocence.

Kill. Destroy. Maim.

The whispers of the engine are vehement, driving into Tyhe's thoughts like hot nails. The pain – the insistence – unnerves him, and he flinches from the contact.

For a fleeting moment he surfaces from the manifold and looks about the Warhound's bridge with his own eyes. Shrivelled corpses lie slumped at the moderati control consoles while flickering energy, sickly and yellow, dances across the panels.

Blood. Let the blood flow.

These are not the voices of his comrades. Cold realisation freezes his heart as he becomes aware of himself. His body is a frail shell, barely alive, kept that way by the unnatural power of *Denola*. He is not its master any more.

'Do not command me! I am the princeps–'

Slaughter. Rend.

The Warhound sends shards of pain stabbing into his mind. Recoiling, Tyhe grits his teeth, battling against the murderous urges filling his thoughts.

'No! No, I am the master of the machine!'

The manifold picks up his defiance, sending it as impulse signals through the Titan's systems.

THE WARHOUND INEXPLICABLY staggers back from the building, stumbling into the middle of the road. Mikal does not hesitate.

'Fire!'

The melta cannon unleashes a focused beam, vaporising the armoured canopy of the Warhound. The surging microwaves incinerate everything inside the Titan's bridge, and the over-pressure bursts its armoured head.

The Warhound topples backwards, guns and legs in spasm, crashing into the hab-block on the other side of the street.

'Again! Full attack!'

Invigilator blasts the crippled war engine with missiles, las and melta-beams, tearing holes through the carapace, severing a leg and shredding its armour plate. Flames engulf the wreck from sheared power lines as the blackened, twisted mess slumps to the ground, leaking burning oil.

Mikal scans the wreck for a few seconds, convincing himself that it is truly destroyed.

'Repair crews – the enemy are closing in on the *Aratan*. I want void shields back online by the time we reach the cordon. Let us hope the Machine-God blesses us with a timely arrival.'

AQUILA DRAGS HIMSELF up the broken rubble and is met by Septival on the floor above. He stands over Varinia and the child. The woman does not move.

'She is dead,' says Septival, looking down at the slender, tattered form at his feet.

Aquila stoops to pick the baby from his mother's dead grasp. Pexilius looks up at the Space Marine with a frown, tiny fingers clawing at Aquila's gauntlets.

'Gaius thought it our duty to protect them,' says Aquila. 'He gave his life for this infant.'

'A one-sided exchange, I fear,' replies Septival.

'He was right. This child will grow up in war and turmoil, but what do we fight for, if not to protect the next generation? One that might know peace. There will be many orphans in the coming years, but we cannot abandon them.'

'And one child will make a difference?'

'If our lives are to be forfeit, it must be for good cause. Gaius believed that this child's life was worth more than his. We owe it to his memory not to make such sacrifice a mere vanity. In time we all will die, but there must be others to bear witness to our deeds. Ithraca is a mass grave, but perhaps one day young Pexilius will know the truth of what happened here, and he will repay that sacrifice a thousand times over.'

'So you have hope for the future of the Imperium after all?'

'Hope is but the first step on the road to disappointment, brother. You can fight for hope if you wish. I will fight to bring honour to the dead. Now, no more delays – we head for the rendezvous.'

Mikal has seen the might of Titans unleashed many times when a world has refused compliance, but the spectacle of two clashing Legions makes all other conflicts pale in comparison. Void shields flicker as the battle rages, blue and purple glares in the smog of war. Shells rip into metal bodies, lasers rupture armour and missiles pound from above. Three Praesagius Warlords have fallen already, their burning wrecks like beacons in the gloom.

Invigilator is just one amongst many, hurling everything it has into the fray. Behind the weakening line of Titans, the crew of the *Aratan* fight to free the main vault doors and see what can be salvaged.

'It does not matter if we are defeated today,' Mikal tells the battle group. 'It is enough that we fight. The artifices of the Machine-God have been perverted to a traitorous cause and we cannot allow that to pass without response.'

A volcano cannon sears into *Invigilator* from the left, blowing out a shield. The brief stab of pain in the back of Mikal's skull subsides in a few seconds. He knows death is near. He is calm.

'It brings to mind a tract from the *Archaia Titanicus*, from the dark days before the Omnissiah brought unity – "It was once held that there was nothing so pure as Man. From Man came Artifice, and so Artifice was deemed pure also. When Man was found to be corrupt, that corruption spread to all that he had created, and all that had been learned was lost." Princeps Maximus Arutis taught me that on the first day I was brought to the Legion. I never understood it fully until now.'

A shower of rockets falls about the Reaver, blanketing the Titan with detonations, another void shield burning out as its energy is expended against the blasts. Mikal replies with the apocalypse launcher, sending his own hail of missiles at the Warlord that has targeted him.

The line is being pushed back, retreating into the buildings around the wreck of the *Aratan*. Mikal looks at the charred hulk and sees swarms of red-robed tech-priests labouring at one of the massive boarding gates. Heavy-duty servitors with arc-cutters saw away at the tangle blocking the vault door.

Two more Infernus Warlords and a Night Gaunt have joined the fight, moving in from the north. The battle group responds, *Victorix* and *Firewolf* striding out to meet the threat, hopelessly outmatched but still defiant. They are prepared to sell their lives dearly.

Just a few dozen metres from Mikal's position, warning beacons blaze into action on the hull of the *Aratan*, flashing red and orange. Klaxons sound as the great gate of the transport finally grinds open. Light streams from the transit bay within.

Its war horn signalling the counter-attack, *Immortalis Domitor* strides from the hold.

The Warmonger-class Titan dwarfs even the Warlords, its main weapons longer than a Warhound is tall. Shells the size of battle tanks are let loose, obliterating an Infernus engine in a single volley. Missiles that can level entire city blocks burst from the launchers of the *Domitor*, streaming out across the ravaged park. They detonate like a dozen miniature dawns.

In the wake of the Warmonger stride four more Praesagius Warlords, fresh and ready for the fight. Cheers flood across the loyalists' comm-net.

Joy singing in his heart, Mikal embraces the manifold once more.

'Get those void shields back online. Battle group, support the Princeps Maximus. Ithraca is not yet lost!'

BUTCHER'S
NAILS

Aaron Dembski-Bowden

BEFORE THE PRIMARCH'S ascension, before his *capture*, the ship had carried a different name. In those more innocent days, it sailed as the *Adamant Resolve*, flagship of the War Hounds Legion.

But time changes all things. Now, the XII Legion were the Eaters of Worlds, and their flagship bore the name *Conqueror*.

It barely resembled the ship it had once been. Ridged by brutal armour plating, spiked by countless weapon batteries, the *Conqueror* had become a crude bastion beyond any other warship in Imperial space.

At the vanguard of an immense battle fleet, it hung in space with its engines powered down, rank upon rank of weapons batteries aimed at a golden warship leading an opposing flotilla.

The enemy ship had never changed its name. Beyond the desecration of the Imperial eagles that once lined its spinal battlements, it remained unchanged beyond battle scars earned in the name of rebellion. Here was the flagship of the XVII Legion, and along its prow, etched in High Gothic, was the name *Fidelitas Lex* – the Law of Faith.

The Bearers of the Word and the Eaters of Worlds stood upon the edge of war. Hundreds of vessels, suspended in the cold void, each side awaiting the order to fire first.

On the bridge of the *Conqueror*, three hundred souls were frozen in their duties. The only sounds were the background mutter of servitors droning about their work, and the omnipresent rumble of the ship's reactor.

Most of the souls, human and post-human alike, felt an alloy of emotion. In some, fear mixed with guilty excitement, while in others, anticipation became a rush of sensation not far from anger. Every set of eyes remained fixed upon the oculus view screen, bearing witness to the fleet that lay beyond.

One figure towered above all others. Armoured in layered ceramite of gold and bronze, he watched the oculus with narrowed eyes. Where others bore a smile, he carried a slit of scar tissue and cracked teeth. Like all of his brothers, he resembled his father as a statue resembles the man it was raised to honour. Yet this statue was flawed by cracks and blemishes – a twitch in the muscles around his eye, a scarred ravine running along his shaven skull.

He reached a gloved hand to scratch at the back of his head, where an old wound would never quite fade. At last, he drew breath to speak, in the voice of a man distracted by pain.

'We could open fire. We could leave half their vessels as cold husks, and Horus would be none the wiser.'

Behind him, seated on a raised throne, Captain Lotara Sarrin cleared her throat.

The statuesque warrior didn't turn to face her. 'Hnnh. You have something to say, captain?'

Lotara swallowed before speaking. 'My lord–'

'I am no one's lord. How many times must I speak those words?' He wiped the beginnings of a nosebleed on the back of his hand. 'Say what you wish to say.'

'Angron,' she said, choosing her words carefully. 'We can't go through with this. We have to stand down.'

Now the primarch turned. A tremor shivered its way along the fingers of his left hand. Perhaps a suppressed need to reach for a weapon, perhaps nothing more than the misfiring synapses at the core of an abused brain. 'Tell me why, captain.'

The captain's eyes flickered to the left. Several of Angron's warriors stood by her throne, their helms turned to the screen, the very avatars of cold indifference. She eyed one of them in particular, imploring him to speak. 'Khârn?'

'Do not look to Khârn to argue on your behalf, girl. I asked *you* to speak.' The primarch's hands were twitching, the fingers shaking like serpents in spasm.

'We can't go through with this. If we attack their fleet, even if we win, we'll be crippled behind enemy lines with a shadow of the force we need to carry out the Warmaster's orders.'

'I did not force this confrontation, captain.'

'With the greatest respect, sir – yes, you did. You have pushed Lord Aurelian's patience time and time again. Four worlds have fallen to us, and each one was an assault declared against our primary orders. You knew he would react eventually.' Lotara gestured to the oculus, where the enemy fleet – dozens of warships that had been allies only hours before – drifted ever closer. 'You forced this engagement, and both the crew and the Legion have obeyed you. We now stand upon the precipice, and it mustn't go any further. We can't cross that line.'

Angron turned back to the oculus, his scarred lips curled into something like a smile. He wasn't blind to the truth in her words, but therein lay the problem. He hadn't expected his brother to react. He'd never imagined Lorgar would suddenly grow a backbone.

'Khârn,' murmured Lotara, turning to the assembled captains again. 'Do something.'

The primarch heard his equerry approach from behind. Khârn's voice was softer than many of his kindred; not gentle by any means, but soft, low and measured.

'She's right, you know.'

Such informality would be anathema within the other Legions. The World Eaters, however, obeyed no traditions but their own.

'She may be right,' the primarch conceded. 'But I sense opportunity in the winds. Lorgar was always the weakest of us, and his Word Bearers are no better. We could wipe this miserable Legion and their deluded master from the face of the galaxy right now. If you tell me that doesn't appeal to you, Khârn, I will call you a liar.'

Khârn removed his helm with a faint hiss of air pressure. Given his life so far, the fact that his face was unscarred seemed nothing less than miraculous.

'Lorgar has changed, as has his Legion. They have traded naivety for fanaticism, and even outnumbered, they would bleed us.'

'We were born to bleed, Khârn.'

'Maybe so, but we can choose our battles. We've pushed our luck with the Word Bearers, and I agree with Lotara. We should rejoin the fleet, cease attacking worlds on a whim, and continue sailing into Ultima Segmentum.'

Angron exhaled slowly. 'But we could kill him.'

'Of course we could. But would you win a battle and cost Horus the war? That doesn't sound like you.'

The primarch smiled. It was a slow, sinister thing – a curving of the gash where his lips had once been.

'My detractors would say it sounds exactly like me.' As he spoke, he rested his fingertips to his pulsing temples. His headaches never ceased, but they were always at their most vicious when his blood ran hot. Today, the primarch's blood burned.

Lotara ignored the warriors as they conversed. She had other matters to deal with, such as three hundred bridge crew caught between staring at Angron, awaiting his orders, and watching the enemy fleet growing in the viewscreen.

'The *Fidelitas Lex* is matching us. She's accelerated to attack speed, and crossed into maximum weapon range. Her void shields are still up, and her weapon arrays are primed. Her support squadron will reach maximum weapon range in twenty-three seconds.'

Angron snorted blood onto the deck. 'We won't back down.'

'Maintain all ahead full,' Lotara called out. Then, quieter, 'Sir, you have to reconsider this.'

'Watch your tongue, human. Ready the Ursus Claws.'

'As you wish.' She relayed the order, and the shout was taken up across the bridge, officer to officer, servitor to servitor. 'The Ursus Claws will be ready in four minutes.'

'Good. We will need them.'

'Incoming hololithic transmission from the *Lex*,' Lotara called out. 'It's Lord Aurelian.'

The primarch chuckled his bass rumble again. 'Now let's see what the serpent has to say.'

The hololithic image appeared in the air before Angron, casting the master of the World Eaters with a flickering mirror image. Where Angron was broken, Lorgar was flawless; where one brother snarled a smirk, the other offered a cold, fierce smile. When Lorgar spoke after several long moments, he had only one question to ask.

'Why?'

Angron stared at the distorted, crackling image of his brother. 'I am a warrior, Lorgar. Warriors wage war.'

The image stuttered as interference took hold. *'The age of warriors is over, brother. We need crusaders now. Faith, devotion, discipline...'*

Angron barked a laugh. 'I have never failed to win a war my way. I buy my victories with the edge of my axe, and I am content with how history will judge me.'

The image of Lorgar shook its tattooed head. *'The Warmaster sent us here for a reason.'*

'I would take you more seriously if you did not hide behind Horus.'

'Very well.' The rasp of vox interference stole Lorgar's voice for a moment. *'I brought us here, and my plan stands on the edge of failure because you cannot control your rage. We will lose this war, brother. How can you not see that? United, we will take the Throneworld. Horus will rule as the new Emperor. But divided, we will fall. You may be content now, but will you be content if we lose? If history paints us as heretics and traitors? That destiny awaits us if we grind our Legions together out here in the void.'*

Lorgar hesitated, studying the other primarch as if he could glean some hidden answer. *'Angron. Please, don't force this battle, as you've forced so many others.'*

Angron's hands began to shake again. He cracked his knuckles, to keep his fingers busy. The ache at the back of his head had become a rolling, tidal throb now – an unscratchable itch within his brain.

'The Ursus Claws are ready,' Captain Sarrin said softly. 'Ready to–'

Her words trailed away as the deck sirens wailed.

They burst into the void in a silent storm. The violence of an Imperial arrival was nowhere to be seen: no vortices of howling light, no battlemented warships of dark iron spilling from wounds torn in reality. These vessels shimmered into existence, as if melting from the backdrop of distant stars. On they came, already cutting ahead at impossible speeds, each one a sleek paragon of bladed majesty.

The *Lex* and the *Conqueror* came about first, each reacting to the new threat in their own way. The *Fidelitas Lex* lessened its thrust, slowing enough for its support squadron to keep pace. As the destroyers and escorts moved into attack formation, the *Lex* led them right into the enemy.

The *Conqueror* powered ahead, heedless of the danger of going in alone. Gun ports rattled open, and the ship's hull thrummed with the massing rise of its weapon batteries priming.

The alien vessels swooped and rolled past the Imperial warship, not even bothering to fire. The faster ships, black against the infinite black, stirred the void around the *Conqueror* without committing a single volley. The World Eaters flagship was already unleashing its rage, spitting payloads in futility, consigning ammunition to the void. The deck guns shuddered as they fired, striking nothing.

The alien vessels ghosted aside, as laser fire streaked the space between stars. More and more of the bladed warships joined the dancing formation, slicing around the surrounded *Conqueror*.

And then, with precision that could never be born of Imperial technology, they opened fire in the exact same moment, in the time it takes a human heart to give a single beat.

Hunting alone as she was, the World Eaters flagship lit up the darkness when her void shields caught fire. Pulsar streams lashed at the energy barriers, breeding violent colours across their domed surface, reflecting the flames back against the shadowed hulls of the alien raiders.

The sirens still wailed on the strategium. The deck shook, as if at the mercy of great winds.

Sarrin reviewed the ship's tactical displays. 'Shields holding,' she called.

Angron wiped his lips, grunting at the painful tics twitching the muscles in the left side of his face. When he spoke, his voice was a low, dangerous growl.

'Someone tell me why we are vomiting all our ammunition into the void and missing every single enemy ship.'

'We're firing blind.' The captain sounded distracted, hammering in commands to the servitors on her throne's keypads. 'The enemy's shields allow them to slip out of target lock.'

'At this range? These bastard eldar are on top of us!'

'The rest of our fleet is almost ready to engage from maximum range. The *Lex* is closer – she'll be with us in under a minute.' Captain Sarrin swore as her head cracked against the back of her throne. 'Shields holding,' she said again. '*Though not for much longer,*' she added in a whisper.

The primarch roared as he aimed his axe at the oculus screen. One of the raiders shivered past the screen, while the slower *Conqueror* struggled to turn and keep it in sight.

'Enough! I'm tired of shooting at ghosts! Fire the Ursus Claws!'

The *Conqueror* shuddered again, though not because of the assault raining upon its shields. From ridged battlements and armoured ports along the warship's hull, a tide of what looked like spears burst out into the void. Each of the lances was the size of a smaller escort ship in its own right, and of the dozen fired, seven punctured home in the hulls of alien vessels. Once impaled, the immense spears came active, locking to their prey's ravaged insides with magnetic fusion.

But while they were effective against conventional foes, the alien vessels were forged from synthetics beyond mere metal. Two of the ships managed to slide free, dragging their ruined carcasses away from the Imperial warship, their cores holed right through and open to space.

They were the lucky ones. The five eldar cruisers still impaled shook as they were dragged off-course, stalling in the void. Their engines burned in silent heat, but each of them remained anchored in place. The spears driven through their bodies were more than projectiles, lances launched to cripple. They were harpoons, fired to claim prey.

With malicious slowness, the *Conqueror* recalled its spears.

The lances began to ratchet back towards the vessel that fired them, dragged home on massive chains. Only the World Eaters would deploy something so barbarous and primitive on such a scale, and only the World Eaters would make such crude weaponry into something so efficient.

Link by link, the *Conqueror* dragged the five ships closer, its massive engines straining against their stagnant thrust. The other eldar raiders broke away, finding it increasingly difficult to fire at the Imperial warship now using five of their own ships as barriers to protect itself.

One ship sought to cut its flailing kindred free, focusing its weapons on the great chains reaching between the *Conqueror* and its prey. Diving close enough to fire brought it within range of the warship's laser batteries, and the eldar raider's shimmering shields collapsed in an anaemic sigh. A moment later, the vessel itself came apart under the *Conqueror*'s rage.

Angron watched all of this taking place, a smile on the slit of his lips.

'Release the hounds.'

Boarding pods spat from the *Conqueror*'s hull, crossing the short distance in the blink of an eye, and disgorging World Eaters into the bowels of the impaled eldar vessels.

'Retract the Ursus Claws that failed to strike. Khârn?'

'Sire.'

'Come with me. Let us greet these eldar.'

As HE STRANGLED the eldar warrior, Angron reflected on an unpleasant truth: perhaps Lorgar had been right.

The warrior kicked in the primarch's grip, struggling against the one hand Angron had wrapped around his throat. A tightening of the fist ended all struggle with the muted wet crackle of ruined vertebrae. He cast the corpse aside, bashing its skull open against the sloping wall.

The eldar vessel sickened him. The sight and smell of it was an assault on the senses. As soon as he'd pulled his way from the boarding pod, chainaxe revving in his hand, the sheer alien foulness of the place set his mind aching. The bizarrely sterile, spicy scent that teased the nose. The odd angles of the walls, the twisting rise and fall of the deck, and the strange un-colours that seemed formed from a hundred shades of black. Beneath it all was the sickly-sweet smell of fear, and the copper tang of vein-fluid, leaking from broken skin. Even alien vessels could smell of blood, when their bellies were sliced open to reveal what lay within. There was purity in the smell – purity and purpose. He'd been born for such things.

Splinters of alien metal clattered against his armour, tearing fresh scars along what little of his skin remained exposed. But what was a scar, really? Neither evidence of defeat, nor a medal of triumph. A scar was nothing more than a mark to show that a warrior faced his enemies at all times, never once showing his back.

Angron shoved his own men aside as he chased the retreating eldar. Their crackable armour and stick-thin limbs had a perverse grace when they moved, but it was a sickening, alien thing. One could admire a snake's lethality, but one could never be deceived into finding it beautiful, let alone worthy of emulation.

His axe fell without heed, without care, each of his merest blows slaying wherever it fell. Ahh, the Butcher's Nails hammered into the back of his head were buzzing now. His muscles burned, and his brain boiled with them. All that mattered was keeping the feeling going. Each sensation was reddened by the delicious justification of honest anger. This was what it meant to be alive. Humanity was a wrathful species, and anger vindicated all of its sins.

Nothing was as honest as rage – throughout the history of the human race, what release of emotion had ever been more worthy and true than depthless anger? A parent confronting their child's killer. A farmer defending his family against raiders. The warrior avenging the deaths of his brothers. In rage, anything was justified. It was the highest state of sentience. With rage came vindication, and with vindication came peace.

Angron charged through another cannonade of splinter gunfire. Blood bathed his neck as he felt the stinging crashes against his head. A sudden nerve-sharp coldness made him wonder, just for the shadow of a moment, if his face was blasted open to the bone. No matter. It had happened before. It would happen again.

He charged on, screaming without realising it, hearing nothing and feeling nothing beyond the disgustingly pleasant whine of the Butcher's Nails in his brain.

The wrath brought clarity. At last, with the spikes buried in the meat of his mind finally spitting their most waspish outpourings, Angron was allowed to drift, to dream, to remember.

Serenity. Never peace, no, never that.

But serenity in rage, like the calm at the heart of a storm.

THREE MONTHS BEFORE, when they'd started this Shadow Crusade, Lorgar had asked him why he mutilated his own Legion. The Butcher's Nails, of course. He meant the Butcher's Nails.

'Do you know what these things do to you? Do you know what they really do to your men?' Lorgar had asked.

Angron had nodded. He knew better than anyone.

'They let me dream,' he admitted. It was one of the few moments in his life he'd ever risked admitting such a thing. He still wasn't sure why he'd said it. 'They make it difficult to feel anything except the most fierce righteousness.' A headache thudded behind his eyes, coiling all the way down his spine. He wasn't in the right frame of mind to have such a talk, but Horus had sent them into Ultima Segmentum to work together. At this stage, so early in their journey, the cracks of tension had yet to show.

Lorgar had smiled sadly and shaken his head. 'Your Butcher's

Nails were not made for a primarch's mind, brother. They steal the healing hours of sleep from you, not letting your brain process the day's events. They also cauterise your emotions, feeding everything back into your basest urges. To kill. To fight. To slay. That is all that gives you pleasure, isn't it? These implants, crude as they are, have remapped the cartography of your mind.'

'You don't understand.' Perhaps they did do all those things, but they also brought a maddening peace that had to be chased, and the purity of absolute fury. 'They are not simply a curse, though they may seem that way to you.'

'Then enlighten me. Help me understand.'

'You want to remove them. I know you do.' He'd die before he allowed that. For all the pain, for all the twitches, tics, spasms and aches right to his bloody bones, the Butcher's Nails brought clarity and purpose. He'd never sacrifice that. He was not weak enough to even feel the temptation.

'Brother.' Lorgar had sounded disheartened then, his eyes cooled by concern. 'They cannot be removed, not without killing you. I had no intention of trying. If it is possible for us to die, you will do so with those wretched things still inside your skull.'

'You know we can die. Ferrus is dead.'

Lorgar looked away, as if staring through the metal chamber wall. 'I keep forgetting that. Events are proceeding so very quickly, are they not?'

'Hnnh. If you say so.'

'So why would you inflict this upon your Legion? Answer me that, at least. Why would you order your Techmarines to hammer these Butcher's Nails into the heads of every warrior in your service?'

Angron hadn't replied at once. He owed Lorgar no answers. But a thought took slow bloom in his mind – the idea that if any of his kindred could understand, it might be Lorgar. After all, the lord of the XVII Legion had inflicted punishments of his own upon his favoured sons. Even now, the Word Bearers in the Gal Vorbak were severed beings, existing with daemons trapped in their hearts.

'It is all I know,' he admitted at last. 'And it has never failed me. This is how I win my wars, Lorgar. You've done similar things to win yours.'

'That is true enough.'

From there, the memory grew hazy and indistinct. The degeneration followed over the course of weeks, as the two Legions suffered the rise of their masters' tension. Forty thousand warriors in Word Bearers crimson, and seventy thousand in World Eaters white, filling the decks and holds of a vast flotilla.

In the beginning, the clashes between Legion ideology had manifested in manageable ways. Word Bearers warriors had been honoured to be invited into the XII Legion's gladiatorial pit fights, and World Eaters had been offered entrance to the XVII Legion's training chambers. It was only as the primarchs' discontent filtered down to their warriors that divisions arose.

The first crack in the alliance had happened at the world of Turem, a planet loyal to distant Terra. The unified fleet had only dropped from the warp to resupply, refuel and move on deeper into enemy territory. The Legions had cast aside the pathetic excuse for planetary defences with no effort at all, and ransacked the world's refineries for everything they required.

Within a week, the Word Bearers had been ready to move on. The principal cities were put to the cleansing flame, and all icons venerating the Imperium were broken beneath ceramite boots.

But the World Eaters weren't finished. What followed were the long days and longer nights of bloodshed and butchery, as the XII Legion, led by their primarch, pursued the ragged remains of the population across the globe.

Lorgar's initial disagreement gave way to disgust, and in turn became the cold anger for which he was now becoming known. Angron couldn't be summoned, couldn't even be contacted, as he laid waste to what little life remained on the planet.

When the last World Eaters returned to their vessels, the flotilla was ten days delayed, lagging behind its targeted estimates.

Then came Garalon Prime. The first world of the Garalon System turned about its sun at the ideal distance not only to sustain human life, but to allow it to flourish. A rare jewel, a mythological Eden, Garalon Prime stood out as a beacon of Imperial compliance, providing vast numbers of men and women for the oh-so-glorious regiments of the Imperial Army.

After annihilating the modest orbital defences, Lorgar had ordered a portion of the population enslaved, and the world burned. He vowed to leave Garalon Prime as nothing more than a blackened husk, with his fleet's indentured crew and servitor contingents swollen by fresh meat.

But once more, the primarchs' desires diverged. Angron led the World Eaters down to the surface, ransacking the cities and destroying all hope of a cohesive assault. As ever, his tastes ran along bloodier lines. He had no desire to leave a charred cinder of a planet as an example to the Imperium. He would leave a grave-world, a planet of silent cities and a billion bones bleaching in the sun.

And so it continued. World after world, forcing the brothers apart through desire and ideology, bringing two of the Traitor Legions close to a civil war of their own. When Angron ordered his fleet to break from the warp to attack a fifth world, the primarchs at last came to the edge of violence.

'If you seek to stop me, Lorgar, you and your deluded Legion die first.'

'So be it, brother. We will not fire the first shot, but we will not allow you to pass us and waste lives and resources on worthless butchery.'

'It is not worthless. They are the enemy.'

'But not the true enemy.'

'All enemies are true, Lorgar.'

Strange, how Angron could remember those words with such biting clarity, but not the look upon his brother's face. It had only been a few hours ago, yet it felt as intangible now as a childhood dream.

'SIRE.'

The voice reached him from a great distance, faint through the coppery euphoria of absolute anger. Rage that deep left its taste on the tongue – something not far from fear or ecstasy, but sweeter than both.

'Sire,' the voice said again.

He turned, but for a moment he couldn't see, until he wiped the blood from his eyes.

One of his warriors stood before him, carrying a black iron chain-axe, its teeth-tracks clogged with meat.

'Sire,' the warrior said. 'It is done.'

Angron's sigh released the last of his clinging fury. In its place, pain swept back into his skull, filling the void once more. The muscles of his right hand spasmed, and he almost lost his grip on his own axe.

'You know I despise that title, even in jest. Hnnh. Back to the *Conqueror.*' He hesitated a moment, looking about himself, at the dark walls streaked with blood dappling. 'The ship is still. No movement. No shaking. No thunder.'

Khârn stood with his boot on a fallen alien's breastplate. The dead warrior's armour was sculpted in the image of the spindly, thread-thin musculature beneath.

'The battle is over.' He knew better than to ask if Angron had failed to hear the vox-net broadcasting the void battle's resolution. The primarch never took kindly to reminders of his wandering mind. 'The enemy flotilla disengaged. Our combined fleets were more than enough to break them.'

Angron watched the blood dripping from his chainaxes. 'The battle made no sense from its very beginning. What did they hope to achieve?'

'Captain Sarrin believes xenos witchery allowed them to foresee the moment that the *Conqueror* would be vulnerable, as it charged ahead of the fleet. Perhaps they sought to strike at us, kill the Legion's command structure, and run back into the night.'

'How many escaped?'

'Most of them. Once the ambush failed, they ghosted back into the void before our fleet could engage.'

Angron mused upon this, as he watched the red droplets fall from the edge of his axes. Each one bred tiny ripples in the pool of blood by his boots.

'We will chase them.'

Khârn hesitated. 'Lord Aurelian has already ordered the fleet to form up and proceed deeper into the segmentum as planned.'

'Do I look like I care what he wishes, Khârn? No one runs from the *Conqueror.*'

HE FACED THE hololithic image, doing all he could to bite back the pain and keep his temper in check. The Butcher's Nails itched and thumped with their own pulse, and concentrating through their maddening beat was a trial in itself. They never ceased, for they were never appeased. Even with bloodshed so recent, they wanted more.

In truth, so did he. The Nails' curse was to make him crave that serenity at the heart of rage.

Lorgar's image wavered with distortion, crackling in the interference of his flagship readying its warp engines.

'Need I remind you that our Legions were on the brink of battle before that pathetic alien diversion? Angron, my brother, this is our chance to reunite and let calmer thoughts lead us onward.'

'I will pursue the eldar. Your consent is irrelevant to me. Once we've hunted them down, we will rejoin your fleet.'

'Divided we fall,' Lorgar sighed. *'You are supposed to be the warrior between us, yet you ignore the most basic tenets of staying alive in battle. If you leave me with a third of my Legion at the edge of Ultramar, do you believe there will be anything left for you to rejoin after your idiotic void-dance is concluded? Do you think what remains of your World Eaters will be able to withstand a full assault if you are caught by the Thirteenth Legion? Or Russ? Or the Khan?'*

'If you fear being outnumbered, perhaps you shouldn't have sent countless thousands into the meatgrinder at Calth.' Angron sniffed back another trickling nosebleed. 'Then they would be here with you now, instead of sailing towards death in the Ultramarines stronghold. Why not call them back before they strike? Perhaps they will hear you shouting from the moral high ground.'

Both brothers stared at each other's hololithic images for a long moment. It was Angron who broke the pregnant silence, but not with another insult.

This time, he laughed. He laughed for a long time, until tears ran down the ruination of his statuesque face.

'I fail to see what is so amusing,' Lorgar spoke through the vox-crackle, more irritated than confused.

'Have you ever considered the easiest way to resolve this, my priestly brother, might be to just *come with us?'*

Lorgar said nothing.

'I am not making some foolish jest,' Angron laughed again. 'Come with us. We'll crush these alien bastards beneath our boots, and burn their fragile ships from the inside out. Tell me, do your crusaders have no wish to punish the filthy aliens that dared attack us?'

'We have a duty to perform here, Angron. A sacred duty.'

'And we will perform it. Our duty is to bleed the segmentum dry, to cleave right into the heart of the Imperium's far reaches. We will do it together. You, I and the Legions that follow us, but in the name of the gods you claim are real, let us spare *no one*. And let us begin with these foul eldar. *Vengeance,* Lorgar. Taste that word. *Vengeance.'*

And, at last, Lorgar smiled. *'Very well. We will play this game by your rules, for now.'*

CAPTAIN SARRIN HAD never tried to track an eldar fleet before. She was finding that it didn't compare to anything else in her experience.

'Warp signature?' she asked.

'Negative,' came the servitor's dead-voiced response.

'Not even from a focused auspex sweep with the coordinates I gave you?'

'Negative.'

'Well... Try again.'

'Compliance.'

She tried not to sigh. Lord Angron – her master and commander, whether he liked to be addressed as 'lord' or not – had demanded she lead the combined Legion fleet in pursuit of the enemy. The problem with that was simple: she had no idea how. The eldar hadn't run. They'd vanished.

The keen rumble of active armour drew her attention to the side of her throne. Khârn was approaching, his features masked by his crested helm as usual.

'Angron's patience is wearing thin.' He sounded calm, casual, almost resigned.

'So is mine.' Lotara narrowed her eyes. 'And I don't take kindly to threats, Khârn.'

'That is one of the many reasons you were given command of the *Conqueror*. And it was not a threat. Merely an offer of information.'

'He's asking me to chase phantoms. Eldar ships leave no warp signature, so how am I to follow them? My Mistress of Astropaths senses nothing. My Navigator can find no warp-wake to pursue. The auspex sees nothing.' She looked at Khârn, her own temper mounting. 'With the greatest respect, what does he want me to do? Fly the ship around in wide circles and hope the enemy returns?'

Khârn said nothing. He merely watched her impassively.

'I have one idea,' she confessed. Lotara reached back to tie her hair into a loose ponytail, keeping it from her eyes. 'We can still punish the eldar. Angron wishes to see the enemy dead before him. I think I can arrange that.'

'And how do you plan to do it?' Khârn asked at last. 'If you cannot chase them...'

'They attacked when the *Conqueror* moved ahead alone, outpacing the rest of the fleet. Their target was us. More specifically, their target was our primarch. When they struck, they'd been waiting for the chance to catch us while we were vulnerable, and they were willing to risk a great many lives to see Angron dead. I'm betting they'll run the risk again.'

'I believe I see where this is leading.'

'Sometimes it seems that Angron cares not from whence the blood flows. But he wants revenge, and I will give it to him. Order your warriors to battle stations, and ready your elite companies for when we prime the Ursus Claws.'

'The Devourers will undoubtedly be ready, captain.' He sounded amused, pleased with her plan. They knew one another well, for Lotara had served on the flagship as a helm officer for years before her promotion. Captain Sarrin enjoyed risks as much as any warrior in the Legion she served. 'What brings that smile to your lips, Lotara?'

'We're about to prove the great truth of the Twelfth Legion, Khârn. No one runs from the *Conqueror*.'

✠ ✠ ✠

THEY SAILED ALONE, deeper into the void, farther from distant Terra and away from their own fleet. Lotara didn't know when the aliens would strike again, only that they would. Eleven hours into their sedate drift into isolation, she was still on the strategium, reclining in her throne and staring into the reaches of space. She ardently refused to give rest to her aching, bleary eyes. Not while there was a job to do.

'*Come on,*' she whispered, little realising the words had become a murmured mantra. '*Come on.*'

'Captain Sarrin?'

Lotara turned to her first officer. Ivar Tobin wore the same crisp white uniform as his captain, and looked considerably less tired. The only difference in their attire was the red palm print in the centre of her chest – a rare mark of honour awarded to the Legion's most worthy servants. She'd earned this accolade from the Eighth Captain himself upon her ascension to the *Conqueror's* command throne.

'Something to report, Tobin?'

'All auspex tracking shows nothing but dead space.' He spoke again after a brief pause, unable to keep the concern from his voice. 'You should sleep, ma'am.'

She grinned. 'And you should watch your mouth. This is my ship as much as the primarch's, and I'll not sail into the enemy's clutches with my eyes closed. You know me better than that.'

'When did you last sleep, captain?'

Rather than admit the truth, she chose to hide behind a lie. Perhaps it would make Tobin leave her alone. 'I'm not sure.'

'Then I will tell you. You last slept forty-one hours ago, ma'am. Would you not rather be well-rested when we engage the xenos?'

'Your concern is noted, Officer Tobin. Back to your duties, if you please.'

He snapped a sharp salute. 'As you command.'

Lotara breathed out, low and slow. She stared at the stars panning past the oculus, and let the hunt continue.

SIXTEEN HOURS LATER, once the *Conqueror* was well and truly out of range of its support fleet, the bridge sirens began to wail again.

Lotara sat forwards in her throne, smiling despite her bone-aching weariness.

'Let's try this again, shall we? Voxmaster Kejic?'

'Aye, captain.'

'Open a focused pulse transmission to the largest eldar vessel, if you please.'

'Opening, ma'am. Priming now. Transmission ready.'

Lotara rose from her throne, moving to grip the handrail at the edge of her raised dais. 'This is Captain Lotara Sarrin of the Twelfth Legion warship *Conqueror* to the miserable alien fleet ghosting into existence across our bow.' She smiled, and felt her heartbeat quicken. This was what she lived for, and why she'd been given command of such a mighty vessel in the first place. Let the legionaries fight with axe and sword. Her arena was the void, and the ships that danced within it. 'I wish to offer congratulations on the last mistake you will ever make.'

To her surprise, a voice crashed back over the vox. Flawed by incompatible communication systems, the words barely emerged from a tide of churning noise.

'*Mon-keigh filth. You will bleed for the thousands of sins your mongrel breed has committed in its pathetic lifespan.*'

'If you wish to kill us, alien, you are more than welcome to try.'

'*Dog-blooded mon-keigh. It is a miracle you mastered even this crude speech. Your mutilated prince with the pain engine inside his skull must die this night. He will never be given the chance to become the Blood God's son.*'

'Enough of your religious madness.' She was smiling now, not bothering to hide her malicious amusement at their arrogance.

'History will be so much cleaner when you are erased from its pages.'

'Brave talk from a race on the edge of extinction,' she replied. 'Why not come closer? Bring those pretty ships in range of my talons.'

With a shriek of wounded noise that may or may not have had organic origins, the eldar severed the link.

'A charming species,' Lotara gripped the handrail.

'Enemy fleet inbound,' Tobin called from across the strategium.

'Deck Officer Tobin, prime everything we've got – all gun ports open, all weapons live, all engines burning hot. Tactical hololithics are to update in two-second pulses to compensate for the enemy's speed. Gunnery, fix primary targets by threat level and assign secondary targets by range. Void shields to full layer extension. Helm, accelerate to attack speed, and be ready to kill thrust with inertial resistors when we fire the Ursus Claws. All stations, status report. Deck officer.'

'Aye, ma'am.'

'Tactical.'

'Hololithics live, captain.'

'Gunnery prime, secondary and tertiary stations.'

'Aye.'

'Aye.'

'Ready, ma'am.'

'Void shields.'

'Compliance.'

'Helm.'

'Aye, captain.'

Lotara sat back in her ornate throne, feeling all traces of tiredness wash away with her racing heartbeat. She keyed in the eight-rune code to activate shipwide vox.

'This is Captain Sarrin. All crew to battle stations. We are engaging the enemy.'

✠ ✠ ✠

THE CONQUEROR CLEAVED through the alien flotilla, broadsides booming, stinging lashes of enemy fire dancing in mad colours across the abused void shields. This time, the warship focused its hunt on a single target, chasing it down with the lumbering inevitability of a mammoth's charge.

The enemy flagship was a contoured thing of arched wings and curving blades, all reaching from a lengthy, ridged hull – a torture device, given size and power enough to sail the stars. It rolled with insidious grace, dancing aside from the *Conqueror*'s dive. In its wake, its knife-winged support ships unleashed their crackling fire against the World Eaters warship's shields. They sparked with unnatural fire, glowing as bright as Terra's own sun, and burst with a brutal lack of ceremony.

The *Conqueror* dived on, heedless, uncaring. It rammed one alien vessel aside, crashing into it amidships and sending the shattered hulk spinning away into the void. The raider vented air in a long, final breath, and spilled its crew into space as though they were drops of blood running from a wound.

Still, the *Conqueror* dived. Its armour earned new scars, new burns, new injuries carved along the dense plating by the cutting kiss of alien lasers.

The enemy flagship was running now. It recognised the warship's intent: not to fight off the entire fleet, but to ignore the lesser craft in favour of crippling the only one that truly mattered. With impossible agility, the eldar cruiser banked and rolled away again, boosting away from its bulky pursuer.

The *Conqueror*'s engines roared white-hot, wide open beast-mouths screaming into the silence of space. As the warship's immense shadow eclipsed the fleeing raider, Captain Lotara Sarrin gripped the armrests of her shuddering throne, and through the smoke streaming across the strategium, she shouted a single command.

'Fire the Ursus Claws!'

No wide dispersal of fire, this time. No attempts to puncture several enemy vessels and separate the boarding forces. The *Conqueror* fired all eight of its forward-arc spears. Every one of them struck home, punching right into the body of the nimble enemy flagship. For a single second, it jerked the *Conqueror* ahead, before the Imperial ship's thrusters asserted their greater, more stubborn strength.

Like a bear gripping a wolf, the *Conqueror* began to pull, to crush, to heave. The immense chains ratcheted back, clanking link by clanking link, hauling the eldar flagship closer.

Boarding pods were already spilling between the ships, pinpricking into the enemy's hull.

Lotara heard two voices crackle over the vox. Two brothers, fighting together for the first time.

'*We are in*,' Lorgar voxed. '*The smell of these wretched inhumans is toxic to my senses.*'

Angron replied with a grunt. '*Follow me, brother.*'

FEW WERE THE archives that could claim a legitimate record of two primarchs battling side by side. Even in an age of war and wonder, it was the rarest of events.

Angron perceived all his actions through the wrath-haze of the buzzing Butcher's Nails. In those long moments of berserk clarity, he saw his brother fighting for the first time.

They couldn't have been less alike in how they moved, and how they killed. Lorgar advanced in slow, driving steps, gripping his spiked crozius mace in two hands, and letting it fall in wide, sweeping arcs. Each strike tolled long and loud, as if some great temple bell heralded every death blow. When the maul crashed into packs of the slender, shrieking eldar, it sent their broken forms flying aside. These unfortunate wretches impacted against the ship's curved walls, and slid down in the aftermath, like a horde of ruined puppets with cut strings.

In contrast to Lorgar's lucid, meticulous fury, Angron was lost to his emotions and the mechanical tendrils vibrating inside his brain. His twin axes, Gorefather and Gorechild, fell in frenzied, hacking chops, ripping his foes apart, killing through decapitation as often as by cleaving the enemies in twain. Blood misted around him in gouting sprays, flecking his bronze armour until it became a crimson akin to Lorgar's.

As the brothers advanced through a vast domed chamber, Lorgar drew alongside the Eater of Worlds.

'You should just paint it red, brother.'

Angron's focus was on the flow of blood, the rending of meat and the breaking of bone. It took him several seconds to tune back to being able to comprehend others' words.

'What?'

'Your armour,' Lorgar paused, turning to hammer his crozius down at an eldar carrying a spear. He pounded the warrior almost flat, and crushed the remains beneath his boot. 'Your armour. Just paint it red.'

Angron felt a grin peeling his lips back from his replacement iron teeth. His brother was far from the first person to speak those words, but the fact Lorgar had actually been serious earned him a chorus of fraternal laughter.

The World Eater kicked another eldar aside, and bisected a third with a backhanded swing of his chainaxe. He saw Lorgar at his side, slaying three aliens with a single swing.

'You kill well now,' Angron said. Saliva stringed between his teeth. Blood ran in hot, slow trickles from both nostrils, and his right eye was weeping red, making a mess of his cheek. 'You've changed, Lorgar.'

The Word Bearer took the compliment with silent grace, killing at his brother's side, but he could only hold his tongue so long.

'Those implants are killing you.'

Angron roared in the same moment, surging ahead, butchering his way down the angular corridor and painting the walls red with the chemical stink of alien blood.

'I know you hear me, brother,' Lorgar said quietly, into the vox. 'Those implants are killing you.'

Angron didn't even look back. He was a blur of gore-streaked bronze armour, both toothed axes rising and falling in efficient, rhythmless murder.

Rather than defend the ship in hopeless desperation, the eldar captain awaited his uninvited guests in the comfort of the bridge. Angron came through the door first, after sawing through the xenos metal bulkhead with the snarling edges of Gorechild and Gorefather.

A withering hail of splinter projectiles clattered and clashed against his ceramite armour, blasting chips and scraps from the war-plate. Venomous barbs sank into what little of his flesh was exposed, but Angron ignored the poison pumping through his veins, trusting his genhanced physiology to purify his blood.

Oh, how the Butcher's Nails sang. They pounded at the core of his skull, as if drilling deeper into the brain-meat to avoid the caress of eldar venom.

He endured this savage hail of fire, and amidst the second volley, he levelled his axe at the figure seated upon the throne of sculpted alien bone.

Lorgar came through after him, a tepid disregard written plain across his golden features. The merest raising of his gloved hand formed a kinetic barrier around them both, psychically shielding them from the hail-fall of eldar splinter shells.

'Have you ever set foot on the *Nightfall*?' Lorgar asked, his calm eyes drinking in the foul scene. Corpse pits ringed the central throne, with the husks of men and aliens impaled on unclean spikes. Hooked chains dangled from the ceiling, many of them ripe with stinking fruit, in the form of inhuman bodies hanging without limbs or skin.

Angron could barely reply. Wracking twitches pulled his features tight, and forced his fingers to gun the triggers of his chainaxes in muscular spasms.

'No. Never been on the Eighth Legion flagship.'

Lorgar's lip curled. 'This... This looks like Curze's bedchamber.'

The World Eater crashed his axes together. 'Let this be *done*, brother.'

'As you wish.'

The primarchs raised their weapons, and charged as one. First, the white-masked wielders of klaive swords. Angron sawed his path through them, while Lorgar hammered them aside with his maul, or sent them reeling with bursts of psychic fire. For the first time in either of their lives, the two brothers fought in unity with another being. Angron turned, disembowelling a dark-armoured bladesman seeking to attack Lorgar from behind. In turn, the Bearer of the Word protected his blood-spattered kin, deflecting an eldar's thrust with his maul's head, and killing the warrior on the backswing.

The union was an effort to control and maintain, for it didn't come naturally to either of them. But they held it until only one other soul remained alive on the bridge.

'Any last words?' Lorgar asked. The ship shook around them with greater force now. The Ursus Claws had bitten too deep. The *Conqueror* was pulling its prey apart purely by the strength of its grip.

Angron staggered to his brother's side, drooling and dizzy – a flawed statue of the perfect warrior, ruined by mistreatment. As bloodstained as they both were, they could almost have been twins.

The alien prince was a thing clad in baroque, ceremonial armour – a creature of angelically consumptive features and the foul stench of impure blood beneath oiled skin. The eldar lord's final words hissed into the air, spat from pale lips.

'Two mon-keigh god-princes. There was only supposed to be one. The one to become the Blood God's son. The pain engines bend the soul to the Eightfold Path. That path leads to the Skull Throne.'

'The Blood God's son...' Lorgar's focus drifted to Angron, as the possibilities played out behind his soothing eyes. 'It cannot be.'

Angron raised his axes. The raider didn't move a muscle.

'Wait.' Lorgar reached for Angron's shoulder. 'He said–'

But the axes fell, and the alien captain's head rolled free.

THREE DAYS LATER, the *Conqueror* limped back to its fleet. While its hull had sustained extensive damage, most of it was superficial. The real losses had been in terms of crew; fully half the indentured serfs and trained mortal adepts were dead. On a ship of such grand size, the several thousand that remained alive were almost counted a skeleton crew.

Of the three thousand warriors Angron took with him aboard the flagship, barely a third had returned. The eldar reaped a bloody toll in their defeat, and the XII Legion's funerary rites lasted day and night, while the ship sailed back to its kindred. The airlocks opened and closed, silent maws yawning into the void, exhaling the shrouded bodies of slain World Eaters and crew.

Lorgar made ready to depart the *Conqueror*, and bid farewell to his brother on the embarkation deck.

'It was good to purge some of the bad blood between us,' Angron said. To his credit, he kept his rebellious muscles from twitching, no matter how the Butcher's Nails stabbed at his nervous system.

'For now,' Lorgar agreed. 'Let neither of us pretend it will last forever.'

Angron wiped his bleeding nose on the back of his hand. 'You said something on the enemy ship. Something about the Nails.'

Lorgar mused for a moment. 'I do not recall.'

'I do. You said the implants were killing me.'

Lorgar shook his head, offering his kindest, most sincere smile. In his mind, he heard the eldar reaver's words once more. *The one to become the Blood God's son. The pain engines bend the soul to the Eightfold Path. That path leads to the Skull Throne.*

'I was wrong, and my concern was foolish. You have survived this long. You will endure into the future.'

'You are lying to me, Lorgar.'

'For once, Angron, I am not. Your Butcher's Nails will never kill you, I am certain of that. If I could ease some of the pain you must be suffering, then I would, but they cannot be removed, and tampering with them is likely to kill you just as quickly as removing them. They are as much a part of you now as the weapons you wield and the scars you carry.'

'If you are not lying, you are at least hiding something.'

'I am hiding many things.' Lorgar spoke through a smile, deceitless in his regret. 'We will speak of them in time. They are not secrets, merely truths that cannot bloom until the moment is right, and the pieces of this great puzzle begin to fall into place. There is much I do not yet understand myself.'

The World Eaters primarch bared his teeth in a metallic smile. It contained nothing of warmth.

'Back to your ship then, crusader. It was a pleasure to shed blood with you, while it lasted.'

Lorgar nodded, not looking back over his shoulder as he ascended the ramp into his gunship.

'Farewell, brother.'

Angron watched the gunship leave the docking bay, and streak away towards the *Fidelitas Lex*.

'Khârn,' he said quietly. The equerry moved forwards from his master's honour guard, who stood silently in their hulking Terminator armour.

'Yes?'

'Lorgar has changed, yet he still keeps his secrets beneath a forked tongue. What is the name of the Word Bearer you duel with?'

'Argel Tal. The Seventh Captain.'

'You have known him long, yes?'

'Decades. We fought together in three compliances. Why do you ask?'

The primarch didn't answer at once. He reached up to scratch the back of his head. The flesh felt raw, swollen. The headache was worse than usual, coming to a crest. He could feel a trickle of blood worming a warm trail down his neck, running from his ear.

'We have many months of difficult unity with the Word Bearers ahead of us. Remain vigilant, Khârn. That is all I ask.'

THE TWO WARRIORS duelled the very next night: the sons of the crusader and the gladiator facing each other in the pit, chainaxe against power sword. Argel Tal's crimson war-plate was undecorated, missing the scrolls of faith and devotion he wore in battle. Khârn's white ceramite was similarly unadorned, but for the chains binding his weapons to his arms.

Both warriors ignored the cheers and cries of their comrades at the pit's edge. Helmetless, they duelled in the sand, blade cracking against blade.

When their weapons locked again, the two warriors squared against each other, boots grinding back through the sand as they sought leverage. Their faces were inches apart, breathing acid-stinking breath as they struggled to break the deadlock. Argel Tal's voice betrayed a curious duality, his twin souls speaking through one mouth.

'You are slow tonight, Khârn. What steals your attention?'

The World Eater redoubled his efforts, muscles straining to throw his enemy back. Argel Tal responded in kind, ichor forming stalactites along his upper teeth.

'Not slow,' Khârn forced the words through a sneer. 'Difficult... to fight... *two* of you.'

Argel Tal gave a toothy grin. As he drew breath to speak, it was all the edge Khârn needed. The World Eater leaned into a turn, letting his adversary overbalance. The revving chainaxe howled through the air, only to crash against the Word Bearer's golden sword edge yet again.

'Not slow,' he chuckled breathlessly, showing his exhaustion as plainly as Khârn showed his own. 'But not fast enough.'

The accursed implants sent a bolt of jagged pain sawing down the World Eater's spine. Khârn felt one eye flicker, and his left arm spasm in ungainly response. The Butcher's Nails were threatening to take hold now. He disengaged, backing away with his axe raised, taking a moment to spit out the acidic saliva brewing beneath his tongue. Chains rattled against his armour as he came *en garde*.

The chains were a personal tradition, spread even among the other Legions after their popularity had escaped beyond the fighting pits of the World Eaters. Sigismund, First Captain of the Imperial Fists, had taken to the custom with his usual zeal, binding his knightly weapons to his wrists on dense black chains. He'd made an impressive name for himself here in the bowels of the *Conqueror*, duelling with the XII Legion's finest warriors late in the Great Crusade. The Black Knight, they called him, in honour of his prowess, his nobility and his personal heraldry.

The Flesh Tearer was another to earn great glory in the World Eaters pits – Amit, a captain of the Blood Angels, who'd fought with the same savagery and brutality as his hosts. Before Isstvan, Khârn had counted them both among his oath-brothers. When the time came to lay siege to Terra and bring the palace walls tumbling down, he would regret slaying those two warriors above all others.

'Focus,' Argel Tal growled. 'You are drifting, and your skill fades with your attention.'

Khârn disengaged with a twist of his axe blade, and attacked in a series of vicious, howling cuts. Argel Tal wove back, dodging rather than risk missing a block.

The Word Bearer caught the last strike on his sword's edge, and locked Khârn in place again. Both warriors stood unmoving as they pushed against one another with equal force.

'The war to come,' said Khârn. 'Does it not feel ignoble to you? Dishonourable?'

'Honour?' Argel Tal's twin voice was throaty with amusement. 'I do not care about honour, cousin. I care about the truth, and I care about victory.'

Khârn drew breath to reply, just as the chamber's vox crackled live. *'Captain Khârn? Captain Argel Tal?'*

Both warriors froze. Argel Tal's stillness was born of inhuman control over his body. Khârn was motionless, but not entirely still – he trembled with tics from the Butcher's Nails cooling in the back of his skull.

'What is it, Lotara?' he asked.

'We're receiving word from the fleet. Lord Aurelian is sending a mass-pulse from all Word Bearers vessels, focused by the Lex. *Kor Phaeron's armada has just launched its assault on Calth.'* She paused, taking a breath. *'The war in Ultramar has begun.'*

Khârn deactivated his axe and stood in silence.

Argel Tal chuckled, a threatening lion's purr in his daemonic twin-chorus. 'It is time, cousin.'

Khârn smiled, though the expression held nothing of amusement. The Butcher's Nails still hummed in the meat of his mind, flicking out their pulses of pain and irrational anger.

'Now the Shadow Crusade begins, while Calth burns.'

WARMASTER

John French

'*Warmaster…*'

The word hung in the silence as it left Horus's lips. Beyond the high crystalflex windows, the light of distant stars hung in sickly folds of gas and dust. Armoured and enthroned, the Primarch of the XVI Legion gazed into the shadows as though waiting for an answer.

'The title is heavy around my neck. Horus. Lupercal. Father, son, friend, enemy – all are lost beneath the weight of that one word.'

He turned his head, looking to the black iron arms of the throne. His eyes moved over the bronze of a mace as tall as a mortal man. It was called *Worldbreaker*, and he had accepted it from his father's hand along with the title of Warmaster and command of the Great Crusade. His gaze came to rest upon the eagle-head pommel. A ghost of a smile touched his lips.

'Our father never spoke of what it meant, only the limits of its authority. A dangerous word to leave unqualified. Perhaps he intended me to discover its meaning. Perhaps he did not care what it meant, as long as it freed him from us, his sons. Perhaps he did not know what it would mean for *his* Imperium.'

Horus raised his hand, and a column of hololithic light filled the air before the throne. The shapes of men and women formed in the grainy projection – twisting, shouting, dying, their pleas and screams looping over and over as the thunder of bolter fire rolled through the silence.

'He knows now.'

He nodded to himself, the reflected light of the hololith flickering across the liquid black of his eyes.

'The fire is lit, and all that was is cast to the wind. We are committed – he and I, my brothers and our Legions. All humanity's futures bound together in this circle of blood. We are all the storm now. The Imperium will fall and rise by my hand. Or fall, and fall, and fall.'

Slowly he stood, his armour whispering and clicking. He gestured again, and more cones of cold light surrounded him, turning with images of blind faces. Some screamed, with words, blood and smoke spewing forth from their mouths, while others droned on in their dead, monotonous voices. Horus inclined his head, listening.

'All is blood and the screams of change. Anarchy is this age's king. We fall apart and this war slips from our fingers to spin into oblivion,' he said, his voice clear even over the cacophony.

Horus turned, watching the holographic recordings bloom around him, and the throne room danced with the ghost-light of a thousand messages.

'Isstvan was supposed to burn in silence so that our war could be won before it ever truly began. The Angel's wings were to be broken at my feet. And still failures come tumbling one over the other. And on, and on.'

He paused, his eyes fixed upon the image of a shrunken astropath.

'Calth burned, yet our brother lives. Roboute. Wise Roboute.

Roboute with his scratching quills, his plans and his hope. Too understanding, too strong. Too damned *perfect!* Horus let out a long breath, and turned back to his empty throne. 'I wish he was with us.'

With a flick of his bladed fingers, the throng of images vanished and silence flowed back with the returning shadows. Horus shook his head, his eyes still fixed upon the throne.

'You would say that I listened too much to Alpharius and Lorgar – that a war fought with deceit is doomed to fail. Perhaps you would be right. The Hydra does not see all, and now his blindness places a knife at his own back. Corax would not have made such an error.'

He gave a mirthless laugh.

'Strange is it not, that so many I wish beside me stand against me, while at my back are only the flawed and damaged. I am a master of broken monsters.'

Slowly he began to circle the edge of the great hololithic table, the sound of his footsteps lost in the echoing silence.

'I cannot control them or their sons, and they know it. Mortarion and Perturabo and the rest, they can all feel it. They all know that this war is no longer something that can be guided, only ridden out. But they never understood me, not truly, and they understand less with each passing second. They doubt. They think that I have lost my way. I can see it in their hearts – the pettiness, the pride, the seeds of ruin driving them on, feeding the tempest. With such creatures must I remake the future!'

He stopped again at the foot of the throne, and reached out. His hand closed over *Worldbreaker*'s haft. With casual ease he raised it up, so that the chamber's thin light caught every dent and scar on the polished metal.

'A thousand battles. Ten thousand. Ten times ten times *ten* thousand, to bring about the new age. All of the certainties of the past torn down, all the beliefs that made them turned to ashes. War on every front, stretched across time until none can know when the final blow will come. There is no disaster, for all disasters serve me alone. The storm rises only so that the thunderbolt may fall.'

He looked down at the throne again, shaking his head sadly. His arm relaxed and *Worldbreaker* rested at his side. His gaze shifted, as though he were looking at something beyond what lay in front of him.

'No other would have dared this. Not even you. Perhaps that is why our father chose me. Perhaps that was his only moment of honesty.' Then his gaze focused and hardened, black eyes like reflective pools in the face of an unforgiving king.

Upon the arm of the throne, the skull of Ferrus Manus stared back at Horus with empty sockets that had once been eyes. A thin fracture-web of cracks ran across the perfect dome of the slain primarch's crown, spiralling back to a splintered pit in its temple. Even reduced to polished bone, the skull still seemed to radiate strength and defiance.

'It does not matter how the galaxy burns, only that it does. Warmaster – that is what it means, my brother. The strength to do what must be done.'

KRYPTOS

Graham McNeill

ATOMIC SKIES BURNED with violent electromagnetic flares, arcing up from ruined tesla-coil energy stacks as the dying machines of Cavor Sarta screamed in terror. The air was filled with the static burr of unimaginably complex mechanisms being tortured, a planet-wide screeching of noospheric dissolution.

Sprawling ore-fields ran molten and mountainous refineries slumped as the volcanic hearts that had empowered their industry now destroyed them. Continent-sized assembly yards and manufactoria were reduced to scrap metal in the blink of an eye by nuclear detonations, and construction hangars that once rang with the relentless hammering of worthy endeavour now echoed to the beat of a far darker drum.

Loyal forges that had once helped build the Imperium of Man were now enslaved to monstrous, inhuman masters who sought to tear it down. Thoroughfares of hard-won knowledge wrested from Old Night now echoed with yells of shouting soldiers, random barks of gunfire and the pounding tread of hybrid creatures wrought from wormflesh and iron.

The Venomous Thorns Chapter of the Word Bearers had brought war to Cavor Sarta, a war the fief-world of the Mechanicum had lost before the first shots were fired. A nameless, unseen foe that struck without warning and left only carnage in its wake had isolated Cavor Sarta from the Imperial strongholds of Heroldar and Thramas. Striking from the shadows of the great asteroid belt around Tsagualsa, this nameless enemy had crippled Cavor Sarta even before the Word Bearers and their billions-strong armies of mortals had dropped through the nuclear firestorms burning the sky.

No fear is as great as the fear of the unknown, and the panic that held Cavor Sarta tight in its grip had already done more than any orbital barrage in weakening the defenders' resolve to fight. The forge world fell in six days, its limitless resources perverted to serve strange alchemy and nightmarish purpose. Forbidden vaults were reopened and buried sciences from the age of Iron and Gold were dragged from dusty tombs to rush hideous war-machines of warp sorcery into production.

Cavor Sarta screamed as it was reborn in a hideous new form.

It would go on screaming until its towering stacks burned out and the fiery core at its heart was cold and lifeless.

The Imperial world was dying, but its death did not go unobserved.

THE CREATURE MOVED with a rolling, mechanised gait that was at once graceful and unnatural. It had an odd number of legs, which offended Nykona Sharrowkyn's sensibilities. Concealed in the shadows of a collapsed smelting tower, his body was utterly immobile, his armour's emissions and the vents of his compact jump pack kept below the threshold of detection by custom-designed stealth systems.

He was as invisible as it was possible for one of Corax's sons to be.

Sharrowkyn scanned the ruins of the wrecked forge for more of the creatures, even though he knew it was alone. The forge was little

more than smouldering scrap metal, blasted brickwork and unbend-
able girders twisted around like steel wool. Magnetic squalls swirled
like miniature dust devils, and the atmospherics were lousy with
echoing machine screams and random detonations of discarded
munitions. Violet light spilled down through the skeletal steelwork
of the roof, and drifts of radioactive shavings fogged his visor.

The creature paused by the wreckage of a pressing machine, its
burn-scar face twisting on a neck of metallic tendons and wet gristle.
Implanted ocular orbs glowed in a triangular pattern, pulsing briefly
as a bray of sound bellowed from the cavernous vox-lungs buried in
the flesh of its chest. Vaguely simian, its upper body was massively
muscled with cultured slabs of meat and pistons, coiled magnetic
enhancers and heaving chem-shunts. Its head was a pyramid-shaped
horror of steel tumours and bloated flesh. Its broad back bristled
with a number of missile pods, though Sharrowkyn had never seen
anything quite like the warheads that jutted from the launch tubes.
Each forearm carried a wide-bore weapon, one a hissing flame-
lance, the other some form of harpoon-cannon.

It moved by means of three over-articulated limbs that writhed
like tentacles, and Wayland had christened these monsters ferrovores, thanks to their habit of devouring mouthfuls of scrap metal
to excrete as exo-armour plates. They were fast, faster than anything
else they had encountered in the three days since their stealthy
insertion onto the planet's surface.

Penetrating the ruins of Cavor Sarta had been child's play. Even
a novice Raven Guard could have evaded detection. The armies
that had taken this planet were rough and unprofessional, dancing around revel fires of vast promethium lakes. Mushroom clouds
of exploding ordnance shook the ground on an hourly basis, and
Sharrowkyn's greatest fear had not been capture, but getting caught
in the blast of an accidental detonation.

Both Sharrowkyn and Wayland had cause to hate the foe that had conquered Cavor Sarta, but too many lives were at stake to risk the mission for hate's sake. Since his youth as a freedom fighter in the tunnels of Deliverance, Sharrowkyn had learned to use hatred, to keep every breath of it bottled up ready for release, but Wayland's Legion wasn't like the Raven Guard. Sabik Wayland was a warrior of heart, and that thought almost made Sharrowkyn smile at the irony.

He itched to bring his needle-carbine to bear, but Wayland had elected to take the shot.

A cascade of scorched metal and a billow of irradiated dust billowed around the tentacle-limbs of the ferrovore, and it screeched with abominable satisfaction as it inhaled great lungfuls of metallic debris. It moved onwards, stomping through the forge temple with a grotesque, peristaltic motion. The creature was almost at the edge of the manufactory, and Wayland had yet to shoot.

'Is something wrong?' he said over the encrypted vox-link. 'Shall I take the shot?'

'Can you compensate for the radioactive cross-wind, or the flux variables inherent in the magnetocline layers?' asked Wayland. 'Is your weapon linked to your nervous system to better compensate for biological variance?'

'Just take the damn shot.'

'When I'm good and ready,' said Wayland, and Sharrowkyn heard a hiss of augmented machine exhalation.

A bloom of burning violet fire shot skywards behind the far wall of the manufactory, and a rolling wash of hot wind surged through the ruins. Sharrowkyn tasted strontium and potassium chloride in the fallout, a chem-silo's destruction or a buried reactor stack reaching critical mass.

Sharrowkyn's armour registered lethal levels of radioactivity, but nothing to trouble him. Though his armour was a patchwork creation that would either horrify the Shadowmasters of the Ravenspire or earn him a commendation, it was proof against such toxicity.

The echo of Wayland's pulse round was lost in the crackling rush of air sucked into the vortex of combusting gases and radioactive meltdown, but Sharrowkyn heard it as clearly as an ice-drill on a frozen promethium face. The ferrovore slumped to the ground as its sinuous legs folded beneath it. The furnace light of its eyes faded and it let out a long wheeze of chemical breath.

Even as Sharrowkyn heard the clatter of a ratcheting bolt action, he was moving.

He ghosted from cover, vaulting onto a tumbled mass of twisted metal. His practised eye knew exactly where to place his weight, and he leapt from solid ground to solid ground, finally springing onto an angled roof girder. He landed lightly and sprinted up the flattened edge of the fallen beam.

'Four seconds,' said Wayland.

Sharrowkyn didn't answer and triggered the jets of his jump pack, powering over the wide vent chute of a pulverised milling machine in a fiery arc.

'Two seconds.'

Sharrowkyn unclipped a fist-sized device the size of a melta charge from his belt before he slammed down onto the broad shoulders of the ferrovore. The red glow of its eyes swelled, but before it could do more than twitch its limbs, he clamped the device to the base of its neck. Injector needles pistoned into the creature's neck, and the device gave out a piercing binaric whine.

'One.'

The ferrovore reared up and Sharrowkyn was thrown from its back. He turned his fall into a controlled descent, twisting his body and spinning his carbine around himself. He landed lightly, with the weapon's hand-crafted stock pulled into his shoulder. His finger put pressure on the trigger, but trained reflexes kept him from tightening too far.

The ferrovore's red eyes burned into him, but its missile pods remained sheathed and its weaponised arms hung limp at its sides.

Sharrowkyn let out a breath.

Wayland emerged from his position, hidden in the wide air vent that cut through the forge's one remaining wall. His heavily augmented bolter was slung casually over one shoulder, as though he'd just brought down a grazing herbivore and not an enemy battle servitor.

'You cut that one fine,' said Wayland.

'If you hadn't waited so long to shoot, I wouldn't have had to travel so far.'

Wayland shrugged. His battleplate was black like Sharrowkyn's, but where the Raven Guard's was stripped down and compact, Wayland's was bulky and enhanced with multiple augmetics. Where Sharrowkyn's shoulder bore the white raven of his Legion – albeit obscured by ionised particles of dust – Wayland's bore the silvered gauntlet of the Iron Hands. One of Wayland's arms was a bionic replacement, and much of his internal biology had been replaced in the wake of injuries suffered at the hand of the Phoenician himself.

'I anticipated that detonation of chemical and radioactive elements, and reasoned I could use the thermal and electromagnetic wash to cover my shot,' said Wayland. 'I calculated that you could still reach the ferrovore in time.'

'I wish you'd stop calling them that,' said Sharrowkyn. 'Giving things like this names reeks of permanence.'

'How little you know,' said Wayland, shouldering his rifle and clambering onto the immobile form of the ferrovore. 'Bestowing a name upon a machine allows me to know it. If I know it, I can understand it. If I can understand it I can overcome it. Now, hurry up and get on before the creature's cognitive architecture burns through the spinal block inhibitor.'

Sharrowkyn swallowed his distaste and climbed onto the ferrovore's back alongside Wayland, using the growths of excreted

armour plating to haul himself into the oozing cavity between its
missile pods and rotten-meat back. Wayland's gauntlet extruded a
long spike of silvered metal, and Sharrowkyn instinctively winced
at the reflections it gave off.

Wayland rammed the spike into the base of the ferrovore's spine,
and though Sharrowkyn could see nothing outwardly different, he
felt the tremors wracking the cybernetic creature's body as it fought
to retain dominance over its control functions.

Wayland nodded and said, 'It's ours.'

IT HAD BEEN a plan of desperation to pair Sharrowkyn with Wayland, but so far the Iron Hand had acquitted himself well. His
stealth abilities were sorely lacking, but he more than made up
for that with his more specialised skills. Sharrowkyn and Wayland were as different in expertise and outlook as it was possible
to imagine, but they had one shared experience that united them
with a bond that would only ever be appreciated by a handful of
Legiones Astartes.

They were survivors of Isstvan V.

Cut off from his primarch and his battle-brothers, Sharrowkyn
escaped the Dropsite Massacre in an Iron Hands Stormbird, one
of only a handful that had blasted its way through the firestorm
of rockets. Sharrowkyn was near death, torn up by traitor bolter
shells that had penetrated his war-plate with sickening ease. Sabik
Wayland had dragged his wounded body onto the Stormbird and
screamed at the pilot to lift off. Even a hair's breadth from death,
Sharrowkyn had felt the hammering impacts on the armoured skin
of the Stormbird as it fought to escape the disaster.

Months of healing followed, though Sharrowkyn remembered
little save blurred memories of a gravel-voiced form looming over
him in the apothecarion.

'You will not die, Raven Guard,' the voice had said. 'Do not let the weakness of flesh betray you, not when you have survived so much. I took a blow from the Phoenician, yet I live. You will live too.'

He remembered the authority of the voice, and Sharrowkyn hadn't dared disobey. He heard the bitterness, but hadn't understood it until he learned that Ferrus Manus was dead, slain by the same hand that had wounded Sabik Wayland.

In the wake of the disastrous counter-attack against the Warmaster, the Iron Hands sought a way to retaliate. Despite the devastating loss of their primarch, the sons of Medusa were combat-ready within a day of rendezvousing with following forces that had managed to evade the Warmaster's trap.

Over the next six months, the fragmented Iron Hands task force harried enemy fleets in a manner that would have made Corax proud. Attacking, withdrawing and attacking again, they struck wherever an opportunity presented itself. Like a punch-drunk pugilist who just won't stay down, the Iron Hands kept coming back to the fight.

And now they had a worthy target for their rage.

BY THE TIME the Imperial forces regrouped to face the threat in the Thramas sector, it was already too late for Cavor Sarta. Its vast resources were already in enemy hands, and the traitors were already coordinating their considerable assets to pluck the remaining forge worlds from the Martian priesthood's grip. Imperial commanders were horrified at the masterful coordination displayed, and sought to break intercepted astropathic transmissions flowing between captured worlds and the traitor fleets.

Such methods were a tried and tested means of thwarting enemy plans, but something was very wrong. The transmissions were encrypted of course, but the Thramas Mechanicum boasted the finest cipher-breakers, and the carrier-codes were quickly unravelled. But instead of transmissions revealing fleet movements, dispositions and strengths, the revealed text was a garbled hash of corrupt binary woven into an unidentified strain of linguistic communication that conformed to no known language family that could be translated.

Only after the capture of a traitor flagship did further information come to light. The vessel's warp engines had failed as it fled an aborted ambush, and warriors from the First Legion had boarded it and killed everyone on board. One of the discovered bodies was that of a heavily modified hybrid creature that bore the hallmarks of genetic manipulation and augmetic surgery of a kind never before seen. Though the creature's brain had been liquefied and its communication organs ripped out, a detailed post-mortem had led the Adepts of Mars to an inescapable conclusion.

The creature was an artificially-engineered, hybridised life form with a language set of its own and a method of articulation that could only ever be interpreted by one of its own kind. It was the perfect code carrier, one whose ciphers the Mechanicum could never hope to break unless they were somehow able to take possession of a living specimen.

Mechanicum adepts codified them as Unlingual Cipher Hosts.

Wayland called them the Kryptos.

THEY SQUATTED IN the ruins of an ore refinery, a bubbling quagmire of hissing petrochemicals and toxic fumes. Located amid a towering collection of relay towers that crackled with fizzing bursts of electricity, the refinery was as close as the ferrovore could take them. It had carried them through the layered defences around the forge temple, past corpse-hung habitation towers and fire-gutted manufactories that echoed with sourceless machine-cant burbling into static as it was corrupted. They saw machine shops ringing with the hammers of re-tasked construction engines, and a landscape changing from soaring silver and gold to scorched iron and altars of bloodstained bronze.

Dozens of ferrovores had come close, but none had so much as looked in their direction thanks to Wayland's manipulation of their creature's power output. Mortal patrols and vehicles gave them a wide berth, for the ferrovores were capricious things and were as likely turn their hunger upon friend as foe. It knew the safe routes through the razor mines, the blind spots of motion detectors, and had the locomotive dexterity to negotiate the fields of laser trips.

Beyond the relay towers was the walled heart of a forge temple, a blocky arrangement of cubes, pyramids and spheres. Strange symbols and arcane equations were daubed on the domed roofs with unguents of blood and oil, the sacred architecture of the Omnissiah corrupted by non-Euclidian geometries and distorting Escherite algebra.

The ferrovore squatted behind them, its brutal mechanical growling swallowed by the penetrating bass thrum of the towers in which they were concealed. At least fifty similar creatures stalked the battered wasteland of sabotaged industry around the temple, moving in overlapping patrol circuits and augmented by several hundred armed soldiers equipped with modified skitarii auspex gear.

'Defence towers, pict-scanners, motion sensors, pressure differentials, interlocking fields of fire. And a single entrance,' said Sharrowkyn, noting one defensive measure after another. He lay on his belly in the shadows, peering through shielded magnoculars. 'From the security around this place, I'd say our sources were right. The Kryptos is in there.'

'And you know a way we can defeat that level of security?' asked Wayland, kneeling behind a giant ceramite insulating dish that had fallen from a wrecked tower. He had his bolter clicked into place at his shoulder, though the barrel and sights were retracted.

'Think you can take out fifty ferrovores?' asked Sharrowkyn.

'No, but if we had a company of Iron Hands too we could fight our way inside.'

'Getting what we want out of there isn't about battering rams and guns. Charge through those gates, and the Kryptos will be lying on the floor with its brain melting out of its skull.'

'So how do you propose we gain entry?'

'We don't,' said Sharrowkyn. 'There's no way to get in there without being detected.'

'So has this mission been a waste of time?' hissed Wayland. 'I thought you Raven Guard were experts at this sort of thing – covert intrusions and operating around enemy defences.'

'We are, but there are some insertions you just can't make. Some defences are so tight that no tactical approach is going to get you past them.'

'Meaning what?'

'Meaning that if we can't get inside, we get the enemy to bring the Kryptos out.'

GIVEN THE DEVASTATION wrought around the forge temple, it was a simple matter to locate exposed data trunking that linked the temple to the planetary network. Much of the wiring was damaged or melted beyond repair, but a few bundles of oily cable still functioned, and it was upon these that Wayland directed his efforts. Numerous wiring clips and clicking devices extruded from his scrimshawed gauntlet, and even the tiny sparks of corposant arcing between his tools were making Sharrowkyn nervous.

'They won't detect this, will they?'

'Only if you keep distracting me,' answered Wayland, running a cable from the tangle of wiring to a boxy device clipped to his belt. The Mechanicum cipher engine whirred as it chewed through high-level encryption with a touch soft enough to avoid detection.

'I'm in,' said Wayland, as a blurt of coded binary hissed from the cipher engine. 'High-grade noospheric intercommunications. Only the best for the Kryptos...'

'Keep it light,' said Sharrowkyn. 'If the traitors so much as *think* we're out here, this mission is over.'

'Just because I am Iron Hand does not mean I cannot be subtle when the occasion demands it, Nykona,' said Wayland, deliberately using his first name. 'I trained on Mars and Adept Zeth's innovation in noospheric networks is not unknown to me.'

'So you've interfaced with this kind of system before?'

'I have studied it extensively,' said Wayland.

'*Studied* it?' said Sharrowkyn, spotting the deflection. 'You mean you've never actually used something like this?'

'Not as such, but I am confident I will be able to interface successfully,' said Wayland, lifting a connector plug and sliding it home in the base of his modified gorget.

'I'll remind you of that if we have to run for our lives,' said Sharrowkyn.

Wayland didn't answer, stiffening as a flood of information surged from the golden cables into his augmented cortical implants.

The Iron Hand moved his gauntlets through the air, manipulating operating systems, power and data flow only he could see. Haptically-enabled fingertips sifted reams of noospheric data with each blink of an eye lens as the barrage of information filled him.

Sharrowkyn left Wayland to his infiltration of the forge temple's data systems, and returned his attention to its defences, looking for any sign their intrusion had been detected.

'It helps me...' whispered Wayland, and Sharrowkyn inclined his head to listen.

'What?'

'The forge,' said Wayland, his voice sounding distant and strained. 'It hates what it has become, and wishes me to end its suffering. Its systems are overwriting my data footprints.'

Sharrowkyn shifted uncomfortably at the idea of the forge temple exhibiting anything that might be construed as sentience. Though the Mechanicum were an invaluable part of the Imperium, their belief in a divine force behind the machines they maintained and built was at odds with the Imperial Truth.

But as with most useful things, expediency and utility outweighed conviction.

'I have it,' said Wayland, twisting one hand and punching in what looked like an access code on an invisible panel. 'Expect to see some activity soon.'

Sharrowkyn returned his attention to the temple as a number of warning sirens blared throughout the complex. Emergency lights flashed and barking announcements in gurgling cant brayed from klaxons mounted on defence towers. Streams of armed men poured from the iron structures, a mix of feral skitarii cohorts and panicked Army units.

'I don't know what you did,' said Sharrowkyn. 'But it's got them running scared.'

'With the temple's consent, I disengaged the control rods from the atomic core of its reactor and altered the composition of the catalysing elements to bring the isotopes to critical mass at an exponential rate. When that happens, everything within a hundred kilometres is going to be vaporised.'

'Including us?'

'No,' said Wayland, tapping another Mechanicum device attached to his belt. 'Not us.'

The enemy troops converged on a point just outside the main gates of the temple, assuming a defensive formation as they stood waiting. A palpable sense of fear gripped the enemy, and when an opponent was off balance was the perfect moment to strike.

'There,' said Wayland. 'That's got to be it.'

Sharrowkyn looked to where Wayland was indicating. A warrior in burnished red plate, awash with fluttering, wax-sealed scrolls, escorted a nondescript adept in a flowing black robe. Bereft of the reticulated machine arms and augmentation common to most tech-priests, there was nothing to outwardly mark this adept as special.

'Word Bearer,' said Sharrowkyn, his voice tight with controlled hatred.

'The magnetic discharge will block vox-traffic,' said Wayland. 'But we have less than five minutes to take possession of the Kryptos.'

'Then let's move,' replied Sharrowkyn, jerking his thumb over his shoulder. 'Is it ready?'

Wayland engaged the slave mechanism of their captured ferrovore.

'Oh, it's more than ready,' he said.

BOOMING GEYSERS OF superheated, radioactive steam blew out domes and walls of the forge temple, and burning traceries of inverted lightning arced through the volatile atmosphere. As the atomic core of the temple boiled itself to destruction, venting systems and dispersal protocols were wilfully deactivated or simply failed to function. The few adepts that remained at their stations found their efforts to avert the temple's impending destruction thwarted at every turn.

Nor was the chaos of the temple's doom confined to its structural elements as Sabik Wayland and its dying machine-heart took their vengeance. Automated gunfire blitzed from defence turrets to strafe traitor positions with armour-penetrating shells. Trip-switches designed to detonate buried mines when certain parameters were met blew out in a rolling series of thunderous explosions that shook the earth and toppled nearby structures in roaring fireballs. The ferrovores convulsed as their cortical implants received contradictory orders, opening fire and scooping up swathes of skitarii to devour their metal-sheathed bodies.

Sharrowkyn and Wayland ran through the strobing hell of explosions and gunfire with the cool precision of hunters.

Wayland moved with his implanted rifle barking out deafening sub-sonic rounds. Each shell detonated explosively within the carapace armour of a skitarii warlord or discipline master, each target carefully chosen to hinder the command structure of the enemy from regaining control. He moved in mechanical precision with the bellowing ferrovore as its guns unleashed arcs of searing fire and electrified harpoons to cut a path through those few traitors that recognised them as enemies.

The launchers on its back sent salvos of air-bursting rockets into the gathered traitors, multiple shells exploding and showering the ground with hundreds of plasma bomblets. Searing bursts of blue-hot fire crackled among the traitorous Army units, fusing metal and flesh and bone with a grotesque hissing sound.

Sharrowkyn's carbine was lighter than Wayland's, but no less deadly in the hands of a master marksman. Each pull of the trigger shattered an enemy skull or tore out an exposed throat; kill shots that took a target's life before they were even aware there was a danger.

'He's running,' said Sharrowkyn, as the Word Bearer threw the robed adept over his shoulder and bolted for a low-roofed structure at the corner of the temple compound.

'Can you catch him?' asked Wayland, pumping a bolt-round through the chest of a screaming skitarii warrior with a bloodied animal pelt draped over his fanged shoulder guards.

'*Please*,' said Sharrowkyn.

'Find me in sixty seconds or you won't make it off this world.'

Sharrowkyn nodded and triggered his jump jets, soaring away from Wayland and the berserk ferrovore. The Word Bearer was too distant to reach in one jump, and Sharrowkyn slammed down on the run, firing on full-auto as he built speed for his next leap. The jets blazed and as he arced up into the air Sharrowkyn saw the Word Bearer had reached the structure, its roof irising open to reveal a silver-bodied flyer with enormous engine nacelles.

'It's not the enemy you see that gets you,' hissed Sharrowkyn. 'It's the one you don't.'

His carbine blazed and the Word Bearer staggered as high-velocity needles punched into the side of his helm and shoulder. Mangled metal and ceramite flew from the impacts, and Sharrowkyn slid the weapon around his shoulder as he landed with a crack of stone in a billow of heated smoke.

Sharrowkyn drew two black-bladed gladii from shoulder-sheaths and threw himself at the Word Bearer. The traitor tossed his ruined helmet aside, and Sharrowkyn saw his face was grey and ashen, covered in a writhing mass of tattoos that slithered beneath his skin like worms of sentient ink.

The Word Bearer dropped the Kryptos and brought his bolter to bear. Sharrowkyn hacked through the barrel with his first gladius and buried his second in the centre of the Word Bearer's plastron. The warrior grunted in pain and fell back as the shell in the breech of his weapon exploded. He lashed out with a clubbing fist, but Sharrowkyn was already moving. He spun around the Word Bearer and drove the monomolecular tip of his gladius down through the warrior's neck.

Sharrowkyn's blade clove the Word Bearer's spinal column. He wrenched the sword up, and his foe's head lolled to the side as it tore free. Even before the body fell, Sharrowkyn turned and lifted the black-robed adept from the ground. Its hood had fallen back, and he flinched as he saw the creature's horrific face. Its flesh was as pale as his own, the lower half of its face a nightmarish arrangement of moving parts, augmitters, vox-grilles and sound-producing elements that bore no relation to anything Sharrowkyn had ever seen. What remained of its skull was like the punch-interface of a cogitator, a brass and flesh arrangement of alien anatomy meshed with glass compartments that left portions of an augmented brain visible.

The Kryptos brayed with a sound that screeched like iron nails on slate, and a stream of garbled machine noise grated from a mouth that moved with abominable mechanised clicking and a wetly animal gurgle.

'Just what I was thinking,' said Sharrowkyn, hauling the Kryptos onto his shoulder and calling up the icon that displayed Wayland's location. The Iron Hand was in the thick of the fighting, keeping in the shadow of the ferrovore as it tore into its erstwhile allies. Sharrowkyn leapt through the air on a trail of fire, landing in the crater of a sonic mine's detonation. A second leap carried him over a group of cowering mortals and his third landed him beside Wayland.

'Cutting it fine as usual,' said Wayland. 'The core is at critical mass.'

'How long?' asked Sharrowkyn, pulling the Kryptos from his shoulder.

Wayland unclipped the second device the Mechanicum adepts had given him and placed it on the ground between them. He flipped up the trigger mechanism, his thumb hovering over the activation stud.

'Ready?' he said.

'Do it,' said Sharrowkyn as the sky flashed impossibly bright, and furious radiance wiped the forge temple from the face of the planet in a bellow of nuclear fire.

TIME CEASED TO have meaning.

An age or the blink of an eye passed for Sharrowkyn, a span of time impossible to gauge. Light and shadow billowed and faded, the world beyond the shimmering bubble of unreality that sheltered them from atomic annihilation moving like a picter reel in overdrive. He couldn't move, he couldn't think, and – for all intents and purposes – he didn't exist.

And then the world snapped back into focus as the timer on the stasis field generator reached zero. Hot winds surged around them, irradiated and laden with toxic poisons that would render this region of Cavor Sarta uninhabitable for millennia. Nothing remained of the forge temple, only a glassy plain and a deep gouge in the earth where its molten core had sunk deep into the rock of the planet. A kilometres-high mushroom cloud seethed with fire, and the hammer-blow pressure waves of its power rumbled through the atmosphere. Caustic tornadoes of heavy metals twisted in the nightmarish ruins of the atomic explosion, and lightning storms surged and roared in electromagnetic melees.

Wayland still knelt beside the stasis field generator, but stood and shook off its lingering aftereffects. Sharrowkyn swept his gaze around the devastation, amazed they had survived ground zero of a nuclear holocaust.

'I think that went satisfactorily,' said Wayland.

'We're alive and we have the Kryptos,' agreed Sharrowkyn, watching as the cringing adept creature curled into a foetal ball, babbling in its unnatural, inexplicable cipher-language as the radiation worked upon its frail body.

'And the traitors will be none the wiser to our involvement. As far as anyone will know, this was simply an accidental meltdown.'

'Do you think the enemy will believe that?'

'Given the lack of cohesion and mechanical expertise among the occupying forces, such events are far from uncommon,' said Wayland. 'I believe our involvement will go undetected.'

Sharrowkyn nodded and activated the integral teleport homer of his armour to signal the Iron Hands vessel concealed in the orbital debris surrounding Cavor Sarta. The electromagnetic storms would cover any trace of the teleport beam, and they would be gone before any enemy forces arrived to search the ruined site.

'Good work, Sabik Wayland,' said Sharrowkyn.

'Good work indeed, Nykona Sharrowkyn,' answered Wayland.

All in all, thought Sharrowkyn, it was a bad day to be a traitor.

WOLF'S CLAW

Chris Wraight

His enemy wore the scaled, blue-green livery of the traitors. He was massive, a heavy-treading monster in Tactical Dreadnought plate, with twin chainblades slung under combi-boltered fists. Already three Wolves of Fenris lay at his feet, bleeding and broken.

Bjorn crouched low, hugging the wall of the corridor. Ship combat was a close, claustrophobic thing – a matter of thick shadows and tight spaces. Only four remained of the pack he had brought with him onto the Alpha Legion frigate *Iota Malaphelos*. There was nowhere to fall back to, no cover to use. Three more traitor legionaries advanced in the shadow of the Terminator champion, crunching over the bodies of the fallen as they came.

Bjorn tensed, readying for the counter-charge. He felt the hunt-spirits of his surviving brothers prepare for the same.

And just then, just as his muscles flooded with hyperadrenaline and his hearts thudded with kill-urge, he remembered how it had been before. He remembered going to Slejek for the tools of war he needed, and what answer he had been given.

What would the Blademaker say, Bjorn wondered, now that the
tide of murder had risen again? What curses would spit from those
burned and blunted fangs, once he realised what had been done?

DOWN IN THE depths of the *Hrafnkel*'s forge-level, the fires never
went out. Calderas of molten iron poured ceaselessly, flaring as the
liquid metal hissed into the formers. Hammers rose and fell against
adamantium anvils, and the whine of the conveyers was broken
only by the steel-thin benediction of crimson-robed tech-priests.

Bjorn pushed his way through the toiling masses, heading with
singular purpose towards his target. The flagship's forgemaster,
glowering in a near-black array of scored and ancient battleplate,
was waiting for him before the open maw of a glowing furnace.

'I wondered how long it would be,' said the priest of iron, his
face hidden behind a slope-grilled deathmask.

'I seek the one they call Blademaker,' said Bjorn.

'We're all called that, down here. But you've found the one you're
after, and he already knows what you want.'

Bjorn looked up at Slejek Blademaker's towering servo-arm, slick
with oils and bearing the chip-marks of recent work.

'I need a gauntlet,' Bjorn said.

Slejek laughed, his voice as dry as brazier coals. 'The Wolf King
likes you. Sent you down himself, I was told.' He drew closer, and
Bjorn smelt his acrid smoke-stench. 'It won't do you any good. You
could be Lord Gunn himself, and you'd still have to wait in line.'

Bjorn raised his left arm. It terminated in a tangle of scorched
and broken metal spars. Since losing his hand on Prospero there
had been no opportunity to forge an augmetic replacement, and
his last combat against the Alpha Legion had mangled what
remained.

'I can't fight like this,' Bjorn said, turning the stump in the light
of the fires. 'Not again.'

'I heard you'd been doing fine.'

'I need to grasp a blade again.'

For a second time, the forgemaster laughed. 'More than one?'

'This was my sword-arm.'

'Best learn to use the other, then.'

Bjorn squared up to Slejek. 'Don't jest with me, hammerer.'

'You think I jest? Look around you. I have four thousand warriors to clad and arm. Every hour that passes brings me another bloodied tally of cracked armour and broken blades. I have worked my thralls to death to meet the thirst for iron, and it will not cease while the Snakes have us by the throat. You have your sight, your strength and you can carry a bolter. That makes you one of the lucky ones.'

'It is not *enough*,' snarled Bjorn. 'I need a gauntlet.'

Slejek stooped, lowering his blackened helm until it was a hand's breadth from Bjorn's. 'Get... in... line,' he said.

For a moment, Bjorn didn't move. He flexed the fingers of his right hand, considering forcing the issue. It was a possibility. Slejek was big, but Bjorn had taken on bigger.

But then, grudgingly, he backed down. Brawling with his own kind would only accelerate their likely doom amid the rust-red stars of Alaxxes.

'I *will* return,' he promised, stomping away from Slejek. 'You will not refuse me again.'

Slejek merely shrugged, and returned to his work. His servo-arms whirled into action, and the fires blazed anew.

Bjorn strode on past rows of labouring thralls, barely noticing the flicker of arc-welders against their heavy masks. His every nerve burned with fury. He would have to enter combat again as a half-breed, a liability, a cripple. His own death held no fear for him, but the thought of failing his pack-brothers soured his blood.

Then, in the final reaches of the forge-chamber, he saw it. It hung on adamantium chains, half-lost in the darkness, glinting sharply from the reflected light of the furnaces. It was complete, pristine, and savagely beautiful.

'You,' Bjorn said, picking out a mortal thrall. 'Who was this made for?'

The thrall bowed clumsily in his thick forge-armour. 'I know not, lord. Shall I beg knowledge of my masters?'

Bjorn looked at it again. The alloy was flawless. This was a singular thing, the work of an artisan-genius. The bearer of this would slay and slay until the stars burned out and darkness howled across an empty void.

'Can you fit it?' asked Bjorn, extending his withered arm.

'Yes, but–' began the thrall, uncertainly.

'Do it,' said Bjorn, reaching for the hanging chains. His pulse was already quickening. 'Do it now.'

ROARING DEATH-CURSES FROM the Old Ice, Bjorn leapt out at the enemy. His four adamantium talons snarled into energy-shrouded life, harsh blue against the gloom around him.

The Terminator champion came at him hard, chainblades juddering in a bloody shriek. The two warriors crashed together, and Bjorn felt the raking pain of adamantium teeth cutting into his pauldron. He took a bolt-round close to the chest, nearly hurling him onto his back. He veered, swerved and thrust, twisting to keep his foe close.

He thrust his wolf claw upward, catching the legionary beneath the helm. Lesser talons would have cracked and splayed, breaking on the reinforced gorget-collar and opening Bjorn up to the killing blow.

But these talons bit true. Their disruptor shroud blazed in a riot of blue-white, tearing into the thick ceramite. The claws pushed deeper, slicking through flesh and carving up sinew, muscle and bone. Hot blood fountained along the adamantium claw-lengths, fizzing as it boiled away on the edges.

The champion staggered, pinned at the neck. Bjorn twisted the blades and the enemy fell, his throat torn out, thudding to the deck with the heavy, final crash of dead battleplate.

Bjorn howled his triumph, flinging his claws wide and spraying blood-flecks across the corridor. In his wake came his brothers, firing freely, locking down the surviving Alpha Legionnaires and driving them back.

Godsmote, Bjorn's second, chuckled as he ran past.

'One-Handed no more,' he remarked, glorying at the deed. 'We shall have to find you a better name.'

Bjorn paid no attention. He was restored, ready to rip and tear and pierce, crippled no longer by fate and the whims of war.

Blademaker could curse all he liked – he would not be getting these claws back.

'Slay them!' Bjorn roared. 'Slay them all!'

And, with a grind of battleplate and the crackle of disruptor energies, he strode out, whole once more, into the shadows.

THIEF OF
REVELATIONS

Graham McNeill

OF ALL THE truths Ahzek Ahriman had learned as a scholar of the Corvidae, this was the most galling – the understanding that real knowledge came from knowing the extent of his own ignorance. He had believed that he understood the mysteries of the Great Ocean and its myriad complexities, but events on Prospero had shown him that his every certitude poured through his fingers like wind-blown dust.

Ahriman's tower, a spiralling horn of white stone raised on the edge of a geomantically volatile plateau, was a thing of beauty. The glittering ruins of Tizca had been transplanted to this world of warp-charged rock, but Ahriman could not bring himself to reoccupy his former chambers. That time of his life was over, and Ahriman had chosen to wield the power that this world offered to craft a new demesne for himself.

A devil's bargain perhaps, but one that might see the Thousand Sons elevated to their former glory, and vindicate their actions in the eyes of the fools who condemned them.

The Book of Magnus, his primarch's last gift to him, lay open on a lectern of glass and silver, its heavy pages rustling with a life of their own.

Precious little else remained of the accumulated knowledge contained within Prospero's burned libraries, but what he had saved was stacked in one endless shelf that spiralled from the base of the tower to its topmost spire.

It was here, at the summit, that Ahriman worked.

Held immobile by coruscating chains of light, a bound figure was spread in a cruciform pattern. The body had once been that of a legionary, a perfect representation of all that humanity could achieve. A paladin of enlightenment, but now little better than a monster.

His name had once been Astennu, and he had been a brother of the Pyrae Fellowship until the flesh change had taken him.

He hung a metre from the reflective floor and fire crawled across his skin. Phosphor-bright traceries limned his veins where aetheric energy oozed through translucent flesh. Daemonic coals burned in sunken eye sockets, and his lips were stretched in the rictus grin of a burning reaper.

The mouth moved, but no sounds emerged from Astennu's throat, only furnace-hot blasts of superheated air.

Concentric circles enclosed the transformed legionary, wards that had been used by the Practicus of the Thousand Sons for centuries when releasing their subtle bodies into the aether. By such means were the denizens of the Great Ocean kept at bay, and by such means could a creature of the abyss be contained.

Nine circles of lunar caustic were described around Astennu, six of which had already burned away, the argent gleam of each ring slowly fading until it was black and inert. The lustre of the seventh ring was already dying.

Ahriman had learned much from the bodies of the flesh-changed that he had captured, marrying his own visionary talents to the bio-transformative empathy of Hathor Maat. Together they had examined the hybrid architecture of forty-five of their former brothers, each time learning something more of the mutations wracking the Legion's warriors.

Ahriman circled the seething fire-creature that Astennu had become, letting his senses push through to the raging cauldron of energy within.

Astennu's voice echoed in his head.

+Again, Ahzek? Why do you persist in this foolishness?+

Ahriman made no attempts to justify what he was doing – this warrior was already lost. Those who benefited from his labours would hear any justifications, and by then it would not matter how he had affected their salvation.

If Ahriman felt any hubris at such presumption, it did not show.

+You are doomed to fail, Ahzek. You know that, of course. Shall I tell you why?+

'You are going to tell me anyway, so why bother asking?'

Astennu's burning grin spread wider. +You will fail because you think the flesh change is to be feared. You think it's a curse, but you can't see it for the boon it is.+

Ahriman let his Corvidae sight penetrate the outer layers of the warrior's burning flesh.

'A boon? Is it a boon to have all that you once were stripped away? To stand on the precipice of enlightenment only to be dashed down to mutant ignorance? These are boons? No, you *were* once glorious, but now you are a monster.'

+A monster?+ Astennu chuckled. +The flesh change has shown me that there are few monsters that warrant the fear we have of them. You dread what I and others like me are becoming, but everyone carries around their own monsters. Especially you, Ahzek.+

Ahriman knew that Astennu's every word was calculated to slip through the cracks in his psyche, and the best barbs were those that came loaded with the truth. He forced Astennu's words from his mind and traced the myriad paths into the future that followed the degeneration of Astennu's flesh.

While the fiery creature remonstrated and taunted him, he watched a thousand iterations of Astennu's hyper-evolution. In some, the fire eventually consumed him, in others, it waxed and waned, but in none of them did it reverse. Without intervention, Astennu's body would only ever devolve further into its warped state.

Ahriman pulled his power back into himself, feeling the cold of the lunar caustic in his bones as he withdrew into his own mind. His armour felt heavy upon his frame, every plate of ivory-trimmed ceramite shimmering in reflected flame-light.

He should have killed Astennu a long time ago, but the things he was learning were enabling him to understand the progress of the flesh change.

And what could be understood could be mastered.

Such was the suddenness and violence of Astennu's change that Ahriman had discovered in him with relative ease. The Thousand Sons Chief Librarian's consciousness lay across this planet like a web, and a warrior's degeneration plucked at its threads like nothing else.

+You can't stop it, Ahzek. It will come to us all. In time, it will come to you. The ninefold gift is already in you, I see it already.+

Anger touched Ahriman, and he stepped closer to the edge of the circle as the gleaming light at his feet diminished. 'The flesh change will not take me, Astennu. I will not let it.'

Astennu paused for a long moment.

+Whoever said it was up to you?+

Too late, Ahriman realised that the last of the wards around Astennu had burned down to black. The fire-creature hurled itself at him, the shimmering veins of its body flaring with retina-burning brightness.

Fiery claws gouged at his plastron.

Ahriman swatted Astennu aside with a hurried kine blow, but his former brother sprang to his feet like a cat, his body wreathed in a rippling corona of white flames.

The air blurred with heat haze and a wordless babble of un-syllables dripped from Astennu's lips like curses.

Ahriman's senses flickered into the immediate future, and he swayed aside as Astennu leapt across the chamber. Flames sprang up in his wake, each afterimage of his presence imprinting its shrieking echo onto the world.

Ahriman extended his arm and summoned his heqa staff to his hand. He swung it like a broadsword, the curved crook catching Astennu in his midriff and doubling him up. Ghostly flames rippled along the length of the staff, but Ahriman snuffed them out with a thought. Astennu lunged again, and a burst of flaming breath went ahead of him.

Before it struck Ahriman, a glittering sphere of freezing air surrounded Astennu – he screamed as his fires were extinguished and the light burning in his veins dimmed to the faintest glow.

Held immobile by an orb of purest chill, Astennu raged impotently in his barbarous daemonic tongue. Ahriman felt restless ambition in his biology that spoke of powerful biomancy.

A voice came from behind him. 'A creature of fire and you *don't* think to use the Pavoni arts against it? You're forgetting how to use your powers, brother.'

Ahriman turned to see Hathor Maat with his hands extended before him, a frost-white radiance blazing at his fingertips. Sobek and Amon stood behind him, their auras alight with channelled power. Although his subtle body had been within the protective circle, he had not sensed their approach.

The venerable Amon approached the hissing, defiant form of Astennu, studying the warrior's disfigured physiology with an expression of horror.

'Astennu…' he murmured, sadly. 'Astennu, what has become of you?'

'What will become of us all, if we fail,' Ahriman replied.

Amon nodded, accepting his words, but unwilling to say so.

'Not to sound petulant,' Hathor Maat strained, 'but there's only so long I can hold this cryo-sphere. So hurry up and kill him.'

Ahriman drew his power back into himself, rising into the Enumerations to focus his thoughts. He nodded to Hathor Maat, who dropped his hands. Astennu flew at them, but he was halted mid-leap as Sobek trapped him in a kine web.

Ahriman's will was a physical thing, an extension of his force and strength, multiplied many times over. It took hold of Astennu and broke him in two.

A hideous crack of splitting bone filled the chamber and the firelight in Astennu's body faded like a snuffed lumen.

His aetheric aura dispersed like wind-blown smoke, and a sliver of Ahriman's heart turned to stone at the loss of another of the Thousand Sons.

Hathor Maat saw his anguish. 'Don't waste your sorrow on degenerates like him.'

Ahriman rounded on the Pavoni, angrily.

'The man of knowledge must be able not only to love his enemies, but also to hate his friends.'

Amon turned the dead body's head from side to side, as if to find something to explain its degeneration. Sobek knelt, and ran a finger through the powdered lines of lunar caustic.

'You take too many risks delving into the flesh of the Changed Ones,' he said.

'I risk more by *not* delving,' Ahriman replied. 'We all do.'

'And did you learn anything of use from him?' asked Amon.

Ahriman hesitated. 'I now see how the corruption spreads.'

'But not how to reverse it?'

'No, not yet.'

Amon shrugged. 'We should take this to the Crimson King.'

'You know we cannot,' Ahriman snapped.

'Why? Tell me. He stopped this once before. He can do it again.'

'He did nothing but postpone our degeneration. In his arrogance, he thought he had mastered what the powers of the Great Ocean started.'

Amon laughed derisively. 'And you think *we* can stop it? Now who's being arrogant?'

'You have been away from the Legion too long, Amon,' Ahriman growled. 'Your wanderings take you to the farthest corners of the world, but what have you learned? Nothing.'

Amon stepped close to him.

'Then I have learned as much as you, Ahzek.'

Sobek was quick to step between Amon and Ahriman. 'The primarch could help.'

Ahriman shook his head, and flipped the Book of Magnus to a page of half-completed formulae and esoteric calculations.

'We have been down this road before, brothers. When the Rubric is ready, we will bring it to our father. If he should learn of the Great Work while it is incomplete and untested, he will stop it.'

Hathor Maat touched the yellowed pages of the Book of Magnus as though it were a holy relic. 'You presume he cares enough to stop it. When was the last time any of us saw Magnus, or felt his presence abroad in the world?'

Their silence spurred Maat to loquaciousness, never a difficult task, and his features subtly shifted to assume a more stately look.

'Magnus broods alone in the Obsidian Tower. Who knows what thoughts fill his head? Certainly not the fate of his few remaining sons.'

'You presume too much, Hathor Maat,' said Amon. Once the

equerry of the primarch, he was always first to rise to his master's defence when words became heated.

'Do I? Then what do you suggest we do? Meekly await what the tides of the warp decree for us? Damn that, and damn you.' Hathor Maat strode to where Astennu's twisted corpse lay, the nobility and awesome majesty it had once possessed now ruined and corrupted. 'This will *not* be me. And if I have to go against the primarch's wishes, then so be it.'

Amon's cheeks flushed with colour and his aura shifted into the higher Enumerations of combat. But Sobek amplified his Corvidae powers to project futures of broken bones, burned flesh and their own ruination into each warrior's mind. 'Enough.'

Amon and Hathor Maat flinched at images of their own deaths. Both adepts earthed their power and the dissipating energies flared from the psycho-conductive spire of the tower in a burst of aetheric fire.

Ahriman stepped to the chamber's centre.

'We are embarked on this course and our purpose is set. To forget one's purpose is the commonest form of stupidity.'

'And to repeat the same thing over and over again and expect different results is the very definition of insanity,' said Amon.

'Then what do you suggest?'

'You *know* what I suggest.'

Ahriman sighed. 'Very well. I will speak with the Crimson King.'

THE OBSIDIAN TOWER was well named, a crooked spike of black rock that towered above all else. Its impossible construction had been achieved in moments, a passing fancy of the Crimson King made real. Its substance was angular and glassy, like napped volcanic rock, and striated with darting lights. No windows or openings marred its surface, save those willed into being by the primarch.

At its peak hung a pellucid radiance, part illumination, part eater of light. It was impossible to look and not feel the gaze of the Crimson King, an all-seeing, all-knowing presence that left no shadows in which to hide secrets.

Ahriman kept his gaze averted.

On a world saturated with warp energy it was a matter of supreme ease to travel from one place to the next in the blink of an eye, yet Ahriman still chose to travel via Thunderhawk. Like everything on this world, the aircraft had not escaped the transformative energies of their new home. Its structure had become altogether more avian in plan, more raptor-like in profile. The power in its name had wrought a transformation all of its own.

Ahriman brought the craft around in a slow turn, circling the tower for a place to put it down. Vivid electrical storms raged like the afterimages of titanic battles in the heavens, and the jagged peaks on every horizon were limned with electrical fire that spat traceries of lightning into the sky.

Sentient zephyrs chased the Thunderhawk, scraps of febrile consciousness that flocked to men of power like acolytes to a high priest. Millions of them attended upon Magnus's tower like the accretion rings of planets or bloodsharks with the scent of prey in the water.

Ahriman angled the Thunderhawk around as an opening shaped itself in the upper reaches of the spire and a shelf of glassy rock extruded from its substance. He feathered the engines and raised the craft's hooked nose as he brought it down with a gentle pressure of thought. He allowed the engines a moment to cool before making his way to the assault ramp and descending to the tower.

As always, he felt the charge in the air, the sense of potentiality that existed in every moment. Here breath had power, and his was seized upon by the invisible zephyrs that flocked to him.

Ahriman ignored them and strode into the tower through an elliptical archway with edges that curved like a dancing flame. The

space within was enormous, too vast to exist within the circumfer-
ence of the tower, and lit in the soft glow of a librarium.

Spiralling stacks and shelves groaned under the weight of myriad
forms of knowledge: parchments, scrolls, data-crystals, hide-bound
tomes, psy-songs and haptic-memes, each bearing a fragment of
priceless knowledge borne from the sacking of Prospero.

To an outsider, such a collection would appear extensive, a repos-
itory of knowledge unmatched by any beyond the great vaults of
Terra. But to the Thousand Sons these were scraps, a fraction of
the accumulated wisdom gathered from the corners of the galaxy
over the last two centuries.

It made Ahriman weep to know that such irreplaceable wisdom
had been lost for the sake of spite and jealousy.

'Was it worth it, Russ?' he muttered.

A voice came from above, resonating with the sorrow of the ages.
It was a voice that knew neither surprise nor joy, and was all the
sadder for having once basked in such wonder.

'Don't speak his name.'

'Father.'

'Why do you disturb me?'

Ahriman could see no sign of his gene-sire. The voice emanated
from everywhere and nowhere, a disembodied spirit that could
have been whispering in his ear or shouting from deep inside the
librarium.

'I wish to ask you something.'

'You did not need to travel to the Obsidian Tower for that.'

'No, but some things are best spoken face to face. Father to son.'

There was a pause, then a sudden swelling of presence; a funda-
mental change in the secret physics of the world. The librarium
vanished, and Ahriman found himself at the very summit of Magnus's tower, raised above it as a god above his domain. The world
curved away, as though he were a giant stood upon a globe, and

he saw the fiefdoms of the warrior-sorcerers who had escaped the final slaughter at the Pyramid of Photep.

From a Legion of thousands, these paltry few remained.

'We would like to live as we once lived,' Ahriman said. 'But history will not permit it.'

There was a crack of lightning and a sudden surge of power, and then the primarch was simply *there*. He looked down at Ahriman.

'But a small body of determined warriors fired by an unquenchable faith in their mission can alter the *course* of history.'

THE CRIMSON KING, he was called. The Red Cyclops. Magnus of the One Eye. All these epithets and more had been heaped upon him – some in praise, most in fear.

The Magnus that towered above Ahriman was clad as he last remembered him, going out to battle the Wolf King in a howling storm of black rain. A blood-red breastplate, sheathed in twin horns of bone and draped in a mantle of amber mail. A kilt of sun-baked leather, edged in gold and stamped with an ivory representation of the Legion's serpentine symbol.

His crimson hair was wild, the mane of a visionary or madman. The primarch's features were bronzed and ruddy, yet beneath it all was a fiery light, the sun at the core of his being simultaneously filling his fictive body with its radiance and reflecting it. That light shone strongest through his eye, a singular orb of gold, flecked with undreamed colours and hardened by the sorrow of one who rued the day he saw further than he ought.

This was Magnus as he wished to appear: a demigod wrought in the image of a lost past by the memories and emotions of his favoured son. Magnus was a being on the cusp of some great transformation, but where that would take him was a mystery that not even he could answer.

Ahriman fought the urge to drop to his knees. Since coming to the Planet of the Sorcerers, Magnus had demanded that none of his sons bend the knee to him, but some habits die hard.

Contrary to outward appearances, the top of Magnus's tower was open to the elements, and the kaleidoscopic storms raging overhead were close enough to touch. Blistering energies of unimaginable power danced overhead, their potency an elixir in Ahriman's blood.

'It's quite something, isn't it?' asked the primarch, speaking with the pleasure of a shared secret.

'It's incredible.'

Magnus walked a slow circuit of the tower, and capricious arcs of lightning slithered around him as though he were a lodestone. 'Like attracts like. The power in me is that of the Great Ocean. Distilled through my reborn flesh into something purer, but still… chaotic.'

In the presence of Magnus, it was impossible not to feel like a helpless student at the feet of an omnipotent master. There was so much Ahriman wanted to ask, but he forced his tumultuous thoughts into the placid Enumerations to focus himself.

'I have been working on something I think you should see.'

'Yes, I know. You have been working tirelessly upon the flesh-changed of late.'

Ahriman fought to conceal his shock. 'You… You know?'

Magnus turned and gave him a skewed look.

'Did you *really* think I wouldn't?'

Ahriman realised he had been naïve to believe the Crimson King would be ignorant of his Great Work, but was still surprised at how transparent he must have been.

'This is why you intrude on my labours?' Magnus asked.

'Yes, my lord. I have read everything in the grimoire you entrusted to my care, and there is a spell that I believe will–'

'Why have you really come here, Ahzek?'

Ahriman walked to the edge of the tower, his cloak flowing around him in the winds from the volcanic plains below. Jagged rocks reared up from the base of the tower like black fangs in the mouth of a predator.

'Because I need your help,' he said. 'We cannot do this without you. We have learned much, but we are blind men searching for revelation in all the wrong places.'

'So you wish my blessing and my help? Well, I do not give it. You are walking a dangerous path, my son. Trust me, I know the nobility that drives you, I felt it myself. But you would think that you had broken the curse of the flesh change only to be deceived by the very power you believed had brought you success.'

'But surely, together, we could finally find an answer?'

Magnus shook his head. 'No, I cannot help you. Moreover, I *will not* help you. And you are to cease all efforts in this matter. Do you understand?'

Ahriman felt his control of the Enumerations slipping as he rose into a higher, combative stance. 'No, I do not.'

Without seeming to move, Magnus swelled to become a towering giant, a feral beast of blood-matted fur with hardened skin. His single eye became a molten sun that pinned Ahriman in place, a carcass set for the spit.

'Your little cabal is no more,' he boomed. '"And woe betide he who ignores my warning or breaks faith with me. He shall be my enemy, and I will visit such destruction upon him and all his followers that, from now until the end of all things, he shall rue the day he turned from my light".'

Ahriman recognised the words and the bitterness that dripped from every syllable. Only one question remained to be asked.

'Why?'

The awful threat and terrible danger faded from Magnus's eye as his physique returned to its former stature. 'Because matters of greater import occupy my thoughts.'

'Matters greater than your Legion's end?' Ahriman demanded.

Magnus did not answer, and cast his eye to the raging storms of light above him, as though the answer lay within them. His features softened and took on a thoughtful cast.

'Much more important,' he said at last.

'Tell me. Tell me, that I might understand why you abandon us.'

Magnus nodded and reached out to place a bronze-skinned hand upon his shoulder.

The Planet of the Sorcerers fell away like a shining bauble dropped down a darkened well.

'I will do better,' the primarch said. 'I will *show* you.'

Ahriman felt a terrible dislocation, like the wrench of a teleport, but a hundred times worse. His genhanced frame, bio-engineered to resist the extremes of any environment, was suddenly that of a frail mortal as his subtle body was ripped from his flesh.

His body of light soared through the Great Ocean, borne upon the back of a fiery golden comet, a presence of such power that he dared not look directly upon it. He knew that this was Magnus, but in the trackless wildernesses of the Great Ocean, it was no longer constrained by any constancy of form.

Stars and galaxies spiralled around him, an endless parade of random events that were not random at all. Everything proceeded to the design of fate's architect, a pattern so grand it could only be glimpsed from beyond the farthest extremes of existence. Even then it was beyond Ahriman's ability to comprehend, its complexities too subtle and its intrigues too tightly woven to be understood.

Sickness built in Ahriman's belly, a bone-deep vertigo and a dizzying sense of falling. He struggled not to cry out. He was nothing to this universe, an insignificant grain amidst a desert of wind-scattered dust formed from the inconsequences of the galaxy.

He was not special. He was not anything.

'No!' he cried out in desperation. 'I am Ahzek Ahriman!'

And with that thought he was whole again, a warrior-scholar of the Thousand Sons. He forced his mind into the second Enumeration, where bodily concerns were put aside in favour of the pursuit of enlightenment.

His body was gone, and in its place was a shimmer of light; a conglomeration of wheels turning within wheels, eyes by the million and a form as immaculate as it was unknown. This was the purest expression of his being, a creature of light and thought.

The voice of Magnus came to him through senses unknown, each word freighted with terrible foreknowledge. 'Come, my son – we will be thieves of revelation. See what I see, and tell me I am wrong to think beyond your concerns.'

Suddenly, Ahriman did not want to look. Once he looked, nothing would ever be the same. But he could not refuse his primarch's demand, and the comfort of ignorance was something to be shunned. His shining body flew close to the radiant form of Magnus.

'Show me *everything*,' he said.

'Everything? No, not that. Never that. But I will show you enough.'

'Enough for what?'

'Enough to know that we still have a choice before us, one that will affect how we are remembered by the tides of history.'

THE STARS WHEELED around them, streaking by in a blur.

They travelled at the speed of thought, and where thought willed them, they arrived in an instant. The sensation was spellbinding. Like gods they bestrode the galaxy, travelling its length and breadth with each moment.

Ahriman had just begun to appreciate the wonder of his primarch's power, when he realised that they had stopped moving, the world resolving around him in the familiar patterns of stars and the elliptical orbits of planets.

'Where are we?' he asked.

'This is Tsagualsa, the carrion-world of the Night Haunter. A place of murder and torment, where the screams of the dying are never-ending. A place from which my brother wages a campaign of genocide. It is from here that he was sent to fight the First Legion of the Lion.'

They spun through the system, past worlds dead and worlds ravaged by conflict, mayhem and the collateral damage of two Legions at war. Ahriman felt his gaze drawn towards the system's edge, where a vicious battle raged in the void, two fleets battering at one another at close range. Intermingled warships engaged in broadside brawls, filling the space between them with high explosive ordnance and criss-crossing las-fire. Wrecks blazed from prow to stern and split apart as their keels broke under intense gravometric pressures.

Ahriman saw thousands of soul-lights flickering out of existence, lives lost by the hundreds every second.

'This is the death rattle of the Thramas Crusade,' said Magnus, grimly.

Ahriman spun around the battle, a ghost of light bearing witness to the cold, airless slaughter. The black ships bearing the winged sword were in the ascendance, reaping a dreadful tally among the midnight ships of the Night Lords, but it seemed the VIII Legion was not seeking a decisive engagement. Magnus went on.

'For two years they have beaten themselves bloody against one another, but with this battle, the war is over and my brothers retire to lick their wounds.'

'Who was the victor?'

'That remains to be seen, though the Dark Angels still bear with them the seeds of their own destruction. In such times, can anyone be called the victor?'

The heavens blurred again, and this time Ahriman felt resistance to their passage.

One by one, the stars went out, snuffed like candles in a novitiates' dormitory until all was darkness. Beyond the black curtain, Ahriman saw a burning world, cracked and ravaged by fire. Its continental plates had split apart, and an eightfold symbol was burned into its crust.

Beyond this was a planet wreathed in a glittering corona of battle, a red world bathed in blood and madness. Ahriman made to fly onwards, to see what new insanity was at play, but a gentle psychic pressure from Magnus halted him.

'No, my son. To come any closer would see you tainted by the madness that would drag Sanguinius and his Angels to their doom.'

'The Blood Angels, destroyed?'

'Time will tell, for Sanguinius stands at a crossroads. He knows both paths end in blood, but he is stronger than anyone understands. Well... *almost* anyone. Guilliman knows, but even he does not truly know his brother's wounded heart.'

The image of the blood-red planet faded, replaced by the vast gulfs of wilderness space between worlds – emptiness that the human mind was incapable of grasping.

'Why are you showing me this?' asked Ahriman.

'Because I will not be made a fool of, again,' Magnus spat. 'Prospero burns because I thought I knew more than anyone else. If we are to choose a course for our Legion, I would have it be the right one. And to that end, I travel the stars and time itself to find my brothers, to know with whom they stand.'

Ahriman felt the emptiness around him grow ever more claustrophobic, like the walls of a meditation chamber inexorably closing in. What had felt unimaginably huge and spacious a moment ago, now felt cramped and constricting.

'That is the weight of our decision pressing in on us, Ahzek,' the primarch said. 'War has come to the galaxy – a war like never before, and soon I will have to choose a side.'

'*Why* must you choose a side? We were betrayed by the Emperor, and Horus Lupercal has nothing to offer us.'

'Think you so? Then let me show you Ultramar.'

The glittering form of Magnus flared brightly, dragging Ahriman in his wake as they plummeted through space once more. This time they travelled to a blue world that withered in the hell-storm of its doomed star. Its cities were flayed by radioactive winds, and those souls not yet below in the subterranean arcologies were already dead.

'I know this world,' said Ahriman, horrified at what he saw. 'I came here after visiting the Crystal Library on Prandium. This is Calth.'

Ships of war scattered from the doomed planet, the gold and azure of the XIII Legion and the bruise-red of the XVII. The Ultramarines vessels regrouped, while the Word Bearers used the chaos of battle's end to scatter into the darkness between the Five Hundred Worlds.

Even as Ahriman watched, a storm exploded from the planet's surface, like the most terrible eruption on the surface of a star. Invisible to the naked eye, it was a vast outpouring of inchoate energies to those with a link to the aether. It engulfed Calth, and soon spread beyond its system boundaries, a ruinous storm of epic proportions that burned like a voracious forest fire.

Uncontrolled, raw and bleeding-edged, the storm tore through the immaterial realm without direction, a raging barrier of hatred and spite that was impassable to all but the most powerful individuals. The energies expended in its creation beggared belief, and Ahriman found it hard to comprehend that something so devastating could come about naturally. But who except the Thousand Sons had the power to summon anything like it?

'They burned Calth...' he murmured, incredulously. 'For Monarchia?'

'Monarchia? No, Calth was but a prologue. Lorgar's vision is grander and wider than the death of a single world, and the cold logic of Guilliman's "practical" is yet to play out in all its majesty and tragedy. Already the pieces are moving, and I sense that this will be the key to everything.'

Ahriman could scarcely believe it. 'Lorgar dares to assault the Five Hundred Worlds? Has he gone mad? Guilliman's armies are Legion. Lorgar could never defeat the host of Ultramar.'

Glittering amusement passed through the luminosity of Magnus's form. 'I will pass your sentiments to my brother when I see him next. After all, history teaches us that there is no such thing as an invincible army...'

He paused, seeming to consider that truth for a moment.

'But sometimes, history needs a push.'

THE DIVINE WORD

Gav Thorpe

'The Word of the Emperor must be Read and Heard with Diligence, so that you may arrive to the Knowledge that is needful for you.'

– from the *The Lectitio Divinitatus*

THE SKY ABOVE the city flashed and cracked with arcs of lightning, starkly silhouetting the army retreating from the shattered out- skirts. Thousands of men and women pulled back from Milvian, bloodied and despondent. The burned shells of tanks and trans- ports were left in their wake as the soldiers of the Therion Cohort responded swiftly and gratefully to the retreat order.

Shellfire and las-blasts followed them, further thinning their num- bers, until covering barrages from hundreds of emplaced guns fell upon Milvian, stalling any pursuit. In the growing gloom of twi- light, the Therions streamed towards their waiting comrades.

The display view faded to static as the recon-link was cut by the observation officers accompanying the assault. Marcus was relieved that he did not have to look at the downcast columns trudging back to the Imperial lines; the view was replaced by a strategic schematic of lines and symbols and target designations that cast a clinical veneer over the whole, depressing affair.

It was not the first setback that Marcus Valerius had faced in his military career but he wondered if it would be the last. The The-rion vice-Caesari pulled his attention away from the main screen on the command deck and returned his gaze to the small commu-nications monitor in the panel beside him.

'The batteries at Milvian must be silenced by midday at the latest. There can be no further delays. Our success depends upon it.'

Looking at the stern face of Commander Branne in the moni-tor display, Marcus knew that the Raven Guard captain was not employing hyperbole. If Branne said the campaign hinged on his army seizing Milvian in the next eighteen hours, then he could be sure that it was the truth.

Though Branne kept his tone even, free from accusation, Marcus was well aware that he deserved far harsher treatment. The initial attack on Milvian had stalled early on, and the Therion Cohort had been forced back in some disarray.

But it was a setback that the vice-Caesari was determined to rectify.

'Everything is being prepared for a fresh assault at dawn,' Marcus assured the Raven Guard commander. He had rushed the initial attack, perhaps out of overconfidence, or simply eagerness. More than seventeen hundred Therions had paid for the mistake with their lives. 'I have determined a new attack approach that should see us break through to the batteries this time. We will engage with full force and nothing less. Your ships will be clear for low orbital attack.'

'We are poised to strike a deadly blow,' Branne continued, labouring a point that he had made several times before. Marcus accepted the reminder in silence, head bowed. *'Your advance on the second capi-tal, Milvian, has sent much of the traitors' higher command fleeing to a bunker complex thirty kilometres south of the city. They will not remain there for long. The Raven Guard will fall upon the renegade commanders with gunship and drop pod in eighteen hours' time; providing that the Therions and their auxiliaries can take Milvian and silence the defence*

lasers and other anti-orbital weapons guarding the city's surrounds.'

Branne did not need to reiterate what was at stake. With the taking of Milvian and the elimination of the traitor command, the world of Euesa would be returned to the Imperial fold and with it control of the Vandreggan Sector.

There was nothing Marcus could say that would not sound like excuses or argument to the Legiones Astartes officer. 'Yes, commander. The Milvian batteries will fall.'

'Confirmed. Is there anything else?'

There was, but Marcus kept his thoughts to himself. There was the dream.

But the bustling command centre was no place to discuss a private matter between Valerius and Branne.

'Nothing, commander.'

'That is reassuring, vice-Caesari. Fight well.'

The display shimmered and then disappeared. Marcus issued a few orders for forces to move forwards and cover the retreat. Assured that all was being done that could be done, the weary vice-Caesari left the command deck and returned to his chambers.

A gentle cough attracted his attention and he stopped to look at Pelon, who was waiting expectantly by the closed curtains across the window. The youth was maturing into a slender but muscled young man, and bore his rank of sub-tribune with pride. It was hard to reconcile the determined figure accompanying Marcus with the easily-startled boy who had been assigned as his manservant ten years before.

'Yes, Pelon?' said Marcus.

'Shall I let in some light, vice-Caesari?'

Valerius waved a hand in ambivalent reply, dismissing the distraction as he started pacing, exhausted in body but his mind whirling with the implications of the defeat. Pelon took this as permission and drew on the cord that pulled back the heavy drapes. The last rays of bluish sunlight streamed in through a trio of arched windows, revealing wooded hills and slate-grey clouds.

Marcus stopped, taken aback by the view. He had been so occupied with the attack that he had not looked out at the landscape of Euesa for several days. He strode to the window and watched as a tree-crowned hill slid past.

Of course, the hill was not moving; the relative motion came from the massive Capitol Imperialis transport that served as Marcus's headquarters. Eighty metres long and fifty high, the *Contemptuous* trundled relentlessly forwards at no more than a brisk walking pace, carried on long tracks, its slab sides dotted with viewports and weapon sponsons. Five kilometres away was another lumbering Imperialis – the *Iron General*, commanded by Praefector Antonius, Marcus's younger brother.

Each of the super-heavy war engines carried two companies of the Therion Cohort – one hundred men and accompanying battle tanks – while a host of Mechanicum tech-priests, adepts and servitors tended the massive behemoth cannon and hundreds of secondary weapons.

Around the pair of transports the rest of the Therions advanced, on foot and in troop carriers, seven hundred thousand men in all. Amongst them strode the Scout and Battle Titans of the Legio Vindictus, supported by several thousand mechanically augmented skitarii, sagitarii, praetorians and heraklii, along with dozens more strange war engines and service vehicles.

There were other super-heavy vehicles in the army – Baneblades and Shadow Swords, Stormhammers and Leviathans of the Capricorn 13th Suppression regiment – alongside hundreds of Leman Russ tanks, Chimera transports, Hydra anti-aircraft cannons and many other tanks and war engines. With them came Gryphons and siege bombards, Basilisk assault guns and mobile missile platforms.

In the two and a half years since the new Therion Cohort had been blooded at the Perfect Fortress of the Emperor's Children, Marcus's army had grown strong indeed.

The route of the advance was being paved, in some places *literally*, by the Lothor Pioneer Corps. Fifteen thousand men and as many engineering vehicles cut a swath through the woods, levelling hills and cutting ramps down the cliffs and escarpments to ease the passage of the host that followed them. Rivers were dammed or bridged by cunningly-designed machines. Swamps had been drained and roadways laid for hundreds of kilometres on end across the plains and low-lying foothills.

The only part of the force not represented were the Raven Guard themselves. The Legion of Lord Corax was dispersed across Euesa and in orbit, but it had been the Raven Guard that had heralded the arrival of the Emperor's forces, and the Raven Guard that had seized the space port at Carlingia to allow the Therions and their allies to land their immense war machines.

'The command council is in two hours,' said Valerius, turning away from the military spectacle. He crossed to the cot made up in one corner of the chamber, the constant rumble of the massive transport's engines no longer a distraction. 'Wake me in one hour.'

He shrugged off his heavy coat into Pelon's waiting hands. As he sat on the edge of the bed and Pelon knelt to remove his boots, the vice-Caesari noticed that his attendant was unusually pensive.

'Something is on your mind. Speak it.'

The attendant hesitated, concentrating on his task. He did not meet his master's gaze as he spoke. 'You did not mention your dreams to Commander Branne this time, I assume.'

'I did not,' Valerius replied. With his boots removed, he swung his legs onto the bed and laid back, hands clasped across his chest. 'He made it clear after the debacle with the Raptors that I was not to speak of them again.'

'The last such dream saved the Raven Guard from annihilation, vice-Caesari. Do you not think this latest experience might be pertinent to the campaign?'

'I am fortunate that Lord Corax has appeared to have dispensed with any curiosity over our timely arrival at Isstvan, and Branne would have it remain so. It is clear to me that the primarch did not send me the visions and I am not about to raise issues that could lead to uncomfortable questions. We have seen some strange things in this war already. An Imperial Army commander who has dream-visions would not be tolerated.'

'But what if the dreams were sent by another, higher power than the primarch?' There was slight admonition in Pelon's tone.

'Nonsense,' said Valerius, sitting up. He looked at his attendant. 'There are no higher powers.'

'I can think of one,' Pelon suggested quietly.

The valet delved into a pocket of his tunic and brought forth a sheaf of tattered papers and plas-prints. He became more animated.

'I was given these by one of the Lothorians, in respect to an entirely different concern. There is truth in these writings, deeper than anything I have read before. The Emperor has not abandoned us, but continues to watch and guide his followers. It is all in here.'

He proffered the bundle of sheets to Valerius, but the vice-Caesari waved them away with a contemptuous snort.

'I expected better of you, Pelon. I thought you had been raised a Therion and taught the wisdom of logic and reason. Now you seek to peddle these superstitions as a deeper truth? Do you not think I have heard these prattling of the divine before? It is an affront to the Imperial Truth, and everything we have fought for.'

'Apologies, vice-Caesari, I did not mean to offend,' said Pelon, hastily stuffing the texts back into his pocket.

'Wake me in one hour, and we'll say no more about god-Emperors and divine guidance.'

✠ ✠ ✠

Sleep had not come easily to Valerius for several days, and today was no different. As soon as he started to slumber, his thoughts were assailed by a frightening tableau. The vice-Caesari stood upon a grassy plain, with storm clouds gathering overhead. Around him the grass parted and rustled as something slithered close by.

Serpents rose up, their slick, green scales shining, the beasts baring fangs as long as daggers. Valerius was surrounded, unable to flee as the snakes closed in on him, sinking their teeth into his legs and arms, burying fangs in his chest and gut.

As he writhed in torment, Marcus saw a greater body heaving into view and realised that the creatures attacking him were but the multitudinous heads of a single monster. The hydra beast of ancient Terran myth subdued him with its venom, and looped its coils about him as it withdrew its fangs, squeezing the life from him...

Marcus woke with sweat dampening his brow.

Through the windows he saw that the sky had darkened further. Pelon sat on a stool by the dresser, hastily pushing something back into his pocket as he turned at his master's wakening. There was concern in the attendant's eyes, and something that Valerius had not noticed before.

Wonder.

Whatever nonsense was written in those scraps of text had clearly had a profound impact upon the young man, but Valerius no longer had the energy to berate him. The vice-Caesari dragged himself upright, his shirt and breeches moist with perspiration.

Pelon crossed to the curtained wardrobe and pulled out a freshly pressed uniform. Valerius wordlessly nodded his thanks.

Situated behind the bridge of the Capitol Imperialis, the command chamber was a broad room twenty metres by thirty, dominated by the glowing hololith display at its centre. A line of communications panels manned by servitors and adjutants lit one wall, while the opposite bulkhead was filled with a live-feed visual display from the transport's scanners and the strategic network.

The hololith was centred on Milvian, a sprawling city that had burst past its curtain wall decades ago, creating a mish-mash suburb of manufactories and habitation tenements encircling the perimeter defence towers and main garrison buildings. Large palaces of the planetary elite dominated the hill that rose inside the walls at the western edge, protected by four keeps overlooking the tilt bridge that spanned the river bisecting the city. Overflights by recon craft and orbital surveys had confirmed that all of the other crossings had been destroyed by the defenders.

Counter-battery fire from macro cannons and wall emplacements was falling only a few kilometres away, so that the command council was conducted to a backdrop of continual shelling against the earthworks and trench lines thrown up over the last days by the Pioneers and their engines.

As Valerius spoke, sub-tribunes manipulated the display on the hololith, assigning formations and manoeuvres with blinking arrows and icons.

'The plan has not changed,' the vice-Caesari told his command council. 'The taking of the city comprises four phases. The first has been already completed – the establishment of a siege line two kilometres from the outskirts of the suburbs. Colonel Golade's guns and rockets of the Capricorn Thirteenth have pounded the inner defensive line. The curtain of fire laid down has held the main force of the traitors inside the central city, leaving the outskirts vulnerable. Led by their praefectors, the men of the Therion Cohort will seize the outer city, ready for an assault on the walls, clearing the streets for the tanks and Titans that would form a spearhead for the main attack.'

Valerius paused as a flashing blue dome appeared on the hololith.

'All was well, we thought, but the earlier attack met something we have not encountered before. A force screen shields the approaches to the city wall, capable of turning aside shells and lasers, ripping into living flesh with great sprays of energy. The men call it the 'lightning field' and it stopped them in their tracks.

'The lightning field is the greatest obstacle, but once it falls,' – Marcus was confident that it *would* fall, once they located the generators and disabled them – 'the inner city districts on either side of the river form the final two objectives. The orbital defence weapons inside the hill keep will be silenced, and the Raven Guard can launch their drop attack on the fortifications beyond the city.'

'Orbital support?'

The question was asked by General Kayhil of the Pioneers, a short, wiry man in his later years dressed in nondescript camouflage fatigues.

'Not until we silence the defences,' replied Marcus. 'We cannot risk any ships in low orbit and any other strikes would be too inaccurate. We need precision strikes to remove the lightning field. Once we have taken out the energy screen we will have air support, but the objective is to take the city, not level it.'

The vice-Caesari waited to see if there were any other questions from the assembled officers. At the back of his mind he could still feel the hot breath of the hydra upon his skin and the sting of its fangs piercing his flesh. He tried to ignore the sensation but the latest dream had been more vivid than before, leaving him in a state of deep unease.

He reviewed the holo-schematic once more, seeking any area of vulnerability.

His gaze settled upon the small town of Lavlin, four kilometres to the west along the main axis of advance. It had been hit heavily by the Capricorn 13th and an orbital attack in the previous days, and a sweep by the Pioneers had confirmed that it was clear of enemies.

And yet, now Marcus's eye was drawn to it once again.

'We are sure that the flank at Lavlin is secure?' he asked Kayhil.

'No enemy troops there twelve hours ago,' the general said with a shrug. 'We could perform another reconnaissance sweep into the ruins, but that would take time. I cannot spare men from the main attack.'

Valerius considered his options, stroking his freshly shaven chin. For all that the plan seemed to be secure – as secure as any plan could be – he could not rid himself of the doubts caused by his nightmare, and the retreat earlier that day.

Again and again his eyes flickered back to Lavlin.

'I will detail ten companies to act as a reserve, in case a flank is threatened.' He turned his attention to one of the screens, showing the face of Princeps Senioris Niadansal of the Legio Vindictus, who had joined the council from the bridge of his Warlord Titan. 'Please assign two engines to the reserve, princeps.'

'It seems a waste of resource,' the commander replied brusquely, brow furrowing. 'Ten companies and two Titans might be sorely missed during the main assault.'

'We can breach the lightning field without them,' Valerius countered. 'They can move forwards and support the main attack once the flank is secure.'

'Do you have some intelligence that we have not seen, vice-Caesari?' asked Colonel Golade of the Capricorns. 'Why the sudden doubt over Lavlin?'

'No intelligence,' Marcus said quickly. He took a moment, calming himself. 'It is imperative that we advance on the city unmolested – that is all. Better to be sure now than regretful later.'

'Perhaps you are being overly cautious,' suggested Golade. 'Casualties are an inevitable consequence of war.'

Valerius bit back his first reply, reminded that the Capricorns were not in the assault force, but safe behind siege lines located kilometres from the city. Instead, he grunted and shrugged.

'Cautious, yes, but not overly so, colonel,' he said evenly, keeping his temper in check. Golade did not know what Marcus felt deep inside and could not be blamed for his doubts.

'Who is to command the reserve?' asked Antonius. Dressed in the colourful uniform of the Therions, complete with the red sash of office across his breastplate, the praefector reminded Marcus of himself a few years ago when he had been bringing planets to compliance; more than two years of war against the traitors had not marred Antonius's optimism. Marcus envied his younger brother's hopefulness, but after seeing what had happened at Isstvan and experiencing the treachery of Warmaster Horus first-hand, Marcus had given up any thought of ultimate victory and simply accepted each battle as it came.

'You will,' Marcus replied. There was nobody he trusted more, and the presence of the *Iron General* was not essential to the main assault. 'I will send details of the detachment – six infantry companies, four armoured – before you take your shuttle back.'

Antonius accepted the responsibility with a nod, and a curious look in his eye. At first Marcus thought that he saw suspicion in the expressions of the others, but realised it was his paranoia. The other officers were dubious of the sudden change of plan, but nothing more.

'Any other considerations we have not covered?' he asked, changing the subject. The assembled council offered no further comments or questions in the brief pause. 'Good. Golade's bombardment commences in thirty minutes. We attack in forty-five.'

THE BRIDGE OF the *Contemptuous* buzzed with comm-net feeds and vox-chatter being monitored by Valerius's subordinates. Every minute or so the main cannon fired, causing the Capitol Imperialis to shudder, the deafening boom barely muffled by audio dampeners.

Marcus concentrated on the main display, which had been divided into seven sub-screens showing the battle-telemetry across the five kilometres-long front. One display was hooked into a live-feed from the reconnaissance craft in the upper atmosphere above the city, showing the pulverised defences. The fire of the Capricorns continued to rain down, shells and missiles concentrated on the pillboxes and weapons batteries.

Five more displays were schematics of the Pioneer and Therion advance into the outskirts of Milvian. Infantry brigades moved swiftly from building to building, covered by Vindictus Warhound Titans. Progress was swift, and it seemed as though the bulk of the enemy had been withdrawn to the wall as Marcus had expected. Even so, the attack was methodical and thorough, leaving nothing to fortune.

A kilometre behind the infantry came the tanks and assault guns of Therion and Capricorn. In long columns they crawled forwards along the main boulevards and avenues, accompanied by more infantry to ensure they were not ambushed.

The remaining screen was a serialised pict-feed around the headquarters transport, the vista of smoke-shrouded streets slightly blurred by the six banks of void shields protecting the massive command vehicle. Flickers of las-fire, blossoms of explosions and columns of smoke painted the scene. The blur of artillery shells sped across the cloudy sky and plumes of dust from collapsing buildings billowed along the streets. From across the comm, a constant background wash of innumerable reports and conversations and the chatter of small arms fire was punctuated by louder detonations. Men and women exchanged terse reports, swore and cursed, reeled off target grids and barked orders to their subordinates.

It felt quite distant, almost a step removed from Marcus as he listened and watched. He would catch a snippet of a sergeant berating his squad for falling back and then the sonorous chant of a

Mechanicum servitor churning out scan vectors, broken by the crackle of static and the hiss of cipher dampening. There were shouts, cries of pain, and on the screens tiny symbols would flash or disappear as the battle ebbed and flowed. Miniscule markings wormed their way along back alleys and were baulked at enemy-held junctions. Arrows of projected advances, triangles of tertiary objectives seized and circles denoting cannon fire zones covered the screens in a seemingly random pattern.

Marcus did not try to comprehend it all; less than tenth of what was going on filtered into his conscious thoughts. Now and then he would ask for clarification from one of his tribunes, but it was not his part to manage every detail of the conflict. His eye was on the broad sweep, and in this regard all was progressing as he had hoped.

Now and then his attention was drawn to the last sub-screen, over which scrolled the casualty listing of the eighteen Therion Cohort phalanxes. Two thousand and thirty men had fallen in the first attack – not all of them dead – but the rate of loss had slowed as the army progressed past the outer line of defenders.

Four kilometres behind and three kilometres to the west, on the right flank of the advance, the *Iron General* and attending companies waited for the command to attack. The assault had begun an hour ago and there was no sign of threat from Lavlin, but Marcus was not yet ready to shake off his misgivings and commit the reserve.

THE CONTEMPTUOUS SUPPORTED the main attack, ploughing along the main thoroughfare of Milvian towards the outer limits of the lightning field. The defensive screen had not been tested against the void shields of a Titan or Capitol Imperialis, and Valerius had determined the super-heavy mobile fortress was the best means of destroying one of the generators. Once a breach was made in the field's coverage, other forces would target the rest.

There was more to Valerius leading the attack than simple prag-
matism. After the repulse of his earlier assault he wanted to prove
to his men, and more importantly to Lord Corax, that he and his
Therions could still be relied upon. When they had been founded,
they had served the Emperor himself, and the primarch of the Raven
Guard deserved no less.

The *Contemptuous* ground forwards, pulverising deserted groundcars and abandoned tanks that lay in the fortress's path. The
batteries on both flanks were unleashing their fire into the surrounding city blocks, the main cannon levelling structures even a
few hundred metres distant. The shells of the defenders detonated
around the advancing behemoth. Now and then a direct hit would
shimmer across the void shields, engulfing the *Contemptuous* in a
blazing aura of purple and gold.

In the wake of the gargantuan engine, Therion tanks and infantry waited to pour forwards to exploit any breakthrough.

Valerius knew that the battle was at its hinge point, with success
or failure of the entire invasion in the balance of the next hour.
Though the advance through the outer city had been swift, the traitors had been wise to marshal their resources inside the lightning
field and the attack had almost ground to a standstill. There were
numerous requests from Valerius's subordinates to commit the
reserve – the added firepower of the Titans and companies were
in demand all across the front.

'Generator site within range, vice-Caesari,' reported one of the
tribunes.

'Target main weapon systems. Fire for full effect.'

As the order left Marcus's lips, another tribune blurted out a warning from his position as the sensor panels. 'Enemy Warlord Titan,
eight hundred metres, sector four, targeting us!'

A sub-screen blurred and brought up an image of the traitor war
engine, its outline hazy beyond its void shields.

'Shall we redirect fire?'

'Negative,' snapped Marcus. 'Concentrate all weapons on the field generator. Our void shields can weather the enemy attack. Our Titans will respond.'

The *Contemptuous* shook as it unleashed a full barrage from its cannons and heavy weapons. Half a kilometre ahead, the generator complex exploded into a micro-storm as the lightning field detonated, sending rockcrete and gobbets of molten metal hundreds of metres into the air amongst arcing shafts of energy.

A triumphant shout across the command deck was silenced by a call from the sensorium tribune.

'Warp missile, vice-Caesari!'

The sub-screen zoomed in on one of the traitor Titan's carapace weapon hard points. A missile ten metres long launched in a plume of blue fire. It covered the first hundred metres in seconds before its miniature warp engine activated. The missile disappeared for a moment, leaving nothing more than a contrail of wavering white and green warp energy. A second later it reappeared, less than two hundred metres from the *Contemptuous*.

'Brace for impact!' roared Valerius as the incoming ordnance skipped into the warp again.

The vice-Caesari grabbed hold of the command console as the warp missile appeared *inside* the Capitol Imperialis's void shields and detonated. Valerius was flung to the deck as the *Contemptuous* rocked on its tracks, teetering for a long moment before crashing back onto the road.

Warning sirens blared, deafening Valerius as he pushed himself to his feet. Blood streamed down his face from a cut on his brow. He wiped it away with the frocked sleeve of his shirt.

'Damage control. Return fire.'

'Vice-Caesari, we have confirmation – the lightning field is down,' reported one of the tribunes. 'Shall we commit the reserves?'

Marcus was on the verge of issuing the order, knowing that any significant delay risked the enemy recovering from the lightning field's failure, delaying the assault on the anti-orbital guns. His men and their allies were dying in the hundreds to push on, but their deaths would be for nothing if the batteries on the far side were not secured.

He was about to contact Antonius when his personal link chimed. To Marcus's surprise, it was his brother.

'Vice-Caesari, we are detecting movement through the ruins of Lavlin. Infantry companies. They are broadcasting Raven Guard Legion authorisation identifiers, and are requesting passage through the line.'

Valerius could barely concentrate amongst the blaring of the klaxons, the barked reports of his tribunes and the throbbing from the wound on his face. 'Are you sure? I have had no report from the primarch or his commanders that the Legion is operating in this area.'

'Comm-checks and sensor sweeps confirm a sizeable force of infantry and vehicles moving on our position. Perhaps there has been a change of plan?'

Marcus was taken aback by the news. While it was possible that a contingent of Raven Guard *had* sent additional forces to join the battle – several of the Legion's companies were spread across the planet fighting independently, as was Corax's usual strategy – it stretched credulity to think that he would not be informed of their presence on his battle front.

'You are sure they are transmitting the appropriate call signs and ident codes?'

'They are Raven Guard signals, vice-Caesari. A few days old, but they clear our protocol servitors.'

The vision of the many-headed serpent fluttered through Marcus's thoughts and his gut writhed.

Old call signs. It was more than coincidence. It had to be.

'The signals are false, Antonius. Open fire.'

'*Brother? You want us to fire on forces sent by the Raven Guard to aid us? Have you gone mad?*'

Marcus considered the accusation for a moment, and drew no conclusion one way or the other. Perhaps he was mad, but perhaps not. If the arriving force were enemies then they would have a clear attack into the rear of the Therions. The whole army would have to be pulled back to counter them. Though Marcus was not sure of his sanity, his instincts were screaming at him to be aware of deception. The primarch himself had given strict orders concerning communications security since the crisis at Ravendelve. Marcus was well within his authority.

'Open fire on approaching forces. Traitors have breached our protocols. This is an enemy attack!'

'*Marcus–*'

'Open fire, or I will have you removed from command!'

The comm went silent. Marcus waited nervously, fidgeting with the red sash across his chest, yet there was no doubt in his mind that he had done the right thing. He watched as the enemy Titan's void shields flared and failed under the pounding of the main cannon and converging fire from friendly Warlords arriving from all directions.

Nearly three minutes trickled past, during which Marcus was expecting to receive an irate communication from Branne, or perhaps even from Lord Corax himself. He wiped the sweat from his face with the cuff of his jacket and stared at the screens, forcing himself to observe the ongoing battle.

'Vice-Caesari, reports of fighting on the western flank.' One of the tribunes delivered the message breathlessly, face reddened with shock. 'Praefector Antonius has engaged an enemy force of Imperial Army renegades on the outskirts of Lavlin. Reserve phalanx and Titans are moving forwards to engage.'

Marcus forced himself to remain calm. He let out a long breath, and spoke in a measured tone. 'I understand. Send word to all commanders. Focus on the assault. The threat is being dealt with. Any confirmation on the identity of the enemy?'

'Nothing confirmed, vice-Caesari, but initial visual reports indicate Imperial Army warriors with defaced insignia. Rebels.'

Marcus nodded, the news unsurprising. There were bound to be pockets of enemy resistance everywhere.

'Send word to Legion command. Inform them that security protocols have been compromised. Recommend immediate evaluation of all forces and plans.'

The comm-link beeped again in his ear.

'*By the Emperor, brother, that was fortunate!*' exclaimed Antonius. '*I was going to let them walk straight into range and attack us.*'

'Fortune had nothing to do with it, brother,' Marcus replied before he could stop himself.

'*You knew? Why did you not tell us you suspected a traitor attack?*'

What could Marcus say? None save for Pelon knew about the dream, and Marcus was not about to broadcast such confidences to the entire army.

'Simply prudence, brother, nothing more. Do you need additional forces?'

'*No, vice-Caesari. The Titans and tanks are pushing them back already. Prudence be praised, eh?*'

'Something like that.'

WEARY BUT VICTORIOUS, Marcus flopped onto his bed. It was past midnight and there were still forces fighting in the city but he could leave the mopping-up to the others. He had received word from Branne that the drop assault upon the enemy bunker complex had been a complete success. Four thousand enemy had been killed and a number of traitor commanders had been captured. Amongst the enemy leaders had been spotted a lone legionnaire from the Alpha

Legion who had doubtlessly been coordinating the defence, but the traitor had killed himself rather than be captured. Branne had been earnest in his praise of Marcus and the efforts of his army. The commander had, thankfully, made no mention of Marcus's timely interception of the Alpha Legion-orchestrated attack.

'Do you wish to undress, vice-Caesari?'

Marcus had not noticed Pelon, who had been waiting patiently for his master's return. The attendant stood by the bed, and Marcus sat up and shrugged off his coat.

'A moment, Pelon,' he said as the manservant turned towards the wardrobe.

'Master?'

'Those scribblings you had. What did you do with them?'

'I still have them, vice-Caesari.' Pelon looked crestfallen. 'I am sorry. Did you wish me to dispose of them?'

'No, not yet,' Marcus said quietly.

He thought of the day's events and knew that he had to find hope from somewhere. He could not continue simply fighting each battle as it came. The emptiness inside would consume him even if the enemy did not kill him. The lightning field, the warp missile and – most of all – the enemy counter-attack all preyed on his thoughts.

'Let me see them.'

Pelon delved into his pocket and fished out the sheaf of texts, passing them to his master after a moment's pause. Fingers tugging at an earlobe, the vice-Caesari began to read under his breath.

'Love the Emperor, for He is the salvation of Mankind.

Obey His words, for He will lead you into the light of the future.

Heed His wisdom, for He will protect you from evil.

Whisper His prayers with devotion, for they will save your soul.

Honour His servants, for they speak in His voice.

Tremble before His majesty, for we all walk in His immortal shadow...'

LUCIUS, THE
ETERNAL BLADE

Graham McNeill

Lucius walked beneath a sky torn and shredded by storms. He had died beneath a sky like this, in a shattered temple far from what the XV Legion called – with stultifying literalness – the Planet of the Sorcerers.

The Emperor's Children had splintered in the wake of Fulgrim's apotheosis on Iydris. Some had followed the primarch to answer a summons from the Warmaster, while others seized Legion ships to strike out on their own.

But a black mood had all but consumed Lucius since Iydris.

He had died, but that wasn't why he brooded. He had been *beaten*.

A Raven named Nykona Sharrowkyn had *actually* killed him, and had taken no satisfaction from that supremely unlikely feat.

That rankled. That *hurt*.

Lucius did not know what intervention had brought him back – whether it had been some higher power or the lunatic science of Fabius – and didn't much care. Now, he had something to prove. To himself more than anyone else.

He was Lucius the swordsman. No one was more skilled with a blade.

Lucius first heard of Sanakht from Hathor Maat, a legionary who reminded Lucius so much of his younger self that he had wanted to kill him there and then. Maat told Lucius that Sanakht was a student of the ancient schools of swordsmanship, a warrior of unsurpassed skill whose defeat remained unseen by the Corvidae's most gifted scryers.

Lucius didn't know who the Corvidae were, but was willing to bet that they had not factored *him* into their visions. And so he had abandoned the rest of his Legion, as much as the rabble Fulgrim left behind could still be called, and set off to find this Sanakht.

The one constant that Lucius came to appreciate of the Crimson King's adopted home world was that nothing was constant. He had been walking for what felt like forever, but his destination came no closer. Sometimes Sanakht's tower appeared to be no larger than a gunship, hovering over glassy plains that reflected a sky that did not match the one above. Other times it rose from distant mountains, a stalagmite of such colossal proportions that it was a mountain itself.

It was always just ahead of him, taunting him.

Drawing him on.

Right now, it appeared as a slender minaret of fluted ivory and mother-of-pearl with a cupola that burned in silver fire. It stood amidst a thick forest of trees that writhed with their own sick radiance. Living flames leapt from branch to branch, giggling with childish amusement as the forest grew and fell back, denying him a way through.

'Scared of me, are you?' Lucius shouted, and the blue flame at the top of the tower flared brighter in response.

He drew his sword, its blade radiant silver. It had been a gift from his primarch; too noble a weapon for hewing, but a necessity in times of need.

Lucius hacked at the glass trees, shattering glowing limbs to fragments with every swing. He pushed deeper into the glittering forest, shorn branches reforming behind him with the sound of windows breaking in reverse.

The capering flames screeched in annoyance, but Lucius ignored them. They darted in and sought to burn him, but he unhooked the barbed whip that he had lifted from Kalimos and lashed them back.

They squealed and fled its agonising touch.

Then the forest parted, and Sanakht's tower was before him. Closer now, he saw the mercury-bright flame veining its structure like a living thing.

A warrior in crimson armour stood in a duelling circle of flattened sand before the tower. Twin swords hung at his waist – one pommel capped with a dark jackal's head, the other with a white hawk. Both were hooked khopesh blades with strange, shimmering curves that gave Lucius a thrill of anticipation.

To face a new blade was always interesting.

'I hear you have been looking to fight me, Lucius,' said the warrior, his face obscured behind a helm with a silver crest and faceplate.

'Are you Sanakht?'

'I am Sanakht of the Athanaeans, yes.'

'Then I've come to fight you.'

'It is your wish to die?'

Lucius laughed. 'I think I did that once already, so I'm not about to try it again.'

Sanakht removed his helm, revealing a youthful face and close-cropped, ash blond hair – innocently handsome in a way that Lucius couldn't wait to destroy.

'Your feelings say different,' said Sanakht. 'You want to know *why* you came back. That is why you sought me out – to find a swordsman as skilled as the Raven. One who revels in the kill.'

'They tell me you're good,' said Lucius.

'I am the best of my Legion.'

'That's not saying much.' Lucius hooked the whip to his belt and entered the duelling circle. Sanakht drew his swords: one crystalline edged and glittering with witch-fire, the other a simple energy blade.

Lucius rolled his shoulders, and swung his blade to loosen his wrist. He had sparred with his own Legion, but had stopped short of killing anyone since Iydris. No such restraint was needed here.

He circled Sanakht, studying his movements, assaying his reach and footwork. He saw strength and speed. Confidence that crossed into arrogance. Sanakht was so like himself, it was almost funny.

'I assure you that I will defeat–' Sanakht began, but Lucius attacked before the Thousand Sons warrior could finish speaking.

All of his strikes were repulsed with casual ease. They broke apart and circled again, studying one another and using obvious cuts and feints to test the other's mettle.

'You have natural ability,' said Sanakht, 'but I have studied every school of the blade since the first swords were hacked from the Dobruja flintbeds of Old Earth.'

They came together again in a clash of blades. Sanakht was blindingly fast, his two weapons moving in perfect concert. Lucius could fight with two swords, but preferred the focus of a single blade. Sanakht's blades cut high and low, forcing him to work twice as hard to keep them at bay.

'Your thoughts betray you,' said Sanakht, and Lucius heard the first trace of amusement in his voice. 'You fight with passion, but I can feel every attack before you make it.'

'Are you actually giving me tips on technique?'

Sanakht swayed aside from a throat-opening thrust. 'I am a scholar of martial knowledge. It is my duty to pass on what I have learned to others, by example.'

'Thanks, but I don't need your help.'

'You are manifestly incorrect,' said Sanakht.

Anger touched Lucius, but instead of controlling it, he let it consume him. An angry swordsman made mistakes, but now he needed that anger. He threw himself at his opponent, discarding any notion of testing his defences, just going for the kill. He wanted to take this arrogant cur apart, to gut him without mercy and without finesse.

To give him an ugly death.

Sanakht turned aside the attacks with lightning-fast parries and ripostes, but Lucius kept up an unrelenting pressure. He forced him back to the edge of the circle, relishing the confusion he saw in Sanakht's eyes.

No longer able to pick out Lucius's emotions from the morass of anger, Sanakht was falling back on techniques learned by rote, and from ancient teachers.

And that just wasn't good enough.

Lucius hooked his sword under the energy-wreathed blade and spun it from Sanakht's grip. As the warrior's arm went wide, Lucius kicked him in the groin and slammed the hilt of his sword into his face.

Sanakht fell back, rolling and bringing his second sword to bear. Lucius smashed it aside, and his return stroke swept down to open Sanakht's throat.

But the silver blade stopped a hair's breadth from Sanakht's neck, as though striking stone. Resistance vibrated up Lucius's arm, and he crashed his other fist into Sanakht's jaw instead.

'Sorcery?' he spat. 'You'd save your miserable skin with sorcery?'

'He wouldn't,' said a voice behind Lucius. 'But I would.'

Lucius spun around, his sword coming away from Sanakht's neck. Another red-armoured warrior stood at the edge of the duelling circle, a cloak of blackly iridescent feathers billowing at his shoulders.

'And who are you to spare his life?' Lucius demanded.

'I am Ahzek Ahriman,' said the warrior. 'And I will soon have need of Sanakht.'

THE EIGHTFOLD PATH

Anthony Reynolds

I STAND WAITING, a duelling axe held loosely in my hand. It is not Gorechild – that roaring monster is purely for killing. The bout is not *sanguis extremis*.

The weapon is bound to my wrist with chain, in honour of the Desh'ean gladiators. I have seen their bones. I have walked the site of their death. I helped enact Angron's vengeance upon their killers.

I never met them, yet their deaths have made known who we are becoming. We are slaves to their memory.

'Third blood, Khârn?'

Borok is stripped to the waist, as am I. His slab-muscled torso is criss-crossed with old wounds. Scars upon scars. All of them are on his front; he has never shown an enemy his back. He is no coward.

'*First* blood,' I respond.

I can see in his eyes that he is disappointed, but he nods in agreement anyway. The Legion has bled enough. There have been too many deaths in the pits since Angron's change, his... *ascension*. That was the word that his brother Lorgar used to describe it, at least.

And as ever, Angron has changed, but so too have his sons.

The circling spectators are noisy. They bray like animals. They hunger for the sight of blood. The Butcher's Nails demand it of us all.

They press into the soft flesh of my mind, grinding and wrenching at my pain receptors. They are getting worse. Even at their most dormant they make themselves known, corkscrewing into my brain. The screws turn and the nails hammer.

The camaraderie of my fellow World Eaters cannot raise a smile from me. Food tastes like ashes. There is no joy to be had but that found in killing. Opening arteries, cleaving flesh, taking skulls – this is what the Nails want from me.

I have shunned my brothers these last weeks. Dark thoughts haunt me. I have taken to walking the decks of the *Conqueror* alone; stalking her corridors compulsively, as though the mere act of walking kilometres upon kilometres will give me some sudden insight. Some direction. Some... hope?

I had not intended to come here tonight. Perhaps the Nails brought me to the pits, but once I heard the sirens' call of clashing blades and weapons hacking into flesh, I was unable to turn away. The promise of even a moment's relief from the incessant grind on my cortex was an offer that was, tonight, irresistible.

The Nails want me to fight again. I have not been here since I humbled Erebus. The wretch's cowardice denied me the kill, and the Nails punished me for it.

But I am here now, and already the pressure has eased.

Borok takes his place opposite me in the circle. He will fight with his usual armament – a pair of long, curved blades.

Swords against axe. Such a fight never lasts long.

I attack. It is the only way I know. My speed takes him by surprise, almost ending the fight in the first breath. He recovers well, though. We are both dancing to the tune of the Nails, and it is an ugly turn. Few within the Legion fight with grace any more.

I block a blade that flashes for my throat, forcing me to sway aside from its twin coming in low for a disembowelling strike. I kick Borok away, slamming my foot squarely into his solar plexus. He staggers back. I wait for him, rolling my wrist, spinning the duelling axe as I adjust my grip.

He snarls as he throws himself at me. I meet him head-on.

Borok is one of the Devourers, one of Angron's 'bodyguards'. The primarch never needed a bodyguard, of course – not before. And now? Chained and bound below deck, the notion that he needs protecting is laughable. The Devourers are little more than his gaolers. An ignoble task for what should have been the Legion's elite.

Block. Sweep. Side-step, strike.

This is not real. These fights are nothing but distractions to ease the pain until the real battle is joined once again, and then the Legion can be unleashed.

The thought of releasing Angron from his prison is not a comforting one.

And what of us, his sons – are we doomed to a similar fate? Will the last of our humanity be bled out as well, leaving us as nothing more than chained lunatics?

The Nails punish me as they feel my aggression falter. They stab into my brain, blinding me with a white burst of agony. Borok almost takes me then. In my distraction, I only avoid his slashing blades by a hair's breadth.

I can see the frustration in him. He wanted to test himself against the warrior that had bested the Dark Apostle, but that was different. That was *true*. This is merely a charade.

One of his blades scrapes along the haft of my axe, almost grazing my knuckles – that would have been first blood, though a result like that would have made Argel Tal laugh.

Perhaps it is the memory of my old friend that adds some fuel to what comes next.

A backhand blow sends me stumbling to the deck. Something drips onto the back of my hand.

Blood. Did he graze me, without me feeling it? No.

We both glance up, the fight forgotten.

The *ceiling* is bleeding.

Another drop hits me, then another. It is trickling down the walls.

Then I hear Angron's roar.

He has been raging for weeks, but this is different. It silences the crowd.

The sound wells up through the grilled deck, vibrating through the steel. It makes the walls shudder and groan. It crackles out through the unpowered vox-horns. It is enough to warp reality itself.

My heart begins to thunder in time with the pounding in my head. It blurs with Angron's din, rising in intensity, a building crescendo. My fingers tighten around the haft of my axe. A growl escapes my lips. The pounding obliterates everything.

I know what is coming but I am powerless to prevent it. It comes on faster than it ever has before. I barely have time to take a breath.

It hits me like a tidal wave, and in an instant I'm drowning. Taking the axe in both hands, I surge to my feet. Everything goes red.

THE STINK OF blood and raw flesh is the first thing I notice. The second is the roar.

Not Angron. The daemon-primarch has fallen silent, but the roar of the crowd is just as deafening.

My vision returns slowly, the red haze lifting to reveal the aftermath of butchery. Blood coats my hands and arms to the elbow. It drips off my axe. There's blood in my mouth, too, caking my lips and chin. It is not my own.

I look at the carnage I have wrought. Borok is no more. What is left is a ruin – the work of a psychopath. The crowd roars its approval. It is sickening.

I want to be away from here, away from the screams and the charnel stink.

A figure steps forwards. My eyes are unfocused, yet the urge to bury my axe in his blurry face makes my fingers twitch.

'Borok was of the Devourers, Khârn,' he says. 'By rights, his place is now yours.'

That actually makes me laugh. It comes out as a bloody cough, spraying spittle and gobbets of congealed gore.

I drop my axe, and it falls with a dull clang. I wipe my hands down my arms. Blood sloughs away, dripping from my fingertips.

I look around like a dreamer waking from a deep slumber. The fury of the crowd, their anger and bloodlust, batters against me. These are my sworn battle-brothers. This is my Legion.

We will no longer walk the Crimson Path. I see that clearly now. We are walking another path entirely – a road far more damning.

I had thought it superstitious nonsense, nothing more than the religious ranting of the XVII Legion. It is not. Sadly, it is not.

We are walking the Eightfold Path, and there can be no turning back.

GUARDIAN OF ORDER

Gav Thorpe

TAKING A DEEP breath to ease the tension that tightened his chest, Zahariel peered down into the opening. He pushed back memories of the last time he had been here, beneath the Northwilds Arcology, and of the terrible things that he had witnessed. He was not sure if it was the emptiness of this primitive new settlement, or some reflection from a deeper, less physical sense that caused him to baulk at the threshold.

He turned to his companion and gestured towards the rock surrounding them, carved by drill and laser pick.

'Someone dug this recently.'

Like Zahariel, the other Space Marine was unarmoured, dressed instead in the heavy robes of the Order. He bore no symbols of rank or title: he was an enigma, the Lord Cypher, and guardian of their secretive traditions. He glanced around and shrugged. 'Scavengers?'

'After so many years? Why would they run from us? Flight suggests guilt.'

Cypher turned back. It was not the first reluctance that he had shown since Zahariel had joined him.

'The Order razed this place,' he said. 'It is natural that the inhabitants might think they are breaking our laws simply by returning. There is nothing of importance here.'

Zahariel disagreed. 'I think it bears further investigation. It was you, after all, who wanted to come to the Northwilds. I am only here as… an "interested party".'

It was Luther that had ordered Zahariel to accompany Lord Cypher in his many secretive comings and goings of late, though Cypher himself had been hesitant to oblige. This was merely the first chance that had presented itself for them to travel together.

'I do not wish to return to the Grand Master without a full report,' Zahariel added.

'What is there *to* report?' asked Cypher, waving an arm to encompass the deserted settlement behind them. 'Some vagrants have raised their slum here. That is all.'

'We have only seen the surface. We should look a little deeper, if only to assure ourselves that there is not another rebellion growing in these decayed tunnels.'

Lord Cypher looked uncomfortable. 'Did Master Luther share the circumstance that prompted his sudden interest in this region?'

Zahariel did not have to lie. 'Briefly. The number of recruits raised has almost outstripped the facilities at Aldurukh. He is thinking of raising a new fortress here.'

'An odd choice, considering its history.'

'I disagree. It is the most obvious choice – a sign that the Order has returned to mark the lands with its presence.'

THEY PASSED DOWN tunnels that had once been gleaming metal, now marked by stains and corrosion. The air turned acrid, tainted by some unidentified source.

Zahariel paused for a moment, one hand to the side of his

head. He felt something stirring beneath them. *Something that he had not felt for a long time, but familiar all the same...*

After a few seconds he plunged into the darkness once more, the lamps of his explorator harness springing into life.

They followed the tunnel for some distance, encountering more signs of recent excavation and construction where toppled walls had been dug away and bulkheads erected to improve the structure. As they descended, the air grew hotter, becoming almost stifling. The stench grew with it, though there seemed no cause for the reek; the passageways and chambers that they passed were free of filth and spoil. Lord Cypher made no remark on this fact, though he continually glanced back at Zahariel.

With the heat and stench also came an oppressive sensation. Zahariel could not shake the feeling that each step was taking him closer to a ghastly fate indeed. The feeling grew the further they delved, though Cypher seemed unaffected.

Or perhaps, a suspicious part of Zahariel realised, *forewarned.*

'Wait!'

Zahariel's warning caused the Lord Cypher to stop in his tracks, hand moving to the bolt pistol at his belt. A moment later a long, low breath resonated up the tunnel, issuing from a distance, the rank air stirring with hot breeze every few seconds.

'*Do you feel it?*' Cypher whispered.

An unnatural dread began to seep through Zahariel's body, a chill spreading up his spine. Zahariel extended his will, motes of psychic energy dancing in the pupils of his eyes, and he reached out a hand, fingers splayed, as though probing an invisible wall. Cypher drew his weapon.

It was better not to speak of what had happened before, so the Librarian lied.

'An after-echo. Nothing more. You look... uncomfortable. What is wrong?'

Lord Cypher shook uncontrollably, eyes darting to the left and right, seeking the doom that was coming for him. 'I... I cannot go... I must...'

He started to retreat up the corridor.

'We have to go back. This was a mistake.'

Zahariel took a deep breath. *'Ghosts of the past...'*

The words were as much for his own benefit as his companion's. He had never seen another legionary act in such a manner, but then Cypher had not faced the terrible thing in the depths of the Northwilds in the same way that Zahariel had.

The Librarian filled his voice with false confidence. 'There is nothing here to be afraid of. Just memories.'

Shuddering, Cypher staggered away. Zahariel did not go after him, the dull thud of his boots fading back up the tunnel.

Zahariel had grave misgivings, his memories crowded with visions of voracious worms and *something* terrible and unnatural, but he pushed on. Luther had sent him here, and the Lord Cypher had been drawn back to this place too. Zahariel did not need his psychic sense to feel the waves of strangeness emanating from the passages ahead.

There was familiarity here: a voice, a presence to which Zahariel was no stranger. The foulness around him did not feel like a warning – though Lord Cypher had taken it as such – but more like a *welcome.*

But why now? Had the settlers unearthed something that had been missed by the purge? It seemed unlikely that they would have remained, had that horrific, pervading aura been noticed when they chose this place.

Was it *really* the two Space Marines that had caused them to depart their homes with such haste? *Why* had Lord Cypher come here...?

Too many questions without answers.

Cypher. He had to have known what was happening here. Perhaps he had been warned that Zahariel was watching him, and lured the Librarian to this place.

Zahariel's superhuman hearing picked up the sharp echo of their shuttlecraft's engines firing. He broke into a run, heading back towards the surface.

Something was coming. He could feel it now, like foetid breath on the back of his neck. The others had to be told. He had to raise the alarm.

The Ouroboros was returning.

HEART OF THE CONQUEROR

Aaron Dembski-Bowden

THE EMPEROR CHOSE her.

In the wake of that choice, honour and pride, those most insubstantial of currencies, were lavished upon her bloodline. Many of her cousins – hundreds of them, in a tangled cobweb of legitimacy and bastardry – offered their best wishes, brought warnings, or simply seethed in jealous silence.

Others were more overt in their reactions. She received a small fortune in gifts, bribes and favours, read through almost one hundred formal petitions for her hand in marriage, and survived three assassination attempts.

None of it mattered. The Emperor chose her.

He hadn't come in person, of course. His decision came in the form of a scroll sealed with Malcador's Sigil. The Imperium's Seneschal had recorded the Emperor's mandate in writing, despatching it with patient haste to the territories of House Andrasta. She didn't need to read the scroll to know the Emperor's choice. Nothing else would bring a full phalanx of golden custodians to the spire-palaces of the Navigator Quarter.

Before her father had time to open the scroll before his gathered courtiers, word had spread like wildfire throughout the city's spires. He spoke two words to the Captain-General of the Legio Custodes. The only two words expected of him; the most important two words he'd ever spoken in all the many long decades of his life.

'She accepts.'

A Gloriana-class battleship, one of only twenty ever constructed. She accepted because there was no possibility or precedent for refusal. This was what she was born and bred to do.

A whirlwind of preparation gripped the following days, passing by in a blur of other people's effort. Less than a week later, pampered and harassed by a small army of slaves and retainers, she set sail for Mars. Waiting in the skies of the Red Planet was a ship eclipsing all others nearby, casting its shadow across them all as it endured the final days of void-dock.

She sensed its impatience even before setting foot on its hangar deck. Its noble hunger was obvious in every metre of dark, fortified iron.

'The *Adamant Resolve*,' she said aloud. Flagship of the War Hounds. Her first ship, and her new home.

That had been an eternity ago. Now they were the World Eaters, and her ship was the *Conqueror*.

The rebellion confused her. She was a sailor, not a soldier. Her gaze rested elsewhere, above and beyond mortal concerns of war and territory. A war fought in the Emperor's name was no different from a war fought for the Warmaster.

Her thralls and feeders began bringing word from the *Conqueror's* crew, telling conflicting tales of loyalty and treachery. Some said that Horus's ambition had driven them to declare war on Terra itself. Others brought word of the Emperor's tragic death, praising

Horus for fighting his way through the crumbling Imperium, back to the Throneworld where he would end the civil war and rule in his father's place.

She didn't know who to believe. Not at first. Over the weeks and months, rumours became reports and reports became facts. She was still unsure of how to act, or if action was required at all.

Yet she came back to one resonant truth, again and again and again. The Emperor had chosen her.

Not the Warmaster. Not Lord Angron. Not Lord Aurelian, with whom they sailed now. They used her and respected her when they acknowledged her at all, but they hadn't chosen her. They had rebelled against He who had forged the Imperium. They had declared war against He who had elevated her kind into lives of splendour, and allowed the Navis clan-families to sail the black gulf between the stars.

Now they sailed to Terra to kill Him – He who had chosen her.

The immaterium was an ocean of scalding, shrieking light. Faces boiled up out of the migraine madness, faces from her past that wept and laughed and raged and screamed as they melted away. Looking through the hull revealed the shadow of the *Trisagion* sailing nearby, hulking and grey and swollen with life, rocking and crashing through the unquiet tides. Waves of aether broke against Lorgar's colossal battleship, setting it groaning and rolling as surely as the *Conqueror* groaned and rolled. Like any ship caught in a storm, the surest way to survive was to sail through the rising waves, fighting them with hope, skill and trust in sanctified iron. Yet the *Conqueror* laboured where the *Trisagion* did not. The former wallowed and took tidal blows to its belly, while the latter cut the aetheric ocean like a great, defiant blade.

Blackness pressed at her from outside the ship – a blackness that no eyes could pierce – not just the absence of light but the death of it. A Navigator intuitively knew what no other human could experience: the deepest tides of the warp *ate* light. This was where illumination came to die.

Her beacon was the Emperor's light. Dimmer now, dulled as if by pain, but still the only light by which to sail. She bathed in it, just as she always had. She followed the Astronomican as it lit the darkest edges of the unreality behind reality.

Captain Sarrin had come to her chambers not long ago, to speak of the warp's roughening tides. She liked Captain Sarrin, who called her 'My Navigator' as was proper, not 'Mistress Nisha Andrasta' like her fawning thralls.

The conversation had not lasted long, for Nisha had no answers to give her captain. The warp was rougher, the Emperor's Light fainter, and she knew no reason why either was true, only that they were.

Lord Lorgar Aurelian came to her some time after. The *Conqueror* was slow, he told her. They were holding the fleet back. She had apologised to him, and he'd smiled with the radiance of his Imperial father.

There was nothing to apologise for, he had promised. Some lessons took time to learn, that was all. Then he spoke of other paths through the warp. Other illuminations, other lights to sail by. The *Trisagion*, he said, was guided not by the Astronomican, but by the songs of distant gods. And could she hear them? Could she, if she really tried?

His words were the soft tones of a teacher, but she saw her death waiting behind his kindly eyes.

'Do you hear the gods' song, Navigator Andrasta?'

'Yes,' she had said to the Bearer of the Word. Lord Aurelian left her in peace, but the *Conqueror* still struggled through the tides. Her lie would not last long.

In her palatial chambers within the *Conqueror*'s heart, she cradled the ornate laspistol in lace-gloved hands, keeping it hidden from sight. Her fingernails were pristine, brushed each morning and night by her attendants. Her slaves always kept her fastidiously clean; to prevent infection or to adhere to their ingrained courtly standards, she'd never been sure.

Her regal robes clung to her skin with a void sailor's honest sweat. Her throne interpreted her silent impulses and the slightest of muscle twitches, forcing the ship to follow.

Through her bond with the *Conqueror*'s changing, mutating machine-spirit, she felt the rage of the *thing* chained in the ship's deepest dark. The thing that had once been the primarch, and whose existence now reshaped the ship's sacred metal into an image of Angron's fury. What use was a Geller field when the warp already lived inside the *Conqueror*'s bones?

Through her third eye, she watched the *Trisagion* cutting ahead once more, already an infinity of distance away. The *Conqueror* moaned and laboured and slowed in the larger ship's wake.

When she had been chosen by the Emperor – and not these monsters and men that now sailed to murder him – she had believed that she would pay any price to see stars and worlds never before witnessed by mankind. Time had made a lie of that belief. She wasn't willing to betray the man that had chosen her.

She pressed the muzzle of the stolen pistol to her temple. Her attendants were running, shrieking, weeping.

'For the Emperor,' she told them.

Navigator Nisha Andrasta pulled the trigger and tore the *Conqueror* from the warp in a cascade of screaming, tortured metal.

CENSURE

Nick Kyme

Vhetok Raan sights the target through his scope, carefully angling the crosshairs over its back. There's a strong side wind blowing that reeks of radiation decay, and he adjusts the aim to compensate when his spotter whispers, reading from a brass gauge.

'Eighteen millimetres left, elevate three millimetres.'

Raan makes the adjustments without acknowledgement. He does not nod, nor even blink. It would spoil the shot and he knows he will only get one. Miss, and they will have to run. He doubts they would escape. He and Scarbek would be dead – or worse, left for dead for the Unburdened to feast upon.

The target is one of *them*. A genetically enhanced killing machine, bent on revenge. Ever since the world burned under the light of its own sun, they have been out for blood. A humming power pack attached to the target's armour creates a heat haze in the air above it. It feels close even through Raan's rad-suit. He can practically *taste* it.

A smirr of rad-dust occludes his vision for a few seconds, his finger moist in his glove just caressing the trigger of his sniper rifle. The rebreather fastened to his face and neck starts to pinch.

Raan holds his breath. The target is crouched, barely moving, as though he might be patiently digging for something in the dirt. The sniper's eye line is a tunnel, myopic and focused, and narrows just a fraction as the moment arrives...

Cobalt-blue flashes in the pre-dawn light, and the crouching figure shifts a little.

'Now,' Scarbek hisses through the vox.

Raan squeezes the trigger.

Like lightning on the sun, a heavy calibre shell scores the rad-hot air as a low cough escapes from the rifle. It seems to pass in slow motion. He fancies he can see the bullet turning, air particles dislocating at its passage through them, a faint and long-lived spark as it strikes metal and penetrates...

But there is no blood.

There should be blood, even through all that armour, a sign that his shot was a mortal one.

He's turning, mouth opening in a half-shout, world slowing further as if in partial suspended animation.

No blood, he tries to shout. *No–*

A cold ball of pain flares in Raan's back. Then Scarbek's throat is bulging open like a burst water main and gushing red all over his rad-suit, soaking the robes beneath.

Cobalt-blue flashes again. Only this time it is behind them, around them, stabbing into them.

In his eye line, which is no longer confined by the rifle scope, but myopic all the same and ever shrinking to black, Raan sees the target still crouched down, as lifeless as it has been ever since they first sighted him.

Now there is blood. Lots of blood, but it is all theirs.

Darkness rolls in, incongruous during the rad-scarred day, and Vhetok Raan realises – too late – that they have been tricked.

AEONID THIEL TAKES an ankle of each corpse in either hand and starts to drag. He has slung the guns across his body already, widening the straps so they will fit his broader and more heavily armoured frame. He doesn't enjoy this grunt work, but it is the practical thing to do. Hide the bodies, bury them in the sun-bleached desert.

Finding a good spot, he starts to dig. Gauntleted hands make for surprisingly good shovels. Bury the dead deep enough and even the Unburdened can't sniff them out. Thiel suspects the radiation is fouling their senses, just as it is fouling his. Auspex, scanner, even his closed helm's retinal display are all unreliable in Calth's scorched atmosphere.

Graves dug and then covered back up, a chrono warning flashes up on his left lens. It is brief and marred by visual static, but about the only thing actually working that provides him with useful information. Radiation levels are spiking. A fresh solar event blazes on the horizon. Burn-up is due in eight minutes, eighteen seconds and counting.

'My gratitude for your assistance, Brother Akanis,' he says to the distant, blue-armoured corpse, 'but I must be on my way.'

No need to bury him – the Unburdened hollowed Akanis out days ago. Only armour and bone remains. There was a time when Thiel would have been reprimanded for such disrespect, using a dead battle-brother as a lure, but Thiel is no stranger to censure. He still wears the red proudly across his battle-helm, though it no longer means what it once did. Had he not defied his superiors, then Marius Gage and even Lord Guilliman might be dead. As it is they live, but they have left Calth behind.

Thiel thought that he had too, but now he is back. Another act of insubordination on his part.

It isn't that Aeonid Thiel lacks respect, he simply acknowledged more quickly than his brothers that the rules of engagement had changed. Old tactics laid down in his primarch's *Codex*, as it is being called, were not always practical. Thiel wears the practical upon his armour, a ceramite and battle-scarred treatise of all the ploys and stratagems he has utilised in this most unconventional underworld war.

One more stretch of hardline cable to check for this tour. He marks it upon his armour with a short stylus, including coordinates, depth and time. Thiel runs, staying low, away from the dead Akanis.

Reaching the dig site, he pulls a seismic stave from his equipment belt, plants it deep and activates the subterranean mapping pulse. Takes a few seconds to kick in. Checking the countdown in his left retinal lens, he realises he has but a few to spare.

'Come on, come on…'

Radiation levels are rising faster, a red and fatal dawn is already burning the horizon in a shimmering line of fire. Thiel feels the temperature increase, even as he shuts down the warning chime in his battle-helm to silence his armour's plaintive urging.

'Not yet.'

If he finds the break in the hardline cable, he will have to come back. No way he can dig now – the ambush took up too much time. That particular stratagem is written on his left shoulder guard. It is not the first time he has employed it, nor will it be the last.

Seismic stave comes back negative.

'Damn.'

Thiel tweaks the depth gain and boosts the signal pulse, knowing that radiation and several metric tonnes of earth, stone and steel will be clouding any weak returns.

Another few seconds lapse, and the chrono goes from amber to red. Time is running out.

Stave beeps again.

'Negative... damn it!'

An actual wave of fire is boiling across the surface of Calth, once a shining frontier of the Ultramar Empire, now rendered into endless desert. Numinus City is a husk, inhabited by corpses and predatory shadows. Gone are the Dera Caren Lowlands, their forests turned to ash. Above, Veridia blazes, not so beautiful now. She is a harbinger, a pearl transformed into a fiery coal of hellish retribution.

Aeonid Thiel was marked for censure, but now Veridia seeks to mark him anew. She has marked him for death, her paint a solar flare that will burn away the red and blue, and leave his armour black.

Leaving the stave and much of his equipment behind, Thiel runs.

NARROWED, BLOODSHOT EYES watch the Ultramarine's flight. Even with flare dampeners dialled to maximum, the warrior is still a haloed silhouette through the scopes, with the hell-sun burning bright behind him. Though, not so bright that the eyes don't see him crouch and activate a panel obscured in the dirt. A few seconds later a crack opens in the desert, prompting a cataract of sand to roll over and into an expanding black chasm.

Ignorant of being watched, the Ultramarine hurries into the darkness of the hidden shelter, smoke rising in grey whisps from his battleplate.

Kurtha Sedd cuts the visual feed, retracting the periscopic viewer back into the cavern where he and his cohorts are waiting. His power armour growls as he turns, and he regards the seven cult warriors before him. Even in the low light of phosphor-lamps, the sigils carved into their bare arms shimmer and coil.

Not Unburdened, not yet. But soon. It has been pledged. Promised.

'Well?' asks one of the cult, speaking roughly through his battered vox-grille.

Lorgar left these men to die on Calth, loyal servants of the Word who chose the wrong demagogue to follow.

Sedd rasps, the smile in his voice easy to detect, 'By Erebus's blood, we have him.'

CRACKING CERAMITE COOLING in the subterranean air interrupts the silence of the underground world that now exists beneath the surface of Calth. That was close. The readings on Thiel's armour went below the red-line, and his radiation levels are perilously close to acceptable maximums.

After the gate, he kept running. Down into the bowels of the earth, where a new and entirely more ugly world awaits him. This is Calth now, cavernous arcologies, no better than tombs.

At the bottom of the tunnel, Thiel slows to a walk and then stops. He slumps down onto one knee to catch his breath. Already battered from the fight aboard the *Macragge's Honour* almost two years ago, he balks at the additional damage inflicted upon his war-plate by the solar flare, imagining the many minute fissures reducing its combat efficacy.

'Every time you leave the compound,' a stern voice echoes from the darkness, interrupting Thiel's thoughts, 'you risk our secrecy and safety.'

Wearily, Thiel reaches for the seals affixing his battle-helm to his gorget, disengages them and lifts it away to breathe fresh air.

He is youthful, but has a face with hard edges made that way by war. Sweat lathers his forehead and temples, sheening his short blond hair. His eyes are blue, like bright sapphires and they find the speaker in the darkness at once.

'And each second we remain isolated and alone, we risk annihilation. Are you keeping such a close eye on my movements now, Captain Vultius?'

An Ultramarine steps from the shadows into the light of a single hanging phosphor lamp. He is gilded, a laurelled helmet in the crook of his right arm, a gladius sheathed upon his left hip.

Three platinum service studs shine, embedded in a forehead like a granite cliff. Vultius has closely cropped dark hair, and wears full battleplate. His wargear is pristine but betrays the battles he has fought, despite his artificer's best labours. A short, crimson cape extends from his power generator, ending just below the joint at the back of his knees.

The eyes of Captain Vultius are emerald green, cold and unforgiving as the sea.

'Do I need to, sergeant?'

'Practical – the longer we go without further reinforcement, the greater the chance we will be overwhelmed. The communications hardline is our only means of signalling the fleet. With it severed, the command hub is cut adrift. I cannot help but wonder what broke it, sir.'

'That's not your concern.'

'It's my *only* concern, sir. As I believe it should be yours.'

'Were you this obstreperous before Lord Guilliman?' Vultius snorts derisively. His question, Thiel realises, is rhetorical. 'I can see now why you still bear the old mark. It was always a badge of honour for you, wasn't it? To be defiant, insubordinate.'

'I am neither, sir. This is an unconventional war, requiring unconventional tactics to wage it.'

'Surely you mean win it?'

'May I speak freely, sir?' Thiel sighs.

Vultius cocks his head to the side, incredulous. 'Are you not already, sergeant?'

Thiel answers the previous question.

'No, sir. I do not mean "win it". There is no winning Calth. It has no strategic significance beyond propaganda. Calth is already lost.'

Now Vultius scowls, his patience having reached its end. 'Perhaps you should have stayed on Macragge.'

'Perhaps, sir. Thought I could be more use here.'

'You were wrong, sergeant.' Vultius is already turning his back, moving from the glow of the phosphor lamp and disappearing into the shadows again.

Thiel nods. 'Seems I was.'

'Get yourself rad-scrubbed, and I'll come to debrief you in an hour.'

'I'll try not to be late, sir.'

Vultius pauses, perhaps about to fashion a fresh reprimand, but decides against it.

'See that you're not.' He waits a few more seconds, half swallowed by the dark, 'I thought Lord Guilliman sent you here as a punishment for defying his will, but I see now that I was wrong.'

'How so, sir?'

'Because it feels very much like *I* am the one being punished.' Vultius walks on, his footsteps echoing away as he leaves Thiel to the darkness.

SITTING ON A bench in a post-purification cell, Thiel watches two servitors through dirty armourglass as they scrub his war-plate. Radiation cleansing is painful, long, but necessary. Ever since the enemy attacked Calth's sun, any trip to the surface brings with it the hazard of radiation poisoning. Even the Legiones Astartes are not immune, but can withstand greater and more prolonged exposure than their ordinary human counterparts.

Thiel's last trip would have killed a normal man several times over. As it is, he will live and overcome the effects of Calth's radiation.

Dressed only in partial undermesh and a white training vest, he still dwarfs the lone trooper standing beside him. The trooper's uniform jacket identifies him as Rowd, in the colours of the old Numinus regiment. Of course, there is no Numinus regiment anymore, nor any battalion for that matter. The survivors of Calth's old Army divisions were subsumed together into a guerrilla force, supported by the legionaries of the XIII where possible.

'How much longer, trooper?' Thiel asks.

Rowd turns, shocked at first. Thiel gestures to the servitors through the dirty glass.

'My armour, how long?'

He knows the answer, but the silence underground bothers him, and allows his mind to wander.

The trooper checks his chrono. He's wearing a partial rad-suit, gaiters and boots but with his jacket unzipped to reveal his old Army designation. A rebreather and concomitant face-mask hang around his neck on a loose strap. A hood gathers over his shoulder blades.

'In a moment, sergeant. The servitors are just finishing up now.'

Thiel nods as though this were news.

'Tell me, trooper – are you supposed to be my keeper?'

Rowd is aghast for a moment. 'I... uhh... No, sergeant. Captain Vultius asked that I ensure you remain here until he can return.'

Thiel gets to his feet, a simple act that sees him loom over the trooper.

'You *are* my keeper then.'

'Sergeant, I'm just–'

Laughing out loud, Thiel waves his hand in apology.

'You may relax, trooper. I am only joking with you. Just a little humour to help pass our time together.'

Trooper Rowd relaxes. He tries a smile, but his fearful eyes give away his game. Before he can reply, a klaxon sounds, accompanied by a flashing strobe lamp above the door to the scrub chamber. Seconds later, a hiss of pneumatic pressure presages the door opening, and a servitor appears with Thiel's rad-scrubbed war-plate. He's pleased to see that his improvised markings are still engrained upon it.

Rowd sees them too.

'What are they?' His eyes narrow, scrutinising – trying and failing to discern their meaning.

'The Legion would call them practicals. I use them as a record of every tactic, every stratagem and ploy I have utilised on Calth since my posting.'

'Doesn't your suit have internal systems for that?'

Thiel smiles, taking a vambrace proffered by the servitor.

'Already full. I've been busy. Here, help me put this back on.'

Rowd obliges, just as the dull echoes of violence sound in the tunnel ahead.

IT TAKES THREE minutes for Thiel and Trooper Rowd to armour him. Another three minutes sees them halfway up the tunnel, en route to the command hub where Thiel hopes that Captain Vultius is still in charge.

Three hard bangs sound in the phosphor gloom, louder than before. Thiel slows to a light jog, armour clanking dully.

Rowd catches him, out of breath. 'What was that?'

'Bolter fire.'

All the colour drains from Rowd's face, illuminated starkly by the fizzing lamp overhead. 'That's a Legion weapon.'

'Yes.'

Rowd checks the power gauge on his lascarbine, and clicks off the safety with his thumb.

Thiel has drawn a bolt pistol from a side holster. In his other hand, he has his gladius.

The gunfire is joined by shouting. Some of the voices he recognises. One belongs to Captain Vultius as he bellows orders. Others are more guttural, harsh. He knows the language, even if he cannot actually speak it.

Colchisian.

Word Bearers.

Thiel's grip tightens around the handle of his pistol, and the hilt of his gladius. He wants to reach for the electromagnetic longsword sheathed down the side of the generator upon his back, but he doesn't yet know what he's facing. No practical to gauge his response, no theoretical worth formulating during these strange days of fratricide.

'Get behind me,' Thiel warns, prowling the last few hundred metres of the tunnel. There are blast doors at the end of it; a key-coded panel prevents entry, but somehow an enemy force has found and infiltrated their base of operations.

The sounds of battle are getting louder, even through the thick plasteel of the doors. Thiel pauses at the threshold, tapping in the precise numeric sequence to disengage them. He wishes there was another way, but this is the only clear route into the command hub. The opening blast doors will announce his presence – he must be ready for whatever lies beyond. Memories of fighting aboard the *Macragge's Honour* return to him in cold flashes. Thiel tries to suppress them, hoping to face only mortal foes this time.

'Every door, a new horror...' he mutters.

Rowd looks up. 'What?'

'Nothing.'

Loud even over the din of weapons fire, shouts and curses, the blast doors grind open.

'Stay with me, Rowd!'

Head low, Thiel darts for the side wall, absorbing snatches of tactical data in his first brief glance at the room.

Much of the command hub is destroyed, its cogitators and strategium consoles wrecked. Flickering overhead lumen strips suggest that the power generator is on backup too. A pair of blast doors on the opposite side are blown-in and lying broken on the fire-black ground, the obvious point of ingress. Three Ultramarines are behind stone support columns towards the centre of the room, chips of ornate filigree and baroque lapidary exploding around them as they take cover.

One of them is Captain Vultius. Blood is leaking into his eye from a savage head wound that must also be spoiling his aim. He is hunkered down, reduced to making snap shots, the hollow echo of his pistol a sign that the magazine is close to empty.

Fifteen targets spread out across the other side of the large chamber, advancing in pairs. Thiel counts seven wearing power armour, but stripped down to leave their arms bare. The other eight are human cultists – flak armour, robes, carrying solid-shot weapons and stolen lasguns. Poorly equipped but well motivated, they move with a precision uncommon in the zealot brotherhoods.

A three-shot burst from Thiel's bolt pistol clips a Word Bearer in the gut, and he spins with the sudden flesh wound, stunned. Rowd gets off a shot too, taking a cultist through the neck, dropping him instantly.

'Good aim,' shouts Thiel.

'I was going for the torso.'

The pair of them are pressed against the chamber wall, using the natural alcoves to shelter in. Blistering return fire is keeping them pinned.

Static crackles over Thiel's vox-feed and the grainy voice of Captain Vultius resolves a moment later.

'*They bombed the door, Thiel. Numetor and Hargellus are dead. Practical – we are ambushed and outgunned.*'

'I count seven legionaries and seven cultists.'

'*Negative. There are at least double that number of human auxiliaries.*'

Thiel grits his teeth. 'I'm sorry sir, this is my fault. They must have followed me.'

Theoretical: they are losing, and in a few short minutes the command hub will be overrun.

Thiel is still formulating a plan when the voice of the enemy leader is broadcast into the room, above the tumult of the firefight.

'*This is Kurtha Sedd, Apostle of the Third Hand, Seventeenth Legion.*'

You are outgunned and outmanoeuvred. Surrender, and your lives – and the lives of those in service to you – will be spared.'

The command hub is part of the wider arcology network, the centre from which the Ultramarines have coordinated the local shelters these past years. There are no refugees here, but there are still civilians. Fourteen men and women, only a third of whom are soldiers, the rest logisticians, engineers and cooks, cower with their failed protectors. Some clutch laspistols in shaking fingers. Others lie dead, hit by stray shots or ended by their own hand. Like Thiel, Vultius is responsible for them.

They are the blood of Calth. Or all that's left of it.

Static fills Thiel's vox-feed as Vultius gives his final order.

'Get out, Thiel. You're the only one who can.'

'You're giving up?'

'They want prisoners – that gives you time, sergeant.'

'Time for what, sir?'

'To mount a rescue.' He laughs, enjoying a moment of black humour that Thiel doesn't share. *'It's like you said, sergeant – this is an unconventional war, requiring unconventional tactics. These are mine. Now go.'*

Thiel's mouth becomes a stern line as he realises what he has to do. 'Fall back.'

Rowd looks at him questioningly. 'Sergeant?'

'To the blast doors. Now. We're leaving.'

Thiel shields Rowd as he leads the retreat out of the command hub and back into the tunnel. He winces as a slew of snap fire follows them through the gap.

'Move!'

Risking a stray bullet, he reengages the locking sequence and puts a bolt-round into the panel before he leaves. The blast doors are still closing when an explosion sounds behind them, putting Rowd on the deck and staggering Thiel so that he has to brace himself against the wall.

Looking back, he sees several figures advancing eagerly through the smoke. Twisted metal lays strewn either side of the ragged doors. He hauls Rowd to his feet. 'Get up, soldier. Hold here.'

The Army trooper is dazed but follows orders, recovering his composure quickly, and firing from a kneeling position. Three screams reward their efforts, one kill definitely Rowd's. The rest of the cultists are more cautious after that.

Thiel holds up a clenched fist, signalling for Rowd to stop. 'Go to overwatch.' He then listens as the resonance of las and bolter fire fades.

The silhouettes gathering in the dissipating smoke are falling back, though a voice lower than the rest still seems to be issuing orders.

'They're retreating.' Rowd cannot help but sound relieved.

Thiel continues to listen. More muttering, the sharp clink of metal against metal. His eyes widen as he recognises the sound of a grenade pin being pulled.

'Down!'

His warning is swallowed by a painful blare of white noise, intensified by the close confines of the tunnel. Rowd cries out as pellucid light fills the space, as bright as Calth's angry sun.

'They've got... stun grenades...' Thiel's speech is slurred. He feels groggy, ears ringing, head like the inside of a pounding drum. The detonations have overloaded his auto-senses, feeding back directly into his cerebral cortex.

He hears a high-pitched pop, followed by the aggressive *whoosh* of expelled pressure and released gas. Fresh smoke is filling the tunnel, spilling out from a new clutch of grenades. Grunting, Thiel drags himself upright. His battle-helm's retinal lenses have overloaded so he takes it off, mag-locking it to his belt and leaving it to auto-calibrate.

Everything gets louder, the stench of cordite igniters more potent. Vision still blurred, he stays low in case the cultists come out shooting.

They don't. Hurried footsteps resolve through the still-fading echoes of combat instead.

Thiel pulls the dazed Rowd to his feet.

'Something's wrong.'

The cultists are backing off. Beneath the sound of their movements, Thiel swears he can hear chuckling. He blinks, willing the harsh sensory afterimages to fade. With the effects of the stun grenade and the smoke, his targeting ability is severely compromised.

Something is coming. Blurred silhouettes, he can't tell exactly how many from this distance, are barrelling towards them. He fires off a shot, but misses. Grainy, crimson ovals emerge through the dense smoke. They are the lenses of pioneer infra-goggles, burning in the murk with heat-targeting certainty.

Closing his eyes, Thiel listens.

Three attackers, running full pelt.

He brings up his pistol two-handed, his eyes closed. He pinpoints a figure – one shot, followed by a grunt of pain.

'Two to go,' he breathes, focusing.

The next shot only wings the target. He hears the shell ricochet, the target yelping as it stumbles. Another shot takes it centre-mass, bringing it down hard.

'One more...'

The cultist shrieks, so loud, so close that Thiel realises he has run out of time. He opens his eyes, and sees that the madman has just triggered the incendiary device strapped to his torso.

The blast rips Thiel from his feet and throws him into the tunnel's ceiling. The thunder of falling rock is almost deafening. As darkness takes him, he imagines himself tumbling down into the maw of a creature that lives beyond reality, through the veil.

A SCRATCHING SENSATION against his breastplate wakes him.

Thiel opens his eyes to darkness, the reek of earth and wet stone.

Something intensely heavy is pressing down on his back. He tries to move, but he is pinned; breathing is hard enough.

'Trooper...' The word is nothing more than a croak, made flat and dull by the ton of rock on top of him.

It is Rowd scraping Thiel's war-plate, arms flattened against his chest by the Ultramarine's armour, fingers locked around a tiny knife, desperately scoring the metal in hope of a response.

'Thank the Emperor,' Rowd breathes.

Thiel is crouched over him, the Ultramarine's pinned body the only thing between the trooper and being crushed to death. At least Rowd had the sense to fit his mask and rebreather before the cave-in.

'Can you lift it?' he asks.

It feels like a tank is squatting on Thiel's back. Experimentally, he pushes. Grunting, he raises the slab of rock that is slowly flattening them both by just a few millimetres before letting it down slowly again.

'Can't get it any higher.'

'Even Space Marines have their limits then?' It is intended as a joke, but Rowd doesn't sell the humour well. 'I don't want to die here, sir.'

'Nor I. That's why you're going to reach down to my belt and unclip one of my grenades. Can you do that, trooper?'

Rowd nods, letting go of the knife.

Thiel's arms are braced either side of him, bearing the load. His legs are similarly trapped. His body is arched just enough that the trooper has a small amount of space to manoeuvre. Thiel feels the grenade disengage, hears it scrape against his breastplate as Rowd brings it up to his face.

'Now what?'

'Adjust the timer to thirty seconds, then reach up and push it into the gap between me and the rock on top of us. Push it deep. You're not wearing power armour, and a blast this close will almost certainly kill you if you're unshielded.'

Rowd sounds uncertain at this plan. 'And what will it do to you?'

By contrast, Thiel is resigned. 'Hurt like hell. Now do it.'

Rowd obeys. He sets the thirty second timer, engages it and plugs the grenade as deep as he can so that Thiel's body will be between him and the blast.

'Done.'

'Good. You have less than twenty seconds. Make yourself as small as you can, and do me a favour – cover my ears.'

With Rowd's trembling hands pressed against the sides of his head, Thiel feels the grenade counting down, each minute tremor of the timer rippling through his armour. With three seconds left, he closes his eyes.

Heat, pressure, the sound of splintered rock, the stench of burned metal and the taste of blood in his mouth – it all hits him at once in a whirlwind of agonising sensation. Thiel has weathered the blast, though his limbs are numb and his war-plate's integrity has been severely compromised.

Above, the air is brighter and he is able to turn, albeit with an intense amount of pain. Rubble and dirt tumbles from his back.

'You alive?' he rasps to the trooper. There's blood on his teeth. He can taste it.

Rowd's reply comes with a strange lack of conviction. 'Yes.'

'Then help me up, trooper. I can hear the cultists scouring the rubble. They're coming for us.'

Alone and without an apothecary, it is difficult for Thiel to ascertain the full extent of his injuries. It feels like internal bleeding, some bone fractures around the rib-shell, and possibly the left shoulder. With his helmet now back on, the retinal display reveals blast damage to both the plate and seals of his armour, as well as his power plant couplings.

Thiel limps to his feet, shucking off the split sections of fallen rock shattered by the grenade. He stares through a cloud of displaced earth and dust, finding enemies.

'Four contacts, thirty-three metres.' He pulls out his pistol, three rounds still in the clip according to the ammo gauge.

A single burst echoes loudly, harsh muzzle flash lighting up the half-dark. Three cultists are reduced to blasted chunks of meat. A fourth dies more elegantly to a well-placed las-bolt from Rowd.

Thiel nods. 'You're actually a pretty decent shot with that.'

Rowd is still wiping the grit and sweat from his face, having pulled off the mask to make the kill.

'I fight for Ultramar, sergeant, even down here in the dirt. Retribution is also a strong motivator. Helps focus.'

'Justly said. What did you do before joining the Army?'

Rowd hesitates. 'I… I was a convict, sir. Penal conscript.'

Thiel whistles. There's a smile in his voice. 'What are the odds?'

Up ahead, solid shot cracks noisily from the shadows. A bullet ricochets from the wall, spitting debris. Another prangs off Thiel's shoulder guard, leaving a shallow groove in the ceramite. Beyond them, a heavier weapon is being wheeled into position, hunkered down behind the rubble. Crewmen are getting it braced, fixing its magazine and targeter.

Thiel has no wish to test the resilience of his power armour any further. 'We need to move.'

Not waiting to be asked, Rowd supports the Ultramarine's weaker left side and together they stumble down the tunnel, turning the bend just before the autocannon opens up.

Rowd crouches down. Thiel rams a fresh clip into his bolt pistol.

With his hands over his ears, Rowd has to yell to be heard. 'Now what?'

'We can't go back that way.'

Gunfire is shredding the end of the tunnel, chewing up rock and earth like a drill.

'Enemy legionaries won't be far behind them, either.' Thiel checks the chrono count on his retinal display. He has it running all the time, just like the operational mark that has been running ever since the Calth engagement began. 'Solar flare should have subsided by now. There's an egress not far from this point.'

'Head to the surface? But it's–'

'A deadly radiation-scorched wasteland.' It's easy to tell from his manner that Thiel's mind is made up. 'Theoretical – we have to find a different approach of attack, surprise Kurtha Sedd and his men. Practical – we stay here, we're dead and so are the others. Captain Vultius won't fight back if he can't guarantee he'll protect the civilians by doing so. Sedd wants prisoners.'

Rowd looks far from sanguine. 'Seems like both choices are death, one just slower than the other.'

Already on the move, Thiel seems not to hear him. 'Suit up, and watch your rad-gauge.'

'I doubt it'll provide much comfort during another solar flare. Where will we go once we're out there?'

Thiel turns his head, regarding the trooper with cold retinal lenses.

'Somewhere underground, and quickly. If we don't, we both burn.'

KURTHA SEDD STANDS impassively, his armoured form half swathed in dissipating smoke and shadows. The little of his war-plate that is revealed in the phosphor light is barbed, misshapen and wrought with lines of cuneiform script. Much of it has been written by his own hand, for he thinks of himself as something of a preacher. Some passages even spread from metal onto flesh but, unlike his armour, these markings are etched in his own blood and not that of his victims.

Hands clasped across his lower torso, he waits.

Three cultists emerge from the shadows, followed by one of his legionaries. He addresses only the Word Bearer.

'Eshra. Where are they?'

'Escaped, my lord.' The legionary kneels when he reaches Kurtha Sedd, lowering his neck for a punitive ritual beheading.

'Lift your gaze. I won't kill you for this failure, but you must make atonement.'

Since Lorgar left his errant sons to die on Calth, a factionalist mentality has arisen, spurred on by a profound survival instinct and sense of righteous denial. Sedd believes that he has been left behind for some divine, albeit unknown, purpose.

Eshra has no war-helm. He lost his several weeks ago and now goes without it, his scars displayed to all as a declaration of his devotion.

'Name it.'

He slams a fist against his war-plate, an outmoded gesture that Sedd does his best to ignore. The apostle's eyes are like balefires behind the lenses of his skull helm. 'Follow them.'

'Into the rad-desert?' Eshra looks perplexed. 'Without full armour…'

'You will sicken and die, but you will last long enough to catch our prey. Think of it as motivation.'

'But my lord, I–'

The blow is swift, severing Eshra's neck and parting head from shoulders before anyone has even glimpsed the blade drawn from Kurtha Sedd's vambrace.

He hisses. 'Kaeloq.'

Another warrior steps forwards from behind the Dark Apostle. He has the good sense to still wear a battle-helm. A curved horn arcs from his left temple.

'Yes, my lord.' His voice is not one but two, overlaid and just slightly out of synch with one another.

'Noble Kaeloq. Will you also refuse this honour?'

Kaeloq draws himself up. 'Do you want their heads or their tongues?'

Behind his rictus mask, Kurtha Sedd smiles.

A HOT WIND is whipping across the scorched ruin of a city. The solar flare has left fires in its wake. Some are small, flickering at the edges of roadsides or within the shells of blasted buildings like tiny funerary candles. Others are vast conflagrations that burn across entire districts, leaving black soot behind them.

Thiel looks to the horizon, then back to Rowd. 'Mercius District South. See, that statue belonged to the landmaster.'

Before the fires, before Veridia turned Calth into an arid waste-land, there were north, east and west districts too. Agri-farms on an industrial scale, all of them. Carefully cultivated vine forests, tree-lined avenues and great arboreal domes, all now just dust and ash. Over fifty-thousand workers, with only this skeletal monument to mourn them.

Thiel knows of Mercius, and he knows of the landmasters. Before he returned to the surface, his tactical briefings on all of Calth's major cities and districts were very detailed. Now they are little more than historical documents, footnotes to describe a broken world.

Rowd coughs into his mask, fogging up the visor with his spittle-breath.

'Are you injured, trooper?'

'I'm fine, sir.'

Thiel's gaze lingers on him for a moment before he turns his attention back to the ruin. 'Eyes open then. There could be anything lurking in those shadows.'

Rowd frowns. 'What kind of a man could endure out here?'

'It's not men we need to worry about.'

Since arriving at the outskirts of Mercius South, they have not met a single soul. Corpses do not count – or rather the charred, blackened bone remains of what were formerly corpses that litter the ground in every direction.

Thiel advances slowly, ordering Rowd to remain twenty paces behind him. He watches every shadow, every fissure and crack, all of which deepen the further in they move.

Silently, he holds up a clenched fist.

Rowd halts at once. Looking ahead, he sees what has caught the Ultramarine's attention.

A tank, specifically a XIII Legion Rhino APC, is blocking the road.

'Hold here,' Thiel's voice crackles through the vox-link built into Rowd's rad-suit.

The Ultramarine advances alone, an unslung bolter cradled in both hands, held at waist height. No good for the tunnel fight, out here in the open its extra range could prove useful. His pistol is holstered, his gladius sheathed, a combat knife at his knee and the electromagnetic longsword strapped to his back.

Though his auto-senses are fouled beyond usefulness by radiation, his internal chrono counts down towards the next predicted solar flare. Caution is a commodity he can ill afford, but recklessness might also prove costly.

Reaching the armoured transport, Thiel notices that the rear hatch is open. Bolter leading the way, he steps inside. There is some superficial fire damage but the interior is largely unscathed. A driver sits slumped at the controls, certainly dead. A hole is gored into his helmet, rimed with dark, encrusted blood.

Thiel has seen injuries like this before. 'Not a blade wound.'

A shout from outside alerts him. He comes running in response to Rowd's cry.

'Up there…'

The soldier is pointing, jabbing the muzzle of his lasgun like a finger.

Thiel follows it to a graven-looking statue, like an ecclesiastical gargoyle, perched and shrouded by its wings atop the remains of a tower.

Rowd sounds concerned, and has yet to lower his weapon. 'What *is* that thing?'

'A daemon, once. Now it's just a shell.'

As if to confirm it, a strong gust of wind erodes the statue into mere flakes of ash.

At last, Rowd lowers his lasgun, but keeps staring at the pair of clawed feet left behind on the shattered tower. 'What's happened to them?'

Thiel shrugs.

'The veil thickened again, I suppose. Daemons went with it. Tough for them to anchor to the mortal plane. There are no true daemons left on Calth anymore.'

Rowd meets the Ultramarine's gaze. 'How can you know that?'

'Have you seen any?'

'No, I haven't.'

'Just the Unburdened left now...' Thiel exhales, a long reedy breath, and reaches out to the Rhino for support. Something dark is trickling between the joints in his war-plate.

Rowd sees it.

'You're still bleeding.'

'I can barely stand. Help me to the tank.'

Together, they struggle inside. Thiel slumps against the interior wall, his breathing ragged.

'What should I do?' asks Rowd.

'Stay in here,' Thiel rasps. 'If we are being hunted, we may be ignored inside this wreck, but they'll kill us if we're out in the open. I'll recover, just need a moment...'

He grunts in pain, hissing through his mouth grille.

'And you can hope my recovery doesn't take too long. Solar flare's not far off.'

Rowd scowls. 'Anything *practical*?'

Thiel laughs at the attempted sarcasm.

'Tell me about your life on Calth, soldier. Remind me what we fought for after our kinsmen betrayed us.'

Rowd shrugs, staring at the ground. 'Not much to tell. I was a farmer, and worked in the Vollard Meadows, or harvesting grain for the silos.' He pauses, fiddling absently with the seals of his suit. 'I killed my overseer when he tried to assault my wife. Shot him through the heart. Dead instantly.'

Thiel's head sinks back, touching the metal of the interior wall. He lets out another pained breath.

'You were convicted of murder.'

Rowd nods. 'I had no proof of the assault. I was a harvester, he was an overseer.' His voice changes, becomes embittered at the memory, the loss. Thiel can empathise.

'With me gone, my wife and infant daughter were alone. They perished before the war – a blessing, I suppose. I thought I'd die in my cage. Instead I was pressed into service as part of the military. Marked for censure, if you like.' Rowd gestures to Thiel's helmet. 'Just like you were.'

Thiel's mirth is forced, because of pain rather than disagreement.

Afterwards, a charged silence descends. Rowd waits a minute to break it.

'We aren't getting out of this tank, are we sir.'

'Maybe we can get the tank moving. It might have self-repaired.'

Rowd looks around. 'They can do that?'

Thiel doesn't answer. He is under, mind and body making the necessary repairs for him to function again. Ultramarines are particularly good at this recovery. They do it efficiently, rapidly, better than other Legions. It is one of the reasons they are so hard to kill. Of late, they have also had a lot of practice.

THE DULL GLINT of armour, seen through the open ramp of the Rhino, makes Rowd start. He realises that he has been daydreaming instead of keeping watch. Without a chrono, there is no way of telling how long Thiel has been out. Certainly, the horizon line is brightening and the stench of heat and fire is growing in the air.

Neither is a good sign. He slowly shuffles over to the hatch, trying for a better look.

A hunting party have seen them, or at least the possibility of their
hiding place. They are advancing on the wreck, four cultists and a
legionary with an ugly battle-helm mask; a single horn protrudes
from the side of his head. Spiked iron chains rattle against his war-
plate. His arms are bare brawn, slabs of cuneiform-inscribed meat,
baked brown by the radiation. In one hand he grips a saw-edged
ritual knife. The other holds a snub-nosed boltgun, with a second
blade attached to the stock.

Rowd estimates that they have scant minutes before the hunters
descend into the shallow crater where the Rhino is languishing.
Scurrying over, he is about to reach for Thiel's vambrace when the
Ultramarine's hand snaps out and seizes his wrist.

Suppressing a yelp, Rowd gestures to the open ramp.

Still a little groggy, Thiel grunts. 'How many?' He reaches a vision
slit, and shakes his head. 'They're close.'

Then he notices the fiery line of the horizon.

'But *that's* even closer.'

Rowd is back at the edge of the ramp, sighting down his carbine.
'I can kill two before they're close enough to see us.'

Thiel cocks his head slightly. 'You say you were a grain harvester?'

'Lot of time to waste, out in the fields. Used some of it picking off
vittle-cans with my father's long-las. He was a sniper in the Army.'

'Didn't skip a generation then. I feel sorry for the cans. Two it is,
soldier. I'll take the others. Legionary dies last.'

Rowd nods. The plan is set.

The trooper waits another five seconds before taking his first shot.
He blows out the eye of the closest cultist, feeding brain and skull
through the back of the head with his las-bolt. The second one
dies with a burn across the neck, good as a slit throat. Both crum-
ple within seconds of one another.

Two boltgun shots boom out from the opposite end of the Rhino, magnified by the close metal interior, heralding the explosive deaths of the other two cultists. Then Rowd sees what is coming up behind them, and realises that their time has just run out.

Thiel is about to draw a bead on the legionary when the first flare of light blinds him. Coursing over the desert, roaring across the ruins and the ash dunes comes a curtain of brilliant fire. It rolls in waves, one atop the other, undulating, coruscating. It is beautiful and terrifying – a living, breathing embodiment of destruction, and it is coming for them.

Thiel shouts through to Rowd. 'Get us moving. Now!'

Rowd obeys, scrambling to the Rhino's command console as the bolter fire begins again.

'How does it...?'

He trails off, the controls foreign and overlarge for his human hands.

'No different to a grain harvester,' calls Thiel over the crash of arms. 'Put it into drive, then ram the accelerator as hard as you can.'

It's hot in the Rhino now, furnace-like with the approaching firestorm.

Rowd hears Thiel shouting, and the solid *thunk* of shells striking the hull. Another voice invades the chaos, deep and guttural. He doesn't need to turn to know that it's the Word Bearer.

Finding the drive lever, he hauls it back, punches the ignition panel. Incredibly, the wrecked tank sputters... then dies. He tries again. Something heavy lands in the troop hold behind him. A shout from Thiel makes him glance in the rear-view reflector.

The Word Bearer is on board, and the two of them are fighting hand-to-hand.

'Seal the compartment,' snaps Thiel, his attention focused elsewhere.

Rowd tries, but the hatch is buckled and won't slide across.

Desperately, he hammers the ignition panel again, sweat stinking in his rad-suit, hot breath fogging his goggles, the heat threatening to overwhelm him.

It turns over, the Rhino coughs and its engine judders into life.

Something is happening behind him. The fight is changing. He hears grunting, snarling, catches a glimpse of something inhuman and bestial. It reminds Rowd of the statue, the daemon-husk. He realises that this creature *is* the Word Bearer.

'HELLSPAWN!' THIEL ROARS, drawing the electromagnetic longsword from his back. It hums with feral energy, as fierce as the monster unveiling itself before him.

The Word Bearer laughs, his two voices mocking.

'Chosen, Gal Vorbak... Unburdened. So many names, none of them true. How petty your mortal flesh is.'

Armour splits, shifts and remoulds around pinioned wings. A crest of dew-wet bone spurs punches out from the legionary's spine. Skin darkens, brown all the way to black. Pin-prick pupils visible through the monster's vision-slit blaze with a malignant light.

And in that moment of transformation, his injuries weighing him down as surely as any anchor, Thiel knows that he is outmatched.

SNATCHED GLIMPSES IN the rear-view reflector reveal little of the fight between Thiel and the Unburdened. It is brutal, a blur of rapid blade thrusts and claw slashes underpinned by the snarling, growling dual-voice of the monster.

The Rhino is moving through the solar fire. Rubble beneath its rolling tracks makes it violently buck and shift. Dwarfed by the driver's seat, Rowd is almost thrown when he smashes through a wall of heavier debris. He clings on, the temperature in the hold rising, the metal now almost scalding to the touch. All he has to do is hold on, keep moving.

Keep moving.

'Just keep on moving...' he mutters.

There's a crack in the reflector, which splits the view of the battle behind him into two jagged pieces. In the background seen through the gaping rear hatch, Calth is burning. The horizon is gone, obliterated by fire. Thiel and the monster are dark silhouettes carved in the light. Hard to tell with the movement and the violent motion of the battle tank, but it looks to Rowd like the Ultramarine is losing.

He is so engrossed by the struggle, so fearful of what its likely outcome will mean for him, that Rowd fails to see the steep drop opening up right in front of them.

EVEN WITH A day's recuperation and fully-charged suit of power armour, Thiel knows that he would still be on the back foot fighting against the Unburdened. It is swift, its blows hard and resonating. Every parry of its claws, every defensive block sends a shivering impact all the way to his shoulders. Grimacing, Thiel realises that his wound has reopened. First a warming sensation in his back, then cold – a chill that numbs his nerves and slows him fatally.

The tank jolts, throwing Thiel back just as he makes a rare counter. He staggers, the electromagnetic longsword slipping in his grip. Seeing weakness, the Unburdened attacks. Brain strategising with every passing microsecond, Thiel is unable to craft a response as the monster bears him to the deck, its claws pressed against his throat.

'Such petty, fragile mortal flesh...'

The Unburdened is laughing. His spittle reeks of decaying meat and spoiled milk, but Thiel does not gag. Struggling to the end, he shows no weakness and resolves to meet his death with fury in his heart. He feels the bite of the claw against his carotid artery, pledging his life and soul to the Emperor and Guilliman, just as the ground beneath both combatants seems to give way. Belatedly, Thiel realises that they are falling.

Then there is blood. Oceans of blood, enough to drown in.

ALONE, THE WORD Bearer trudges doggedly along the subterranean corridors beneath this dirty little world. In his hand he carries a head: his promise. The helmet still worn by the head is covered in markings, battle strategies scored into the very metal.

He follows the sounds of pain emanating from deeper within the tunnel complex, knowing they will bring him closer to the command hub. Above ground, the inferno will be raging, scorching the earth and turning it black.

The crash saved him. Dumped in an extinct sub-arborea – the vines withered, the hydroponic systems long fallen to neglect – he found a way back. The further down he went, the less he felt the heat. His armour is caked dark with blood.

Heaving open the last of the inner doors, barely visible in the gloom, he finds them.

One of the warriors turns, chuckling. 'Kaeloq? We all thought you were dead.'

The two Word Bearers have an Ultramarine as their captive, a captain by his rank insignia. Vultius's face is bruised and bloody, one eye gummed shut with congealed crimson. They have evidently been torturing him. A rusty table strewn with knives and clamps sits within their reach. A magnesium-white lumen casts the scene in a stark light. It flares intermittently, surging and dying every few seconds.

Kaeloq steps into the torture chamber. 'Not yet.'

The two Word Bearers, who had been intent on their cruel labours, turn sharply at the sound of his voice.

KURTHA SEDD REGARDS the pict screen with quiet interest. With the phosphor lamps extinguished, the pict screen is the only source of light. It paints the Dark Apostle a sickly green. The image crackles, crazes with static and then stabilises for a few seconds before crazing again.

'Perfect,' Sedd purrs, smiling to himself.

They have been digging, planting seismic beacons with every new tunnel excavated. Its pattern is revealed on the screen: a star with eight points. A tribute to the unholy Octed.

At the sound of another legionary entering the chamber, Sedd half turns. He stops himself, confident in his mastery of this place. In his peripheral vision, he sees that Lathek is still 'playing' with another of the surviving Ultramarines.

'Don't bleed him dry, Lathek. Not yet.'

They need this warrior's blood, and the captain's. He resists the urge to send Lathek to check on Vorsch and Methkar. All of their captives must live, for now, and the humans cowering in the far reaches of the chamber, too. Their blood will be important.

'The veil will thin again,' he says. 'Is that not so, Kaeloq?'

The horned figure standing behind him takes a step forwards. Kurtha Sedd sneers.

'You reek of blood. Did you bring me their heads or their tongues, my disciple?'

Something heavy is kicked over to Sedd, rolling around to face the apostle. He stares down into the smashed lenses of an Ultramarine's helmet. It is bloody, with a ragged stump of neck jutting out of the bottom.

'Very good, Kaeloq.' Sedd looks up again to the screen and the ritual tunnels they have hollowed out beneath the rock. Here, an old sewer line. There, a mag-lev track fallen to disuse. All Sedd had to do was join up the points. So much of it was already there, part of the cosmic pattern long before the war even came to Calth. This subterranean bunker of the Ultramarines provided the nexus. A pleasing twist of fate.

He gestures back to the map. 'Miraculous, isn't it?'

'It is.'

Realising that this voice does not belong to Kaeloq, Kurtha Sedd starts to turn again. He recognises the blood-soaked Ultramarine wearing Kaeloq's helmet.

'By the Word!'

'I have a word for you,' Aeonid Thiel replies. 'I'll let my bolter speak it for me.'

MUZZLE FLARE RIPS into the darkness, tearing open Lathek's chest plate and exposing his insides to the air. He crumples with a muted gurgle of pain. The pinned Ultramarine Hadrius, who still has Lathek's ritual knife embedded in his clavicle, stamps down on his captor's neck as he lies supine on the floor.

Screams and cries of alarm echo in the chamber as the human captives scramble to get out of harm's way. Sedd is faster than his warriors, and dives for cover, shouting at his remaining disciples to counter-attack even as another of them is cut down. Word Bearers are not the tactical equals of Ultramarines – perhaps they are not even on an equal footing as warriors, but Thiel knows that to dismiss them all as mindless fanatics is an error.

Hadrius learns this fact to his cost, his throat and right arm exploding into bloody gore when a Word Bearer opens fire, as the Ultramarine attempts to rush Sedd.

Thiel roars in anger and guns down Hadrius's killer. There is only one more Word Bearer left, besides Sedd; the rest of their enemies are human cultists.

Vultius lunges from the shadows, killing two with well aimed shots from his bolter. He's injured, but the captain still manages to square the odds. Another cultist hauls up a chain-stubber, spitting dogma copied from his master's heretic tongue.

A bright las-beam scythes through the dark, striking the gunner in the chest and leaving a burning crater as it passes out of his back.

Rowd has a good eye, and Thiel is thankful that he has the con-vict-turned-soldier watching his back.

Enfilading fire keeps the traitors down behind a command con-sole, Vultius pinning them from one end of the room, and Thiel from the other.

Just below the fire exchange, Thiel discerns the sound of rhyth-mic chanting and recognises Sedd's voice.

'Captain!' he calls out.

Vultius has heard it too, but he is weak and slumped behind a blasted column. Sedd's remaining disciple is switching fire between them, snatching off rapid bursts that are foiling Thiel's aim.

But Thiel is not alone.

'Rowd! Remember those vittle-cans, out in the fields?'

Rowd's reply is nearly swallowed by the harsh retort of the bolter. 'I've never forgotten them.'

Thiel smiles. 'Hit one for me now, would you.'

Stepping from his hiding place in the fallen rubble strewn half-way across the command hub, Rowd fires a single shot. The rifle is pressed into his shoulder to swallow the recoil, his eye squeezed into the sight. The las-bolt travels through smoke and debris, burn-ing across the shadows of the room to strike the Word Bearer just above the eye. It stings, but doesn't kill – makes him shift, turn and seek out his aggressor.

The momentary lapse in concentration is all Thiel needs to put a round through the side of his head. Before the body has even fallen, the Ultramarine is leaping clear and discarding the spent bolter.

Vultius leans out of cover, firing off a flurry of shots into Kurtha Sedd as the Dark Apostle rises. The explosive shells burst against a dark aura now surrounding him, some foul ritual of summoning lending him unnatural protection from harm.

Thiel sees the practical at once, forgetting the pistol at his hip.

Aboard the *Macragge's Honour*, blades and axes smote the Never-born more efficiently than any firearm: something to do with the creatures' ties to ancient times, and the old methods employed to banish them. But Thiel has no knife or blade. They were lost in the Rhino crash, his prized longsword – a weapon from the primarch's own armoury – amongst them.

When the Unburdened died, capricious fate delivering it to the edge of that electromagnetic blade, it exploded, showering Thiel with daemonic gore. As he awoke, the blood cooked to his armour, he fashioned a theoretical that would give him the element of surprise and a practical he could exploit to save his battle-brothers. Kaeloq's borrowed helm, repugnant as it was, completed the subterfuge. Now, as he runs at Kurtha Sedd, as the apostle's skin writhes and shifts with warp-spawned mutation, Thiel uses the helm again. Ripping it off his head, glad to be free of its stinking confines, he wields it like a weapon.

Sedd is delirious, revelling in his burgeoning power.

'The veil thins, and I ascend!'

'You die,' Thiel corrects him, and slams the horned helm into the apostle's skull-like face.

Sedd screams with two voices as the ritual falters and the change begins to reshape and devour. Armour, skin and flesh melts into a gelatinous soup, until even that starts to smoke and wither.

Recoiling from the hideous creature, Thiel draws his pistol and aims squarely at the fleshy mass that used to be Kurtha Sedd.

'Vanquish it, Thiel!' Vultius cries out.

The captain shoots at the same time, and the two Ultramarines empty their magazines into the spawn. Every explosive impact shrinks it, reducing it down until it is little more than a stain.

The echo of bolter fire fades. Calm returns, undercut by shallow weeping and the muttered thanks of the human captives for their deliverance.

Thiel sags a little where he stands, still holding out his smoking pistol as if the thing he and Captain Vultius have just eradicated might yet come back to the material plane. He flinches as he feels a hand upon his arm.

'Easy, sergeant,' says Vultius. 'It's over.'

Men and women are crawling from behind cover, blinking as the emergency lumens kick in. Thiel nudges a dead Word Bearer with his boot, the one Rowd clipped. 'Need to make sure they're all dead. Clear this place out.'

'Give it a few minutes.' Vultius claps him on the shoulder as Thiel sits down on a fallen column, exhausted. 'I misjudged you, Aeonid. I'm sorry for that. You are a credit to the Legion.'

'I didn't do it alone.'

Thiel looks for Rowd. He sees him, slumped against the wall, legs out, head off to one side. There is a gash in his rad-suit, one that has been there ever since the tunnel collapse. He is not moving, but there is blood on the rebreather mask hanging loose at his neck. Rowd's eyes are open, but they do not blink.

'You brave and foolish man. You followed me onto the surface anyway.'

Vultius follows Thiel's gaze. 'A conscript? Penal legion?'

Thiel shakes his head. 'A farmer, a husband and a father.' He gestures to the stuttering green pict-feed and the Word Bearers' mapped excavations. 'We'll find the break in the hardline along one of those tunnels.'

Vultius nods. 'We'll lead teams, effect a repair and call for reinforcement. You and I can't run this hub alone.'

Grunting, Thiel gets to his feet.

'You'll have to do it without me, sir.'

'What?'

Thiel's eyes are weary, and not just from the fight. 'As soon as the next wave of reinforcements arrive, I am leaving for Macragge. I made a mistake coming back here, to this.'

'We must keep fighting, Sergeant Thiel.'

'Yes, we must. But not here. This is propaganda, and I'm not much for politics. I'll only do or say something that'll see red on my armour again.'

Vultius looks about to protest, when he nods and smiles.

'You're probably right.' He salutes, and Thiel returns it. 'For the Emperor. For Calth.'

Thiel spares a final glance for Rowd.

'Aye, for Calth.'

THE GUNSHIP POWERS up from a bare landing field on the surface, several kilometres outside Numinus City. The legionary reinforcements have already been deployed, and now only a single warrior besides the pilot remains aboard.

'*Brace yourself, sergeant,*' a voice crackles through the vox-feed in the hold.

Thiel is fastened into a mag-harness. His bolter is stowed in the overhead weapons locker, along with his electromagnetic longsword. After the arcology was secured, he went back to retrieve it from the wreckage of the crashed Rhino – he could hardly return to Lord Guilliman without it. Thiel's armour is cleaned, though the practicals etched into the ceramite remain. He doesn't need them to recall his battle plans – they are for the purposes of legacy, to preserve his combat logic for future generations.

When he gets back to Macragge, Thiel thinks that he will present them to his primarch.

As they break for orbit, the pilot's voice crackles over the vox again.

'*Are you glad to be leaving, Sergeant Thiel?*'

'Glad to be getting back to the war. Has much changed in my absence?'

There's a pause as the pilot makes the necessary adjustments for void flight.

'You haven't heard?'

Thiel looks up, paying proper attention for the first time since the ascent.

'Heard what?'

'Our Lord Guilliman is building.'

Thiel frowns. 'Building what exactly?'

'Imperium Secundus.'

LONE WOLF

Chris Wraight

As HE RUNS across it, the earth ignites. He goes so fast that he might be flying, barely touching the charred plates, tearing through the blue-tinged tongues that ripple out from the fissures below. The sky is alive ahead of him, riven by the aurorae of a thinning veil.

He has seen the prey, towering above the boiling mass of bodies, and that is enough. Axes rise, silhouetted against fire, hurled into the faces of the damned as they scream, but none are his.

The entire Rout fights across the sprawling battle plains of Velbayne, its fury set against a host of madness. The Wolves are loosed, thrown into the furnace, just where they wish to be. The packs fight, covering one another, forming shieldwalls and axe-wedges. Screaming night-creatures crash against them, though such shrieks freeze in unholy mouths as they face the wrath of Russ. The primarch still fights, though his immense presence cannot be seen – there are horrors enough on this battlefield to keep even the Wolf King busy.

As for him, *he* has no pack to protect his approach, none to cover his desperate charge. He has been alone for long enough now that he no longer feels the strangeness of it. His axe whirls around him like a bolas, whistling, accelerating, ramping up for the strike.

The prey looms over him. It is massive and crustaceous, boiling with black-hearted fire. Its wings unravel into the tortured night, ragged and skin-stretched. Its hooves crack the earth beneath it, its blade rips the air itself, its bellows make the world shake.

It is a vision of mortal terrors, merged and bulked into colossal proportions and forged in madness. It strides across the fields of murder, lashing out with smouldering strikes. The fires leap up to greet it, rippling across blood-dark muscles and reflected in oil-slick spines. A long taurian face is crammed with tusks, weighed down by a crown of horns, wrinkled into a snarl of wrathful contempt.

He accelerates. He has seen the creature before. He recognises the curl of the daemonic skin, the axe it carries, the runes of destruction hammered into iron ingots. He remembers what it did the last time their fates crossed.

How could he forget? He remembers almost nothing else.

It sees him, and its roar of challenge shivers the battlefield. Its leading leg crashes down, sending cracks racing out over the fire-edged plates. Its weapon moves heavily, trailing streamers of boiling blood from the edge.

By then he is going too fast to stop. He jumps, vaulting past the lesser ranks of terrors, shouldering them aside and breaking through their ineffective cordon.

He calls out for the first time in years. He frees his tongue, held silent since the last of his pack brothers burned on the pyres. They are declaimed in the order they went into battle. He promised their ghosts as much, back when the funeral embers still glowed like dying stars.

Alvi. He shouts the name as he smites the creature for the first time. Gore the thickness of magma spouts across his axe-blade. Alvi, who had no deed name, who was the purest of them all.

Alvi had died when his breastplate was crushed under the creature's hooves, still hacking at its unnatural flesh even as his helm filled with blood.

The daemon howls, arcing down its own axe-edge, but he is too quick. He is moving like storm-lightning now, spinning out of contact and spearing in close – uncatchable, unhaltable.

Byrnjolf, Teller-of-Tales. The pack's skjald, heavy-limbed but agile-tongued, the carrier of the pack saga and the memory of its slayings. Byrnjolf had died as the creature's fist had dragged low, thrown back into the mire of Gryth's eternal miasmic plague plains. With the Teller gone, the tales fell into silence.

The daemon tries the same trick on him, but he is too wily for that now. He is older, tempered in fires far hotter than those that harrow this world. He hastens aside, already coiled for the next thrust.

Eirik. Golden-haired, vital. Eirik had cut it deep before the end, clambering up the creature's own body to stab at it.

He does the same now – he uses its massiveness against it, countering bulk with speed. The daemon's axe sweeps around, heavy as a pendulum, missing him by a finger's breadth. He plunges his blade into its chest, catching on to the chains of iron to arrest his fall and haul himself higher.

Gunnald Shieldbearer. How could Gunnald have died? What force could have ended such a bastion of defiance? Gunnald had weathered the worst of it until the end, wielding his thunder hammer and spitting curses even as his throat was throttled.

He does not try the same thing. He does not have the heft of Gunnald and so sticks to speed, clambering up the daemon's hide of iron plates. It tries to shake him clear and fails. He can feel its mounting fear. It knows who he is now.

Hiorvard. Hrani. The twins, fighting together as always, levelling bolters and filling the air with curtains of explosive power. They had only been taken down when the creature had broken the assault and cast aside the last of the blade-bearers. He remembered the way they had cast aside their guns, drawn swords and charged. They had died as they had lived – shoulder to shoulder.

No more names now. He is fighting as if maddened, clinging to the daemon's shoulder with his artificial clawed hand, working the axe with the other. It tries to throw him off, to hurl him away like it did before, but his talons are sharper now.

Everything is harder, deeper, older, wiser, tougher. In killing his pack, it has made him into a slaughterer of apocalyptic stature. He is like the old huntsmen of legend – drawing in the strength of the slain.

The creature bats away his axe and bellows in triumph. It watches the blade tumble clear, flashing red before it hits the seething earth. In pausing to watch, it has erred.

He has been waiting for this. His wolf claw reaches for the creature's neck. Adamantium blades, each crackling with actinic energy, clench tight around daemonic thews, pressing the stringy muscle together.

It thrashes. It claws at him. Its talons rake down his armoured back. All he has to do now is hold on. He presses harder, digs deep, pushing the physical air from un-physical lungs. He grits his fangs. He is bleeding now from the wounds it has inflicted upon him.

Its skin bursts, its vessels swell and flood, its strength ebbs. He hangs on, strangling the life from it even as it falls to its knees. The battle rages around them, a whirlpool of unfettered rage, but even the daemon no longer sees this.

Its red eyes glare at him a final time, and he stares back into them. It chokes, it writhes, but he never lets go.

Only when the creature is gone, its mortal frame turned to unmoving slag and ash, does he raise his bloody claw in triumph. He tears his helm from his head and lifts his shaggy head to the sky. Tasting unfiltered air, he howls in triumph.

His living brothers howl with him. They know that he will be coming back to them now. They know what manner of thing he has really killed.

He stands upon the smoking corpse of the daemon, grinding his boots into its slumped shoulders. Only one name remains to be declaimed, the last member of the pack, the one who hunted through the sea of stars for vengeance, the one they have called the Lone Wolf for too many years.

Bjorn.

ABOUT THE AUTHORS

David Annandale is the author of The Horus Heresy novel *The Damnation of Pythos*. He also writes the Yarrick series, consisting of the novella *Chains of Golgotha* and the novel *Imperial Creed*. For Space Marine Battles he has written *The Death of Antagonis* and *Overfiend*. He is a prolific writer of short fiction, including the novella *Mephiston: Lord of Death* and numerous short stories set in The Horus Heresy and Warhammer 40,000 universes. David lectures at a Canadian university, on subjects ranging from English literature to horror films and video games.

Aaron Dembski-Bowden is the author of the Horus Heresy novels *Betrayer* and *The First Heretic*, as well as the novella *Aurelian* and the audio drama *Butcher's Nails*, for the same series. He also wrote *The Talon of Horus*, the popular Night Lords series, the Space Marine Battles book *Helsreach*, the Grey Knights novel *The Emperor's Gift* and numerous short stories. He lives and works in Northern Ireland.

John French has written several Horus Heresy stories including the novellas *Tallarn: Executioner* and *The Crimson Fist*, the novel *Tallarn: Ironclad* and the audio dramas *Templar* and *Warmaster*. He is the author of the Ahriman series, which includes the novels *Ahriman: Exile* and *Ahriman: Sorcerer*, plus several short stories. Additionally for the Warhammer 40,000 universe he has written the Space Marine Battles novella *Fateweaver*, plus a number of short stories. He lives and works in Nottingham, UK.

A prolific freelance author and journalist, **Guy Haley** is the author of *Space Marine Battles: Death of Integrity*, the Warhammer 40,000 novels *Valedor* and *Baneblade*, and the novellas *The Eternal Crusader*, *The Last Days of Ector* and *Broken Sword*, for *Damocles*. His enthusiasm for all things greenskin has also led him to pen the eponymous Warhammer novel *Skarsnik*. He lives in Yorkshire with his wife and son.

Nick Kyme is the author of the Horus Heresy novel *Vulkan Lives*, the novellas *Promethean Sun* and *Scorched Earth*, and the audio drama *Censure*. His novella *Feat of Iron* was a *New York Times* bestseller in the Horus Heresy collection, *The Primarchs*. For the Warhammer 40,000 universe, Nick is well known for his popular series of Salamanders novels and short stories, the Space Marine Battles novel *Damnos*, and numerous short stories. He has also written fiction set in the world of Warhammer, most notably the Time of Legends novel *The Great Betrayal* for the War of Vengeance series. He lives and works in Nottingham, and has a rabbit.

Graham McNeill has written more Horus Heresy novels than any other Black Library author! His canon of work includes *Vengeful Spirit* and his *New York Times* bestsellers *A Thousand Sons* and the novella *The Reflection Crack'd*, which featured in *The Primarchs* anthology. Graham's Ultramarines series, featuring Captain Uriel Ventris, is now six novels long, and has close links to his Iron Warriors stories, the novel *Storm of Iron* being a perennial favourite with Black Library fans. He has also written a Mars trilogy, featuring the Adeptus Mechanicus. For Warhammer, he has written the Time of Legends trilogy The Legend of Sigmar, the second volume of which won the *2010 David Gemmell Legend Award*, and the anthology *Elves*. Originally hailing from Scotland, Graham now lives and works in Nottingham.

Anthony Reynolds's work for Black Library includes the Horus Heresy novella *The Purge* and short stories 'Scions of the Storm' and 'Dark Heart'. He is perhaps best known for the Word Bearers trilogy and the Knights of Bretonnia series. Originally from Australia, Anthony moved to the UK where he worked within Games Workshop for many years before returning to his homeland. He is currently settled on the west coast of the United States.

Gav Thorpe is the author of the Horus Heresy novel *Deliverance Lost*, as well as the novellas *Corax: Soulforge*, *Ravenlord* and *The Lion*, which formed part of the *New York Times* bestselling collection *The Primarchs*. He is particularly well-known for his Dark Angels stories, including the Legacy of Caliban series, and the ever-popular novel *Angels of Darkness*. His Warhammer 40,000 repertoire further includes the Path of the Eldar series, the Horus Heresy audio dramas *Raven's Flight* and *Honour to the Dead*, and a multiplicity of short stories. For Warhammer, Gav has penned the Time of Legends trilogy, *The Sundering*, and much more besides. He lives and works in Nottingham.

Chris Wraight is the author of the Horus Heresy novel *Scars*, the novella *Brotherhood of the Storm* and the audio drama *The Sigillite*. For Warhammer 40,000 he has written the Space Wolves novels *Blood of Asaheim* and *Stormcaller*, and the short story collection *Wolves of Fenris*, as well as the Space Marine Battles novels *Wrath of Iron* and *Battle of the Fang*. Additionally, he has many Warhammer novels to his name, including the Time of Legends novel *Master of Dragons*, which forms part of the War of Vengeance series. Chris lives and works near Bristol, in south-west England.

John French

TALLARN: EXECUTIONER

The battle begins

The scattered forces of the Imperial Army strike
back against the Iron Warriors

An extract from Tallarn: Executioner
by John French

'KILL!' SHOUTED LACHLAN. Tahirah winced as his voice roared from her headset. She felt sweat rolling down her skin. The temperature inside *Lantern* had spiked an instant after the weapon had fired. Inside her enviro-suit the hairs rose across her skin as the plasma destroyer began to recharge. The hull was shaking and bucking as it accelerated into the engagement. Engine noise vibrated through her head.

Crammed into the turret next to Lachlan, it felt like she was riding a boat in a stormy sea. All of the crew wore sealed suits of rubber and treated fabric. Breathing air through a mask plugged into the tank's air supply, it felt as if she was drowning in the heat and the brain-numbing snarl of *Lantern*'s engine. She could barely see anything that was not directly in front of her eyepieces, and moisture from her breath was already beading on the circles of glass. The only reason she could talk to the rest of the crew was because of the internal vox.

Outside on the hull a sheet of burning vapour vented from the cone of the cannon. The slime clinging to its hull ignited. Flames crawled across *Lantern*, scorching the Amaranth stripes from its turret. Black liquid splattered up in its wake, as it dragged a cloak of guttering flame.

For Tahirah everything had started to move very fast from the moment she had targeted the enemy vehicle and Lachlan had fired. She had trained in war machines for half a decade, been through live fire drills and logged over a hundred machine hours. But this was like nothing she had ever felt. Information and sensations washed over her. Dozens of thoughts, fears and possibilities formed and fled in a second. It was like trying to catch hold of a storm. It was the gap, she realised, the gap between training and reality, the gap she had always wanted to cross.

Plumes of heat and gas blurred her view out of the periscope. Red icons painted the point where the enemy machine had been. It was not moving. Good enough.

'Kill confirmed,' said Tahirah. The auspex was screeching. A shape had emerged from the green pixel fog. 'Enemy, left flank, sixty degrees, engage when you see them.'

'I can't see them,' shouted Genji.

'Traversing,' said Lachlan next to her, and the turret began to turn in its collar.

'*I can't see anything.*'

Genji, thought Tahirah. Terra, she wished the girl would stop shouting. Tahirah did not answer; she had no idea what was going on. The enemy had vanished off the auspex. Flashes of amber, green and red danced across the black screen. She tried to focus on the auspex screen, flicking glances out of the periscope blocks. She could not see a damned thing either.

She turned her view to the green icons of *Silence* and *Deathlight* on the auspex screen. Together they formed a wedge with *Lantern* at the tip. The first kill had been straight ahead and even then they had only been able to see it because of the heat bloom. Now they could not pinpoint the rest of the enemy force. She knew that there was a very real chance of the squadron falling apart, of doing something fatally stupid and hitting each other as they tried to kill the enemy. She pushed the right-hand cup of her headphones over her ear and clicked to transmit.

'All call signs, this is *Lantern*, engage only with visual confirmation.'

Hector and Brel acknowledged the command, their voices almost lost in the rising jumble of sound around her.

'Where the hell have they gone?' said Lachlan. His face was pressed against the rubber eyepieces of the Executioner's main weapon targeter.

'I've got one,' came another shout. It was Udo, in the right sponson. She glanced at the auspex and saw the angular red return of metal and heat to their right. A target.

Sharp-eyed little rat, she thought.

'Turn, right, right, right. Target, right flank, eighty degrees narrowing, visual confirm to engage.' The tone of the engine changed and the turret began to turn.

'I've got it,' shouted Udo.

'Confirm enemy,' said Tahirah, but the right sponson's firing light was already glowing amber on her control panel. She opened her mouth to shout.

'Firing.'

'Udo! Confirm, damn you.'

The lightning-crack of the lascannon echoed through the compartment.

'Hit,' whooped Udo.

Tahirah pressed her eyes against one of the periscope viewers. She could barely see ten metres. Ochre clouds swirled in front of her eyes like silt in churned water. She switched to infra-sight and the world became a haze of grey. The heat of the las discharge was a fading line through the fog.

'*Lantern, this is Deathlight.*' Hector's voice spat from her headset. '*I have las flare to my front. Almost hit us. What's going on?*'

'Udo!' shouted Tahirah.

'It was them, I saw,' called Udo. She could almost see his face twist with denial, as if shooting the front off a friendly was just another understandable mistake.

'Shut up,' she snarled. Icons were dancing across the auspex now, fading from red to amber, overlaying and contradicting. It was like trying to punch someone you could only hear in the middle of a rain storm. The enemy were there, they were right–

Red blossomed across the auspex. The *Lantern* rocked. White light flashed from the eyepieces of her periscopes. Lachlan swore. She glanced at him. His hands were pressed against his eyes. Genji and Makis were shouting. The auspex cleared. She stared.

Deathlight's green icon had vanished. A white smudge of heat rolled where it had been. *Lantern* kept driving forwards, its turret traversing so that it faced back towards Hector's last position. Tahirah's fingers slipped as she thumbed the comm-stud.

'*Deathlight*, this is *Lantern*,' she began.

'It's gone,' shouted Lachlan. She did not want to look at him. She could hear enough in his voice.

'*Deathlight*, respond.'

'It's gone.'

Her skin suddenly felt very cold. Sounds seemed to be louder and further away.

Genji's voice cut through her. 'Target. Firing.'

'Wait,' said Tahirah, but the word was lost as the left sponson fired.

Akil closed his eyes against the glare as the fog outside lit up. Rashne was screaming into the vox. The world was all vibration and sudden noise. For a second when the oncoming tank had vanished in a ball of fire he had thought it was them – that they had been hit, and that he was trapped in his last second of awareness.

Then the light had turned red, and black smoke had stained the firelit fog.

More sound and light, and teeth-aching tremors spun around him as he pressed his eyelids shut and Rashne screamed on and on.

'STOP,' SAID BREL calmly. The rest of the crew said nothing, but he felt the engine disengage and the tone of the noise drop in the compartment. Jallinika was looking back at him, waiting for him to tell her if there was a target worth trying to see; they both knew that if she had her eye to gunsight without reason she would start firing at ghosts, or her own side.

Old ways, and old tricks, thought Brel. *And here we all are again. Home, like we never left.*

The fight had begun just how they always had, with a roar of death and then the hurtling descent into anarchy. He had felt *Silence* rock when *Deathlight* had gone up, and had heard Tahirah calling for a response. Tahirah's machine had no idea what was going on, but they were still moving and firing anyway, at an enemy of unknown strength and unknown nature. All they had were the blips on their screens and the images skidding across their sights. They might get another kill, but they were dangerous to stay close to.

Brel watched the auspex display. The *Lantern* had one confirmed kill, and the enemy had fired back and killed the *Deathlight* in reply. That meant a minimum of one enemy machine still out there, as well as the lost scout machine. The enemy were good. They must have broken formation as soon as they were ready to engage, and they were using the fog and auspex interference to hide themselves.

Or they were jamming our scanners and comms, he thought, *reducing both to unreliable junk. Very good indeed.*

'Jal,' he said into the intra-crew vox. 'Strength of an elite hunter unit in these conditions?'

'Three.' She shrugged. 'No more than four.'

'Two?'

She laughed. 'Only if you had no choice.'

Brel nodded, and let out a long breath.

'Yeah. I was worried you would agree.'

He thought for a moment longer, and then gave one order.

'Shut down the engine. Keep the load in the main gun. Keep comms, air, sights and auspex up, but close down the transponder.'

There was the barest moment of hesitation. The transponder sent out a constant signal telling all other friendly units set to the same frequency where they were and that they were not something to fire at. Without it the *Silence* would appear as an unknown return on friendly auspex screens, and in a battle like this they would be a target to everyone.

'Now,' said Brel, and a second later the *Silence* became an inert slab of cooling armour.